SIZE ZERO

Published in the United States by Visage Media, LLC, Los Angeles

The Library of Congress has cataloged the edition as follows:
Names: Mangin, Abigail, author.
Title: Size Zero / Abigail Mangin.
Description: First edition. | Los Angeles: Visage Media, 2020.
Identifiers: LCCN 2020932706
BISAC: Fiction / Thrillers / Suspense. | Fiction / Satire. | Fiction / Fantasy / Urban.

Visage Media Trade Paperback ISBN: 978-1-7345534-1-3

eBook ISBN: 978-1-7345534-0-6

Cover art by Megumi Mizuno

www.visageny.com

SIZE ZERO

ABIGAIL MANGIN

VISAGE

NEW YORK

1

―――

"Think of me as your father," the model agent said. "I'm going to take such good care of you."

"Dads are dicks." Ava kicked a pebble at his shins.

"I'll be your mother then."

Ava pointed to her so-called mother, who was leaning against their dilapidated double-wide trailer. She slurped wine from a McDonald's soda cup. Her eyes blinked in a flurry, trying to stay open. "Moms are worse."

The model agent reached into a leather bag and pulled out a heart-shaped music box filled with golden-wrapped chocolates. "How about a lover?"

Ava crunched strawberry Pop Rocks between her teeth. She stuck out her tongue, and the candies let out a crackling hiss. "That's creepy. I'm eleven." She spat the Pop Rocks in his face. The little red candies sprayed like soggy confetti.

"Ava. Don't be a brat," her mother said in a drunken slur.

But he laughed it off, swiping the spit from his stubble. "Not a lover in a *romantic* way. I'll *care* for you. It looks like you could use some love."

She took the chocolate box from him. Golden ballet dancers were engraved into the casing, and a beautiful melody played when she twisted the lever.

It was the nicest thing she had ever been given.

The model agent handed her mother a small stack of hundred-dollar bills and a Ziploc bag of white powder. She gave him two plastic takeout bags. Inside were Ava's birth certificate, three outfits, and a toothbrush. Those were her mother's parting gifts.

"I'm *not* going." Ava stomped. "You can't sell me. I'm a person."

"I gave you life. The least you can do is get me some money," the mother said.

Ava dropped to the ground and curled up into herself. She put her head to her knees, and her lower lip jutted out. She didn't have the energy to cry.

The model agent squatted next to her on the dirt path. His arm wrapped around her shoulder, breath smelling of cigars masked with spearmint. "Fashion Week is so fun, you know. Tyra Banks. Twiggy. You'll make lots of friends. You'll wear diamonds. And paparazzi will take your photos. You'll make so much money. Magazine covers. Big parties at the Plaza Hotel."

And then she noticed his teeth. They were so white they looked fake, like the plastic vampire dentures she wore at Halloween.

"I don't care about diamonds."

"What *do* you want?"

Ava thought for a moment. She rushed into the trailer and came out with a McDonald's Happy Meal box. She opened up the golden arches to reveal a fluffy brown hamster. There were miniature chairs made out of paper. And she had put popcorn and French fries inside for him to eat.

"Can you get Mr. Puffles a cage?" she asked. "And some hamster food?"

"We'll get him a castle."

She scooped up the chocolate box and Mr. Puffles and went straight for the Mercedes. She didn't say a word to her mother. She didn't even look at her.

The agent chased her with a childish giddiness. His feet spun out like a cartoon character's, kicking up dust.

"I'm proud of you," he said. "You made the right choice. Besides, modeling can't be worse than *this life*, can it?"

It could. And it was.

Fashion Week, 2019. Ava was twenty-four.

A mirrored runway drenched the world in reflective silver, washing away all the depravity and filth of Manhattan. Snowflakes rained upon eyelashes and coated the tips of tongues, like a dusting of sugar.

The snow was real. The white peacock feathers were freshly harvested.

Everything Visage made was earthy. But it felt like a dream.

New York Fashion Week was an arctic wonderland. Dresses covered in white winter moss. Icicles frozen into flower crowns.

Pine trees rose from the mirrored runway floor, sparking golden fireworks from their tips.

Backstage was not as pretty. Ava's fellow models were hunched over in makeup chairs, a halo of golden branches keeping their innocence intact. Cigarette smoke hung in the air like smog above them, as artists masked the jaundiced hue of the girls' cheeks, the shadows around their eyes, and the baby fat that clung to their young faces. Their plush cheeks were swaddled in fur scarves, shielding their faces from prying eyes.

A model's face never mattered. The bodies were all that had value.

The girls couldn't text. The agencies had confiscated their phones. But the few who borrowed the stylist's cell managed to text their families: *"Te amo,"* "I miss you," *"Je t'aime," "Ik hou van je,"* "I love you."

But Ava was not covered in golden glitter, flower crowns, or fake snow.

She woke up in a dark closet backstage. The room cocooned her, roughing her elbows with gritty brick. Her hands were invisible in the blackness. But handcuffs weighed heavy on her wrists.

She kicked up her legs, and a chain rattled. She was shackled in the room.

The smell of body odor and hairspray seeped under the door. Her head throbbed, and her fingers traced over the blood pooled at her hairline.

When she tried to scream, her breath got trapped inside her chest. Her rib cage heaved up and down.

Stars flitted before her eyes, marring the darkness. But there was not even a glimmer of light dancing on the broken glass embedded in her neck. An air vent kicked on with a rumble behind her. As the cool gust blew over her body, she realized she was naked.

Three minutes until showtime.

A thumb stroked her shoulder in lurid circles. She wasn't alone. Ava shrieked, but the commotion outside made it impossible for anyone to hear her.

Two minutes until showtime.

The door cracked open just enough for Ava to see someone holding a Visage dress bag, the perfect size to fit her body.

She thrashed and writhed, hands tied in front of her chest. When she tried to stand, her body was crushed to the floor. A needle found a vein in the crevice of her arm, and a numbing warmth shot through her.

A slimy leather coat slid onto her back as she tried to fight through the nausea.

She had never smelled anything worse than that cape—a decaying animal splashed with gasoline, the fabric moist against her naked skin.

When the coat's hairy hood dangled securely on her head, she was pulled to her feet, and the door opened to the runway.

Sweet tones of Vivaldi's "Winter" played, accompanying the ballet of champagne glasses and hors d'oeuvre that sashayed through manicured fingertips. Ava held her breath as the room spun, Crevier crystals blinking mockingly at her in Technicolor.

There was the runway, glimmering and calling to her like a skywalk.

Ω

In the audience, the elite fashionistas sat like cameras with open shutters, passively watching life drift across their lenses.

Sparklers shot up around ice sculptures of cranes and jaguars. Feathers on white gowns floated as they moved, threatening to fly away, as white fur glimmered with a golden hue beneath the twinkle lights adorning ice.

Tazia Perdonna, designer of the luxury brand Visage, sat with her eyes closed behind Lazard sunglasses, rose-gold hair rippling down her back.

One model after another strode down the runway with quick stomps, wearing scowling disguises to make the audience feel inferior. Their bones jutted out like toothpicks under chicken skin, the simultaneous embodiment of youth and death. They were modern art, bodies galloping in a straight line with no destination.

But the thunderous stomping came to a halt. There was an abrupt pause in the mannequin parade.

A mistake.

People shot sideways glances at Perdonna. Camera crosshairs flashed at a violent pace, the photographers excited to catch a void Visage stage.

Though the silence did not last long. A shrill scream echoed from the corner of the room. And Ava Germaine stumbled onto the runway, wearing a corpse coat bleeding red onto the mirrored glass.

Some in the audience covered their eyes. Others clapped, hoping the skin coat wasn't real. They prayed it was Perdonna's idea of deconstructionist art, a grander statement about society.

Ava collapsed to her knees in a splash of blood, and a grayish eyeball rolled down the runway, stopping directly before Perdonna.

She removed her sunglasses, revealing vicious red scars and clouded eyes of her own.

That was the moment the front row knew the skin coat was real.

A flayed human body was made into a coat. Purple beads and evergreen sequins were embroidered into skin. Human hair was braided into a bun on the hood. And one dull eyeball remained stitched into the human face.

A gas mask, a condom dress, and even an animatronic T. rex had debuted at prior Fashion Weeks. But never before had a dead body.

2

Everything at St. Joseph's Abbey had a purpose, which is precisely why Brother George hid inside of it.

Mountains surrounded the chapel, a natural cradle protecting it from evil. The closest house was five miles away, and nothing could be heard but quacking ducks and wind sizzling against the trees. The Benedictine monks were happy to pray, sing, and work together in their own tiny town they called an abbey.

A canopy of bright red autumn leaves hung over Brother George's daily reading space. He preferred to overlook the pond, full of blooming lily pads and adorably obese stray cats. Nothing smelled like life more than wet grass and lavender.

Brother George brought his crossword close to his eyes to avoid seeing anything but his own words written in minuscule capital letters.

A pen was cradled in his hand, stroking letters across black and white squares. Unlike the other monks who practiced ceramics and stained glass, Brother George was an artist only with words.

Cigar smoke puffed from his lips. Ink violently smeared from his pen's nib.

Demesne. Chatoyant. Bucolic.

His fingers tangled through his brown hair, coating the tips in ink.

The clue "Half of a dance" made the answer CHA (half of the cha-cha), and "Is it acquired by breaking the law?" made WEALTH.

Not enough things in life were black-and-white. The murky crevices, the obscurities of day-to-day living, were not in Brother George's vocabulary. He preferred the world of crosswords, where for every block *down*, there was an *across* to be made.

The Bible and black habit might've helped him fake maturity, but his teal-blue eyes only highlighted the boyish pinkness that still clung to his dimples.

It was only in the darkness that one could see the depth behind his shallow, daytime eyes.

A black-and-white yo-yo fell from his hand in sync with his tapping pen. Scrawling crosswords allowed him to order his own chaos, to bring everything to a conclusion.

His word was SKIM. The clue: "It's less rich than the one percent."

The sound of footsteps came from behind him, and he turned toward the woods to find an adolescent, frizzy-haired boy staring at him with bulging eyes. He quickly hid the crossword puzzle inside his Bible, snuffed his cigar out on the porch deck, and pretended to be humming hymns.

The boy was spooked by the sight of a monk. *The cape. The crucifix.*

He froze at the edge of the walking trail, mouth agape as though he'd just seen a centuries-old relic come to life. When Brother George waved, the boy turned red-faced and ran down the muddy hill, sliding on his butt, and scampering to the edge of the abbey pond.

Ducks quacked and flew out of the water, running away from him. Even the abbey's stray cats, the freeloaders who purred their way to chicken wings and obesity, kept their distance from the boy as he flailed downward. He looked back at Brother George who pretended to be reading. And then he dunked his head into the lily pads, holding his breath under the water. Brother George put down his book and walked toward the pond, completely confused.

By the time the boy came up for air, gasping, Brother George stood over him, black habit flowing like a cape.

"Jesus," the boy yelped, falling back onto the grass. "Please don't kill me. *Please don't kill me.*"

Brother George put his hands up. "I'm a monk, not a ninja."

The boy folded his hands and raised a skeptical eyebrow. "But you look like a Jedi. The black hood, the belt, the cloak. And the cigar! I don't believe you."

"Let's not mention the cigar to anyone, please."

The boy picked a slimy piece of algae out of his hair. "I thought monks were old bald guys."

"Some are. *Most* are, actually. The church isn't exactly *en vogue* right now so I'm the youngest monk here." Brother George's Levi's jeans peeked out beneath the slit in his habit, and the boy lifted it to find the white T-shirt to match. "See, a ninja or a Jedi wouldn't wear such boring jeans, now would he? I come in peace."

"That's exactly what a ninja would say," the boy whispered.

Brother George folded his arms. "What were you doing in the pond?"

The boy shrugged, taking off his wet shirt and fanning it in the air. "Mom said I needed holy water because I'm a sinner."

Brother George chuckled, putting his hand out to help the boy to his feet. But he stomped and pouted. "Hey. Don't laugh. Mom says I'm going to hell. Like *real* hell. With dragons and fire and Satan." Tears welled in his eyes as the boy turned away. He picked up a pebble and tossed it into the water, trying to preoccupy his thoughts.

Brother George's smile quickly faded, and he knelt down. "Do you want to talk about it?"

"No," the boy said, pouting. His eyes slowly drifted up to Brother George's.

"Well, as pathetic as it is, my only superpowers are listening and forgiveness." When Brother George didn't get a response to his poorly formed joke, he whipped off his belt cincture and cracked it like a whip. "Or we can have a duel, and I'll go to hell in your place if you kill me."

"Whoa." A smile crept up despite the boy trying to hold his frown. "You are so not what I expected monks to be."

"Don't worry. I'm not a very good monk. I don't think I'm a very good person, either."

The boy folded his hands and looked up at the sky, praying. "The priest at my church wants to send me away from my parents for what I did. He wants me to go away for months."

"To prison?"

"To Jesus camp. Do you know what they make you do there? I once spent three hours decorating a cross with sequins and colored cotton balls. I don't understand what a rainbow crucifix has to do with Jesus bleeding all over a cross."

"What did you do? Smoke marijuana? Steal your mom's car for a joyride?" Brother George asked.

"So much worse."

The small smile left Brother George's face. He placed his palm on the boy's shoulder. "Did you kill someone?"

"*Worse!*"

"Just tell me."

The boy leaned forward, looking at himself in the water. His freckles reflected against the backs of turtle shells, making him look even more innocent.

"I kissed a boy," he whispered. "My friend Brett. Just one time." His lips twisted and trembled, shaking faster and faster as he tried to hold back the tears. "Mom says I'm gay. She hasn't looked me in the eye in three weeks. When she told my dad... He, um. He hit me."

A lump slid down Brother George's throat like a snake writhing beneath the skin. He noticed a greenish welt peeking out from beneath the boy's collar, right around his neck.

Suddenly a woman appeared from the wooded pathway behind the pond. "Good, Billy. You've found someone to help you."

Brother George stood, meeting Billy's mother with a solemn face.

"It's a tragedy, isn't it?" she said. "Please help us. What should I do with him?"

"I have a solution. Do not worry." Brother George put a hand on the woman's shoulder. "But you have to follow my instructions very clearly. That's the only way either of you will find salvation. Understand?"

She nodded enthusiastically, even pulling out her iPhone to take notes.

"You're going to go home," he said, "and talk to your son with a nice smile."

The woman typed enthusiastically.

"You're going to tell your husband never to lay a hand on Billy again."

She typed slower, looking up at him with worried, wide eyes.

"You're going to go home and show Billy the classics that are *Flashdance* and *Grease*. You will buy him sequined shorts if he wants them. You will love Billy no matter whom he loves when he's older. And if your husband lays a hand on this boy again, I will personally shove those sequined shorts up his ass."

"Brother George!" Abbot Joseph barked, standing atop the grassy hill with all of the abbey monks in tow.

He gave one look to his brothers, who stood staring down at him, both literally and figuratively, with scowls on their faces. The mother shook in place, hands quivering as her son's had when he first saw Brother George. "God bless you," he whispered.

As Brother George walked toward the monks, cape flinging around him like a royal train, Billy grabbed his hand. "You were wrong," he said. "You are a ninja."

Ω

In a few weeks, the monks would attend Brother George's solemn profession. After a six-year formation period, studying Scripture, the Rule of St. Benedict, and life at the abbey, Brother George would give his solemn vows to commit the rest of his life to the monastic community at St. Joseph's Abbey. He would live, eat, and pray all for God, never leaving the abbey walls. Once he spoke the vows, he could never go back to normal life.

Brother George was terrified.

The monks silently sat on long benches in the refectory as dinner was served. They received only two meals a day. Food moderation was key to Benedict's Law. No meat of mammals was ever served, except to Brother George's obese stray cats.

The tubby cats, Mochi and Muffintop, sprinted toward his feet, stumbling over their own stubby legs at each dinner. The cook made two chicken wings just for them. They sat at Brother George's feet as he peeled the wings and fed them by hand.

He missed meat. But even more, he missed pepperoni pizza. Of all the sins that tempted him, it was pepperoni pizza that he was sure would lead to his demise. In his dreams, he'd imagine standing at Grimaldi's Pizzeria beneath the Brooklyn Bridge, shoving two whole pizza pies into his mouth at once.

In reality, he'd do with just one slice. But in dream-form, those two whole pizzas were carnivals of cheesy-tomato goodness. Dreams didn't punish gluttony.

Brother George was served a slice of bread, a kale salad, and ginger tea. He split the piece of toast into twelve tiny chunks, so it felt like he had a dozen bites instead of one, and dipped the pieces into the ginger tea.

The other monks stared at the twenty-four-year-old novice, hoping he'd somehow get lost on the way to the chapel before his solemn vows.

But Brother George reveled in the silence of the meals. As a teenager, he held French fries in one hand and his phone in the other, eyes scrolling through text messages, never looking up. He watched YouTube videos of cats skateboarding, instead of feeling the cats' warm purrs against his legs.

The holy isolation of St. Joseph's Abbey kept Brother George sane.

In the refectory, each sip of ginger tea felt meaningful. Each bite of bread was savored. And the shared energy of his brothers radiated through the wooden walls.

The monks even found a way to communicate around the

silence. If Brother George needed a knife, he would slice or rub one finger over the other as if carving. If he wanted a napkin, he'd set two hands over his lap and spread them. To ask for apples at dessert, he'd bend his right thumb to the middle of his palm, seize it with his fingers, and raise up his fist.

It felt like theater, with each player actively reacting to another's needs.

When the silence ended, the plates were cleared, and a projector screen rolled down from the ceiling. It was the only occasion monks used the internet.

Prayer requests.

It was a time for monks to interact with the outside world, to personally meet and help the people for whom they prayed over online video. It was Brother George's idea. Some of his modern tech was helpful.

A church volunteer managed Skype, answering people's calls and putting them on screen before the monks.

The first person to ask for prayers was a skinny young woman sitting in a rundown trailer, cradling a crying two-year-old tot in her arms.

"My boy… I have a two-year-old, and he has brain cancer. Two tumors." The woman shuddered, hiding her face in her elbow. "I'm…I'm not askin' for God to keep him alive. I know he'll do what's best for my son. I just…I pray I can get the money to get him some treatment."

The woman put her baby down in a homemade cradle and wrapped him in a bundle of old T-shirts. "I work two jobs. Cashier. And I can't pay for chemo. It's either chemo or food at this point."

The monks soothed her worries and conspired to set up a fundraiser for the woman. She'd have the money in two months. Ceramic pipes and beer made by monks sold well on the internet. The Lord's Work, *Fulfilled by Amazon*.

The image of the crying woman and her messy trailer was replaced by the intimidating limestone structure of Lincoln Center in Manhattan. Red-and-blue lights flashed ominously onto the columns of the building. Sirens blared. Hundreds of New Yorkers crowded around the yellow police tape.

"I'm Margaux LeClaire," said the woman on screen. "In case you didn't know that."

She stretched her yellowish-blond hair into a tight bun, making her look like the wolfish grandmother in *Little Red Riding Hood*. Her New Orleans roots prompted her to tan too often, tinting her skin forever Oompa-Loompa orange. Her jewelry was made of bright pink and yellow stones so heavy that they weighed her neck down.

Like a golden toilet, the look was attractive...in a remarkable way.

Margaux LeClaire looked rich with a side of white trash poking through.

"I don't need prayers," she said. "How much do miracles cost?"

"Excuse me?" Abbot Joseph scoffed as the monks shuffled uncomfortably. "You can't buy miracles."

"Oh, bullshit," Margaux said. "Jesus was Jewish after all." Margaux slinked into a dark Lincoln Center. Rubble from a fashion show covered the floor, Visage purses carelessly tossed aside. Posters for the Visage luxury brand lined the walls. *"You can't buy miracles,"* Margaux chided in a sarcastic tone. "Tell that to my church on Madison Avenue. I have to give them ten grand just to piss in their toilet. If that money's really for Jesus, he's one greedy little Jew."

"Ma'am," the abbot said. "We're going to have to move forward if you keep speaking this way."

Margaux opened the door to the fashion show where a coat made of human skin was being lifted off Ava Germaine's naked body by a small crane. Crevier crystals were sewn into purplish skin. Elaborate embroidery tangled around gemstones and bedazzled buttons.

Margaux wobbled up to the bloody eyeball on the runway and put her phone next to it until a police officer swatted her away.

"That's my model," she said, pointing the camera toward the girl beneath the coat. "I'm a model agent. And somehow, *my* model wore a dead body onto the Visage runway show."

"Is she okay?" Abbot Joseph asked.

"Not the point," Margaux said. "I'd like to pay one of the monks to come down here and tell the police I'm Christian and would never murder anyone. Also, I'll pay extra if he says it on TV to Anderson Cooper on CNN. But only to Anderson Cooper, not Wolf Blitzer. He's an asshole, and he hates me because I always steal his parking spot on Madison."

Forensics took down the skin coat carefully from the crane. Police swarmed the area, taking every piece of clothing from the Visage collection as evidence.

"Ma'am, we don't do that here," Abbot Joseph said. "Also, being Christian alone doesn't preclude you from being a murderer."

Margaux folded her hands in prayer.

Abbot Joseph spun toward the volunteer who manned the video chat. "Can we please move forward?"

The other monks sat slack-jawed, some averting their eyes from the sight of the skin coat.

"Just one question before you throw me back to hell," Margaux said. "Why are priests called Father?"

Brother George leaned toward the camera with a furious red face. "Because it's too suspicious to call them Daddy." He leaned back. "There. Happy? You got your line in."

The monks hid their faces, and Abbot Joseph grabbed Brother George's arm. "You're making your last weeks before solemn vows very difficult, aren't you?"

Margaux turned the camera toward a woman in handcuffs. "Oh goddammit," she said, fanning herself with a fashion show program. "They got Clara. That's my niece, by the way. She's my far, *far* removed niece. Clara Royds. So God can keep everyone straight in the prayers… If you're gonna pray at all, or if you pray to send us to hell. Whichever, as long as there are frosted animal crackers wherever you send us."

The police had dragged Clara Royds out in handcuffs. It must've been difficult for the officers. Not because she threw any punches, but because she hung from their arms like a limp rag-doll, refusing to walk.

Clara was highly altered with a face more sculpted than a pyramid. Her nose had been cut to a small strip of cartilage. Her forehead had received so much Botox that her skin glistened with a plastic glow. And her bright pink hair floofed like a powder puff.

She was less than thirty, and plastic surgery had already ruined her face.

"What do you want, Margaux?" Brother George spat.

"I want my deadbeat child to come home and help his family in our time of need. Instead of hiding and playing dress-up in some fake paradise in the forest, he should keep his family out of jail."

"Based on this, I'd say he was right to leave," Brother George said.

One of the older monks practically fainted, putting his head down between his hands.

"Take off the costume and come home, Brother George. Who needs God when you're Cecil LeClaire?" Margaux asked, hanging up on the monks.

Six short years ago, Brother George was the heir to a multi-million-dollar fashion empire he did not want: LeClaire Model Management.

As the monks gave Brother George bewildered stares, Muffintop flopped onto the table.

"Down, cat. Down," one of the monks barked.

But an undeterred Muffintop pranced down the refectory runway, flabby belly swaying triumphantly like the fringe on a dancer's dress. Her stubby legs barely peeked out from beneath the fat rolls.

"Get her off the table. Off. She's got bloody paws!"

She tilted her head up with pride, showing off her trophy kill, which was a bit presumptuous as Muffintop never actually caught the mice herself. She stole them out of mousetraps and took all the credit.

"Muffintop!" Brother George yelled, climbing off the bench. "Please don't drop the mouse's head on the table."

He stuck his hand out, and Muffintop plopped an object into his palm. But it wasn't a mouse head. It was a piece of blood-soaked cardboard.

Muffintop rubbed her neck against Brother George's wrist, giving off a contented purr.

The chapel bells chimed for vespers, but as the refectory

emptied, Brother George noticed a set of bloody paw prints lead-ing out of the refectory. It was a lot of blood for a mouse.

Brother George heaved Muffintop into his arms. The pads of her feet were printed in red. He followed her prints along the sidewalk.

"What did you get yourself into?" he whispered, cradling her to keep all four dirty paws upright and away from his habit.

The tracks led a few feet from the refectory to where his work-shop stood. There was a cardboard package on the doorstep with a corner chewed away. There was no postage, but the nametag read: To Cecil LeClaire.

When he lifted it, he felt a soggy, wet bottom.

The package was bleeding.

3

"The police are on their way," Brother George whispered to the abbot as the monks gathered outside the chapel. "They said not to worry. It's probably just a prank. Animal bones or something. I put the box in the workshop for when the police get here."

The abbot's eyes drifted away slowly. He wasn't convinced.

The bells rang out a glorious tune, and the chapel doors burst open. It was vespers, the prayer of the shadows.

A monk hugged his harp, pulling at the strings as if he were spinning gold. The melody twinkled around the small chapel, the last remains of sunset beaming through the stained glass windows.

The monks prayed together five times a day, from dawn to dusk, each prayer in tune with the rising and falling of the sun. Vespers happened when the last bit of daylight touched the Earth, the last chance for the monks to meet the day rather than hide in the night.

It was usually Brother George's favorite prayer. Now, sweat pooled beneath his collar. Margaux LeClaire's incessant voice rang through his ears. And he couldn't stop thinking about washing the blood off his hands.

The monks processed down the aisle between the pews like delicate black swans. Their habits swayed to the sound of the harp, mimicking the rhythms of the Earth. It was a runway walk of a different kind. Each step had a purpose. Each pause in the march toward the chapel's nave held a contemplative silence. The farther the monks entered into the small chapel, the more their eyes gave away their peace.

Brother George followed behind the black habits, eyes locked on the brothers who bowed to God. It was only when he saw the little boy, Billy, standing alone in the pews, that he felt at home again. Billy watched in awe, standing straight and stiff, saluting the monks like they were military men.

Brother George bowed to the abbot and to God and took his seat in the wings of the chapel's nave. The monks sat across from him, prepared to sing the psalms. They looked to the cross or to the light that came through the wooden beams of the ceiling.

When the abbot sat, the monks turned to Psalm 109. They sang, "A prince from the day of your birth on the holy mountains; from the womb before the dawn, I begot you."

Their voices joined together into melody. One breath, the same words, in monotone, yet the lyrics flowed light and airy.

Brother George looked out toward the pews, curious about Billy. He sat alone, his shaking hands gripped the printed pink paper as he hid his face behind it. It was intimidating to sit among the monks, to feel small in the presence of the confident chants.

Brother George still felt small.

When Billy stood to leave the chapel, Brother George waved him over.

Billy scurried down the aisle, clumsily stumbling over a floorboard.

"The Master standing at your right hand will shatter kings in the day of his wrath," the monks sang with a lilting glee.

Brother George pointed to the lines in the psalm so Billy could follow along.

"This is like magic. It sounds so pretty," Billy whispered into his ear. "But I feel scared... I don't know why."

Brother George sang the next line alone. He sang it with a

solemn, lower tone than the others. "He, the judge of the nations, will heap high the bodies; heads will be shattered far and wide."

Billy gasped and avoided Brother George's gaze. "Why would you say that?" he whispered.

"God punishes the wicked. It's His judgment."

Billy's hand quickly covered his face, pretending to rub his forehead. "Can I tell you a secret?"

The monks stared at Billy with angry scowls, upset over the whispering. Brother George pretended not to hear him.

"I don't think I believe in God," Billy whispered. "So, I'm definitely going to hell." Billy huffed and again hid his face in his elbows.

Brother George patted his back. "I'm probably going to hell too. So don't feel bad."

"But you're a monk."

Before Brother George could respond, he was called upon to give the incense and thurible, a golden incense burner suspended from chains, to the abbot. He chose the incense and burned it, dispersing sweet-smelling smoke into the air. The wispy smolder danced toward the ceiling where the sun shone, twirling like silk, like the breath of the monks.

It was the scent of the chapel that brought Brother George to St. Joseph's Abbey. It was a perfume that clung to the weathered woods. It mixed melted sugar with the musky scent of rose petals, melting candles with worshippers' Chanel No. 5 and Visage perfumes to make a distinctly comforting scent.

But that peace was quickly shattered by a loud knock. The monks ignored it, as Abbot Joseph continued to swing the incense around the room. But the knocks came louder, like bullets shelling the wood.

The chapel door burst open. Four cameramen and three reporters walked inside. They barreled forward with gelled hair and tired, caffeine-addled eyes. All of the peace and magic of the moment was sucked into their camera lenses.

The reporters shouted over each other:

"Cecil! Cecil, are you a suspect in the murder investigation?"

"How much did you enjoy making the skin coat?"

"Is murder genetic in your family?"

Brother George stood from the pews. "Get out."

The harpist continued to play. He nervously softened his melody beneath the commotion.

"An online Chatter poll shows forty-two percent of responders think LeClaire Model Management is hiding that you're a serial killer. Would you like to comment?"

Brother George clutched his Bible and rushed down the aisle to drive the reporters outside. He was absorbed into the mob. When he pushed past them, they knocked him in the face with camera lenses. Lights flashed so brightly he couldn't see anything but white and the shadowy red outline of the veins in his eyes pulsing before him.

He was pushed outside and knocked onto his knees. The quiet hum of the wind had gone. Geese flew away from the flashing lights and cackling voices. The sun faded behind the trees. And all Brother George had left was the rocky ground that scraped his knees.

"It's the tenth anniversary of Annabelle Leigh's disappearance," a reporter said. "Did you make the skin coat? Kill again to celebrate?"

Brother George felt light-headed. Reporters surrounded him with vicious, glazed-over eyes. They wanted to consume him. There was no lonelier feeling than being trapped by reporters, seeing your own terrified eyes shining back at you in the camera lens crosshairs.

It reminded him of the first time he was mauled by the press.

October 23rd, 2009. Two weeks after Annabelle Leigh disappeared outside of his home.

It was the first time Cecil learned that he was evil.

Fourteen-year-old Cecil LeClaire wore his usual school uniform—an Armani suit jacket two sizes too big. He had read on the internet that people make posters when a friend goes missing. What he didn't know was that he was not "people."

So he stepped inside a dingy Manhattan FedEx and plugged his USB into the printer. Missing person posters shot out, Annabelle Leigh's grin fading and reemerging in each new image, like an animation bringing her back to life. *Missing Girl.*

Disappeared Oct 23. Have You Seen Her? A portrait below featured Annabelle's Shirley Temple curls and adorable wink.

Tears welled up in Cecil's eyes. He noticed the two middle-aged cashiers staring, and he wiped his cheeks.

"That's Cecil LeClaire," one of them whispered. "Holy shit."

"What's he gonna do?" the other whispered. "Hand out fliers on the *street*? They'll maul him."

"We should call TMZ. They'd love this."

Cecil scooped up his fliers and approached a homeless man bundled up in sleeping bags and cardboard, hands trembling, smelling of urine and vomit. He put a one-hundred-dollar bill in the man's paper cup.

"Are you okay, sir?" Cecil asked. "Can I get you a sandwich? A glass of water?"

The man held the cup shakily. "No."

"Um, sir. My...My best friend disappeared. And the policewoman told me that people hand out missing posters to bring their loved ones back. And...And I really love her. So..." He held up a poster and pointed to her photo. "This is her. Her name's Annabelle. Can you please keep a lookout?"

The man grasped the poster, eyes blinking rapidly, face turning green. A flash of recognition, but then he vomited an alcoholic stew all over the poster, and it sank to the ground.

Cecil hugged his posters closer to his chest.

"Leave one with us," the cashier called to him. "We'll post it in the window."

"Thank you." He solemnly placed a stack of posters in front of her.

The cashier whispered, "Poor kid. He doesn't have a clue."

Cecil stepped back into his chauffeured Escalade, which drove him straight toward the black heart of Manhattan, the crowded hell where real New Yorkers rarely dared to venture.

Times Square.

The Escalade parked outside the Visage flagship store. The brand's famous watch cogs and silver wires ran like veins over the windows. White beetles decorated windowpanes. The entire building façade was caked in real metallic blue butterfly wings.

A line of people stood outside the store for hours just for a look inside. The Visage devotees wore T-shirts featuring the Visage icon, a Libra symbol. The setting sun on the horizon.

Cecil stood by the store, worriedly clutching his posters. Hot dogs and garbage roasted beneath the sun. Honking cars, groaning homeless, and the relentless rumble of eight million chattering tourists. People shoving, rubbing against each other like sardines on crowded streets. All while Gap and Amazon advertised on giant, glittery billboards above.

He was an ant in the concrete jungle, shyly holding out a poster.

"Sorry, I'm from out of town," the man said, shoving Cecil's hand back.

"But...That's fine. You might see her. Just in case, please. Please just take it."

He tried again, but the man shook his head and kept walking, checking his subway map to avoid his eyes.

"Missing! Missing girl. My best friend's missing," Cecil shouted, drowned out by the stand owner screaming, *"Hot dogs. Hot dogs, come an' get 'em."*

A conspicuous billboard hung above him—his godmother, the founder of Visage, adorned in a stingray-skin gown. *Perdonna* was signed in delicate red cursive over her bare legs.

Missing posters littered the sidewalk as people discarded them, feet stomping over Annabelle's face.

A girl leaned over from the Visage line, wrapped her arm around Cecil, and smiled, flashing her disposable camera at them. He handed her a poster, and she took a photo of that too.

Pedestrians pointed at him. Cameras flashed like tiny stars.

"Help me! Please. My friend's missing. Why are you taking pictures of me?"

People stopped to watch, a crowd forming around him. Paparazzi swooped in from behind.

"Brah, check your silver cabinets," a stranger jeered. "You totally dismembered that girl."

He tried to ignore it. "Her name is Annabelle Leigh," Cecil said. "She likes the Plaza Hotel...so she might be there."

The people laughed. Some clapped at the absurdity.

A reporter shoved a microphone in his face. "It's been almost two weeks. Time to look for a body, Mr. LeClaire?"

Cecil hadn't left his house in the two weeks she had been missing.

"Were you fucking her?" someone asked. "Was Annabelle Leigh your girlfriend? Were you sleeping with the chauffeur's daughter?"

"She disappeared outside *your* house, dumbass. How did you not see it?"

A large camera came so close to Cecil's face that his nose smudged the scope with oil and sweat. It flashed bright white into his eyes. The people in the crowd seemed to laugh in slow motion, faces disgustingly contorting.

Cecil fell to the ground, holding his arms over his head to shield himself from the blows.

Armed security guards pushed through the mob and shoved the reporters and tourists away. The tall men formed a circle around Cecil.

"Perdonna! Perdonna! Oh my God, it's Tazia Perdonna," people shrieked. The line outside Visage went wild, crying at the sheer sight of her.

Security ushered Cecil into a Mercedes-Maybach. Perdonna joined after signing autographs, her eyes carefully watching Cecil as he gave a despondent stare out of the car window.

"Bellino, what were you thinking? Times Square?" she asked, pulling him close and kissing his head.

The mob banged on their car, eyes glaring down at them, trying to see through the tinted glass. Thunderous hits smashed against the windows, and it felt as if the blows went straight to the skin.

All he could do to escape was look into her eyes.

He wanted her now. As he stood outside St. Joseph's Abbey, his new home, entirely alone.

"You're just hiding here, right?" one reporter asked. "This monk thing is an act."

Abbot Joseph swung open the chapel doors. "I can assure you

it isn't. Brother George is a God-fearing man."

The reporters chuckled at the thought but tried to hold in their laughter in front of the abbot. Even atheists in the twenty-first century respected the monks.

"*Murderous Monk* will make a good headline," a reporter said.

A monk exited the chapel, and the reporters made a dash toward him, camera crew clumsily towing their equipment.

Brother George watched as a camera scope zoomed in on Brother Martin's face, lengthening like a giraffe neck until the camera's glass stared him in the eye. Brother Martin, small and meek, began to cry, shielding his face from the lights.

"Do you know Cecil LeClaire?" they shouted.

"Has Margaux LeClaire visited the abbey? Has Perdonna?"

"I...I don't know these people," Brother Martin whispered.

Brother George stood in front of him, arms splayed out. "These are supposed to be silent hours."

"And what do you think about during silent hours, Cecil? How many seconds it took to suffocate Annabelle Leigh?" a reporter asked, accompanied by a chorus of naughty laughter, like rats tweeting into the night.

"Come on, Cecil. Where'd you bury her? It's been ten years. She has to be dead."

"Get out!" Brother George screamed. His throat rattled, and the veins in his neck squirmed like snakes.

A cameraman pushed toward Brother George and zoomed in on his red face, and he turned, shoving the camera out of the man's arms. The camera whacked the man in the nose. He stumbled backward, clutching his mouth, fingertips covered with blood.

"I'll press charges," he said, holding his face.

Another shook her head. "Go ahead. Perdonna will bribe him out anyway."

Red-and-blue police sirens flashed up the gravel road toward the chapel, reflecting off the tree leaves.

"Private property," the officer said. "Time to leave."

Brother George looked to the sky to ground himself. The stars millions of miles away felt more concrete than his very own existence.

Ω

The abbey was most magical at night. When the pond was wiped clean and transformed into a perfect sheet of black that reflected the stars across the Earth. Heaven fell from the sky each night and onto the abbey lawn.

Brother George knelt down to the trunk of a giant maple tree, knees cradled by the soft bedding of autumn leaves. He stuck a twig into the creases of a notch and cranked open the small door he had built to cover a hollow. Inside was a Visage cigar humidor, decorated with tiny pearlescent-blue mussel shells and a stuffed red dog.

He lit a cigar between his teeth, then used the flame from the lighter to illuminate the pages beneath the cigars.

Newspaper articles read: "Lowly Child Stolen from America's Wealthiest Avenue," "The Disappearance of the Century," *"Pourquoi la famille LeClaire a tué Annabelle Leigh,"* and "Annabelle Leigh, Lost in Her Kingdom by the Sea."

Beneath the articles was Annabelle's diary—mostly schoolgirl erotica and meticulous, albeit disturbing, records of Margaux LeClaire. She wrote about the time Margaux whacked her father, the chauffeur, with a silver platter because he bought the miniature rainbow Swedish Fish instead of the originals. One Christmas, she refused to wear stockings. Her legs froze because Margaux said nylons were for maids and Michael Jackson only.

Ten years ago, at 4:00 p.m., a townhouse camera on Sixty-Third Street caught a video of Annabelle. She paced outside of the LeClaire Mansion, appearing in and out of the security footage. It seemed like she was waiting for someone. But no one knew whom.

Then, at 4:09 p.m., she disappeared from the camera's view, and that was the last anyone had ever seen of her.

One theory had Margaux LeClaire ordering Annabelle's abduction in front of the LeClaire Mansion to raise the celebrity cachet of LeClaire Model Management. Another speculated that terrorists, funded by Margaux, kidnapped Annabelle for military training in the Middle East. But the most popular theory of all was that young Cecil LeClaire brutally murdered his girlfriend, so Visage and LeClaire covered it up.

The case was adapted into a Lifetime made-for-television movie, which further established Cecil LeClaire as a bad boy, teenaged sex symbol.

Brother George held a photo of Cecil and Annabelle as pre-schoolers, riding a kiddie Batmobile. Annabelle with her Shirley Temple curls dressed up in a Catwoman suit with whiskers, a tail, and a giant smile on her face.

He kissed the photo and placed the contents back into the box. He watched as the flame from his lighter scarred the stars in the pond's perfect black mirror, and he chucked the cigar humidor into the reflections of the flame.

"I see you haven't exactly given up your worldly possessions," Abbot Joseph said. He looked down to Brother George's hand, which clutched a red leather dog. It was in tatters with both ears torn midway. The scruffy, franken-dog was adorable to him, but to others it looked like a lab experiment gone wrong.

"I can't throw away the stuffed animal," Brother George said, clutching the dog. "It belongs to someone else."

"I didn't mean the dog. I meant the person. Throwing away some paper doesn't mean you've moved on."

Brother George took the cigar from his mouth and snuffed it out, the smoke floating before his face.

"How can you be married to God if you haven't even gotten over a dead teenaged girl?" the abbot asked.

"I spent my whole childhood with that *dead teenaged girl*," Brother George barked. Unlike the reporters, the abbot didn't flinch at his show of violence. "I spent my whole adult life as her murderer."

"You're angry," the abbot whispered.

"Of course I'm angry," Brother George said, clasping his hands to stop the shaking. "I'm sorry. I'll be quiet."

The abbot chuckled. "I meant you're angry in general. You're holding in a lot of hurt."

Thunder rumbled through the sky, and the tree frogs' bright melody faded into the water.

"Ever since I was a teenager, I always felt cursed," Brother George said. "If the entire world believes I'm an evil psychopath, then there must be some truth to it, right?"

"Maybe." Tiny droplets of rain fell onto the leaves above them. "But you can't figure that out here." The abbot pointed to the water where the box had sunk. "I think you need to go back to New York."

Brother George's eyes went wide, and he clenched the stuffed dog in his hand. "Excuse me? Do *you* think I'm a murderer?"

"Of course not."

"Then give me another chance."

"Give you another chance to do what? Shove another reporter tomorrow?"

"Jesus Christ was violent all the time."

"Jesus Christ wasn't a monk!"

Brother George sat by the pond, dewy moss sticking to his habit's fabric. He placed the stuffed dog in his pocket and put his head in his hands. "I'll stop making sex jokes about pizza. Or if it's about that mother earlier—"

"Admittedly, she deserved that," the abbot said with a sly smile.

"I'm learning the power of God. I'm trying—"

"The power of God *is* suffering. It is about facing your troubles and having the power to overcome them," the abbot said, grabbing Brother George by the shoulders. "The abbey isn't a place to hide."

"What do you think I'm hiding from?"

Water droplets trickled from the sky faster and faster by the second until the thunder came. With a loud roar, rain pummeled the Earth. A lightning bolt feathered down from the clouds and struck the maple tree a few feet over.

"Come on," Brother George shouted, shielding the older man's head.

They ran toward a small cabin beside the pond where Brother George worked on his craft. When they swung open the doors, it was pitch black inside.

"Power lines must be down," the abbot said, teeth chattering, cold and wet.

Brother George crawled beneath his workbench, feeling his way across the ground, to find a kerosene lantern he stashed away. The tub beside him smelled of animal hides and lime. The animal skins were stripped of their fur with lime to create leather. Brother George made medieval manuscripts, recreating the old masters' artwork on parchment paper.

When the kerosene lantern burst with flames, the abbot huffed. "Speak of the devil."

Sheepskins were stretched on a dozen wooden frames, pulled and dried until they became paper. And on clothing lines, large parchment papers sparkled with gold leaf. Intricate illustrations featured a naked Eve, neck arched, seductively chewing the apple among boa constrictors and golden chameleons. Decaying sheep hides were transformed into gold-plated masterpieces that could last over a thousand years.

But the bloody cardboard package took center stage.

The door burst open, and the usually stoic abbot screamed a high-pitched yelp. An NYPD detective shook his drenched head like a drowned rat.

The young male detective stood a foot shorter than Brother George and refused to look up at his face. The man had an innocent, doughboy look, except for the terribly crooked nose that had presumably been bent by the many people he irritated.

"Detective Tom Chandler," he said, eyes scouring the animal skins. "Good with the epidermis, are we?"

"Yes. But I would've never put that corpse on the runway," Brother George said.

"Why not?" Chandler put his hands on his hips, tilting his pelican beak of a nose.

"No artist would embroider a brunette corpse with *purple* beading. Brunettes are autumns, not springs—that's the real crime."

Chandler snarled like a tiny Chihuahua. He raised his foot to stomp but seemed to think better of throwing a full-blown tantrum. "Now isn't the time to be making jokes."

"If not now, when?" asked the other detective as she opened the door, completely dry beneath her umbrella.

The female detective was Chandler's body opposite. She stood as tall as Cecil with a rotund belly and a roll of fat that jiggled like Jell-O when she walked. But despite her domineering size, she had those marble-round eyes that could only depict kindness.

"I remember you. Detective Roosevelt, right? You're the detective on Annabelle's case," Brother George said.

"Was. The FBI took it over several years ago when it became a kidnapping, and it died there. It's been out of my hands," Roosevelt said. "Doesn't mean I haven't been studying it."

Chandler pulled gloves from his backpack and began laying tarps around the bleeding package. He examined the exterior of the box, taking photographs from all angles.

"Do you think the skin coat has something to do with Annabelle?" Brother George asked.

"Possibly." Roosevelt pulled a pair of gloves over her hands.

Chandler stared at Brother George as Roosevelt inspected the package.

"You're opening it here?" he asked, then he caught Chandler's prying eyes and realized they wanted to see his reaction to the items inside. All of the LeClaires were suspects.

Roosevelt tore through the tape to find an invitation to the Visage Collection Presentation wrapped like a scroll. Grasping it was a pale hand.

It's a plastic hand, he told himself, resisting the temptation to poke the bloody flesh.

The abbot held his nose, gagging as he looked away.

A charm bracelet held the skin-vitation together, positioned to look like the limp wrist was wearing jewelry. Dangling from the chain was a cat charm. It was the bracelet that disappeared ten years ago with Annabelle Leigh.

The purplish hand was the same color as the flesh coat on the Visage runway. A bright red scar marred the wrist.

"The skin coat isn't a new murder," Brother George said. "The skin coat *is* Annabelle."

"How do you know?"

"That is her charm bracelet." He touched the scar on her wrist. "And that's her scar. This is her hand."

4

Blood smeared over the silk Visage invitation.

Cecil LeClaire is cordially invited to
The Visage Collection Presentations
On the 23rd and 26th days of October 2019
SHOW SOME SKIN?

"We'll contact the hospitals in Manhattan, see if we can get DNA for Annabelle Leigh to test against the flesh from the invitation and the body on the runway," Roosevelt said.

"But where could Annabelle have been? She disappeared ten years ago. Either she's been alive all those years, or that's a ten-year-old corpse," Brother George said.

Chandler shrugged in agreement and winked at Roosevelt.

Abbot Joseph retrieved suitcases and began packing goods for Brother George to take to New York—raspberry preserves made by the Trappist monks, illustrated Bibles, ceramic bowls made by Brother Martin, and bottles of beer made at the abbey brewery.

"I'm not leaving," Brother George yelled over his shoulder, but the elderly man kept scurrying.

Brother George pointed to the invitation. "Why is Perdonna having another runway show? She just had one."

"Fashion Week is late this year," Chandler said, blushing a bright shade of red. "The second show is a Visage showcase for the investors."

Roosevelt puckered her lips and tried to hide her snickering. "Are you a fashion aficionado, Chandler?"

"What can you tell us about Clara Royds?" Chandler asked Cecil, ignoring Roosevelt's mocking.

"She's my second cousin." Brother George paused, thinking about it. "Or maybe a third cousin? She's from New Orleans."

He grabbed a rounded stone from his workshop desk and began rubbing it along a piece of stretched leather. Flakes of pale white skin blistered off. He rubbed harder and harder, trying to calm his stirring emotions.

"Nervous?" Chandler asked.

"I'm sad. I'm angry. Who wouldn't be?"

"Where was Clara at the time of Annabelle's abduction?"

"She was nineteen. Margaux gave her an internship at the modeling agency for the year as a favor. But she was constantly doing drugs. She taunted the models. She bullied Annabelle. She was a problem."

"We heard Clara Royds told the media *you* murdered Annabelle Leigh. She reported the stories that you dissected cats for fun. She told the world you beat Annabelle Leigh to death."

Brother George stopped rubbing the stone along the leather. He huffed and folded his hands together, listening to the rain.

"She did," Brother George said.

Chandler gave a smug grin and scribbled notes onto his notepad.

"Clara was nineteen when Annabelle disappeared. Where would she have kept Annabelle this whole time—in her bedroom closet? You don't have any other suspects? No idea where Annabelle has been for the past *ten years*? There is no way Clara killed Annabelle on her own."

"The skin coat had a strange mix of medical and decorative stitches. We believe Clara had help," Roosevelt said. "But, right now, we are looking at a few suspects."

"Who are the other suspects?" Brother George asked after a pause. When he scanned Roosevelt's drooping eyes, he knew. "My mother and me?"

Brother George rolled his rosary nervously between his fingers. "Do you have a motive?"

"Assuming you didn't send the invitation to yourself," Roosevelt said, elbowing Chandler. "Someone *invited* you to see the body with this invitation. So Annabelle's murder could be an act of revenge."

"Revenge for what?"

"Unclear," Roosevelt said.

"Any ideas?" Chandler asked, eyeing up Brother George.

"I can't imagine anyone I know sending me this or wanting revenge for *anything*."

"Your mother?" Chandler asked.

"I love Margaux. She's flawed. She's a handful. She says horribly disgusting things. But she did her best to raise me well...given the circumstances."

"As we understand it," Chandler said, "you were raised mostly by Perdonna and nannies, not Margaux."

"Margaux wasn't the best mother. But she wouldn't kill Annabelle."

Chandler scoffed in a harsh, biting way. "You all cover for each other."

Brother George stopped himself from a witty reply. He stormed out and slammed the door. The rain had petered out into a dull drizzle, lightly tapping the pond's black surface and rippling into tiny waves.

He stuck his hand into the pocket in his habit and gripped the stuffed dog, whipping it over his head. But just as he was about to throw it into the pond, Abbot Joseph grabbed his wrist and pulled his arm down.

He was out of breath, body leaning against a bag of jams. "You're not ready to be a monk yet. First, you have to take responsibility. To face the truth, no matter how horrible."

"I'm not leaving. This is my home."

"You don't have a choice. But you will be welcomed back with open arms. *After* you've buried Cecil LeClaire and all that comes with him. *Then* you can take your solemn vows." The abbot presented Brother George with his gifts. "You'll leave tomorrow morning."

$$\underline{\underline{\Omega}}$$

Brother George left his cell early the next morning to avoid saying his goodbyes. It was one of those mornings where the darkness felt infinite, as if the sun would never burn its way over the ground.

He lay with the white crosses in the cemetery, splayed out like one of the dead. Grass stained his white T-shirt, and warm, wet moss hugged his hands. It was the first morning in years he hadn't worn a habit, and he felt naked. He didn't know who he was. He couldn't call himself a monk anymore.

He imagined sinking into the earth and leaving only a white cross as a sign that he lived. At least the pile of white stones would give him meaning.

He had always wanted to be buried. Cremation seemed messy. And he doubted many teaching hospitals could accept the donated corpse of a murder suspect.

Annabelle was always adamant about having her head frozen so she could be restored as a robot in the future. But she only wanted to be brought back if they also managed to revive Walt Disney. Because what was the point of living if she had no hopes of ever becoming a Disney Princess?

Annabelle probably would've thought it pretty cool that her body was turned into a bedazzled coat. Though sequins and embroidery didn't exactly lend to the freezing process.

Maybe Annabelle and Cecil could be buried at the abbey together. Then he could lay among the great monks who devoted their lives to goodness. He'd never have to leave.

But that was only a dream. Instead, he clutched a flip phone that had been donated to the monks and planned to set off in an old Toyota.

He dialed his mother and heard: "You have not reached Margaux LeClaire. Please do not leave a message after the tone unless you are Pierre Lazard, Tazia Perdonna, Tom Gray, or a federal police force. No, not you, Karl Lagerfeld. You know what you did."

When the voicemail greeting ended, a blaring jingle came from behind the trees. He peered behind the cemetery and found a ringing car.

A giant monstrosity.

There was a metallic-gold tank with oversized headlights and armored doors. It sprung on its wheels like a children's bouncy castle. And the doors flapped open and shut, lifting up like wings.

As the morning bells chimed over the chapel, Brother George ran to the car to shut it up.

It made exhaust sounds like a small boy pretending to be a truck.

Margaux LeClaire appeared on the dashboard screen. "You like?" she asked. "Thought you'd need transportation."

"Turn it off!" he yelled.

The car doors closed. The headlights turned off. The tank seemed to cry itself to sleep, softening its blaring ditty to a whimper, then to silence. He climbed inside when it was safe.

"Why was it ringing?" Cecil asked, staring at the reflective, disco ball interior.

"Not ringing. It was celebrating. That was *celebration* mode," Margaux said with a beaming Cheshire Cat grin. "There's no purpose to it, really. It's just fun. Like the car is dancing."

"Don't do it again, please."

"Aaaaand celebrate," she said, clicking a button on her computer. "It's just so cute. So cute. Like a little teddy bear tank." The car doors flew open, and a different, more soul-crushing song played. The backend bucked like a donkey, and the headlights flashed in time. Sitting in the seat felt like riding a bucking bronco.

"Stop," Brother George said, frantically slamming buttons on the car. Monks began peering out of their cell windows, shoving their curtains aside. "Mother! Turn it the fuck off."

"Oh, Jesus. I see you're not *that* Christian."

The car fell back to sleep. It droned as the lights dimmed, the cheesy tune went soft, and the backend squirmed to a standstill. The car seemed sad, a baby crying about his party ending. "What is this?" he asked, tracing the Lamborghini logo with his fingers.

"The Rambo Lambo," Margaux said. "A gift from Gaddafi. He had one leftover from his military, and he gave it to me. I decked it out."

"The Libyan dictator Gaddafi?"

"Yep. That's the one. Saddam Hussein's son had one too. But his obviously didn't have *celebration* mode."

Margaux snarled, playing with her tight blond curls between her fingertips.

"I can't drive this thing into Manhattan," Brother George said. "It's too big for the streets."

"It does great in New York. You'll see. The goddamn bike lane takes up half of Fifth Avenue now. Traffic's terrible. But the Rambo's great. It just plows those Spandex-clad queers right over."

Brother George rested his head against the seat. He spent most of his life feeling guilty for wanting to laugh at her wildly inappropriate jokes. It was her brand. She pretended to be a clown to disarm everyone. She was charming in a backward way.

It was never clear what she meant in earnest, and which lines were just jokes. And so she could get away with saying almost anything. And the public tuned in to listen.

"Have you spoken to Clara?" Brother George asked.

"Can't talk to her. She's in total lockdown," Margaux said. "Our lawyer thinks they're trying to get her to flip on me. Her shithole apartment's closed off, her stuff is confiscated..."

"Why is she back in New York?" Brother George asked. "Why is she back in your life?"

"Um, well...long story."

"I'd like to hear it."

Margaux smacked her cherry lip gloss across her lips. Her

gaze darted away. "Clara is a heroin addict. Some of my models are junkies too. And I was using Clara for supply."

"What!"

"It's why she doesn't have any friends. No leads for the police. I think Clara is just the henchman for whoever abducted Annabelle. She's too strung out to be a mastermind."

"But did she *murder* Annabelle?"

Margaux shrugged. "It was probably a frame job. Clara was high backstage at the Visage show, so the killer probably had her put the coat on my model."

Margaux held up her phone to the screen and showed Cecil the newest Annabelle Leigh headline.

"You were right, though," Margaux said. "It's all over Chatter. Detectives confirmed the DNA from the coat. The skin-vitation is Annabelle Leigh."

Brother George took a deep breath, even though he knew the moment he saw the hand. "Where do you think she was for ten years? Do you think she suffered?"

"No shit. The girl was abducted and murdered. I'm sure they kept her in a candy shop. Maybe a butterfly garden full of monarchs and jujubes?"

Behind Margaux, he noticed a crowd of hundreds of young women. Banners with the LeClaire Model Management logo covered a dull cement building that appeared to be a mall in New Jersey. The girls wore heavy sweatshirts and gloves in the cold fall morning.

"What is that?" he asked. "Where are you?"

"Casting call for the agency."

"It's not even five in the morning."

"Oh," Margaux scoffed, pointing to tents and sleeping bags. "They've been camping out in the parking lot for *days*. Half these little bitches want to be rich and famous. And the other half just want to be told they're pretty."

"A body showing up on a runway yesterday didn't put them off modeling?" Brother George asked.

"Instagram fame is all that matters to these kids," Margaux said. "I can make them a star. I'm a tastemaker. Whichever girls I deem pretty get to walk in Fashion Week and get a million social media followers. My top model looks like an albino hippopotamus with fangs. But I really, really love hippopotamuses. So...guess who's walking all the runways this season? *A hippopotamus.*"

Margaux picked up a black leather binder and flipped through laminated pages of girls' faces. Then she held up the binder to the camera. The model had wide-set eyes and big puffy cheeks. Tiny nostrils and tiny ears framed a broad chin, and her canines jutted over her bottom lip.

"Tell me that's not a hippo?" Margaux asked.

"It's a hippo," he said, laughing despite himself. "A vampire hippo."

"So, I found this adorable hippo in a mall in Amsterdam. I signed it and brought it to America."

"Her. You signed *her*," Brother George corrected.

"Right. As soon as she came, I took photos of her, trained her, and pushed her on all the designers. I told Pierre Lazard she's beautiful and unique. Everyone will write about her in the papers after your show. She's *exotic*... So now, a hippopotamus is on every billboard in New York City. And I have fulfilled my life purpose."

Brother George scanned the crowd of wannabe models. The girls holding their photos in binders, with their hair in tight curls, wearing puffy pink sweatshirts, looked a lot like Margaux herself.

Margaux LeClaire had the most successful model agency in New York City because she came from nothing. She knew how to appeal to the high fashion market while also being aspirational to the whole of America. Fashion designers trusted her to bring them the most beautiful girls to model their clothing.

The prospective models clung to photo albums of themselves, anxiously screaming with glee and excitement every second. A booming voice came over a loudspeaker. "You're all so beautiful! The most beautiful group we've seen *ever*!" The young girls squealed with glee. "Who wants to meet Margaux LeClaire?"

The hundreds of girls screamed bloody murder. Margaux might as well have been a boy band.

A stylist came by to touch up her look, spraying a veil of hairspray that glittered over her hair. "We'll do a press conference when you're back. Try to convince people you didn't murder Annabelle," Margaux said.

"Why do people *still* think I had something to do with her murder? I've been in a monastery."

"It's because you look like a young Clint Eastwood. You're hot, charming, and untrustworthy."

"And yet they love *you*. You. The most—"

"Careful—"

"Awful witch. They think you're a saint."

"Because I can make their dreams come true." She kissed at the camera and hung up the phone.

Brother George carefully placed his bag of gifts from Abbot Joseph in the back seat. The scents of jams and freshly baked bread filled the Rambo Lambo, and it felt a bit more like home. Even though the seats were made of velvet and the steering wheel was lined with twenty-four-karat gold.

When he put the key in the ignition, a chilled drawer popped out, holding glass bottles of Coke along with drawers full of chocolate truffles decorated with raspberry and mint. He reluctantly took the Coke. He was on break from the monastery after all.

He made a deal with himself. Coke and Lamborghinis were acceptable vices for the week. But he'd still refrain from sex and overindulging in food... Well, maybe not pizza. And maybe he'd sneak a hot dog or five.

He drove the gold Rambo Lambo through winding cornfields tinged with the orange hue of morning. The tattered red dog, called Aberto, sat on his dashboard. Sliding his Visage sunglasses over his eyes, he saw the industrial wasteland of Philadelphia through a gray haze.

Time moved in a blur. It seemed one beat of the clock's second hand could take him back to New York City.

Manhattan had no middle class. Hundred-million-dollar condos looked down on housing projects and homeless people peeing on garbage cans. New York was a grid. From thirteen thousand feet in the sky, America's class lines hung like aircraft vapor trails.

But the LeClaires knew nothing of the rats carrying typhoid in the subways or the drug addicts sleeping in Washington

Square Park. To Margaux LeClaire, the entire universe existed between Fifth and Madison Avenues, the land where a size two was average and the ideal was size zero. Where plastic surgeons chopped skin off seventeen-year-olds and made women over fifty look like sallow ducks with pursed lips. Where the "haves" and "have yachts" docked their egos. Where a coat was $20,000, and Pierre Lazard and Tom Gray had castles that sat proudly over their domains.

The neoclassical LeClaire Mansion sat on Sixty-Third Street between Fifth and Madison Avenues on the Upper East Side. Two Ionic columns framed a solid black door. The windows were covered in one-way mirrors, shielding the models from any plebeians trying to look inside.

If you looked into the windows of LeClaire Model Management, you would only see your reflection staring back.

Two marble lions crouched growling with their teeth flashing at pedestrians. Unfortunately, Margaux had hired a cheap sculptor from Ohio to design them, so they looked like disproportioned cats with lopsided ears and missing teeth. Margaux added bedazzled red collars to their necks, keeping things gaudy. Putting the snaggle-toothed lions in front of a Manhattan mansion was like putting a six-year-old's Play-Doh self-portrait in the Louvre. Such was *La Famille LeClaire.*

The deformed lions had turned out to be a decent marketing tool, nonetheless. They were the billboard image for the Lifetime movie. Tourists stopped to take selfies with the mangled monsters, more often after Annabelle's death. Cecil and the LeClaires became bastardized celebrities—famous only for their names.

Visitors put bloody (ketchup-covered) Visage bags and broken Buratti heels at the mansion stoop with newspaper clippings of articles about Cecil with headlines like "Uptown Murderer" and "The Butcher of Fifth Avenue."

Margaux took advantage of this debacle. She set up a Chatter and Instagram photo booth outside of the modeling agency. You could pose with a blood-covered mannequin in front of a mirrored wall of the mansion.

In 1987, Cecil's father, Louis, bought the mansion from a

strange Brazilian man who claimed too loudly not to have Nazi ties. Soon after, Louis became obsessed with eugenics, and Margaux received three sets of perfectly proportioned twin models with whom she started LeClaire Model Management.

Brother George hadn't been home since Margaux had relocated all the model agency operations to the mansion. He had never before seen his family home turned into a modeling empire.

He parked the Rambo Lambo in front of a plaque that read "LeClaire Model Management." Security cameras flickered toward him like the eyes of a skulking monster.

It would've been a lie to say he was filled only with dread. But he didn't want to admit there was the smallest bit of excitement inside him.

He knocked on the door of his former home, the cold metal of his cross feeling heavy on his neck. As the doorman ushered him inside, Brother George didn't recognize the mansion.

The sober Louis XV foyer his father had built was gone, replaced by a two-story fountain that sprayed upward. It had a white coffered ceiling lined with gold, and two opposing marble staircases covered in oxblood carpet, swirling around the lobby like the red cape of a queen.

The mansion had become an empire, the embodiment of a dream.

White orchids existed only to perfume portraits of naked models, and light appeared more from mirrored reflections than from the sun itself.

Nothing could be touched. Not the chandeliers, dangling crystals with modern red spokes jutting out. Not the Venetian-onyx elevator buttons. And certainly not the models.

Their spidery legs swayed atop stiletto heels, lurid eyes peering upward, drunk with the American Dream.

5

"Your mother is in the middle of something right now," said Margaux's assistant, Freddy. He was a short man with bulging muscles on top and bird legs on the bottom, always sporting skin-tight plaid pants and a poufy afro.

"Doing what?" Cecil asked.

Freddy put his lips to Cecil's ear, scooting right up to his cheek, encroaching on his personal space. "It's the po-po. The penguins. The Stasi. She's on the phone with Roosevelt. Not the president, the cop."

"I assumed," Cecil said, inching away from Freddy's face.

Freddy pointed to the staircase where two young models sat in red dresses, legs parted open enough to see white lace peeking between their thighs. "Come upstairs and wait."

Agents spun around them in a frenzy, shouting into their headpieces. Girls sprinted out the doors to get to gigs, photographs and heels in hand. The LeClaire agency had the momentum of a tornado.

Freddy pushed through the former living room door. No trace of Cecil existed. There were no longer apple-cinnamon candles or photos of his high school chess club. It was as if he had never lived at all.

On the television encrusted with crystals, a school photo of Annabelle wearing braces, a Mickey Mouse sweater, and red bows in her hair appeared on the news.

His former home was unrecognizable to him.

It was cold and luxurious. Margaux LeClaire's fever dream.

One wall was covered in black marble, veined with white lightning bolts. A giant mirror reflected the white veins and refracted the shadows around the room. Ottomans featured marble legs strangled by gold chains and jagged pieces of broken mirror. To sit on them, you would have to risk scraping open your thighs.

It looked like a high fashion sex dungeon. Or a ballet studio in a prison castle.

Tarot cards sparkled in etchings carved into the tabletop— goblins and devils and a crowned princess stroking a lion. Twinkling golden chains hung from the ceiling as chandeliers.

It was a room meant to intimidate—expensive, impressive, and shocking. It was a space only to be photographed for *Glamorama*.

A painting, Goya's *Saturn Devouring His Son,* hung front and center. The titan with a ghoulish mane and horrified eyes held the naked body of his son as he ate him like a turkey leg. He had already consumed the head and one arm, leaving a small, bloody, pale corpse in his giant grasp. It was disturbing, yet beautiful, the dark black and gold paint from the canvas melding into the marble walls.

It was Cecil's favorite painting. He had never admitted it. Because it was his mother's favorite too.

Cecil subconsciously wrapped his fingers around the golden cross at his neck.

Then he heard the sound of heels clacking against the floor like horse hooves. Hushed whispers flooded beneath the door.

Cecil stood and pressed his ear to the wall. Citrus and cinnamon wafted up his nose.

He pushed open the door to find mirrors and camera equipment. Silver and golden chiffon flew through the air as models paraded past. White silk was strewn across the floor, stepped on as though it were sawdust. Models were sculpted figures with wasp-thin waists, half-dressed bodies in dainty laced underwear, rib cages so defined they looked like railroad tracks. They were beautiful yet creepy dolls, expensive and fragile, breakable when handled.

Their arms stuck out like tree branches, so thin Cecil could wrap his hand entirely around their biceps. Their collarbones stood on display as necklaces of bone poking through their skin. He'd been surprised by the glowing whiteness of their teeth. They looked as though they had been artificially lacquered with Wite-Out.

Lacy white fringe and transparent bras bandaged their tiny breasts.

Models seemed to be another species altogether, nymphets with sallow cheeks, a coquettish Lolita aspect tying it all together.

Eyes bulging from their sockets were inlaid gems set above cheekbones.

The skin glowed with the sheen of scented oils. And musky dewdrops sat between the rounds of their breasts, like dotted candies.

They did their best work when they stood still. A model's job was to play dead.

They were just as haunting as Cecil had remembered. He had always been cautious of models. They were beautiful but askew, as if they weren't entirely human.

As a kid, he tried to stay far, far away from the models. But being with them now face-to-face for the first time as an adult, was an inhuman experience.

"Um. Ahem." Cecil waved his hand awkwardly. "Do any of you know Ava Germaine? The model who wore the skin coat? Is she here? I'd like to talk to her."

The models' heads turned toward him at once like preprogrammed robots.

"You don't need Ava. I can please you." A tall girl wearing cut-off jean shorts and kidult sneakers held out her hand. "I'm Jordan."

Cecil grasped her fingers. "Excuse me? Oh. I'm not casting."

Jordan walked to the speakers in the corner of the room. She cruised like a shark among minnows. A deep bass began to shake the room as she found the perfect beat. "Every man is casting. You're casting even if you don't know it."

A six-foot-tall freckle-faced girl approached with a camera the size of her torso. She heaved it into his arms. "Test shoot?"

"I...I'm not a photographer," Cecil said. "I want to ask Ava a few questions."

He scoured the room for the girl he had seen wearing Annabelle's body.

"Are you casting a runway show, then?" Jordan asked with a wink.

Cecil heaved the camera onto his knee, taking the weight off his arms. "Does anyone *other* than Jordan speak?"

They stared back in confusion.

"No English. *Eu não* entendo. What?" a few models said.

"Oh," Cecil said.

He realized Ava might not be American. He looked nervously around the room, trying to remember her look. But all models looked the same to him.

Jordan twirled into a catlike pose. Her back curved upward, and her neck seductively rolled. She prowled forward, and her curly hair fell over her breasts. "I'll do the job for a shopping trip to Visage."

Cecil clutched the camera with a death grip, looking through it like a gun sight. He snapped a photo of her to keep her at bay, the flash blinding her eyes.

"Please. *Por favor! S'il vous plait!*" they shouted.

"There's no job."

They tugged on dresses, stepping in and out of scarves and silks, frolicking with the clothes like little girls playing dress-up. The girls lined up before his camera to audition for a job that didn't exist. Cecil whipped the camera up to shield himself as the girls prowled toward him.

Scents of vanilla, cinnamon, and lavender grew stronger. He had entered a purely feminine wonderland, one where passions flowed freely through the air like wisps of cigarette smoke.

A model bounced onto the sofa next to him, whispering, "*Wat zeg je, wat bedoel je.*"

Before she stroked his hair, he aimed the camera at her eyes. Her fingertips were whacked by the camera lens. Suddenly she leaned her head over the couch, fluffed up her hair and froze into a pose. "I shall do job for winter coat."

"Um. I'm sorry. I swear there really isn't a job."

"Do you work out?" Jordan cooed, pressing her sneakers into Cecil's navel and inching closer to his thighs.

"Whoa, whoa," Cecil said. "I'm a monk." He looked to the door. It was a distant ten yards. Far, at least, when he considered the possibility that the models would strip him of his shirt the moment he stood up.

"I don't care." Jordan winked. "You're hot."

A beautiful white gown approached with a petite freckled girl drowning inside of it. She innocently waved at him, as if to say hello.

"Nice to meet you," Cecil screamed over the music, wiping sweat from his brow.

"No English," the girl said, the bodice of the large wedding gown almost coming over her head.

Cecil pointed the camera, and she lifted the gown over her knees. She showed off her legs, turning them in like puppet limbs. She blew a kiss at him through the glass.

Jordan straddled his lap entirely, thighs rubbing against his. Bare breasts pressed into his torso as she traced her hands around his waistband. He wriggled the camera between their chests and used the machine to wrench her backward.

"You should check out my comp card," she said. "Maybe you'd want to have dinner with me?"

Another girl poked his arm. "Do you travel a lot?" she asked in a heavy accent. "Have you been to Russia? My family is there; I want to go see them."

"Can't you visit?" Cecil asked.

"Not enough money."

"What's your name?"

"Karolina."

He tried to hide his disappointment. She looked almost like Ava.

Jordan rubbed her hands across his chest. "So strong... You can touch me too, you know."

He stood up from the couch, wiping his lap. Flirtation wasn't entirely comfortable for a twenty-four-year-old monk.

The girls carried lavish laces and heels in crates, flowing purples and pinks, and dresses covered in chiffon. They shoved each other to fight for a place in front of the camera.

Cecil ran his fingers over the fabrics in the chest. "Whose dresses are these?"

"They're for Visage. Perdonna's ateliers haven't finished them yet."

He studied the shape of the garment, eyes focused on the angles. This would all be easier if their bodies were covered. "Let's get you dressed."

He ran his fingers over the girls' arms, testing the fabric already pinned to their arms. He placed new dresses overtop them, ripping tulle to shreds. His hands traced the girls' waists, feeling the pins, studying the shape of the dress.

There was nothing sexual about his hands gliding over the girls' legs. There was absolutely nothing arousing about cutting the neckline off of a long-sleeved gown, fingers stroking collarbones. Shaking skirts around their hips was a chore.

He removed the pins that kept the chiffon dresses half-formed, letting the fabric whip around them like a daydream.

The pins and needles sticking from their bodies no longer constricted them. They were free. He had turned the half-formed dresses into flowing masterpieces with a few simple cuts and tugs.

When loose fabric fell to the ground, he tied it around Jordan's shorts, making her a makeshift dress, pinning it to her curves. He carved the Venus de Milo out of a young girl.

She removed her T-shirt and jean shorts from beneath. Half-naked and covered in transparent pink cloth, she became a goddess. The flash of a camera lit up her eyes, no longer void of passion.

They looked like happy girls instead of disturbing creatures cocooned in silk.

Now they were ballerinas twirling in a rainbow, his photos capturing the beautiful line of a woman's body.

"What are your favorite snacks?" an American model with

freckles and a gap between her teeth asked Cecil. "Did you bring anything with you?"

"Um…excuse me? Are you hungry?"

"Chocolate! God, I miss chocolate," another American said. "I'll do the job for chocolate."

"Are you Ava?" Cecil asked.

She shook her head. "But I'm a better model than she is."

The model lunged toward his camera and he fell back onto the couch. He pointed the camera crosshairs to her head and she posed like a ballerina, one leg in the air.

Jordan's coquettish stare stuck out in an ocean of pink. Her green eyes twinkled through the camera lens as she posed her jaw perfectly to the shot.

He noticed a half sheet of paper on the mirrored coffee table. It was Jordan's comp card, her "resume" for modeling, showing Polaroid pictures taken without makeup or photo editing. She looked particularly young, cheeks rounded and pink, hair in knots on her head.

"How old are you?" Cecil asked.

"Eighteen," Jordan answered.

"What's the age range here?"

"Like fourteen to eighteen."

He stood frozen in the sea of girls. *Fourteen years old.*

The room spun around him as the music slowed.

"What's wrong?" Jordan asked.

"What are you trying to do? Flirt with me? If you know I'm Margaux's son, you know I can't hire you for anything."

Jordan brushed up against his arm. "I know you're Margaux's son," she said, kissing his cheek and whispering in his ear. "Sorry to hear about Annabelle. At least she had a good last show."

"Excuse me?" Cecil asked.

"I knew Annabelle. Take me outside to Central Park tonight, and I'll talk." She placed her hands on his jaw in an aggressive, flirty way. He aimed the camera lens to push her back. She put her hands in the air, like a fugitive faced with a cop's gun, and pouted her lips in a pose for the photo.

"Can't we talk about it now?"

Jordan's eyes darted. "I want to go to Central Park for a few minutes tonight. For some fresh air," she whispered. "You're her son, so I figured you have some power."

"Why do you need permission? Central Park's a block away."

"It's too dangerous for us to walk around Manhattan alone," Jordan said. "We can't leave the mansion without a chaperone."

None of the girls uttered a sound. One model wanted a winter coat. Another wanted plane tickets home. The saddest girl only wanted chocolate.

These were not the luxuries he expected high fashion models to crave.

The doors swung open, and Margaux stood at the entrance.

"Only girls play with dolls, Cecil. Men should play with women." Margaux pounded her cane to the floor, and the reverberations shook his entire body.

6

―――――――

"Think of me as your father," the model agent said. "You have to tell me everything."

Ava Germaine bit her chipped glittery pink nails. She was eleven years old.

It was 2006. Thirteen years before she would walk onto the Visage runway wearing a skin coat.

Andre Blancas's office was rigged like a theater stage, lacking windows but sweltering under the stage lights above. A cube so small a model could spread her arms and touch both walls. The model agent was a kind of vampire who outfitted its coffin with blinding light, a Polaroid camera, and twelve-year-old girls.

Ava covered her eyes from the blinding stage light, hands trembling. "Ugh...I killed my hamster."

"Not what I meant."

"I'm really sad... See, it's about Mr. Puffles. So, I snuck him into my bunk. Because...you know how sometimes people toss and turn and can't sleep? Well, that was me. So I put him with me in bed to cuddle. He bit my chin a little, but they were love bites, and they actually felt really good. So I kept him in bed with me and when I woke up, I couldn't find him."

"A stuffed animal didn't seem like a better idea?" Andre asked.

"I wanted someone to talk to... But then I woke up. And...and, when I rolled over, I felt, like, a little lump under me. And there was Mr. Puffles with his tongue sticking out. At first, I thought he was just tired, so I put him on his wheel to see if he'd run."

Ava quivered. "He didn't. So, then I spun the wheel, and he just sorta slid with it all limp-like. So, yeah. Then I...I got it."

"I don't think I can add hamster killer to your resume."

"You said you wanted to know about me. I thought...I thought you loved me."

Tears pooled around her burnt-caramel irises. *Glamorama* once wrote that Ava Germaine looked like "a baby doll on the brink of death." Her lips were bee-stung and pouty, but the color of a purplish corpse. Her eyes could've been painted by Goya— big and glassy, but with dark circles cradling them in half-moons. Cellophane pale skin covered her body, so emaciated it seemed to wither away beneath her plush pink cheeks.

She was the most beautiful eleven-year-old to walk the Earth.

"I do love you, darling." He took her hand and rubbed the palm as she wiped her tears on her shoulders. "I'm sorry. I'm sorry Mr. Puffles died. I'll buy you a new one after we get your nose fixed."

Ava touched her nose and scrunched it up. "My nose isn't broken."

Andre looked up with the "model agent gaze." Model agents had a way of studying girls. It was the same look butchers had when they eyed cows to be cut into New York strips. "It's too wide. Throws off the symmetry." He ran the edge of his car key across her face, tracing the distance between her eyes and nose. "I told your mother agent about a nose job. We can afford it. The cost can be deducted from your last editorial paycheck."

"I'm pretty sexy, I think. You're wrong. Everyone says my eyes are pretty." She put her hands on her hips.

"They're bug-like. But it's great for the Asian market."

Ava frowned, trying to squint her eyes to make them smaller. "Do you think I'm pretty, though? Like, overall?"

"You're expensive." He flashed the camera, shooting a Polaroid out. "No better compliment than that.

"Take your top off," he said, as bluntly as if he were asking her to pass the butter.

She whipped her camisole off to reveal a polka-dot string bikini top above her jeans. The photos flashed to blinding whites.

Squinting with only the lower half of your eyes—that was the model's secret. Suddenly, an eleven-year-old porcelain doll transformed into Lolita. A pout of the lips, a curve of the neck, a vacant, scolding, I'm-too-good-for-you-shopper stare. The high fashion shopper wanted youth in its purest form, a body void of puberty.

The model agent ran his fingers through her hair with a clinical touch. "We might straighten your hair."

She stuck her tongue out, and he grabbed it between his fingers, pushing it back inside.

"Don't smile. Pout. Seduce them," he cooed.

His palm pushed against her ass, lining the hips with her shoulders. She posed geometrically, like a machine devoid of life. She had become so accustomed to his hands on her body, she didn't flinch.

"Pants off," he said.

The zipper roar cut through the slap of photographs shooting out of the camera. The jeans crumpled to a pile in the corner.

Andre removed red stilettos from his bag. When she slid her foot inside, her heel was inches from touching the back of the shoe, like a daughter traipsing around in her mother's shoes during dress-up.

Ava could smell the skunk scent of marijuana on his collar as he kneeled before her to take photos of her body.

"You promised you'd take me to the movies this weekend."

His hands reached between her thighs, pushing her legs farther apart for a pose. His index finger scraped along the lace border of her underwear.

"I will."

"Promise?"

He yanked a measuring tape from his pocket and wrapped

it around her breasts. With a sigh, Andre scribbled down the reading.

"What?" she asked.

"You just...you have to be careful not to turn into a woman too quickly. We don't want curves."

Ava looked down at her chest as the agent placed a bottle of pills in front of her.

"Just keep taking your pills and you'll be fine," he said.

Ava nodded. "Why am I taking these again? Am I sick?"

"No, no, darling. Of course not. Nothing like that."

His lips caressed her forehead, and she smiled. She wrapped her arms around him in a hug.

"If you can't do the movie, can you take me for a slushee, at least?" she whispered.

"I'll try. Promise. But stop complaining, darling. Most girls would kill to live in a mansion. With models. Come on. Your biggest problem is a dead hamster."

He left the room with a thump of the door.

Ava swallowed three pills with a dry gulp.

2013. Ava was seventeen years old.

Ava suckled a Snickers bar in her prison cell, holding it like a chipmunk protecting its winter stock. Why was she in prison? The answer depended on who you asked.

She stood on sanitary pads in the showers to protect her feet, rubbing a detergent-like soap through her hair, taking extra time to massage her sensitive scalp. Penis drawings, telephone numbers, and gang signs were carved into the yellowish paint that covered the stalls.

None of the showers had doors, so she had to watch herself in the mirror, fingers brushing soap over a body devoid of sexuality. She was a broken machine, sharp angles with weak muscles connecting the bones. With a body that felt more like a cage than a vehicle, she was a breathing cadaver.

She wanted her Snickers bar back. She needed something sweet.

Wet hair up into a bun, a clean jumpsuit, and a smack of the cheeks for some color. She wanted to look pretty on the off chance someone came to visit her. But no one ever did.

Ava was the only girl to sit alone at an empty table in the visitors' lounge. She pretended to read a copy of *Lolita* while a crying mom gave her daughter Fritos and a Diet Coke from the outside. Ava wanted Fritos too.

"Ma'am, are you lost?" the guard asked. "If you're here to file a missing person report, it's down the hall."

"I'm visiting," a woman said. "Ava Germaine."

Ava slammed her book closed. She looked up to see a cascade of rose-gold hair falling in loose curls down a forest-green dress.

The rowdy room went silent. No more crying, no more screaming. Everyone stared at the porcelain model of a fairytale queen.

She tilted her Lazard sunglasses down, revealing the red scars along her blinded eyes. The guard walked before her. She snaked through the tables. Perdonna's height had her towering over the prison guards, gown swiveling around her like a coral in water.

The waft of vanilla overpowered all the body odor in the room. Ava placed her hand over Perdonna's balletic fingers, feeling the raised veins, the only sign that she was a day over thirty.

Somehow, even her hand was luxurious.

"She's famous, right?" a girl whispered. "Is she like...a princess?"

A chorus of whispers ensued, until one girl, with a big bright smile, decided to show off. "Dayum, girl. You so hot, I'd *fuck* you," she shouted.

"Ohhh," the inmates cooed, slapping their tables.

"I've been known to dip into the honeypot sometimes," Perdonna replied with a coy smile.

Girls stood up from their tables, chanting "Ayyy," as even the parents held back laughter until a guard blew his whistle.

"Sit down, sit down, everyone."

Ava, still shaking, avoided Perdonna's cloudy eyes when she finally turned to her at the table.

"I love inmates," Perdonna said, lips smacking a nude lip gloss. "They're *primal.*"

"Do you know many inmates?"

"I know many people who should be."

Her voice lilted like a song, the accent not quite Italian, not British, but a blend of the two. The red scars around her eyes seemed to melt the frames of her sunglasses, like hot coils brushing up against gold.

"Detective Roosevelt told me you're quite innovative. I see you've memorized *Lolita.*"

Ava gave her a skeptical glare.

"You've cut out the pages," Perdonna said. "I assume you're either hiding a knife or a candy."

"A shiv and a Reese's Peanut Butter Cup." Ava looked around the room as people continued to stare. She lowered her head self-consciously. "Why are you here?"

"*Why are you here?*" Perdonna repeated. "That wasn't quite the warm welcome I was hoping for."

"Sorry. I meant... How do you even know who I am?"

"You were a top model, darling."

"I was?"

Perdonna's mouth curved into a withered half-moon. When she lowered her glasses, sympathy managed to seep through her grayed out eyes, like sunlight beaming through the clouds. "There was a time one couldn't drive down Fifth Avenue without seeing your face. Do you think *all* the models are driven in limousines? Housed in the Peninsula Hotel?" Perdonna slapped down a copy of *Glamorama*, Ava's fourteen-year-old face adorned in Visage lipstick on the cover. "You were living the *dream.*"

"The *dream?*" Ava clenched her hands. "*Jail* is a dream compared to the hell I went through."

Perdonna brushed her fingertips across Ava's, a gentle caress almost unnoticeable. "I know. That's why I'm here to make it right. I want to give you some money."

Ava swallowed the lump in her throat. Her hands stopped

shaking, but they were coated in clammy sweat.

"You're paying me off?" Ava asked. "To keep my mouth shut? I don't want your money."

Ava's eyes locked on Perdonna's rose-gold hair. It was the epitome of her greed, a golden hue with soft rosy highlights. More striking than the sunset, it was the twenty-four-karat gold equivalent of hair.

Ava wanted it. Or hair made of diamonds…chains and chains of diamonds.

"I want to help you," Perdonna said. "You were treated poorly. I employed you. It's my responsibility to make it up to you."

"I don't take money I don't earn," Ava said.

"Then model for Visage. I'll put you up in your own place so you don't have to live in models' apartments."

"I'd rather die than model again."

Perdonna shook her head. "I don't see people as clothes hangers."

"Why would you want a convict?"

"The word *convict* does not mean anything to me. You were an abused child. A strong, beautiful girl who defended herself against a terribly evil man."

Ava twirled the tips of her hair, curling it into knots. The bad habit was a physical manifestation of the cogs churning in her head, of the anxious thoughts that became too complex to bottle inside. She had childlike mannerisms, stunted from an upbringing full of very adult work.

"I sort of have a precarious relationship with life," Ava said, looking at the cracked skin around her toenails, the yellowish jaundice of her feet. "I feel like I'm on one team, and life is on the other. I always try to get the better of life, and it tries to get the better of me." She held her gaze, staring straight into Perdonna's glasses.

"Then consider my offer a second chance," Perdonna said.

"I won't be a slave again. Models are always slaves." She touched Perdonna's wrist and tilted the watch face to her eyes. "The hands don't move from 11:04," Ava said.

"Oh, it must be broken." She tugged her wrist away. "How unfortunate."

"It's not broken."

"No?"

"Your watch has been at 11:04 forever. The hands never move. Every year at Fashion Week, I'd stand backstage and look up at the screen projector to check the time on your watch."

Perdonna sat back in the oval chair. "All these years, no one else has noticed... It's my birth time."

"No, it isn't."

Perdonna slid her sunglasses back over her eyes, as if she was worried some secret would slip through.

"You also didn't live in Italy most of your childhood, either," Ava said. "But you tell every interviewer you're from Venice."

Perdonna twiddled her fingers, staring at the table. "And?"

"Your Visage watches are modeled after the clock in Santa Maria Novella—from the bombing. And 11:04 was the moment the bomb went off. So I always thought Visage was somehow inspired by the Bombing of Florence."

Perdonna stroked the top of Ava's head and held her cheek in the crevice of her palms.

"I want a fighter. I need a pair of eyes," she said, tapping her sunglasses. "You know the fashion industry. You can take your pain and turn it into something. Model for LeClaire and keep an eye on Margaux for me."

Ava twiddled her thumbs, hunching over. Her eyes darted back and forth.

"Would you join the security team? Be a spy?" Perdonna asked, folding her hands. "Hardly a slave's role."

"Why would a fashion brand need a security team?"

"Why would a designer base her brand on a massacre?" Perdonna retorted.

"I don't know."

"Hopefully you'd like to find out," she said as she revealed an illustrated collection of the stories of Edgar Allan Poe with a compartment drilled into the pages. Inside were beautiful dried butterflies. "Put me on your visitor's list, darling."

It was the first gift Ava had received in years. It was one of the few items Ava ever owned.

As Perdonna reached the exit, Ava called out, "Wait."

Despite the guards telling her to sit down, she ran to Perdonna. With a few shakes of *Lolita*, the Reese's Cup fell out of the book. Her fingers traced over Perdonna's palm and dropped the candy into her hand.

"It's not much. But it's the only thing I have."

7

The sound of a clacking cane trickled across the marble floor as Cecil followed after Margaux. Her collection of erotic canes was Margaux's fashion signature. The ivory handles were molded into naked ladies with their backs arched into Margaux's hand. They also featured naked ladies spooning. Or a stripper dancing with the cane as the pole.

From a distance, the pornographic scenes looked like finely crafted Rodin sculptures.

Her second favorite weapon was an antique revolver. She never used it. But it was always there, nestled in a golden holster around her thigh.

In the lobby, the models practiced their runway walks in skin-tight jeans and black camisoles. Their spidery legs kicked out like pinwheels. Their hips led the strut, pelvis leaning forward. They were puppet soldiers. Their bodies seemed to move like human ones, but something was *off.*

When Freddy pulled away Margaux's attention, Jordan rushed up to him and whispered in his ear, "We'll finish our conversation about Annabelle when you're done."

"Are you having dinner with us?" Cecil asked.

"The models eat in the basement," Margaux said, spinning back toward them like an angry squirrel.

She yanked Cecil away from Jordan as the models continued to pace around each other in a circular formation. Their heads bobbled forward like soccer balls on the ends of giraffe necks.

"You better not sleep with my models," Margaux said.

"I'm a celibate monk. Sex is sort of off-limits."

"Yeah. Right. We'll see how long that lasts."

"So, the girls live here now?" Cecil asked.

"Yeah. Too many models got raped in their Bronx apartments...and shot. I couldn't afford the losses." Margaux fondled her breast-cane.

Cecil studied her flat-lined smirk. No, she wasn't joking.

"Welcome home, my monk." Her eyes twinkled with a hint of sadness. She looked up to him, seemingly tracing his height with her eyes, like she had forgotten he was a grown man.

"What were you doing answering questions from reporters at the monastery? *Never* take questions. You really dug yourself a hole," Margaux said. "Punching a reporter?"

"It was only a shove."

"They made you look like a douchebag. It's all over the TV. No more reporters. No more interviews. If you want to talk to the public, you pre-tape. It's all about the pre-tape. You hear me? *Pre*-tape. Then you can edit your image to look however you please."

Cecil followed Margaux to the sitting room through a side door.

Gold-and-pink lamps looked like giant bubbles glistening in the sun. A sculpture dangled from the ceiling like golden rain. And plush hot-pink carpets surrounded French antiques.

Margaux collected anything and everything she liked. And even though no single item was tasteful alone, the pieces worked together in a very Margaux way.

She sat before blinding lights and camera tripods, tan concealer running down her face, sweating, drooling from nervousness.

"We'll explain away this Annabelle nonsense. Got it? You look into the camera and tell the *people* why you're a good person,"

Margaux said. "Then Freddy will edit a tape together for the press."

Straight at the camera, Margaux raised a crooked eyebrow and said, "Success is sex in excess… I built a fortune on cunts."

"Cut," said Freddy. "Keep it PG, babe."

"So, pussy instead of cunt, right?"

Freddy's tongue flicked out in disgust. "Not what I meant, but sure."

Margaux's head careened out so she had a view of the lobby. Her eyes traced over the girls like a soccer coach studying her athletes. "Hey, you. The one whose nipples look like cigarette burns." Margaux clapped her hands together. "Walk on the goddamn beat. You're too fast."

The model slowed her steps.

"You shouldn't talk to them that way," Cecil said.

"Meh, meh, meh, meh, meh," Margaux mouthed. "They need motivation. Motivation gets you Visage shows."

Freddy flicked on the camera and counted down with his finger. "Look," Margaux said to the camera. "I hate to say this, but my niece, Clara Royds, she's troubled. She's got bipolar."

Cecil shook his head.

"And ADHD, schizophrenia, Down syndrome, autism, asthma, you name it. She didn't know what she was doing when she did the skin coat."

"Cut," Freddy said. "Cut, cut, cut. She can't have all of those. You have to pick a mental illness if that's the excuse you want to use for Clara kidnapping Annabelle."

"What's the most pitiable? I mean, could we claim she's been made psycho by Botox? Clara's had so much Botox it looks like a snake bit her in the face and shot venom into her eyes."

Cecil sat back, folding his arms. He poked his head out to watch the models. "It's extremely offensive to blame murder on a fake mental illness. Also, I don't think we should blame Clara for murdering Annabelle in the press. I know how that feels."

Margaux stood from her interview seat and walked up to Jordan. She stomped her foot and smacked her on the butt with her cane. "Tuck in your giant ass. I say it one more time, I swear I'll break your legs."

Margaux spun away with a smile on her face. When she noticed Cecil's glare, she shrugged. "It motivates them. That's how you make money. Carefree runway walk, carefree life."

Cecil flashed a baffled frown at Freddy, who just closed his eyes.

"Rolling," Freddy said.

Margaux looked at the camera. "It's not just Clara. It's the whole millennial generation. They're deficient in vitamins A, B, C, D, E, love and attention. My models can't even talk."

"Okay. Okay. Let's move off the 'crazy' excuse. We shouldn't even accept Clara's guilt," Freddy said. "Who else might've murdered Annabelle?"

Margaux folded her arms and stuffed her face with frosted animal crackers. "Fine. New route." She licked a giraffe with a long, wiggly tongue. "The LeClaires didn't abduct Annabelle. It was a pedophile. Just took her off the street. Like…bang. Grabbed her by the pussy," Margaux said.

"PG!"

"Like…bang. Grabbed her by the cunt!" Margaux tried again.

Freddy took a deep breath and turned away from the camera.

"No? Not good?" Margaux whispered. "I'm just trying to keep it fun. Lighthearted. These subjects are kind of dark. Won't people be turned off?"

"I don't think America is satisfied with a random pedophile theory," Cecil said.

"Well," Margaux said, mouth full of frosted hippo, "they're not satisfied with who shot Bush, either."

"You mean who shot JFK?"

"I thought you were supposed to be helping me here." Margaux thumped her erotic cane onto the floor, scowling. Her fingers moved from the handle to reveal a black-and-white marble sculpture of a couple having sex doggie-style.

Cecil stood up from his chair. "I give up. I'm not giving an interview for this."

Margaux waved her erotic cane at him. "Fine. We'll just edit you in later," she yelled.

As Cecil walked by the models, he clapped his hands and said,

"Girls, dinner is in an hour."

"They eat in the basement," Margaux yelled from the sitting room.

"Not tonight. Tonight they're my guests," Cecil said.

The girls tried not to cheer and giggle. The agents corralled them back to focus on the pacing, but Jordan winked at him.

♎

Cecil stayed in a guest bedroom so stylishly dreary it felt like a vampire's coffin. Even the aquarium was cast in a black light and covered in dust. Fish blended into the scene as shadows in a rain puddle. The only light came from a white koi with a broken fin, helplessly swimming through the darkness like a drunken man, the threat of drowning looming over him.

He pressed his nose to the cool glass, tracing the koi's path.

Suddenly he heard a rattle from the doorknob. As Jordan walked into his bedroom, the aquarium sprung to life. Neon colors illuminated the seaweed, and each fish glowed like pieces in a rainbow. The koi no longer looked so helpless.

"The light. I doubt the fish like swimming in the dark." Jordan raised an artfully sculpted eyebrow. "Dinner time." She waved him out of the room.

Cecil remembered a young Annabelle running through the same door, wearing a wooden mask on her face, covered only in red and black body paint. He chased her with a toy spear as she banged on a drum, giggling and dripping paint around the lobby fountain.

"Will you give me this elusive information *now*?" Cecil asked.

"Not yet," she said, giggling. Her eyes darted up to the ceiling where cameras hung in crystal casings.

He followed Jordan back downstairs. In the corridor outside the dining room were three square Visage mirrors. Each displayed a rotating series of famous paintings as etched carvings. But Jordan paused in front of one.

"It draws your reflection in the mirror as a famous painting," Jordan said.

The mirror became a touchscreen. You could choose from twenty famous artists. She pressed "Manet" and the mirror began etching over her face in gold.

"Fun, right?" She giggled.

Cecil selected "Goya." The mirror turned him into an eerie ghoul with hollowed cheeks around his sharp cheekbones and sunken eyes. His gold cross shone brightly around his neck.

"Fun and creepy," he said.

The dining room featured a chandelier with wiry gold branches extending outward across the ceiling like a wild tree. Small twinkling lights dangled downward from the branches. Crevier crystal butterflies hung from the ceiling as if in flight. An aged, white-gold brick covered the walls, and a glass dining table had silver ivy twisted throughout.

To an outsider, the room might have felt ostentatious. But the amalgamation of twinkling lights and golden trinkets transported them to somewhere otherworldly.

Perdonna was carved into one of the dangling butterflies. He wasn't surprised she'd designed the chandelier. It was the only room in the mansion with taste.

The models wore their regular uniform of skinny jeans and camisoles. But they clearly dressed up for the dinner. Their eyeliner was heavily applied with blue eyeshadow, making raccoon eyes; it looked as if it were the first time the girls had applied their own makeup. There was so much paint on their faces that their pores did not exist.

The models didn't seem to be made of skin or muscle or bone. They were silver and gold, satin and cashmere.

When Cecil peeked into the kitchen, he found a series of masterpieces—a lobster frittata made with a pound and a half of lobster meat, three ounces of Beluga caviar, and a dessert modeled after Serendipity 3's Golden Opulence Sundae: Tahitian vanilla ice cream infused with Madagascar vanilla beans and drizzled with the world's most expensive and rare chocolates and candied fruits, covered in edible twenty-three-karat gold leaf with a side of caviar, served in a Baccarat Harcourt crystal goblet with a gold spoon. Serendipity required you order it forty-eight hours in advance so they could fly in the ingredients from around the world, and they sold it for $1,000 a pop.

He sat at the head of the table as the chefs, dressed in yellow and black like bumblebees, placed both the ice cream and the lobster together at Cecil's place setting.

A girl with bandages covering her head, and a puffy, bloody mouth, sat on his other side.

"What happened to you?" Cecil asked.

Jordan patted the cheeks and pulled on them like an overzealous auntie. "Margaux had her back teeth pulled out to make her face thinner."

Cecil didn't know how to respond.

Some of the girls were served three egg whites, with minimal sea salt sprinkled on the edges. While others were served chocolate and rib eye.

"That's all you eat?" Cecil asked.

"It's in our contract."

"If we gain more than four pounds, we're fired. And then we have to move out of the mansion."

Jordan dipped her fingers into the sundae, slurping up the ice cream like a vacuum. The models heaved lobster out of the shells, whipping the meat over each other's faces. They laughed hysterically, practically starting a food fight.

"We're measured once a day—"

"Or twice, depending on the season—"

"By a body scanner that compares weight and height to the golden proportions."

"But," Jordan mumbled with her mouth full, "we can eat whatever we want if we're naturally skinny."

A glittery purple paste sat on tiny gold dishes. Jordan dipped her finger into it and rubbed it over her teeth before swallowing. "Tooth Goo. It tastes like cake batter mixed with Play-Doh, and it whitens your teeth."

Cecil begrudgingly dipped his finger into the purple paste and tasted. The Play-Doh flavor gave him a nostalgic, sappy feeling, especially since the cake batter taste reminded him of his birthdays.

He noticed a glass of orange juice beside the freckled model. She had taken nothing off of the buffet.

"At least you get your vitamin C," Cecil said.

She pulled a cotton ball out of her pocket and dipped it into the glass of orange juice. "Helps fill my stomach."

She slid the cotton ball into her mouth, pulling at the fibers of cloth and succulently tugging at it with her lips as if it were a marshmallow.

Cecil's stomach came up in his mouth—a sour, acid taste. "When I was in high school, the most radical model diet was Atkins."

"I mean, sometimes I get bloated, but the cotton digests eventually… We use tissues too."

"But it's a taste issue. Tissues sometimes are scented like air freshener, and they leave a chemical taste in your mouth."

"This is disgusting. You can't survive on cotton balls and Tooth Goo," Cecil said.

"I'll gladly pass on chocolate for three *Glamorama* covers," one model said, leaning closer to him as she walked up to fill her plate with cotton balls. "And I kissed Leonardo DiCaprio at the Oscars party."

Eating was central to survival. Food was fuel. But in that room, food became a luxury, an activity to be paraded in food magazines and cooking competitions.

Where you ate, *what* you ate, and *with whom* you ate became the purpose of food.

Cecil noticed gaps at the table. Every twenty seconds or so, a girl stood up, walked into the next room, and never came back.

Sugary steam wafted toward his lips, caressing his mouth. He noticed a white, silken liquid in the Crevier crystal goblets. It looked like white hot chocolate, but with a luxurious foaming top.

He took a nervous sip. "Mmm," he said, wiping his lips. "Jesus."

It tasted like torched vanilla custard, like the caramelized top of a crème brûlée. And it smelled of Tazia Perdonna's perfume.

All of the girls giggled. "Tastes great, right? *And* it's anti-aging," said the freckled girl. "Perdonna's chef, Immacolata, makes it."

He took another sip and blushed with shame.

Gold flakes crinkled between the girls' cherry-glossed lips. Half sucked at the caviar, mixing it with vanilla and glittery purple Tooth Goo. And the less fortunate continued to dip cotton balls into crystal goblets.

Jordan licked her fingers, slurping up the lobster juices and Tooth Goo. She was a jaguar ripping a carcass to shreds. Butter ran down her lips and onto her bare chest.

Suddenly three boxes of pizzas arrived, and Cecil gulped.

"Please eat," Jordan said. "We'll still answer all your questions, Mr. Detective."

He took a bite of celery from the freckled girl's plate. "I won't eat in front of you. Not since some of you can't."

"No!" the models yelled.

"We love food porn," Jordan said. "See, it's all over Instagram and Chatter." She lifted her watch face and suddenly a projection shot in front of her. A holographic Instagram floated before her eyes.

Photos of chocolate tortes and brownies, carrot cakes and cupcakes had thousands of *Likes*. "You see a picture of a cookie, and it's like you're eating it."

"Not really…" Cecil said.

"You can imagine the smell of strawberry and the gooey, freshly baked sugar cookies."

A girl nodded. "But, yeah, watching a person eat the real food is way more interesting."

"So once a month, we make a pilgrimage to the Whole Foods in Union Square."

"Excuse me?" Cecil spat out his food.

"We take pictures pretending to eat organic food at Whole Foods to impress the Instagram followers of LeClaire Model Management," Jordan said. "Little girls need to believe we eat hemp brownies so exercise companies can make money. When the truth is half of us are eating cotton balls, and the other half can be skinny while scarfing down sundaes."

The other models said nothing, too engrossed with their watches to hold a conversation. Cecil realized none of the girls had phones. They only used their clocks.

It was a strange but beautiful shape. The face was circular with a straight bar of gold beneath. It almost resembled an ebony clam shell with a clock.

When the clam-top was lifted, a screen projected as a hologram.

"It's called the Dial," Jordan said. "Perdonna—"

"Invented it," Cecil finished her sentence. "She's been working on it for a while."

The Dial projected a screen onto any flat surface around them so that they could use it as a phone or for accessing social media. They could even type onto the projection and use it as a touch screen. It was an iPhone without the screen.

Some girls projected the screen onto their hands and typed directly onto their palm.

With one flick of a wrist, a girl could smile at the projection and take a photo.

They took chocolate chips from his sundae and put them in their mouths, only to take a photo. Then the slobbery chocolate went back in his sundae, uneaten.

They sent the photos across social media with desserts at their lips, advertising their ability to "eat" sweets and stay thin.

Other models stared at food photos and spied on their model competition. Who had the best fake dessert photos? Who had the best organic detox tea?

Soon the entire dining table was covered with images of social media and glossy idealizations of themselves. The girls barely spoke to each other. It was as if they felt so robotic, so alone, that they forgot how to love.

Cecil could barely see the girls' faces across the table through the holographic social media lights.

Against his better judgment, he opened the box of pizza in front of him. "Is it Grimaldi's?" Cecil asked the butler. He nodded, and Cecil bit his lip. He pulled out a piece and brought it to his nose to sniff. He put the pizza on his plate only to stare at it.

"Are *you* anorexic?" Jordan asked.

"No," he said. But Jordan only kept a raised brow. "It's called gluttony."

"You're not a monk anymore," Jordan whispered.

He took the pepperonis off the pizza and began cutting the slice in half. He cut the bottom portion into twelve tiny bites like a surgeon. All of the girls stopped eating and stared. They were taking notes.

Out of the corner of his eye, he noticed big brown eyes peering into the room. There was a somberness in her eyes, a disdain that made Cecil want to run after her. When he looked directly at her, she flashed him a peace sign and walked away.

"Are all the models at the table?"

"No," Jordan whispered, eyes downcast. "But the important ones are."

♎

Ava Germaine watched from outside the dining room as Cecil meditated on the pizza. He ignored all the models' cries for help. She wanted to strangle him with his belt and shove a whole lobster claw down his throat.

♎

Cecil put a pizza chunk in his mouth, and his eyes almost rolled back into his head. His tongue swirled around the cheese.

Jordan stared in a dazed, hard kind of way at her phone. She leaned in toward a girl beside her and said, "Veronica read in the *Daily Mail* that Annabelle Leigh worked as a waitress for the past ten years in Oklahoma."

The other girl replied, "I read a theory today saying that Cecil killed her. He kept her buried beneath this dining room."

"I can hear you," Cecil said.

The models dropped their Dials, staring at Cecil, waiting with bated breath. Gossip placed second to food porn on the models' list of favorites.

"What do you know?" Cecil said. He finally popped a pepperoni into his mouth.

"Jeremy White trapped Annabelle Leigh in the *Glamorama* basement and used her to write free articles," a girl said.

Everyone squirmed.

"No. People are only Chattering that because they think she did a cover for *Elite* once," another girl said. "She wore a one-piece bathing suit. Very boyish haircut, like a bob."

"I don't think it's that. I think it's more that she worked as a spy. She pretended to be a model but was actually a spy for Dior. They had to delete the fashion editorials after she worked."

"I heard she worked for the Italian mafia as a High Fashion Hit Man."

"Oh, stop. You only make up lies, Victoria. Stop being an attention whore. *Everyone*—and by that, I mean everyone with a life—knows that Margaux accidentally shot poor Annabelle in the head. She twirls her pistols around like she's Jesse James, like they're only meant to intimidate us, but we all know her guns are always loaded. Why else would you walk everywhere with an erotic cane and a pistol...unless you have a plan."

A model with a giraffe neck and skin like coffee grounds threw her fork on the table. "You're ridiculous! You know Margaux wouldn't make that mistake. She shot Annabelle on purpose."

Cecil shook his head. "You all have wild imaginations. Margaux's guns aren't loaded."

Jordan put her hands up. The models froze, heads bowed to the Queen B.

"I'll bet you your Bible that they are," Jordan said. "Here's the real truth. Annabelle Leigh was a model. She was abducted in a van outside of your house after begging Margaux to make her a star."

"How do you know?" Cecil asked.

"I shared an apartment with her. I did. I'm sure it was her. Like five years ago," Jordan said. "I was too young to know anything about the news, so I didn't know who she was."

"Did she seem okay? Was she healthy? Happy? Did you talk to her a lot?" Cecil leaned in closer to Jordan, heaving his chest over the table like he was about to lunge at her.

"We didn't really talk. She was too shy. She seemed fine enough... But I remember a photo of her modeling in lingerie in her portfolio. The picture was signed with VD."

"Who's VD?" he asked.

A blonde girl raised her hand. "Oh! Oh! I've seen that signature before. But... I don't know who it is."

"So she definitely worked in the fashion industry after she disappeared. And no one but Jordan has ever seen her?" Cecil asked.

"People move in and out of the modeling industry like a dick moves in and out of a prostitute."

"We only have a three-year window. Then we're too old to model."

"But this isn't all of us. Margaux's other models live separately. They might know something. More models live on the fourth floor—the new faces."

"Why aren't they eating with us?" Cecil asked.

"They're the girls who aren't quite good enough to be top models yet."

"Bullshit. They'll never be good enough. Margaux hires them as slave labor."

"Honestly. We don't know. We can't get into the models' quarters without Margaux. She has the key."

Jordan put her hands up, stopping all of them. "But we all know Margaux works pretty closely with this VD."

Chimes. Ten o'clock. Margaux entered with a perturbed swing of a penis-shaped, onyx-handled cane.

"You should be in bed, girls," she said.

The models scurried away. Jordan turned back to him and made her fingers into a pistol shape. "Pew-pew," she mouthed.

8

"Enjoying the new amenities?" Margaux asked as she stood by Cecil's chair, dipping the handle of her erotic cane into the melted vanilla ice cream and licking it off.

"Like you've always said, success is sex in excess."

Margaux winked. "Your father's dead. I can have what I please."

Cecil traced his fingers across a diamond-encrusted sconce. "Most of your models come from poor countries, right? Is it fair to flaunt your mansion in front of them?"

"Survival means winning. And winning means there's a loser." Margaux took a tissue from her Visage bag and waved it like a flag. "That's life. I'm surviving, others are losing." She rested her chin on the ebony cane, studying Cecil.

"Can we talk in private?" he asked.

"About what Jordan said to you?" Margaux pointed her cane down the hallway like a band conductor waving a baton. "The Annabelle thing?"

"Were you spying on us during dinner?"

Margaux pointed to the crystal cameras above. "I have them

for a reason." When they reached the elevator, she continued, "There's a simple explanation. But we have to grab some things from the fourth floor."

The fourth floor was where Jordan had said the lower-tier models slept.

The elevator arrived, and the doors opened to classical music. A large, transparent clock, with its innards and cogs showing, covered all four walls, hands twirling rapidly, out of sync with real time.

It was designed by Visage. Shattered bits of purple mussel shells and pearls made up the face with silver roman numerals entangled in the silver cogs.

In the corner, a teenaged model stood in a black bra and underwear, posing in an angular stretch that changed every twenty seconds.

"An elevator model," Margaux said. "Beautiful marketing technique."

Cecil's jaw clenched so loudly that the click of his teeth made Margaux jump.

"What?" Margaux shrugged. "Only *men* can be doormen?"

He held out his hand to the girl, introducing himself.

She said nothing, focused only on posing her body to show off its angles. A long awkward pause ensued as they waited for the doors to open.

"Is the weather nice outside?" the model asked.

"Unseasonably warm for October," he said. "Did you not go outside yet today?"

The girl shook her head. "Don't go out much. Margaux says only beauty makes me free."

"That's...that's not true," Margaux said.

"In here, it is cold." The model pulled down her bra top and pointed to her erect nipples.

The elevator stopped with a feathery pause, and the doors slid open.

"Ah," Cecil said, "what the fuck is this, Mother?"

Margaux slid her hands down her hips and shimmied like an awkward belly dancer. "My girls are comfortable with their bodies."

"Aren't they kind of...young? Where are their parents? Are they okay with you not feeding them?"

"Their little girl is famous, who cares if she eats? And besides, the models are watered thrice a day. Fed on organic Tooth Goo and—"

"And *cotton balls*. You'll give them cancer."

Margaux stroked the testicles on her cane. "Better cancer than a venereal disease. And besides, cotton comes from a plant. It's a vegetable."

"It's not a vegetable!" Cecil held onto her cane when she tried to scurry away. "How much do you pay them anyway?"

"You had all your life to show interest in my business." Her face flushed red. "Do you *want* me to tell you what happened the day Annabelle disappeared?"

"I demand to know."

"Then you better shut the hell up about my agency. Most of these girls would be on the street if it wasn't for me."

She gave him the same look his father used to give him. The one that said *I regret that you're my child*. It was a look that made Cecil believe Margaux could extract potions from the contents of her cane—tongue of wolf, eye of bat, horn of unicorn.

On the fourth floor, silver hourglasses adorned the walls. Translucent chandeliers hung from the ceiling. Even the floors were transparent with indirect lighting from below, reflecting soft golden hues throughout the hallway. Darkened cubicles sat embedded in the walls, like the windows of the Red Light District in Amsterdam.

Cecil knocked on a cubicle window, and a pale hand hit back, shooting out from the darkness. Inside the glass, a young girl stood up wearing black Agent Provocateur underwear. Her body, skinny and pristine, wobbled on her heels. She posed for Cecil, elbows jutting outward. A strange, almost inhuman white mask covered her entire face, only the eyes showing through.

As he walked down the hall, lights turned on, illuminating the cubicles. A dozen models posed in their glass cases. The pre-pubescent bodies, thin and taut, spread throughout the hallway. A beautiful pattern of skin and leg, heels and hair, reflected on every surface.

"Magnificent, right?" Margaux asked.

"No. They're not collectible Barbie dolls," Cecil said. "They're girls. Human beings."

"It's how we train them for mannequin modeling. Each model does an hour a day of posing in the hallway."

She grabbed keys from a safe and scurried away, telling him to wait for her.

Cecil paused in front of a girl who looked like Annabelle. Her curly hair dangled over the white mask. She had bruises just below her bra top, and she subtly held a hand over the thin fabric of her underwear. His fingers stroked the glass. *Take the mask off*, he wanted to whisper. The naked female body without a face appealed to his most carnal feelings—breasts, abs, and thighs. Pure lust without love.

"Do you like them?" Margaux asked, popping out of nowhere.

The hallway felt like a sexual circus, a high fashion freak show. But that was the exact feeling his mother wanted to elicit.

He could only imagine the elation a fashion designer felt walking past a series of girls on display.

"It's disturbing," he said.

"But you must admit...only Margaux LeClaire could've designed it."

Margaux bowed, the weight of her stocky frame resting on her pristine penis cane, the jewels of her gaudy necklace clacking against the head.

Just before she waved him back in the elevator, Cecil noticed a plaque outside a room that read "Models' Quarters." He wanted to see inside, but he knew better than to ask his mother.

The fourth floor was meant to make a visitor feel self-conscious. *Look at yourself and then look at my Photoshopped, perfect models.*

She opened a door to her office. "Come, darling."

Margaux's office was the kind of abandoned pink dollhouse you might find in an asylum. She loved Christopher Guy's Champignon Banquettes, circular couches with pearl cushions. She had ten in her office, with white polar bear cub furs strewn over the tops. Pillows of pinks and pearls sat on desks and dressers, chairs and couches alike. She collected strange music boxes, and so there were at least one hundred of them organized onto Crevier crystal shelves.

She had every kind of music box—from ballerinas twirling to Tchaikovsky to an entire puppet production of *The Wizard of Oz*.

When Margaux's lips brushed his cheek, Cecil realized he couldn't recognize the perfume, couldn't recognize the scent of his own mother.

"You smell like holy water," she said. "That's brave of you…to let Jesus literally rub off on you."

Cecil flopped onto the banquette. "I *am* a monk."

"No, you're not. You grew up in Manhattan, settled by the greedy Dutch, all about big money and bloodsucking. You're not a saint; you're a LeClaire."

He poured himself a glass of scotch from Margaux's drinks trolley. "Speaking of the bloodsucking LeClaires, let's talk about Annabelle."

"It all points to Clara," Margaux said as she clipped her fingernails, flinging red nail polish chips onto her pristine pink carpet. "Poor thing. I hate to say this, but I hope the inmates kill her quickly. Put her out of the misery."

"I meant what Jordan said. About Annabelle being abducted in a van? About you asking her to model?"

Margaux stopped cutting her nails and picked up her cane, twirling. The twinkly starkness left her eyes, leaving only a defensive gray shield. "Jordan's a lying bitch. She's my highest paid girl, and it's made her entitled."

"Annabelle *did* visit the mansion the day she disappeared," Cecil said.

"Jordan probably went snooping and found my pictures. Then she invented this whole story to tell you so she could bribe you."

Margaux pulled out a stack of photos of Annabelle Leigh. She was bare-faced in all of them. Her curly hair paired against a stark white background. At the edges of the pictures, her body measurements were scrawled in serial-killer-style capital letters.

"You know Annabelle desperately needed money, desperately needed a future that her chauffeur father couldn't provide for,"

Margaux said. "Well, she came to me the day she disappeared, asking for a modeling job."

"And you didn't tell the police! Or me?"

"It would've made me suspicious."

"But that could've been the key to her entire disappearance!" Cecil paced, grabbed a pillow from her banquette, and threw it at a chandelier.

"She didn't want to model," Margaux said. "But she needed the money."

"Why didn't she ask me?"

"She probably didn't want you to worry. And you *always* whined about the girls at school asking you if they could model."

Cecil sat back down and took a deep breath. "So, what did you say to her?"

"I told her she would never be a model. I told her to go home."

"Why would you do that?"

"Why? Well, she didn't have the measurements," Margaux said.

On her iPad, she showed her portfolio of models. Solemn, serious glowers glimmered underneath photo filters and harsh lighting. Models were dramatic faces, empty masks with no person behind them.

The girls existed only to be part of a portfolio as collectible stamps.

"It's not *America's Next Top Model*. Models aren't eighteen to twenty-one with jobs at L'Oréal and college degrees. Real models have a combined IQ *and* bodyweight below one hundred. They don't even work at Starbucks; it was a bad path for Annabelle."

"So, what happened? You turned her away, and a man *happened* to abduct her outside?"

"Could have been anyone," Margaux said.

"Detective Roosevelt thinks it was a man."

"Well...I suppose it could've been another model agent. If she submitted photos to the wrong person... Well, bad things could happen."

Cecil noticed the hazy fake tan peeling away from her skin, revealing the paleness, as if she were a transparent wrapper, hiding something inside.

"Do you know who VD is?"

"No. Jordan's making the whole thing up. *VD*. Who the hell would call themselves 'venereal disease'?"

Cecil folded his arms as a music box began to sing in Shirley Temple's childish voice.

Margaux showed him one last photo of Annabelle singing on their Hamptons property. "Found this. Thought you should have it."

He remembered that photo of the Hamptons. It was the day Clara almost died.

9

August 2009. Two months before Annabelle's abduction.

A white canopy fell over the picnic tent, fabric waving in a perfect breeze as the sun sank over the ocean. Waiters served hot dogs and watermelon, beach food Cecil rarely had a chance to eat.

The party had the stuffy formality of Margaux's usual events. Ateliers and fashion editors strode in lace cover-ups and sundresses. Women wore hats with brims that fell below their chins, flopping downward with large red flowers and white bows the size of their heads. They carried punch and pink lemonade. Cecil had never seen so many diamonds on a beach.

A string quartet played "Palladio" beneath the wispy tents.

Perdonna avoided the crowds of babbling women, lounging in a beach chair, painting dress designs in watercolor, her hat tipped just enough to shade her face. Her eyes were still a bright cerulean, the color of the paint that coated her fingertips.

Two guards stood several feet behind her. She didn't trust Margaux's guests. But the guards were mostly there to protect against Margaux herself.

Cecil stared at Perdonna from a nearby beach chair, pretending to play Tetris on his phone.

Her white bathing suit rode up her hips as she kicked with her legs to the rhythm of her brush strokes. Drips of blue paint fell onto her skin and smeared over her stomach.

"You spend too much time looking at that phone," Perdonna said. "How will you be an artist if all you ever see is a black screen."

"Invent a phone that projects into the air." Cecil shrugged. "Then at least I'll see the sky behind YouTube."

Perdonna turned to him, splashing her fingertips in the water. She tore the canvas to the ground. "How would you type? You still need a touchscreen."

"Type on your palm? Like a hologram."

Perdonna took a pencil from her purse. She sketched an arm and a Visage watch overtop the wrist. Rays of yellow paint represented the holographic projection.

"I'd wear it," Cecil said.

Then—*bang!* A soccer ball smacked Cecil on the side of the head. Annabelle giggled and ran to pick it up. Cecil chased after her toward the water, their feet sinking into the hot sand.

"You're so gross," she said.

She bounced a soccer ball on her knees near the ocean's edge, sand slipping into her bikini bottoms. He tried to steal the ball from her and playfully pretended it was too difficult. She pushed into his chest and grabbed his arms.

"Perdonna's like older than...older than Walt Disney," Annabelle said.

"Disney's dead," Cecil said, gently kissing her neck.

"Not when he comes back to life, he's not."

Annabelle's hair whipped his face, and he smelled her oaky scent.

"Well... Perdonna looks twenty, and that's all that matters."

She huffed at him. With a fingertip, he let her knock him to the ground and roll on top of his sandy chest. The waves rushed over their bodies as Annabelle stroked the waistband of his swim trunks. She wrestled him.

"I'm joking. Joking! She's practically my mom," Cecil said.

"Except you'd totally have sex with her."

"Would not!"

She ground her hips into his and stroked her hands across his chest. A daring, lust-filled gaze crossed her face. The water crashed over them, and Cecil raised a questioning brow.

But then a fly buzzed up behind them.

"Margaux said I was supposed to separate you," Clara said.

Annabelle spun off of Cecil. Clara had come out of nowhere, wearing her bright pink hair in Princess Leia buns, holding a stuffed SpongeBob.

"Why did she say that?" Cecil asked.

"She said you were being bad."

"Tell Mom I'm fine."

Clara pouted and tears streamed down her face. Even though she was the older cousin, she crouched on the ground like a toddler and folded her arms. "Why don't you like me, Cecil?"

Clara was nineteen at the time, but she still talked like a tween.

Margaux rushed toward them over a dune, carrying her dress in her hands so the silk fabric wouldn't touch any seaweed.

"The vocalist never showed up to sing the national anthem, and the fireworks are starting in thirty minutes," Margaux said.

"I'll sing," Clara offered.

Margaux shook her head. "No. You can't even *speak* without a lisp."

Cecil saw Annabelle look at the empty stage. "I can sing...if you absolutely need someone."

Margaux opened the door to a portable bathroom. "Audition for me."

Cecil shook his head. "She's not auditioning in a port-a-potty. No."

"Then at least let me put you in something that makes you look like less of a child whore."

As Margaux dragged Annabelle into the house, Clara bent down by the water, salty tears dripping into the ocean. She disappeared when Annabelle took the stage and never came back to the party.

Annabelle's voice sent sweet dulcet tones over the beach, sing-ing the national anthem a capella as the wind blew her dress. With her final note, Cecil embraced her in a hug. He kissed her beneath the blues and reds bursting in the sky.

But Margaux broke the moment with a shrill scream. Perdonna ran into the house. They refused to let anyone inside until the paramedics left.

Margaux had found Clara in a pool of blood, passed out on the kitchen floor. They said Clara had cut herself while chopping watermelon.

♎

Cecil felt like he was in a nightmare. LeClaire Model Management had no similarity to his former home. He had trouble sleeping there, despite the new comforts. He had fluffy pillows and beau-tiful art, and all the food he could ever want. The abbey was prison compared to the mansion. But he slept like a baby at the monastery.

Cecil Googled "VD models" on the iPad in his room. The harsh blue glow reflected off the Art Deco furnishings in the bedroom. The only search results he found were obscure models dressed in lingerie, PSAs about venereal disease, and naked girls dressed as sexy lust fairies with sparkly wings. He tried "VD fashion," "VD lingerie," and still, nothing.

A fresh cigar sat next to him on the bedside table when Jordan appeared in the doorway, wearing a bulky sweatshirt with boy shorts barely covering her ass.

She bounced on the bed and pressed her lower half into his, rubbing her freshly showered hair over his lips.

"I can't sleep," she said. "Can I sleep in here with you?"

"No. But"—Cecil held the iPad out to her—"I searched 'VD,' and I can't find those photos of Annabelle anywhere."

"You think I'm lying?" She leaned toward him, rubbing her

cheek against his. She shuffled into his sheets and rested her head on his pillow, nudging him aside so she could fit right up against his neck. "Whoever VD is killed Annabelle. And I'm sure Margaux had something to do with it. I swear."

Her breath tickled his ear.

He liked the feeling of her warm body in bed, and it made him feel guilty. Her heat against the sheets. Her eyes. Her smile.

The black silk sheets snaked around her shoulders, and she rolled herself up in a cocoon.

"Why do you want to sleep here?" Cecil asked.

She ripped the sheet off of them and straddled his waist, coyly running her arms over his chest. "Maybe... I'm interested in you."

"Sex doesn't work so well on a monk," Cecil said.

"Sex always works on men."

Her pelvis moved up and down against his waist as she rubbed against his boxers. He grabbed onto her hipbones to stop her. The bones felt like spikey ridges, threatening to puncture him through her skin.

"It won't," Cecil said. "What is it you really want?"

"You're not much of a man." Jordan raised a quivering eyebrow. "What kind of man refuses sex?"

Cecil lifted her off of him and fluffed up a pillow so she could sit up against it.

"I know you want something from me," Cecil said. "People only touch me when they want something. I spent my whole life being touched. Touched by reporters. By stylists. I got fake hugs from girls in high school who wanted me to make them into models. Fake hugs for photos. Fake hugs from strangers who pretended to feel bad my best friend disappeared. I don't respond well to fake touch. So I might not be a man, but at least I'm not a liar."

Jordan crossed her legs beneath the sheets and sat straight up. She squirmed. "Fine. I really do just want to sleep here. I'm sorry. I'm scared, okay? It's not safe in my room," Jordan said. "Margaux's really mad at me for telling you about Annabelle modeling."

"What's she gonna do? Stuff you with animal crackers? Force you to sing Shirley Temple songs for her while she showers?"

"Shoot me with her revolver," Jordan said.

"Oh, come on."

"Seriously! I don't think Margaux likes me. She calls me Oreo."

"She loves Oreos," Cecil said. "Does she make lip-smacking gestures when she says it? Do her cheeks puff out like she's eating Pop Rocks?"

"Yeah." Her usually firm lips softened. "How did you know?"

"She's threatening to eat you. She calls me beignet when she's mad at me."

Jordan ground her teeth together with a crack that sounded like nails on a chalkboard.

"If she demotes me tomorrow, you'll be sorry for making light of it." She took off her hooded sweatshirt and put it on his pillow. She stood up out of bed, but before she left, she said, "I know what you mean about the touch thing. It's the worst part about being a model too. The hairstylists, the dressmakers. I always wanted a real hug. A real hug so tight you could feel every inch of a person's skin." Tears pooled in Jordan's eyes. "I don't think I've ever been hugged at all."

Cecil opened his arms and stood. She giggled, climbing inside. He cradled her head in his neck and rubbed her back with his hands. She felt so small despite that boisterous personality.

Then she pushed him back onto the bed. And he felt her lips press against his neck.

"You really can't stay here," Cecil said.

In a blur, she slapped him across the face. The sting vibrated through his teeth, jaw aching. He grabbed her wrists so tightly that he felt the tiny bones of her wrist.

She spat in his face, and he flipped her off him and pinned her down with shaking hands. His face flushed red, anger overtaking him.

"What was that?" Cecil shouted.

She anxiously gripped onto the tips of her hair like a scared child cuddling a stuffed animal. Her lower lip squirmed. She threw open the door and sprinted down the hallway before he could process.

He called after her, but she disappeared.

Her sweater still sat beside his pillow. He turned off the last over-head light and curled up into the bed, still smelling her shampoo and feeling a wet spot where her hair had rested against his pillow.

Ω

In the morning, he blinked into the light, waking up to find Jordan's sweater. He'd been cuddling with it during the night, but as he groggily stretched his arms, he heard a crinkling in the pockets. There was a piece of paper.

> **The House of VD   Oct. 22, 2016**
> **I decided it is in everyone's best interest to return Annabelle Leigh to the United States. She has been doing great work in Shanghai, and I felt it worth the risk to return her to the US. She will make more money for us here, and I am confident she will stay quiet and out of sight. Police intervention is not a concern. I have attached your commission of $128,000 for Annabelle's work for the last three months.**
> **With Love.**

Annabelle had been in the United States for three years before her death. She had worked in Shanghai, presumably as a model for this VD. But who was making a commission on her?

Jordan had brought the papers to prove she wasn't lying.

He needed to know how Jordan got the note. He had to find her.

10

The sound of hairdryers, stomping heels, and the rolling thunder of makeup trolleys was the LeClaire Mansion's morning soundtrack. It was 8:00 a.m. on the day of the exclusive Visage show.

Sequins and glitter slid under Cecil's bedroom door, making it look like the floor of a gay nightclub.

Cecil threw on his jeans and T-shirt and rushed into the room called the models' quarters.

If there were a Homo sapien exhibit at a zoo in a third world country, it would be a nicer place to live than LeClaire Model Management's models' quarters.

Cheap metal bunkbeds were stacked four to a tower. Skin-colored makeup stains covered the walls in handprint shapes. And dried nail polish coated the floor like a splatter painting.

It smelled like a high school locker room—body odor and cherry lip gloss.

Girls hunched on their bunk beds, unable to sit up straight in their cells. They sprayed their greasy hair with dry shampoo. It seemed there were only three bathrooms.

They covered their bodies in glitter oil. Dried skin flaked around acne.

When the girls noticed Cecil, they shrunk back into their beds, hiding their faces in paint-covered bath towels.

"Do any of you know where Jordan is?" Cecil asked.

Frail stick fingers covered mouths. Eyes squinted, and skinny arms crossed over bony bodies.

"Where does she usually go when she's upset?" Cecil asked, words rushing out of him in a stream. "Are you really not allowed to leave the building without a chaperone?"

"We can't go anywhere without Margaux's permission."

Cecil huffed and folded his arms. "Come on. You can't go *anywhere*?"

He scanned the soiled sheets and pillows that covered the rickety bunk beds. He stared at the puffy eyes and the burnt, knotted hair that sat thin and oily on the models' heads.

He threw open drawers and closets, sifting through their room, hoping to find personal belongings. But he only found cotton balls, desiccated celery, Tooth Goo, a few ragged stuffed animals, and torn jeans. No family photos or cellphones.

Dress bags from Ami, Buratti, and Tom Gray held unwearable couture clothing. Marijuana mixed with the white glitter across the floor. It looked like reindeer had thrown up on weeds.

"Jordan doesn't live with us," the freckle-faced model said. "Margaux's top models have their own rooms. Those are the models you've been speaking to. We have it a little...less fancy. Until we work our way up."

Cecil sat on one of the bunk beds with his knees pulled up to his chest. He looked out the one window, only to see a limestone wall and an air-conditioning unit.

"Do her parents live close by?" Cecil asked. "Could we call them and see if she's there?"

"We can't call our parents. We only have our Dials," a girl whispered. "And even with those Margaux has them set so we can only Chatter within the mansion."

His eyes scanned the faces of the girls. They were drained and hollow with sallow eyes. White, rusty bars covered the window. Suicide-proof windows. This room used to be his playroom. "Are you all crammed in this tiny room like sardines?"

The girls looked up to him with big, bloodshot eyes. Their limbs tangled in a wiry pile as they sprawled across the ground in plain white underwear and tank tops.

"Is this worth it?" Cecil asked. "For a chance to be a model?"

The girls nodded enthusiastically.

Metal bunk beds were stacked four high. It looked like a military camp, except the sheets looked dirty and the room smelled of body odor. It was a far cry from the glamor Cecil expected when he thought of modeling.

"Margaux's already at the show getting ready. Jordan and the other girls probably left with her," the freckled model said.

"I'll call her."

♎

He had dialed Margaux from the mansion phone four times only to hear her new annoying voice mail. "You have not reached Margaux LeClaire. Please do not leave a message after the tone unless you are God. No, not you, Karl Lagerfeld. You are not God. *I'm* a God. Your cat, Choupette, is a God. But not you. You're a piece of shit." Beep.

Cecil would have to track Margaux and Jordan down at the Visage show. The odds of solving the Annabelle conundrum before the show were stacking against him.

He might not be going back to the monastery so soon.

He dialed 9-1-1 in an attempt to reach Roosevelt about Jordan's VD letter. Instead he heard: "The NYPD is no longer accepting voice calls. Nine-one-one is now text and Chatter only. If this is an emergency—"

Cecil hung up. He reached for the iPad in his room, but then he noticed a black box sitting on his dresser.

Inside was a Dial. It was made custom by Perdonna. Instead of the signature Visage wires twirling in between shattered oyster shells and shimmering blues, this one was customized. Miniature rosary beads spiraled out from the center, tangling with silver wires.

He clasped the Dial over his left hand. The watch face opened up like a clam shell, and the computer sprung to life.

"Welcome to the Dial," the machine said in Perdonna's recorded voice. "Please place the earbud in your ear."

Cecil found a clear miniature earbud in the box and put it in like a headphone.

"You can now use me to make phone or video calls," the Dial said.

A projection shot onto the wall—a full computer screen with messaging, an internet browser, and a camera. Perdonna had set his background to a portrait of a white-tailed deer frolicking in roses. It was his painting.

"The Pearl is my camera projector," the Dial said. "You can drag the dial around your wristband to adjust where the Pearl projects the hologram. Try it."

He grabbed the watch face and the machine slid around the metal wristband until it was under his forearm.

Inside the ebony watch was the shimmery white Pearl. It moved like an eyeball. The lens grew bigger and smaller depending on which surface it projected onto. It was a pupil adjusting to light.

"I will default the screen as a hologram in the air," the Dial said. "If you want to use the screen on a surface, point the Pearl in that direction. For privacy, project onto your palm and type into your own hand. I will compensate for angular differences in projection versus surface."

Cecil projected the holographic screen into the air before him.

He touched the Chatter icon. The Dial projection felt warm to his touch, like the machine was breathing against his fingers. The Pearl seemed to be alive, cradled in the Dial shell.

"The Dial is your friend. Text on your steering wheel so your eyes don't have to leave the road. Let the Pearl take your selfie, so *you* can feel less self-absorbed. Watch YouTube against the backdrop of the ocean. Stop staring at your cold, lifeless screens. Touch your own hand. Feel nature instead of an unconscious black screen. And bring the internet back to the real world."

He pulled the VD letter out of his pocket.

He touched the camera icon on the hologram and took a picture of the letter. Then he Chattered to the police at 9-1-1 through an account Perdonna had set up.

Cecil LeClaire: Found this letter in LeClaire model, Jordan Jones's, jacket pocket. Seems this VD held Annabelle in Shanghai for six years. Jordan is claiming Annabelle was a model and worked in the US. Please tell me you knew this after ten years investigating??? Wonder who he paid the $128k commission to?

Automated Response: Please wait...

Det. Fran Roosevelt: Do you know where Jordan Jones is now?

Cecil LeClaire: Visage flagship midtown. For the show.

Det. Fran Roosevelt: Thank you. I'd like to speak with you after.

Cecil LeClaire: Of course.

And then he noticed a black velvet suit hanging above the giant aquarium. A white silk shirt hung beneath, glinting when the fabric moved. And the cufflinks were crosses made of rubies and pearls. *Bellino* was written in Perdonna's jagged but beautiful cursive on Visage stationery. Her nude lipstick pressed into an elegant kiss in the corner.

Cecil traced the print of her lips with his fingertip. Some of the lipstick rubbed off onto his finger. It was the closest he had been to her in three years—touching an imprint of her kiss.

He had to go to the show to talk to Jordan and Detective Roosevelt. Though he at least wanted to remain in his T-shirt and jeans. Something humble. Perdonna's art was beauty in excess. It was anything but modest.

Yet isn't beauty the most godly thing of all?

He pushed a shimmery silver box on the Dial screen and his wall turned into a digital mirror.

"Because if you're stuck in a hurricane without food and water," Cecil said to himself, "what you really need is a mirror so you can fix your hair."

At St. Joseph's Abbey, he never once looked at his own reflection. And he was at peace with himself.

But then came the mirror. He stared into his own eyes, shimmering back to him eerily from the paint on the wall. He looked like a scruffy, intellectual caveman. So he shaved the scruff off of his face. Then he noticed his hair seemed flat, so he combed it out with some gel he found in the bathroom. And his lips were chapped, so he put on Vaseline.

Before he knew it, he was worried about the dark rings and puffy bags under his eyes.

"Six years building up my inner self and spirituality," Cecil joked to himself, "and it's all gone in two minutes alone with a mirror."

He bent his head in prayer, clutching the cross around his neck. "The heavens proclaim the glory. So day unto day takes up the story, and night unto night makes known the message," Cecil sang to himself.

He stripped off his T-shirt and nervously unbuttoned the silk one. Putting it on felt like lying in a bath of chocolate. It rippled over his chest, highlighting his slender muscles.

"No speech, no word, no voice is heard; yet glory extends through all the earth," he chanted.

The velvet jacket felt like a hug, a warm embrace. This was a different habit. Wearing Perdonna's artwork as a child had felt less sensational. He looked like a kid drowning in grown-up clothing. Now, though, he was James Bond.

"At the end of the sky is the rising of the sun; to the furthest end of the sky is its course. There is nothing concealed from its burning heat."

He put the little red stuffed dog, Aberto, into the inside pocket of his jacket.

It was showtime.

11

The Visage store lit up Fifth Avenue. Silver wires and watch cogs burst through pearlescent oyster shells in the store windows. Golden lizards hugged the turtleneck of a black dress. And a black-and-white-marbled jacket sat beside a faux leather romper. The center window featured the debuting masterpiece: a floor-length black dress that moved like ocean waves even when the wearer stood still.

Perdonna's ateliers had recently developed the technology. Wires ran through the skirt and connected to a minuscule computer at the dress's back. The technology acted like a nervous system. It allowed the dress to naturally flow and react to the environment. The new Visage dress was almost a living organism.

A red carpet ushered celebrities into the show space. They wore Buratti, Lazard, and Louis Vuitton. Hannibal Lecter masks masqueraded as vintage from the Third Reich and hats looked like beasts from *Where the Wild Things Are*.

To make other people feel inferior was to make you stylish.

The bitter paparazzi lived for red carpets. They shouted into their cameras, "That dress looks like a naked Margaux LeClaire.

Globs of orange in the front and a train of pink frosting shooting from the ass."

Paparazzi cameras never showed the audience what actually stood behind the red carpet. The glorious ruby walkway was simply a rug that rolled over the dog urine and cigarette butts on New York City streets. The plastic green bushes hid antiterrorism bollards. And designers snorted cocaine to survive the night.

Celebrities wore makeup so plastered on their skin that, up close, they looked like wrinkly gremlins covered in thick paint. The camera translated the glitter glue on their lips and cheekbones into healthy, glossy skin. Spanx and medieval torture contraptions kept average bodies from spilling out of $30,000 dresses.

Cecil drove the golden Rambo Lambo up to the red carpet. His sweaty fingers gripped the VD letter. Jordan was not on the red carpet, but he had to find her backstage. He had to know how she got the note.

He mustered the strength to exit the vehicle and handed the keys to the valet.

Out of the corner of his eye, Cecil could see the NYPD officers closing a tighter perimeter around the red carpet. Perdonna's security team, dressed in heavy black suits, whispered into their earpieces.

The reporters swarmed Cecil the moment the Rambo's engine stopped.

"Do you believe Clara abducted Annabelle?" a reporter yelled to Cecil. "Or do they have the wrong suspect?"

"Clara didn't abduct Annabelle."

"Then who did?" another asked. "Your mother?"

"Maybe another model agent," Cecil said.

Suddenly a mob of more than fifty people pushed through the crowd of Visage fans. They wore "skin coats" made of typical clothing fabrics.

"I think a man with the initials VD had something to do with Annabelle's disappearance. Do you guys have any leads about that?" Cecil asked the press.

But the reporters completely spun away from Cecil and toward the mob of skin coats.

While Annabelle's coat was covered in Crevier crystals and diamonds, the mob used twist ties and bottle caps as decoration. Yarn made up the hair, and purple beads made up the eyes. The wearers' faces were obscured by the hoods. It was an army of creepy ragdolls.

"Those are bad knockoffs," said a reporter.

"I'd take the real dead body over the cloth one any day. Annabelle's skin coat was beautiful. These look scary as hell."

Police and armed Visage security tentatively moved toward the mob in case it presented a threat.

"No more leather! Say no to fashion! No more abuse! No more death!" the mob chanted. "Don't kill for fur! Don't kill for skin!"

"We ask you at home," another reporter said into her camera, "are these fake skin coats offensive to the memory of Annabelle Leigh? Or are they the best Halloween costumes ever?"

Cecil clapped his hands just to feel the sting. He finally had answers to share with the press about Annabelle Leigh. But they didn't want to hear it.

Cecil yelled to the reporters' backs, "Have you heard of VD?"

"Believe me, kid. They won't listen. PETA protesting with Annabelle Leigh skin coats will get millions more clicks than some initials. The news wants flash. If you, Margaux, or Clara didn't kill Annabelle, there's no story anymore. Nobody's gonna run with a 'VD.' Even if it's true."

It wasn't a reporter speaking. It was a burly, bald Visage guard standing inches from Cecil, hand tightly gripping his machine gun. *Henry* was etched on the gun shaft.

"Welcome to the twenty-first century," Henry said. "There are no facts. Perception is reality. And whoever lies the best is right."

The members of the paparazzi and media didn't seem to have souls. Whenever Cecil looked at reporters, their eyes seemed as glassy and reflective as the camera lenses they shoved in their subjects' faces.

He felt alone in the circus.

Henry ushered Cecil away from the chaos. The security guard took them through the back alley and up the service elevator to the backstage dressing room.

Posted signs in the makeup room read "No Crying" and "No Eating Under 21." Dressers and ateliers desperately sewed naked models into fabrics with safety pins and glue, whatever they could find at the last minute. Cecil had never seen fashionistas sprint so fast. It was chaos.

They only had ten minutes before the show started.

Margaux slapped a Danish girl on the ass with an erotic cane handle shaped like two women scissoring. The girl was no older than sixteen. Her dress was a transparent tulle, a giant tutu covering her body. A streak of blood smeared down the back.

She lifted up the back of the dress and showed the model. "This is why you don't wear pads at a fashion show. *Especially* in a see-through dress. Tampons. Tampons. Tampons."

The other models covered their mouths, trying extremely hard to hide their laughter.

"I wish I could rip out your uterus," Margaux growled. "Goddammit. Perdonna is gonna kill me."

Ateliers poured peroxide on the fabric, desperately trying to scrub the stain away.

But one girl twirled about. She ignored the bloodstain and played with strands of her hair. She danced in a circle, humming to her own music. He recognized her from her bizarre walk. Her legs seemed to wobble beneath her like a toddler's. It was Ava Germaine.

"Hi. I'm Cecil LeClaire."

"No shit," Ava said.

A golden cart of treats was rolled by, clearly for the audience. But Ava stood in front of it. The man tried to stop, squatting and gripping hard onto the handles, but the cart rammed her in the knees. "Ow," she said, rolling her eyes. "I think I deserve some foie gras now, please."

She dipped her fingers in the meaty foie gras paste and handed Cecil a Toasted Vanilla, the steaming drink in the Crevier crystal goblet. The smell of Perdonna's perfume wafted over him.

Margaux suddenly threw powdered sugar over the model's bloodstain in a last-ditch attempt to hide it. The ateliers yelled at her even more.

"When I was a kid," Ava said, "my stepmother told me that women bleed once a month as a punishment for failing to be women. She said girls fail every month that they don't produce a child. So nature stabs them in the gut until they bleed."

Cecil spat out the drink. "What is *happening* right now?" he asked aloud.

Ava shrugged. Her long caramel hair was adorned with tiny copper twinkle lights, and she wore a black suede dress shaped like a cylinder. She moved like a Siamese cat, slinking but clumsy. She looked strung-out but childish. Dead but youthful.

Her eyes seemed to study him through the mayhem. They curved up into half-moons and blinked only whenever Cecil moved.

"Have you seen Jordan Jones?" Cecil asked.

Ava stared in front of herself, sipping her Toasted Vanilla. Her eyes glazed over and she seemed to leave the room. As if some terrible memory was replaying on the floor in front of her.

"Hello?" Cecil asked.

"Yeah?"

"I asked if you've seen Jordan Jones."

Ava twirled her hair nervously until strands fell out. She seemed spooked, like she was still traumatized from wearing the skin coat.

"Are you stoned?" Cecil asked.

"I haven't seen Jordan Jones since she went to your room last night," Ava said, looking him straight in the eyes, suddenly alert.

"How do you know about that?"

Ava shrugged and continued twirling her hair, twisting the copper wires into the strands. The twinkle lights had left indents on her fingertips.

"I've been watching Margaux," she said.

"Why?"

"It's fun. It's a human animal cracker trying to run a multi-million-dollar business."

A male hairstylist with a thick black mustache, piercing green eyes, and spiky white hair waved his hairbrush and pointed it at Cecil's face.

"I've been looking for Jordan for hours," the hairstylist said.

"She's supposed to be the closing girl for Perdonna's show. She has the best piece. Perdonna will personally slice Margaux's throat and cut off my balls if Jordan isn't here in a minute."

"This isn't the first time a girl's gone missing," Ava whispered in Cecil's ear.

"She's not *missing*," Cecil said. "She just didn't turn up for the show."

"Oh, she's *missing* missing. Believe me."

The stylist ran his fingers through his mustache and cocked a cubic eyebrow. "Ava. Get dressed. You're taking over for Jordan."

"What will Perdonna give me if I do it?"

The stylist held his headset close to his ear. Then he leaned into Ava and whispered. Apparently the offer was satisfactory. She held out her arms, and the stylist slid a heap of fabric over her frail bones.

The dress looked like a computer with dull metal wrapped around bloodred chiffon. The stylist removed the twinkle lights from her hair and curled it into angelic waves with an iron.

When the dress turned on, it lit up in a constellation of golds, swerving around her like the wind in the night sky.

A smile slowly spread across her face. Her shoulders pulled up into a proper posture. Her chin tilted up ever so slightly. She completely transformed into a new character—one with confidence and grace. A simple dress took away her strange childishness.

"Do you know who VD is?" Cecil asked.

"I think he's a lingerie photographer," Ava said. "I haven't heard good things. I've been trying to figure it out for a few hours but no leads so far."

"One minute. Showtime," someone yelled.

Ava kicked up her dress, and it lifted into the air. When her foot came down, however, the dress stayed afloat. She giggled like a schoolgirl.

"I have a bad feeling about this show," Ava said with a wink, as if her bad feeling was a good thing. "I hope you find Jordan."

Cecil opened his mouth to ask one more thing, but the dressers pushed the girls out onto the runway, and he was left alone with only makeup artists and a sea of Visage chiffon.

12

The Visage Gallery had been transformed into a mesmerizing black pool. The show floor was covered in twenty thousand liters of purified engine oil. It was a black mirror, reflecting the golden lamps and charcoal-colored silk on the walls. Flames seemed to ripple through the blackness, with scarlet red diffusing after.

Visage was the night sky; it was the universe in chaos.

A narrow walkway led to a circular stage, rotating like a sadistic carousel above the oil.

It was Perdonna's pedestal. She stood center, wearing a black shroud that covered her scarred eyes and long curls. A goddess, more beautiful than the models themselves.

Tragic tones echoed from Mozart's "Lacrimosa"—a chorus of impending doom, a requiem of a dream.

The lights rose to reveal models posturing like Greek statues around Perdonna, changing poses in time with the languid violin cues. Gold and red dresses swirled into a Milky Way around the models' light skin. Limbs reflected like white bones in the mirrored black swamp.

As the music crescendoed, more golden twinkle lights turned

on, projecting stars all about the room—in the oil, on the ceiling, and in Perdonna's hollow eyes.

Perdonna bent her hand gracefully to the floor as a ballerina would. And suddenly, a ring of fire shot up around the circle. She stood in the middle of Dante's Inferno.

Brave, for a semi-blind woman.

Fresh models entered, wearing sheer white dresses that flowed around the curves of their naked bodies.

Solemn white Venetian masks hide their faces. None had identity. None even showed her eyes. Breasts were framed under sheer fabric, fertile bodies on display. Curved thighs left shadows under the translucent white chiffon. Beautifully bowed hips were covered only by a white fig leaf.

They were granite masterpieces, gargoyles in the army of Visage.

It was religious, a ceremonial ritual.

The models bowed their heads in synchronicity, breasts bouncing above the audience.

Cecil made his way around the gallery where viewers stood.

When Mozart ended, a slow piano melody accompanied Ava Germaine's entrance. She walked out in a dress that seemed to swirl around her like a jellyfish in water. The models began twirling around the strip of runway, and Perdonna and Ava ascended on the circular platform.

Perdonna stripped the black cape away to reveal a thin black silk dress that hugged her curves. It was a sexy day dress. No wires showed through the fabric, but they still did their magic. The dress levitated around her, creating a beautiful illusion that she was floating in the air.

"Nervous Fiber," Perdonna said in her gorgeous accent. "Clothing becomes your lover."

Water fell from the sky like rain over the runway, and the torches of fire blew out. Ava's and Perdonna's dress skirts levitated as a pool formed at their feet. The fabric danced above water like translucent ghosts..

Oohs and aahs flooded the space.

"It's intelligent fashion," Perdonna said. "It knows what you need. A miniature computer detects objects surrounding you and adjusts the fabric accordingly."

Ava approached the small staircase leading down from the circular stage to the straight runway. The poufy ball gown of tulle lifted high above her feet so she could see each step. When she turned and walked back up to the stage, the dress collapsed and flowed onto the floor.

Cecil watched from the audience, distracted from trying to find Jordan. The technology felt too sophisticated for a *dress*.

"When you stand still," Perdonna said, "the dress will sway as if you're in the wind. Or in the water. So you look more dynamic than you really are."

Ava twirled with her twinkle lights and fairy dress into Perdonna's arms. She looked like a pixie, cheery and demure as she draped herself over Perdonna's body. The skirts tangled together, Ava's excess chiffon curving to Perdonna's. They became ballet dancers twirling inside a jewelry box.

"You can dance in a whole new way," she whispered seductively. "And when you're done feeling like a little girl, you can change."

She pressed a button on a small remote. The dress fabric fell around her in a molt until her outfit transformed into a domineering jumpsuit. The fabric tore at the seams and melded back together to hug her legs as pants. The shoulders jutted out into an angular curve. She was a boss. A sexy, evil witch towering over her domain.

The audience clapped ecstatically.

"Don't worry, gentlemen. There is something for you," Perdonna said. "If you're cold and rain-soaked. If you need a coat. Then voilà."

Cecil heard a tearing sound by his ear. A spotlight illuminated him, warming his head. His jacket began unraveling and re-stitching itself. It transformed into a stylish habit, hood curved into points, and the draped cloak covered in silver embroidered ivy.

His face turned bright red.

"Or, if you wake up one day and decide to become a monk," Perdonna said.

A crack in Perdonna's voice gave her away. Even blind, she stared in his direction a little too long. It was an undefinable show of emotion. But it was the only show of humanity the public had ever seen from her.

The audience stared back and forth between the two, nervous mouths agape.

"I have you covered," she said.

Ava held her hand out to Perdonna and she turned away as they descended the circular pedestal. All of the models' dresses levitated, and the final parade began. The models traced around Perdonna.

The spotlight dimmed on Cecil, and he let out a breath he didn't even know he'd been holding. His heart raced through his ears. A few eyes remained on him. One watcher was Detective Roosevelt, who stood toward the back of the space.

A final group of models paraded across the stage to a series of claps.

From out of nowhere, his mother's cane smacked him in the knee, making him stumble into the lady in front of him. He knocked her wig off her head. The hairless woman scowled and prepared her purse for attack but coyly blushed when she realized it was Cecil LeClaire.

"Oh. Sorry I was in your way, Mr. LeClaire."

He shoved his arm into Margaux's side. "Was that necessary?"

"It was an accident... I wanted you to stand next to me. You're a famous model now. I need you in my stable," she whispered.

Cecil glared as he felt the smooth suede that made up the Visage habit.

"Jokes," Margaux whispered, shading her eyes with her hand. "This show is ghastly. I mean, naked nipples and fire? This isn't the WWE. If Perdonna is supposed to be a clothing designer, she should sell drapes instead of sex. Sex is *my* job."

"I thought Jordan was supposed to close the show," Cecil said. He looked at her Dial. He remembered there was a tracking system for Margaux's models on it. He just had to ping Jordan.

"She quit. She said it was about you." Margaux raised an eyebrow. "You fucked her?"

"We both know that isn't true," he said. "Everyone says she's missing."

Margaux covered her nose with a pink handkerchief covered

in doilies. "She's in the finale still."

"So someone *has* found Jordan, then?"

Margaux's sapphire-blue eyes dug into his. "She's not missing."

"So she's closing the show?"

Margaux placed an Altoid in her mouth, and the smell of spearmint clashed with Ami and Buratti Black. "No. Ava Germaine closed."

"So where's Jordan?"

Margaux put her hands on her hips and furrowed her lips so he could see the pink exposed underneath her bright red lipstick.

"Jordan was afraid of you," Cecil said. "Why are you being so dodgy about where she is? How could she disappear in a model agency with such intense security?"

"What are you implying, darling?"

Cecil showed her the letter from the VD House. "Do you know anything about this?"

Margaux's hands trembled, making her bracelets chime several notes along with the sound of her models' stomping heels. "No."

"I called in the information to Detective Roosevelt."

"Goddammit, Cecil! Why would you do that?"

"The police are supposed to help—"

"Black lives matter, darling. Black lives matter. Haven't you read the news? Who the fuck turns things over to the corrupt police?"

A tiny bubble of socialites glanced above their sunglasses to look at Margaux, smelling an awkward domestic drama brewing next to them. She quickly put a smile on her Botoxed face.

"I'll handle it," she said, wiping perfumed sweat from her brow. "Go back to the agency and tell my assistant, Freddy, to collect all the cellphones in the chest and dispose of them."

"What?"

"Just do it," Margaux said, clacking her cane against Cecil's knee. And he noticed then that her ebony erotic cane had the same black sheen on it as the pool surrounding the stage.

Oil covered Margaux's cane. Did she slip in it and use her cane for balance? Did she lose her grip while whacking someone else, sending the cane into the oily pool?

"I'm your mother, Cecil. You know what it's like to be falsely accused. I didn't do anything wrong. I'm being set up. You're a monk. Show some trust."

"Yes, though I walk through the valley of the shadow of death, and I *will* fear evil. For *you* are with me. Your revolver and your staff, they abuse little girls!"

"Oh, joking with Psalms. So cool," Margaux chastised.

Cecil grabbed her wrist. He fidgeted with her watch. "I just want to track Jordan."

"After the show," Margaux squealed.

He tried to flip open his Dial, but Margaux stabbed her cane into his foot.

"What are you trying to hide?"

Margaux screamed so loud when Cecil spun the Dial projection onto the floor that half the audience turned to look at her. He pushed an application called Find My Models and scrolled down to the name *Jordan Jones*. When he tapped the name, a deafening alarm went off.

Perdonna tried to keep the models walking, but the girls dropped out of character. The cocky grins left their faces, and their legs wobbled. Perdonna's head turned to the sound.

She put her hand up, and the entire show stopped on a beat. No more music. No more lights. No more walking.

Cecil weaved through the audience, following the shrill beeping. He noticed a faint light underneath the oil pool. He paused before it as Ava stepped into the audience and came to his side.

"Is that Jordan's Dial?" Ava asked.

"I think so."

"Well, go get it."

She thrust all her weight at his waist and knocked him into the oil. She stepped back, avoiding the splash of his body plopping into the oil.

His knees rammed into the bottom of the oil pit. A large object rubbed against his feet. As the crowd watched, he bent down to feel it and cringed when he felt oiled, soft skin. He bit his lip, feeling shivers eke through his spine.

The spotlight never felt more damning.

With all the strength he had, he lifted the body out of the oil.

He held the limp corpse before him, the head dangling like a massive bulb above her neck. Her wrists drooped like wilted leaves on the ends of branches.

The blinding white lights returned. The press jostled for position to take photos of Cecil holding the corpse covered in oil. Now the lights felt normal to him. The camera flashes were soothing compared to holding her dead body—the body of the girl who had kissed him only the night before.

It was Jordan.

He wanted to sink deep below Perdonna's inferno. He felt cold despite standing by the fire. And a tear fell down his cheek.

He flipped open the oiled Dial to turn off the beeping. But as he did, the screen projected onto his hand. And there was a close-up photo of Margaux, the end of her cane pressing Jordan's dead body into the oil.

Cecil contemplated his next move. For a moment, he hesitated to reveal the photo. He didn't want to turn his own mother into the police. Especially if she *hadn't* killed Jordan.

But he flashed the photo overtop the oil. Margaux's worried face glistened like fireworks. Her cane loomed over Jordan's closed eyes and solemn, dead face.

Roosevelt and Chandler pushed through the audience, getting a look.

Margaux was already using her cane as a pathetic blockade.

Roosevelt grabbed Margaux by the wrists and yanked her bedazzled pink revolver from the holster around her waist. "Margaux LeClaire. You're under arrest."

Two doors burst open with a bang, and the NYPD ran through with helmets and vests. Women shrieked, men pretended to look at their phones.

Chandler directed the NYPD, and they converged on Margaux LeClaire.

She threw her cane in the oil before putting her hands up.

With the click of the handcuffs, Cecil felt the corpse in his hands slip back into the oil. His eyes clouded despite the bright lights still shooting at him. And Perdonna faded from his view.

13

Cecil looked like a helpless duck plucked from an oil spill, congealed black gunk drooping from his wings.

He sat in the back of an emergency service vehicle. It was a sad and hopeless sight.

The police barricaded the alleyway between the Visage store and the tower beside it. Dead rats festered in garbage, and mystery juices fell from the air vents of the towers above, splatting on heads. The mystery liquids always smelled like urine, even if it was only spittle from a resident above.

Perdonna stood before the barricade, surrounded by guards several inches taller than her. They towered over the paparazzi. Somehow Perdonna's cheekbones sparkled even with the backdrop of decomposing rats and an oil-drenched Cecil LeClaire.

"Two dead bodies in one week. Visage stock is plummeting by the minute. Anything you'd like to say to shareholders?" a journalist asked.

"In times like this, it is not the money I worry about," Perdonna said, triumphantly kicking around her body, keeping the media at bay. There was a six-foot perimeter around her. She was untouchable. "I mourn for Jordan Jones and Annabelle Leigh. I've directly spoken to Jordan's family and plan to meet with them in person. If Bob Leigh, my dear friend, were still alive, I'd be crying with him."

"I don't believe Perdonna cries. I doubt she even has tear glands," a reporter whispered a bit too loudly to the woman next to him.

"And I love how she refers to her chauffer as a 'dear friend.'"

Perdonna's eyes landed upon them. The empty stare felt more ferocious than any seeing eyes ever could. Their churlish grins disintegrated in a moment.

"Is Margaux LeClaire a suspect in Jordan Jones's murder?" a reporter shouted. "Any idea why she was arrested?"

"Carrying a revolver without a concealed-carry permit? Smacking an officer with an erotic cane?" Perdonna gave a coy half-smile as the reporters laughed. Her charm seemed to silence the wolves. They even bowed to her, hunched over beneath their cameramen, shaking even at the sight of her. They were nervous to ask her questions. "I have no idea," she said.

"Did Cecil LeClaire kill Jordan Jones too?"

"Did Mr. LeClaire plant the alarm to go off?"

"Did Cecil call Jordan's watch?"

Perdonna waved her hands and pointed to one journalist at a time, silencing them like a band conductor. She was practiced in managing the public.

"Jeremy White. *Glamorama*," a voice rumbled. Jeremy White looked like an older version of Cecil. Except he had blond hair and less attractive cheekbones. He walked toward Perdonna, threatening the invisible wall between her and the paparazzi. "Can you define your relationship with Cecil LeClaire?"

"He is my godson."

Other reporters yelled out questions in a bumble of chaotic noise. But Jeremy broke through again. "And have you seen him since he left Manhattan for St. Joseph's Abbey?"

"No."

"A reliable source tells me you vacationed alone together for two weeks in Bolivia sometime in 2016."

The whole crowd went silent.

Perdonna shook her head. "Even apprenticing monks can't leave a monastery for *vacation*."

"But he's gotten permission to be here, hasn't he?" Jeremy asked. He rubbed his hands together and stepped closer to Perdonna. Her guards slowly turned toward her, hands gripping guns with a tighter fist. "Just seems strange you'd take your twenty-one-year-old godson on vacation alone."

"It would be strange. But I haven't seen Mr. LeClaire in six years." Perdonna stepped out in front of her guards. Her long hair fell forward. "Step back, sir."

Detective Chandler's doughboy face reeled up into a carved V shape from all his smirking. With his arms folded, he stood by and watched as Cecil tried to itch the oil off his body. Roosevelt held Margaux in a police vehicle.

"How am I *still* the murderer to the media? I just turned my own mother in."

Ava stepped toward them, wearing her cylindrical black dress once again. Six strands of fairy lights remained in her hair, glistening gold. "Is it true?"

"No! I'm not a murderer!"

"I don't care about that. I mean Bolivia? Did Perdonna take you?" Ava asked, nodding to Perdonna's interview.

"Of course not." Cecil shook his head rapidly and combed his fingers through his hair.

Ava's eyes squinted into crescent moons. "You are a spectacularly terrible liar," she said in a monotone. Her head was always cocked, as if she constantly studied the world around her. But she didn't need answers from Cecil. She'd figure out what they were doing in Bolivia herself.

She scuttled away when her eyes locked on a peculiar white, fluffy rat covered in garbage. Her feet pattered toward it, and she followed it down the city block.

Chandler pretended not to be excited about attending a Visage show, and managed to tear his eyes away from Perdonna to turn his beak-like nose back to Cecil.

"It's interesting *you* pulled the body out of the oil. How did you know it was there?" Chandler asked.

"I didn't. I was trying to find her just like you were."

"That's the first thing murderers do. They want to be involved in the search," Chandler said, nodding. "So they can get off by reliving the crime."

"And you know what detectives are supposed to do?" Cecil asked, feeling that familiar angry heat rising up to his face. "They're supposed to protect little girls. Had you even heard of this VD before I gave you the letter?"

"You could've made VD up. Wrote the letter yourself and collaborated with Margaux to hide the body. But then you got cold feet and turned Margaux in. Or maybe that was your plan all along. Pin Jordan's death on Margaux, just like you pinned Annabelle's death on Clara?"

Cecil slammed his hands against the police vehicle. The sting of metal left red-and-purple marks on his palms. He rose up, looking like a grim reaper covered in black slime. His eyes were obscured as the liquid drained down his face.

"Wait, wait," Chandler said. "Fine. Let's pretend you didn't kill Jordan. Margaux might've killed Jordan to stop her from revealing evidence that Margaux was receiving commissions on Annabelle's work after her disappearance. Margaux clearly knew Annabelle's whereabouts and didn't inform the police. So, she killed Jordan to prevent the evidence from coming out."

"Then who killed Annabelle and who abducted her?" Cecil asked, wringing his hands.

"Well, this VD, whomever he is. And Margaux had something to do with the abduction."

"How could you only be learning all of this *now*? What have you people been doing all these years?" Cecil threw down the monk habit, and it crumbled into a dark oily puddle. "How could you not know Margaux is dangerous?"

"Margaux was the FBI's lead suspect in the abduction," Chandler whispered, beginning to turn his body away from Cecil, afraid of him.

"Margaux's been here screaming at girls. Throwing their bodies into oil and people just *let* her do it? Annabelle was in the United States for four years. *Four years* and no one found her?

Jordan didn't have to die. And neither did Annabelle."

Cecil kicked over a trash can with a loud bang, and suddenly he felt a large hand on his back. Henry, Perdonna's bodyguard, stood overtop him.

"She wants you to bring her the coat so she can dry-clean it," Henry said. He nodded to Chandler. "Can I take him? Or is Cecil under arrest too?"

"He's free," Chandler said with leery little beady eyes.

Cecil noticed that Perdonna was no longer standing with the reporters. Henry opened the side door to the Visage store and led Cecil back inside.

A hallway behind the stage was crowded with vats of oil and torches from the show. Cecil clutched the habit in his hands, heavy from being drenched in oil.

"You good?" Henry asked.

"For what?"

"Wait and stay quiet," Henry said. "I'm leaving you here." He slammed the door behind him and locked it.

The lights dimmed to pitch black, except for a small stream of light that trickled through a tiny crack in the wall behind him. He could see his hand only six inches from his face. Behind the wall was the crime scene.

If he listened close enough, he could hear the sounds of camera shutters. Police boots were stomping across the floor. He heard the loud thump of sets being torn down.

But around him, there was only an eerie silence. And the occasional trickling of water from an air-conditioning unit. He began to worry about Henry. Maybe he shouldn't have trusted him only on the knowledge he was Perdonna's new bodyguard.

He felt his way along the wall, running his fingers over soft furs and rough linens, stucco paint and concrete, until he came to the door. But when he tried the circular knob, it was locked too.

"Hello," he called out. "Hello?"

Cecil slid down against the concrete wall. His heartbeat sped up.

Then he heard the alley door creak. It closed and opened before he could turn around. Heels clanked against the concrete. But instead of wobbly newborn colt hooves, they sounded like staccato drumbeats.

"Hello?" Cecil asked.

A hand wrapped around his collarbone and pushed him back up against the wall. The other hand pressed a finger against his lips, and he tasted salty vanilla. "You have a phone again, love. Stop making a commotion."

She removed her shushing finger and nuzzled it beneath his Dial band, scratching lightly at his pulse.

Her voice was rich and confident, even in a whisper. A voice that sounded like honey swirling into hot black tea. It was Perdonna.

"I suppose wrath isn't a deadly sin anymore?" she whispered, keeping her nails against his jugular.

"What do you mean?"

"What do I mean?" she scoffed, moving even closer. "Screaming at the detective? I'm standing up there trying to save a billion-dollar company from you and your raccoon of a mother, and you're behind me throwing a temper tantrum."

"You're the one who's best friends with that raccoon."

"Raccoons work very, very hard."

"Until they shit on themselves," Cecil said. "And kill people."

As he moved away from the crack of light, he could see her lips curve up from behind her nude lip gloss. "Stop being cute. I'm angry with you," she whispered only inches from his face. Cinnamon mints mixed with her vanilla perfume.

"Why are we whispering?" Cecil asked.

"I can't be seen speaking to you."

"Because I'm a serial killer monk."

"Precisely," Perdonna said with a deep chuckle. He felt her chest bump into his. Her soft rose-gold hair brushed up against his neck. "Let me tell you, monkhood isn't helping your case either. This is Manhattan, darling. Jumpsuits are in, stripes are out. Astrology is back, Christianity is out."

"That's ridiculous."

"I don't make the rules."

"You absolutely do. That's your whole job. Trends."

"Are you admitting Christianity is a trend?" Perdonna asked with wide eyes, taunting him. Her fingertips still sat at his throat.

"I'm sure you're not allowed to do that."

"You trapped me."

"No. I simply—"

The door from inside the show floor opened, and Perdonna whipped the oily habit overtop them. She pushed him down to the floor and climbed on top of him.

"Can you remove your hand from my neck now?" he whispered.

Her fingers dug deeper into his neck. He fake gagged, and she smacked him in the chest with her hand. The hit made a small thud.

"Shit," she whispered, lips pressed against his ear.

Cecil threw back his head, trying not to let out any audible laughter.

"Stop it." Her body shook against his, trying not to laugh.

"Wouldn't it be worse for someone to find us like *this*? Then you'd have a whole different kind of story to worry about."

Her thumb pressed into the underside of his chin. "I'll kill you."

He felt her lip gloss stick to his ear as she pulled away. Her smooth cheek rubbed against his neck.

The feeling clashed with the loud jingling passing by them. It sounded like a shopping cart being rolled over cement.

Cecil felt Perdonna's arms quaking around him, as she tried to keep her body hovering over his without touching him. "You can sit on my lap, you know. I'm a monk, not a priest. I won't rape you."

She paused a few seconds. Then she rested against him, trying not to move the habit. They could feel each other's hearts beat into their chests. Cecil's fingers tangled in her hair without even realizing it. He traced his fingertips through her scalp, lightly massaging her head. And he could feel the goosebumps rise along her collarbone.

Cloudy sunset filled her eyes. He could see her pupil move beneath the fog.

She was not completely blind. Her world was a Monet-world, impressionistic and blurry.

He loved touching her. It wasn't necessarily sexual. It was how they communicated.

The public took so much of her. All he had were the private

little touches. Her pulse. Her scalp. Her breath. The media would never know those.

"I missed you," he whispered into her ear, thumbs resting by her temples.

She let out a little gasp. The moment the passerby jingled her keys and opened the outside door, Perdonna whipped off the habit. She jumped up covered in oil.

Cecil stood and licked his finger. He tried to wipe the oil off of her, but she smacked him away.

"Whoa, what's wrong?"

"I don't like the way you spoke to that detective."

"I thought we were past that?" Cecil asked, folding his arms.

"Chandler and Roosevelt are trying to do their jobs as best they can," Perdonna said. "If you want to blame anyone, blame the FBI."

"I blame Roosevelt for not knowing Margaux had something to do with Annabelle's abduction. For questioning me, a fourteen-year-old boy, more than Margaux LeClaire. They killed Annabelle."

Perdonna shook her head. Her hands skimmed the oil off her arms. "Then you killed Jordan."

"Excuse me?" Cecil asked, face going red. He felt his feet take steps toward her. Their whispers had grown to staccato chatter.

"By that logic. Jordan told you Annabelle was a model. She said Margaux was dangerous. She thought VD worked with Margaux. She told you she was afraid to sleep in her own room the night she tried to sleep with you. What more did you need to confront Margaux?"

"Your guys are surveilling LeClaire? Ava Germaine works for you?"

Perdonna nodded as Cecil stood closer to her. He put his hands on either side of her body, leaning in toward her. "Why didn't *you* call the police?"

"The NYPD doesn't like it when I step on them."

"Are you kidding me?" Cecil shouted. He punched the stucco wall beside Perdonna's head. "A girl is dead."

She smacked him across the face. The sting quaked through

his teeth. "Get back." He stepped away from her. "Jordan is dead because you couldn't admit your mother is a weasel. You didn't look into the truth of what Jordan had to say because you didn't want to know."

"You're right."

"She risked her life to let you know part of what happened to Annabelle. She was trying to hide it from the cameras so Margaux wouldn't know."

Cecil put his head in his hands. "Abbot Joseph sent me here to deal with my unresolved family issues before I become a monk."

"Smart man. Maybe religion isn't so ridiculous after all."

Cecil sighed, looking back to the habit in a heap on the floor. "What happened here? We were getting along so well. Should I not have said I missed you?"

Perdonna chuckled. She licked her hands and traced her fingers over her neck, flicking off the black sheen. "That. And I'm still angry about Bolivia."

"It was three years ago."

"And you clearly haven't spent any time with women since then," Perdonna said. "Women don't give up grudges without a fight."

Cecil leaned over, and the little red leather dog, Aberto, fell from his pants pocket. Perdonna's lips fell open. Cecil leaned over to pick him up, brushing the dirt off him carefully. He put the stuffed animal back in his pocket.

When he looked up again, he saw Perdonna staring wistfully at the pocket. "Do you want him back?" he asked.

"No, no," Perdonna said. "I'm surprised you still have him, is all. I thought you'd have to give him up at the abbey. I was worried."

His eyes lit up. It never ceased to surprise him when Perdonna was vulnerable. "I did have to give him up in theory. But I hid him."

A smile exposed her teeth, gleaming white. Perdonna's lips barely ever crested higher than a centimeter. "I'm sure you were a stellar monk," she said sarcastically.

"Am," he corrected. "I'm still a monk."

Perdonna swallowed the lump in her throat. She put her hand on Aberto and whispered, "*In bocca al lupo.*"

Into the wolf's mouth.

14

Tazia Perdonna was born in Florence, Italy. No one knew when because Perdonna would never reveal her age.

Her British-born mother worked as a cheese whisperer in Italy, tapping wheels to make sure the highest standards of Italy's Parmigiano-Reggiano were upheld. And her father was a master clockmaker.

Perdonna's last years in Italy had been marked by fear known as Strategia della Tensione. During the Years of Lead in the 1960s to 1980s, the communist government of Italy committed assassinations, mass bombings, and street warfare.

Her father rejected capitalism and socialism, finding himself stuck between Italy's two battling parties. So he joined Terza Pozisione, a political and economic Third Position. *Neither red front, nor reaction*. The Third Position was nothing and everything, a dangerous middle ground.

Police found hand grenades, fabricated documents, and carabinieri uniforms on the Terza Pozisione premises. It was soon after that Perdonna's father took her to Florence for a weekend vacation.

On Sunday, her father woke her, telling her to stay in the hotel room the whole day—not to see family, not to call friends. She should pack her bags and be ready to leave in the afternoon when he returned.

He carried a suitcase with both hands, tiptoeing cautiously as though the luggage held a fragile glass trinket. Perdonna assumed he was sneaking out to bring a present to his mistress. But she had to see for herself. She snuck out behind him.

Cobblestone roads and red terra cotta roofs still framed the Medici family coat of arms.

People crowded in piazzas and churches in the morning. The smell of cured pork and sausage mixed with Bolognese sauce being prepared for the afternoon meal. The summer in Florence was so unbearably hot and humid, one couldn't find refuge even under the medieval city's shaded porticoes.

The Arno river twinkled its evergreen sheen over her father's gray hair. Perdonna walked many yards behind. She listened to the cars jingle over cobblestone roads, humming to the rhythm.

They weaved through intimate alleyways, big enough only for a horse. Fresh linen hung from clotheslines and fresh bread baked in ovens. Each passage opened up to a piazza with a church as the centerpiece.

Florence was a Renaissance maze that always led to God, no matter which path you chose to take.

Her father wandered into Piazza del Duomo. And he stopped in front of Santa Maria del Fiore, one of the largest churches in the world. Brunelleschi's red dome towered over Florence. A red crown fit for the Mother of Christ.

Her father knelt down behind a cart of fruits, facing the cathedral and bell tower. He bowed his head, murmuring prayers to himself.

Perdonna studied the pink and green marble that swirled over the white panels of the basilica. She counted the panels to avoid wondering what her father was about to do.

After kissing Michelangelo's masterpiece goodbye, Perdonna followed her father to the final stop. The train station.

Thousands of people passed through Firenze Santa Maria

Novella railway station. Doctors and business owners traveled to countryside villas or the seaside to escape the roasting town. University students on break dreamed of visiting their families for the holiday. Police, porters, and railway workers stood in uniform, prepared for a day of hard work.

Her father arrived at 10:00 a.m., not wearing his regular unlined jacket nor his leather loafers. He wore ragged clothing, a simple shirt and pants so he would blend in with the thousands of commuters—doctors, beggars, and students.

Perdonna followed. She was sure he planned to travel to one of his mistresses. Isabella? Maria? She didn't know.

He walked into the only air-conditioned waiting room in the train station where everyone crowded like sardines just to feel a breeze.

She checked the train departure times to guess which place her father would visit. Milan or Rome?

But when she got back to the waiting room, her father wasn't there. Only his suitcase sat on the floor, abandoned.

Two children, no older than seven, tossed a ball back and forth beside the bag. Mothers flipped through the daily news, the smell of espresso wafting toward their noses. A beggar jingled coins, belting the national anthem while no one paid attention.

Her father wouldn't forget an expensive suitcase. Money mattered. Leaving it behind was no accident. She knew what was in that bag.

Perdonna's dad didn't bring her on a lovely father-daughter vacation. Perdonna was only ever an alibi.

Sweat formed on her brow as she sat in the waiting room with the Florentine travelers, staring at the bag for twenty minutes before accepting the truth.

It was a bomb in the waiting room. Her father planned a terrorist attack on Florence.

Instinct told her to move the luggage, grab the handle, and carefully drag it out of the room. But when would it go off? Could movement trigger it? Was it on a timer? Of course it was—her father was a clockmaker. The blast could happen at any second. And she couldn't tell the police; her mother always said not to trust them.

Perdonna sat beside a young girl who had puffy youthful cheeks framed by loose ribbon-clad braids. In her hands was a stuffed red dog with tan floppy ears, covered in dirt and holes.

She put the toy on Perdonna's lap. "This is Aberto. He says hi."

"Hello, Aberto."

Perdonna looked forward, eyes fixated on the suitcase. Then the girl woofed, using the dog to paw at Perdonna's arm, naïve eyes shamelessly begging for attention.

The mother scolded the little girl for her antics.

"She's fine. I don't mind," Perdonna said.

"Are you a princess?" the girl whispered, flapping Aberto's tan ears through her fingers.

Perdonna would've laughed if she hadn't been so stressed. "Why would you think that?"

"You look like a princess." Her fingers touched Perdonna's blond locks as she had Aberto's ears. "I hope I'm like you someday."

She used the dog as a puppet, dancing Aberto across Perdonna's lap. She felt the girl's hand brush against her knees. "Where are you traveling?" Perdonna asked.

The mother looked over at them with tired, puffy circles around her eyes.

"I'm going to say goodbye to my daddy," the girl said. "Mommy told me he died."

Perdonna's breaths came in shallow huffs as tears streamed down the mother's face. People in the waiting room moved in slow motion before her eyes, as though they did a tribal dance around the suitcase.

"I'm sorry. I have to go," Perdonna said.

The police had to know what her father had done. She went to the security counter, but as she reached to tap the policeman, a hand swooped her up by the waist. Her father dragged her from the waiting room, screaming. His hand covered her mouth.

Perdonna looked back to see the little girl waving her hand goodbye.

At 11:04 a.m., the time bomb detonated. The explosion hit the train that waited at the first platform. And the roof of the waiting room collapsed under the pressure of the blast, killing ninety-two people in total.

Perdonna stepped in the rubble a few hours after, breaking away from her father's hideout. Given the number of casualties, hundreds of civilians helped with the cleanup effort, acting as amateur firefighters, nurses, and taxi drivers.

The smell of ash and char radiated from the bodies as Perdonna climbed over them. She found the spot where she sat with the little girl. Their seats were unrecognizable, covered in jagged metal and a mountain of rubble. She dug to free the family. A split metal pipe sliced her palm. Her blood pooled on a wooden plank.

There she caught sight of a tiny braid, and the holey ear of Aberto.

The little girl's blank, dead eye stared up at her the same way Perdonna had stared at the suitcase bomb.

She rested her head on her knees, gagging until she coughed up only air. It was as if her soul had been ripped out of her.

Aberto seemed to slink out of the rubble as she lifted planks off the stuffed animal. His body had been split down the middle. She cradled the dog to her face like the girl had, and she soaked him in tears.

Perdonna killed Aberto.

She never recovered from the bombing. It was as if she began to see people as animals, bony and sweaty with eyeballs that could be torn apart with only a pencil tip.

She felt like a murderer from a murderous family.

Soon after the massacre, she stole $100,000 in cash from her father's safe and escaped for New Orleans. Then at eighteen years old, she traveled from New Orleans with Margaux and Louis LeClaire to Manhattan. There she would make Visage a fashion empire.

Informal was not in the Tazia dictionary because fashion served to hide her darkest secret—beneath the velvet and the pearls, she was a bloody, sweating animal.

Men of all walks invited her to the oh-so-popular Studio 51. She spent nights with Pierre Lazard and Lorenzo Buratti. But

Perdonna didn't notice the drinks or the so-called fun. She saw how people battled for social supremacy like African lions at a watering hole.

In Studio 51, she recognized the economic importance of style. And in 1997, she debuted her watch collection that she called "Visage" as a snide nod to the superficiality of it all.

The watch featured a maroon enamel rim with a pearly-white interior. The numbers appeared blocky and stylized, small square dots marking the minutes. She added brownish-red second hands as a nod to Aberto.

No one knew that Perdonna had modeled the watch after the clock that still stood in Florence, memorializing the massacre.

Her personal timepiece always read 11:04. Time never moved forward, nor could it ever move back.

After the Visage watch brand rose to fame, she expanded to apparel, defining her style as a seamless unification of the natural world and the human one. Visage abolished unflattering elephant pants and gaudy colors. Nature broke through form. Perdonna made fashion from Mother Nature, but in the most expensive, high fashion sense.

Stingray-skin pants and gowns. Golden lizards and ruby-red maple leaves lined women's suit jackets. Diamond and sapphire pendants resembled dinosaur fossils.

Visage was the future and the past in one.

The masculine and feminine were in harmony. Visage was modern, but with an elegant, classic sheen.

The company soon went international, opening home goods and children's wear lines branded with the Visage Libra. And by 2009, the corporation reached $5.8 billion in yearly revenues.

15

Cecil returned to the fourth floor of the LeClaire Mansion, wearing a baggy NYPD sweat suit. The hallway's red cubicles were empty and dark like the shop windows of a closed store. There were no models to be seen.

LeClaire Model Management was quiet without Margaux. Very quiet.

But then he heard a sound coming from Margaux's office. *"Animal crackers I love you. Chinchillas and Camels two by two. Why are there so few?"* her voice shrilled out from a recording.

Margaux loved butchering Shirley Temple songs. Margaux modeled her entire existence off of the child performer. Shirley Temple was her idol. Her god. Her spirit animal.

Cecil tried the door handle, but it was locked.

"When the hippos are inside me where it's warm, I walk around like a human farm. I stuff my tummy like a pig with animal crackers... I love you."

He had heard enough. With one lunge, he kicked at the door handle. But instead of the door collapsing under his mighty strength as he thought it would, it didn't even budge.

There was a French antique knockoff side table next to him. It featured a plump cherub hand-feeding glitter to naked angels.

With a grunt, he heaved the table at the door. The power of the cherub knocked it down.

He stormed into that pink-covered room like a soldier. He threw open the gold-lined cupboards. In the first, he found shelves of spray-on tan in the shade "Gingerbread Woman." In the second, there were four shelves of Smurf action figures with tiny fairy huts made from coconuts.

He threw stuffed animals all around the room. There had to be hidden keys or damning evidence stuffed up at least one of those hippos' asses. Why else would a grown woman be obsessed with hippos?

There was nothing beneath the polar bear cub rugs. Nothing inside the ten white ottomans. And nothing inside thirty of the music boxes. He gave up on the last seventy.

But when he finally stopped Margaux's karaoke recording on the desktop computer, he saw another video.

It was the result of Margaux's pre-taped press conference.

On the screen, Margaux's miniature movie played.

There was security camera footage of Cecil's first encounter with the models. Girls danced around him half-naked while he sat staring at them. The camera he had been holding was nowhere to be seen. The footage made it look like he had asked the girls to strip for him.

Jordan sprawled out over his lap.

"Look," Margaux's voiceover said. "I hate to say this, but my son, Cecil LeClaire, he's troubled. He's not a monk but a maniac. We sent him to the abbey to reform his wickedness. But he came back even worse."

The news reports of Cecil shoving the reporter at the abbey were edited into the frame. The scene was cut to avoid showing the press attacking him first.

"I'm terrified of him," Margaux's voice said. "That's why I carry a revolver everywhere I go. *He* abducted and killed Annabelle."

Margaux sat before the camera in the lobby as she had during the taping. But instead of makeup dripping down her face, her skin glowed. "He just took her off the street. Like...bang. Grabbed her by the pussy," she said to the camera.

The dark preamble ended when the New York City skyline filled the screen. The LeClaire Model Management logo floated above in golden letters. Models partied on the rooftops of sky-scrapers with champagne in their hands. Girls wore tiny bikinis and danced on top of yachts.

They posed in front of Ferraris in Beverly Hills, palm trees swaying above their heads. They swam on the shores of the Caribbean.

"Think you have what it takes to be a LeClaire Model?" asked Margaux. "Come to a Manhattan casting."

Jordan Jones posed wearing a beautiful ball gown. Her skin sparkled with more glitter than any unfiltered person could rea-sonably apply. Her hair had more volume. Her legs were more balletic than a dancer's. Her arms twisted behind her head, and she smiled at the photographer.

"Be the best you that *you* can be."

Cecil grabbed an erotic cane off the wall and smashed the computer screen with it. He hacked at it like a serial killer stab-bing a body.

He stopped for a breath of air, but then he felt something furry around his ankles. There was something white. But it wasn't a polar bear cub, it was a rat. The tiny teeth dug into his ankle beneath the sweat suit.

"Jesus," he said, jumping away from it. He clutched his ankle. But when he looked closer, he noticed the disheveled white hair. The bedhead rat.

"Figaro," Ava yelled. "Screw you, Figaro. Screw you."

Ava turned her back to the rat. He seemed to pause before her, tail twirling as if begging to be accepted again.

"No. I hate you, Figaro. I hate you. I'm serious. I do."

Ava sucked on a lollypop and wore a sparkly pink boa around her neck. It was a childlike look. And her outfit seemed to trans-form her into an actual child.

She stomped her foot even as Figaro, the rat, climbed up the leg of her black suede dress. Even though Ava's dress was never formfitting, he could see the rat climbing up the whole outfit like a mouse moving through a snake's stomach.

"Figaro is *your* rat?" Cecil asked. "Margaux lets you have a rat?"

Ava shook her head. "I live with Perdonna. Margaux knows I work for her too. It's like how they shared Annabelle's dad, the chauffer. They share me too." Ava twirled around with the boa. And eventually Figaro gripped onto the boa as well, clinging to the feathers as they whipped around like an amusement park ride.

He laughed at the sight. And secretly kind of wanted a rat for himself. It was then that he remembered Ava was also twenty-four. They were the same age.

Ava chucked the lollipop to the ground and took off the boa, plopping Figaro back onto the floor. The white rat scurried onto one of the polar bear cubs and chilled out, blending into the fur.

"Margaux is being questioned at the One-Nine. If they have enough to hold her, she'll be locked up for a long time," Ava said. Her voice was back to its spooky tone, her eyes returning to their dead-eyed expression.

Cecil folded his arms and studied her posture. Like she had backstage at the show, she changed into an entirely different person. She was a child playing dress-up. Whenever she put on a new outfit, she adopted a character. And it seemed she didn't even know she was doing it.

"What's wrong?" Ava asked. "Margaux will be fine. I've been to prison. It's pretty nice."

"You were in prison?"

"Juvie. But basically the same." She opened one of the Advil bottles, probably to see if Margaux had been hiding schizophrenia meds or models' pulled teeth inside. She jingled it and stared into it as if there was no bottom to the container.

"What did you do?" he asked.

"I robbed an important government document."

Figaro climbed on top of a row of music boxes. Each time he hopped onto a new spinning figure—Mickey Mouse, a rainbow teddy bear, or Hannibal Lecter—a different note played.

"That's impressive," Cecil said. "Why did you steal it?"

"I stole the Declaration of Independence from the Archives'

preservation room during a party. Because there was a map on the back of it."

"That's not true."

Ava nodded. Her eyes locked on to Figaro and squinted as he continued to make noise. When he didn't stop, she walked toward him and stood, waiting like a mother with her toddler. Eventually, he climbed up her arm and onto her shoulder. "It is true. I've lived an extravagant life."

Cecil scoffed. "That's the plot of the movie *National Treasure.*"

"I know. It's based on me."

"It's fine if you don't want to tell me why you went to prison," Cecil said. "But you're lying."

"Believe what you want to believe."

A small muscle pulsated and protruded from Ava's neck. It looked like a beetle writhing in her throat, trying to break through the skin and escape into her caramel hair.

"What was that?" he asked.

Ava covered the twitching muscle with her palm. "I'm sick."

"Are you okay?" The muscle in her neck stopped twitching, and Cecil placed a hand on her shoulder.

"Fine."

"Are you dehydrated?"

"My first model agent drugged me with hormones to keep me skinny for years," she said. "Now I'm sick with Ava-itis. No one knows what it is."

That one, he unfortunately believed. "I'm sorry to hear that. I'll pray for you."

Ava's eyes widened, and her mouth twisted into a disturbing shape. She looked disgusted. "Please don't be a monk about it. If you pray to anybody, pray to Figaro. He's got more power than God, believe me."

Ava plopped onto an ottoman and stared out the window, seemingly lost in her own thoughts. It was impossible to read her eyes. Whenever she wasn't dressed in costume, she seemed just a hollow shell of the person that must've once lived inside her.

"So why does Perdonna have you working for her? To steal secrets from her competitors or to frame them for murder?" he asked.

"I'm her eyes. I monitor the industry. I make sure everything's fair, nothing too corrupt."

"So, in other words, you're studying competitors' crimes for Perdonna so she can use the information to out-manipulate her enemies," Cecil offered.

"And I used to be a top model, so she knew Margaux would take me. Even though I'm old."

"Old?"

"A hag."

"You're twenty-four."

"A *really old* hag."

Cecil chuckled. But he stopped laughing when Ava frowned. Her pout wasn't a child's pout. That lower lip seemed to bounce with intention. It was a strangely wise and direct way of guilting people and manipulating their emotions.

"I was trying to find evidence of Margaux killing Jordan," Cecil said. "I guess she was the last person to see Jordan, so I was hoping—"

"She wasn't."

"She wasn't what?"

Ava refused to answer. She petted Figaro instead, curling his tail around her pinky finger.

"Hello?" he asked as she dazed off into oblivion.

Ava scoffed. "I don't have to always answer you. I'm not a dog."

"You mean Margaux was not the last person to see Jordan?"

Ava nodded. "Right. Freddy, Margaux's assistant, was the last person to see Jordan *alive*. I have it on tape. He opened the staff entrance to let Jordan go outside the mansion. She came in a half hour later with a note. Probably the letter VD wrote Margaux."

"Interesting."

Ava raised an eyebrow. "Do you know the code to the basement?"

Cecil shook his head.

"Okay, bye," Ava said. She put Figaro into her black backpack and turned to walk out. But Cecil put his hand on her shoulder.

"Wait, why?" he asked.

"I want to see the basement. It's off-limits, and Gisele, the elevator model, had strict orders never to take me there. But Gisele is missing. So now I might finally have my chance to go to the basement."

"Gisele is *missing*? What?" Cecil asked. "Why are we standing here talking?"

Ava shrugged. "I thought you knew. None of the models are here. The agents are gone. And the security cameras went black about an hour ago."

Cecil ran his hands through his hair. "Well, let's find them. You think they're in the basement?"

"I'm not working with you," Ava said.

"You work for Perdonna."

"And?" Ava put her hands on her hips. "I'm supposed to figure out if VD killed Annabelle Leigh."

Cecil mimicked her aggressive stance, throwing his hands to his hips. "So we both want the same thing."

"I *could* help you. What do you have to offer me?"

"*Offer* you?"

"Money? Any kind of Hershey's bars? We can trade something." Ava cocked her head in her studying way. Her voice lilted up into a cute high pitch. It was a baby voice on a young adult.

"Nothing. I have nothing." Then he thought for a moment. "I have prayers." A joking grin spread across his face.

Ava's eyes remained hopeful and dreamy. They squinted into half-moons. "Anything for Figaro?"

"Does Figaro like prayers?"

She rolled her eyes so dramatically that the iris seemed to slip off the eyeball. "Perdonna said I had to help you anyway. Come on."

A large knot in Ava's hair swung back and forth. It seemed to propel her feet down the hallway like an engine. The knotted hair probably came from the twinkle lights that were strewn into it. As soon as he got a chance, Cecil would pull that rat's nest apart and fix it properly.

Cecil flipped open his Dial and typed onto his palm.

Cecil LeClaire: You sure like to hire eccentric people.

Tazia Perdonna: She has a great eye. She notices everything.

Cecil LeClaire: Like her rat?

Tazia Perdonna: Figaro is not a rat. He's a gentleman.

Tazia Perdonna: Also a good rule: everything Ava says about other people is true, everything Ava says about herself is a lie. Love.

The elevator doors swung open to reveal Freddy standing in a sweat-stained skull T-shirt paired with plaid pants so tight they seemed tattooed onto his calves. His curls clung to his forehead in swirls.

"Ava?" Freddy heaved, out of breath. "What are you doing up here?"

"Breathing," she said, twirling her hair between her fingertips.

"You're supposed to be in the basement."

"Is that where everyone is?" Cecil asked.

Freddy nodded. He rubbed his hands together and tapped his feet onto the marble floor. "Margaux's protocol. If ever she dies or gets arrested, I'm supposed to send the agents home and keep the models in the basement."

"Why?" Cecil asked.

"Because Margaux wouldn't want anyone to talk when the police come searching," Ava said.

Cecil pressed the basement button. But Freddy froze the elevator, shifting levers and pressing a complicated series of buttons quite quickly for someone who acted so stupid.

The clock hands on the elevator wall continued to spin, but the roman numerals began in a slow spiral along with them.

"You can't go down," Freddy said. "LeClaire Model Management staff only."

"Margaux's son doesn't count?" Cecil said.

"It's dangerous down there. There are rednecks doing construction," Freddy said.

"Terrifying. Are the rednecks going to torture me with country music?" Cecil asked.

Ava's eyes drifted toward Cecil, and she nudged him with her shoulder.

"There are exposed beams everywhere. Cement dripping off the walls. Asbestos leaking from the ceiling like pimple puss. It's terrible," Freddy said.

"So you're sending Ava there? And all the models? You put

racehorses in a barn. Might as well put your models in a basement. Save the money, right?" Cecil asked with a sarcastic huff.

"It's a spa," Freddy said, still rubbing his hands together as if
somehow he'd start a fire and burn himself to death just to escape
the elevator. "Monks can't *spa*, right?"

"A spa?" Cecil asked. "So, the girls are getting cement chips
instead of French tips?"

"Cute," Freddy said. "You *are* Margaux's son."

Ava sat down on the elevator floor like a child tired of standing. She leaned her head back against the wall. But whenever the
clock hand spun toward her, she had to lean forward. Eventually
she got so frustrated she tried smacking it.

"The models are sent to the basement for punishment," Ava
said. "It's not a spa."

"You wouldn't know," Freddy said. "You've never been."

"Because Margaux doesn't want Perdonna to know what mess
must be down there."

Freddy restarted the elevator by pulling levers. Once again,
the roman numerals froze in place, but the hands twisted around
the swirling clock. Freddy pushed the button for the lobby. And
this time, Cecil noticed a keypad on the elevator controls.

"Fine. None of us are going to the basement," Freddy said.

Ava nudged him with her backpack. In the side pocket, he saw
zip ties and duct tape. Cecil grimaced, but Ava jabbed him with
her bony elbow. He stuck his hands into the bag and pulled out
the zip ties.

"Hold his wrists together," Ava said.

"Excuse me?" Freddy asked. "Whoa, whoa, whoa. I'm just
doing what Margaux told me."

"We could've done this the easy way," Cecil said.

Freddy flailed, but Cecil easily held his wrists together. He
kicked at Cecil's shins, squirming hopelessly like a newly won
carnival goldfish.

"Ow, asshole," Freddy said. "You guys won't guess the code
anyway."

Ava lunged to sit on Freddy's lap, helping to weigh him down.
She put Figaro on top of Freddy's head like a crown.

"Really?"

"Reveeennnge," Ava whispered.

Cecil tried Margaux's birth month and day, then the month and year. Both failed. Cecil typed his own birthdate to no avail—he didn't know Clara's. He tried Shirley Temple's birthday, which he knew because Margaux celebrated it every year with a fully catered tea party at the mansion.

When he tried Perdonna's birthday, the clock spun rapidly. Alarm bells flashed red, and blaring sounds filled the tiny space.

"The password is incorrect," a robotic voice shouted over the loudspeaker.

"Any ideas?" Cecil yelled over the noise.

"If you get it wrong one more time, the elevator will crash!" Freddy said, lower lip wriggling. His teeth chattered, and his face turned bright red.

"Are you serious?" Cecil asked.

Freddy nodded ferociously. Sweat flung from his curls.

"And you still won't tell us the code? You'd rather die in a crashing elevator than let me into the basement?" Cecil asked.

"We wouldn't die," Freddy said. "Maybe a broken fibula at worst. But, if I let you down, Margaux *will definitely* kill me."

Cecil's eyes traced the swirling lines of the clock. Everything was tangled into a circle, a vortex of decoration. Metal roman numerals rolled out from an inner spiral, intertwining with shattered shells. The rainbow pieces were frozen in a crystal Crevier wall.

None of Perdonna's designs had this *Alice in Wonderland* pattern. None of her clocks or Dials looked as zany as this.

"Maybe the clock is a code. Could the password be the golden spiral?" Cecil asked Ava. He watched Freddy's eyes to gauge whether he was correct, but Freddy seemed too panicked to even register the thought.

"What's that?" Ava asked.

The blaring seemed to grow louder. With the clock's constant spinning, it felt as if the whole elevator car were shaking.

"Margaux's favorite number 1.618, the divine proportion. It's math for being really pretty. Two quantities are in the divine proportion if their ratio is the same as the ratio of their sum to the larger of the two quantities. The golden spiral is in the veining of leaves, conch shells, beautiful faces... It was the number that our family doctor, Dr. Tibolt, used when charting Margaux's face for plastic surgery," Cecil yelled.

Ava began covering her ears with her fingers. "Try it."

"No! Please no. I don't wanna crash!" Freddy cowered into his hands.

Ava wrapped her arms around Figaro to shield him from any fall. "I doubt it actually crashes. Margaux probably says it to scare people."

Cecil took a deep breath and typed 1618. The elevator plummeted downward as Ava and Freddy shrieked.

Their stomachs tumbled up into their mouths.

But then the car stopped abruptly, and they were all jolted up into the air. Cecil hit his head on the ceiling and keeled over.

"It doesn't do that if you get the code right on the first try," Freddy said with a snarl.

A chilly wind struck their faces when the basement door opened.

The sound of the large ticking clock in the elevator mixing with the various heating units in the basement created a deep throbbing sound. Cement bricks and cobwebs surrounded them. But what they saw several yards ahead made them want to go back to the lobby.

16

As soon as Cecil and Ava stepped out of the elevator, Freddy rocketed back upstairs. They were left in the trenches, the foundation of LeClaire Model Management.

"Hey!" Cecil banged on the elevator doors. "Are we locked down here now?"

Figaro climbed down Ava's leg and scurried through the hall. "Probably," Ava said casually. She scanned the hallway.

A checkered black-and-white passage stretched the entire length of the mansion, a wormhole to Margaux LeClaire's dirty business. Orange spongey fabric dangled down from the ceiling. It was a perverse laboratory, the smell of burnt hair and body odor clinging to each antiseptic brick.

"Well, how do we get out?" Cecil asked in a panic. He started knocking on the white brick walls.

"We'll starve," Ava said. "Or we'll be set on fire by Freddy. We'll decay and our seeds will be planted beneath the cement and we'll come back as zombies to murder Margaux... Or you'll just call the police."

Cecil tapped his Dial and blushed. "Right."

Two dozen screens sat beneath a sign that read: Recruitment Center.

Instagram images of teenaged girls flitted across the screens each second. Girls made duck faces with pursed lips and wore fake flower crowns and puppy dog ears. They posed in bikinis with their asses to the screen. Cropped T-shirts and underwear were framed by pink bathroom mirrors.

The teenagers of Instagram were trying to attract praise; really, they were attracting masturbating househusbands and lonely perverts. Even the photos they shot with their friends at Disney World led to two hours of wasted time and irreparable damage to the self-esteem.

Followers posted encouraging comments. *"You're the most unbelievable person ever. You're firrreeee,"* *"OMG you're amazing I'm so proud to be your friend,"* *"You're going to do great things someday."* The comments were written beneath a girl who pulled her bikini bottoms over her butt cheeks to show off her ass.

"You'd think she won the Nobel Peace Prize or something," Cecil said to Ava.

"People comment the praise they want to receive themselves," Ava said. "Social media is a magical circle jerk. Be happy you missed most of that in the monastery."

#ModelMe #LeClaireRecruit

Suddenly, colors flashed on the photos. Computer scanners ran over the images. The system stripped away the filters and photo-modifying elements the girls' employed. The authentic, unedited photos developed. Acne reappeared on their faces. Waists grew back to size eight from size zero, heights fell to the average five-two and five-four. Eyes became smaller, hair thinned out. Even muscled bikini stomachs disappeared in the authentic images.

Numbers shot across the unedited photos. Lines covered the arms and legs, noses and eyes. 1.168, 1.194, 1.888.

"It's calculating for divine proportions," Cecil said.

If the computer deemed the girl mathematically promising, the computer automatically sent the girl a direct Instagram message:

YOU ARE STUNNING.
Have you ever considered becoming a model?
Join LeClaire Model Management
at a casting call in the Big Apple.
Use code "InstaScouted" at www.SIZEZERO.org
The world deserves to see you.

"It's hard for Margaux to find girls willing to take her abuse and miss out on college. She holds these fake, luxurious castings in the Hilton ballroom. Hundreds of girls show up, but none of them get picked. It's a fake casting to get girls excited about her brand. Imagine a Midwestern girl coming to the big city for the first time. They feel like a princess for a moment...the future America's Next Top Model," Ava said.

They heard two footsteps patter behind them and turned to find a girl standing with her hair wrapped in a towel. Her left eye was covered in bloody gauze.

"Are you okay?" Cecil asked.

"Freddy run by, take Gisele," the girl said in a huff. "Scared."

"What happened to *you*?"

"Light. Cooked me."

"Excuse me?"

"Burned," the girl said, remembering the word.

Ava walked away to pick up Figaro. The white rat wrapped himself around her neck.

"A set light burned her eyes," Ava said with a quick shrug. "Happens all the time."

Cecil gently touched the girl's hand, afraid to hurt her. "You're safe now. We're here to help you. Do you know where he took Gisele?"

The girl pointed eerily, mechanically down the hallway. "That way."

The sound of a door closing made Cecil swallow.

Windows peered into a gym, if one could call it that. Mirrors covered all four walls, and large openings lined the wall so the model agents could watch. Treadmills, bikes, and jump ropes filled the small room—no bulking equipment allowed.

The treadmills operated at a brisk walk, keeping the emaciated muscles thin and the fat low.

Sweat covered the ashen, dehydrated faces of the models. Wet hair clung to their foreheads, and their muscles shook like an abused racehorse's. They walked toward Cecil on the treadmills, staring with dead eyes, like zombies hoping to suck the life out of viewers.

Some walked in high heels, raw blisters oozing blood onto knock-off Louis Vuittons.

Models were rats on wheels in the laboratory. Their bodies were a high-priced commodity. And as they marched in black booty shorts and green tank tops, they looked eerily the same. They were faces to be traded and showed.

"How does Margaux get away with this?" Cecil asked.

"It's not just Margaux. It's all high fashion agencies."

"Excuse me?" Cecil asked. "What about Tyra Banks? Naomi Campbell? Kendall Jenner?"

"Commercial models," Ava said. "High fashion modeling has a specific aesthetic. As tall as possible, as thin as possible, as young as possible. They model for brands like Visage, Ami, and Tom Gray. If high fashion is Kim Kardashian, commercial fashion is their overweight, diabetic brother, Rob. The Gap and Old Navy. No girl can brag about a mattress advertisement.

"Supermodels are the ones who make it, or the ones whose parents were rich enough to bypass all this. Think about it—Gigi Hadid, Kendall Jenner, Cara Delevingne...rich parents. The one percent. The other ninety-nine percent of models come from the opposite background, and they do this for survival, not Chatter and Instagram followers."

These high fashion girls were designed by Margaux—perfect humans with the animal removed.

A girl seized and fell off the treadmill. Her eyes rolled back in her head, and she buckled onto the floor, body shaking as though a vibrating motor sat somewhere in her stomach, controlling her.

The treadmill beeped a red alarm, and an automated voice beckoned from the machine, "Please get back on the treadmill. Work will set you free. Please walk a little longer, walk toward beauty. Work will set you free."

It repeated itself like a song as the beautiful blonde girl's lips turned a naked beige.

The other girls stepped off their treadmills to help her. They set off a series of red lights, flashing in a chorus. Cecil threw open the door and helped the girl up. He found a minifridge full of water bottles and put one on the girl's neck. Her eyes slowly opened.

"Everyone off," Cecil said, waving the other models off the treadmills.

"Beep," one girl said with an accent, heaving profusely. "Alarms. We get yelled at."

"It's fine. Freddy's gone," Cecil said.

The girls got off the treadmills and immediately collapsed onto the ground. The alarms blared a vicious sound. The blonde girl across his lap was finally able to sit up. She took a few sips of water.

"Ava, can you get the other girls water, please?" he asked.

Ava looked to the small refrigerator. "What do I get for it?"

"Gratification."

"I don't know what that is," Ava said. "Sounds like a lousy chocolate bar."

Cecil rolled his eyes as he handed out the other waters.

"Freddy took Gisele through a door. He left her in there and went back upstairs," one girl said. Cecil looked up and realized it was Margaux's albino hippopotamus with fangs. Her pudgy face had turned a bright red, and her tiny ears were tinged with sweat.

"What door?" Cecil asked. "I don't see any other doors in the hallway?"

"Don't know," she said. "But I heard a door open and close. Then Freddy went into the elevator without her. She was yelling and crying when he took her."

"We have to move forward," Ava said.

"Wait here," Cecil said to the models. "We'll find a way out."

Cecil was unable to remove his stare from the sweatshop in his childhood basement. His footsteps echoed through the basement hallway accompanied by the voice, "Jogging will set you free."

"Do the designers know?" Cecil asked. "I mean, how can they charge twenty thousand dollars for a coat and not pay a little extra to feed and house these young women? Or at least respect basic human rights?"

"They turn a blind eye. As long as the models are size zero and six feet tall with a one in a million body. Tom Gray said in a *New York Times* interview that 'if a girl is old enough to do the dishes, she's old enough to walk a runway.'"

Cecil deflated. Tom had always seemed so genuine. He had even given Cecil a leather-bound journal for his seventeenth birthday.

Along the right side of the wall, they came upon large wire cages that locked away plastic shopping bags and tattered luggage. A pink stuffed rabbit with one eye dangling held his paw out through the wire openings. Brand-new shoes, cell phones, laundry detergent, and tagged socks—the gifts the models' parents gave them to travel to a new country alone. It was the place where Margaux stored the young girls' hearts, the place where she stole their youth.

A carved-out cubby held the laundry machines, where models not only scrubbed their own clothing but also Margaux's underwear, Freddy's boxers, and the agent uniforms. Ironed shirts by Ami sat folded without a crease. The models wore beige plastic gloves so detergent could not mar their valuable hands. When Cecil saw a girl scrubbing stains from his own jeans, he grabbed them from her hands and threw them in the trash can.

"No doors," Ava said.

Then Cecil noticed a mirror similar to the ones outside the dining room. "Stand in front of the mirror," he said.

Ava looked into the glass, and the scrolling menu of artists appeared. "Yeah? It's one of the Visage mirrors Perdonna makes."

Cecil walked up to it. He tried to take it off the wall to see the back, but it was bolted. When he tapped the frame, nothing happened. In anger, he whacked his hands onto the corner. The mirror shifted to the right, and a golden light shimmered around it.

He twisted the frame more. And the white bricks along the wall sprung forward in the shape of a door.

"Whoa," Ava said. "Are all the Visage mirrors locks?"

"Probably," Cecil said. "Margaux loves Clue, the board game. So I'm sure there are secret passageways everywhere."

But when he tried the handle, the door didn't budge. Ava stood in front of the mirror and pressed her nose almost to the glass. It painted her face like Rembrandt. Deep golds spread across the screen and every natural hollow in her face was shadowed. The puffs under her eyes. The button on her nose. The creases in her forehead.

But the door was resolute.

"So now what?" she asked.

"We call the police?"

"The police are stupid."

"Perdonna told you that."

"I know the police are evil myself. I dealt with them in jail. They're monsters. They put me in solitary confinement almost the entire time I was there just because I didn't have parents to complain for me."

Cecil shook his head, but then he noticed the mirror sketching his face. He had accidentally moved in front of it. And suddenly the Rembrandt of himself had a somber expression. The chipper dimples disappeared into his cheeks. Was that the *natural* version of himself? When the final eyebrow hair was sketched, the door unlocked and swung open.

"Why did it work for you?" Ava asked.

"That's strange."

"You're not an inside agent, are you?"

"Perdonna probably programmed me in."

They stepped inside cautiously and saw a painted world map, drawn in gold and black, covering the walls. Polaroid photos of adolescent girls were pinned to the countries from which they originated.

Ratty hair, sweaty faces, and imperfect yellow teeth sat above bikini-clad bones. None were older than eighteen, and all wore terrified doe eyes. The wall looked like a collage of mugshots or a collection of photos a serial killer would take as trophies before slashing the girls' necks.

A large black metal cabinet sat at the far wall. Ava opened it. Inside were stacks of passports, modeling contracts, and birth certificates.

"Were these taken from the girls?" Cecil asked.

A Dial sat between stacks of passports. Cecil flipped it open. The messaging system only worked within the mansion. The models had no way to call for help.

"So these are minors with no way to contact their mothers. No passports. No birth certificates. What if they want to quit modeling? What if they want to go home?" Cecil asked.

"They can't," Ava said. "Model agents effectively own the models. The parents and child sign the contract. Then the child comes to New York City, and Margaux controls everything they do."

She held up a LeClaire Model Management contract. The name read: Karolina Krün. But on the signature lines, each was signed with an X. Her mother, her father, and herself.

"And most of the families that the model agents target are poor and illiterate. They can't even read the contract they're signing. The parents believe they're doing the best thing for their child. Giving her up so she can go to America for a better life."

Cecil read Karolina's contract carefully. Attached to it was a printout of a run-down farm. *CORN* ⊠ was scribbled across it in Margaux's handwriting. Margaux bought Karolina Krün in exchange for funding the family's cornfield and farm. The Krün family was going bankrupt, so sending Karolina to America to model was their last hope.

But once Margaux seized the passport, the girl could never go home again.

"It's worse," Ava said.

"*Worse?*"

"Margaux always says, 'Well, I'm housing you. I'm feeding you. So that money *Glamorama* paid you for being on their cover, I'm taking that. Oh, that check you earned from modeling in Fashion Week, you don't get that money. That money only covers the cost of your test photos the agency paid for.' The models almost never see their paychecks."

"So, most of the models are actually child slaves?" Cecil

asked. "They don't make money, and they can't go home."

According to the Bureau of Labor Statistics, the average annual wage of a model was $26,000, which was only $13,000 above the poverty line. Poverty didn't convey a picture of lavish lifestyles and yacht sailing. It didn't mean parties in St. Tropez and Milan. Instead, the purpose of modeling was to achieve cheap labor from desperate children.

"We live in beautiful mansions, lay in the sand in dresses that cost more than our parents' houses," Ava said. "But none of it is real."

Cecil found a binder labeled "VD." Inside were empty folders. "Do you think Freddy stole these? It's the only empty folder."

Ava took the VD binder and put it in her backpack. "Probably."

He opened the second set of cabinets to find drawers and hangers full of designer outfits—Buratti, Pierre Lazard, Visage. That was how she dressed them to go out, a dress-up chest for the dolls.

Ava handed Cecil what looked like a photocopy of the LeClaire Model Management, LLC Corporate Bylaws. Under Article 5, entitled Officers, it read:

> 5.1 <u>Designations:</u> The officers of LeClaire Model Management shall be a president and one vice-president. They shall hold office until their successors are elected and qualified.

> 5.2 <u>The President, Margaux Cerise LeClaire:</u> The president may preside at all meetings of directors, shall have total supervision of the affairs of the corporation, and shall perform all other duties as are incident to her office or are properly required of her.

> 5.3 <u>Vice President, Cecil Louis LeClaire:</u> During absence or disability of the president, the vice president shall exercise all functions of the president. He shall discharge such duties that may be assigned to him from time to time.

The LeClaire Model Management corporate bylaws were signed twenty years ago upon the establishment of the model agency, meaning Margaux deemed Cecil heir and vice president to the company when he was only four.

"Hello, Mr. President," Ava said.

"I didn't ask for this. I don't want these girls to suffer." Cecil tore the paper in half. "My mother can't put my name on paper and make me liable for her crimes."

"But she did. If we don't save these girls and figure out where Margaux sent Annabelle Leigh, you could go to prison with her."

And then they heard it. Muffled cries, like a dog's whimper, coming from the closet.

17

"What do you think we're going to find in there?" Ava asked.

The whimpering rang through the closet door. Cecil pushed it open to a shimmery dark space. A plastic factory smell oozed out.

He cautiously stepped inside and glossy latex rubbed against his skin. Dress bags were hanging from the ceiling rack like body bags in a haunted house.

The whimpering crescendoed as he stepped farther into the slippery den.

He stopped at the spot where the groaning was the loudest. One of the dress bags had a bulge. When he poked the lump, it kicked back.

Ava jumped in front of him and unzipped the bag.

Gisele rolled out in her uniform of black underwear, eyes blinking rapidly to adjust to the light. She was curled up in the fetal position, hands and ankles tied together.

"What happened?" Cecil asked as he carried her out of the closet. "Are you okay?"

"Freddy locked me here to steal passports from chest," said Gisele.

"Passports? Why would he want those?"

"I do not know," Gisele said, stretching out her legs. "Took Jordan's file. Not supposed to take."

"Have any girls gone missing recently?" Cecil asked. "Other than Jordan?"

"They go missing all the time." Ava shrugged as Figaro climbed beneath her dress.

"And where is Freddy now?" Cecil asked.

"At his party. At his house. There is a party at his house."

A swirling metal staircase in the back of the closet led to the lobby.

Cecil and Ava freed the girls from the basement and ushered them all upstairs.

"You're Ava Germaine," Gisele whispered before going up the stairs. "My friend worked for Mr. Blancas. Your story... She thinks you're a god. Like Princess Jasmine."

Ava tensed and slid her tongue over her two front teeth. "I don't know any Blancas."

"Every girl wished they had guts to do what you did."

Ava's large eyes danced toward Cecil to see his reaction. She twirled her hair to her lips and began biting the tips between her teeth. Little bits of the dead hair crunched off between her incisors. "It wasn't brave. Jail is better than modeling."

As Gisele padded up the staircase, a deep cuckoo clock sound bellowed from the lobby.

"What is that?" Cecil asked.

He climbed the staircase as the sound grew louder.

A shrill bell, like a fire alarm, blared throughout the house. White lights blinked around the towering water fountain and on the front door.

"The doorbell," Ava said.

"NYPD," said a voice from outside.

Cecil opened the door to find a set of six police officers. Margaux had installed an obnoxious alarm to warn her when the police were coming.

"We have a search warrant for Margaux LeClaire's home," an officer said.

A sergeant patted Cecil on the shoulder. "There's a good chance Margaux LeClaire will be moved from the Nineteenth Precinct soon. She wanted us to give you the message that you should visit."

"Are you allowed to tell me that?"

"She *is* Margaux LeClaire. Special privileges."

Cecil pointed to the lifted tile and down the swirling black staircase by the fountain. "You should really check out the basement."

"The warrant is only for Margaux's home, not the business. The basement is part of the agency, correct?"

"Well, yes but—"

"Is anyone in immediate danger?" the officer asked.

"Depends how you classify *immediate*."

The officer chuckled. "FBI has been trying to take on the LeClaire agency for years, kid. Most of Margaux's crimes are committed on foreign soil. It's harder than it looks."

The men walked up the swirling red staircase, laughing among themselves. Cecil glared at Ava.

"That's why I hate the police," Ava said. She grabbed Cecil's blue NYPD sweatshirt and pulled his ear to her mouth. "Perdonna doesn't want the NYPD digging through anything."

"Does Perdonna know what Margaux's doing?" Cecil asked.

"She's trying to rein Margaux in. But that takes time. She calls it the taming of the shrew."

The officers started in Margaux's office. They bagged each ivory erotic cane in its own plastic evidence casing.

Ava knew Margaux well. She had handwritten notes, camera codes, even the sapphire necklace Margaux stole from Perdonna in 1998. But she chose to keep it all to herself.

To Ava, Margaux was a bit like a pet she found at a freak show, the most awkward criminal she'd ever encountered. Her only list of likes included erotic canes, music boxes, cunnilingus, Shirley Temple, antique revolvers, porcelain dolls, anal sex, and beignets from Café du Monde. She hated everything else. *Everything* else.

The beignets, little delightful donut balls of sugar and fat, were shipped from New Orleans's Café du Monde to the LeClaire Mansion every morning at 9:00 a.m. They even sent her their special frying oil so the donuts could be refried in the authentically fatty, gritty oil.

Ava always arrived at exactly 9:20 a.m. so she could steal one from the kitchen.

Margaux's corruption began forty years ago when she researched French *mannequins* from the 1920s. With names like *Passion* and *Miss Sweet*, mannequins became wax figures with human heads and realistic eyes. The clothing sold well. Margaux realized that human girls would appeal to the financiers navigating the high fashion buying market more than plastic mannequins. She brought a revived modeling industry to America.

She became the first agent to recruit models from the Eastern Bloc when she rushed into Germany and climbed over the Berlin Wall. While most businessmen went to Southeast Asia for textile manufacturing, she went for the heroin, pioneering "Heroin Chic." When the exercise fad of the nineties boomed, Margaux forced models to train like Olympic gymnasts and eat like starving mice on LSD.

Margaux LeClaire felt she had a gilded fate, a manifest destiny in the fashion world. She would never be a housewife.

When the police moved on to Cecil's guest bedroom, Ava lifted the lid from one of the ottomans, revealing several hundred yellow pill bottles stacked like Legos.

Cecil coughed. "Are those for drugging the models?"

Ava showed him the label on one of the bottles. Prescribed by Dr. Tibolt. Adderall and methylphenidate.

"They're to keep the models sedated during gala parties and stuff," she said, stuffing some of the drugs into her bag.

He opened one of the bottles and crushed a pill between his fingers, recognizing the scent of the medication immediately.

Dr. Tibolt was giving the models ADHD meds in high doses.

Cecil wrapped his hands around the shaft of a wooden cane the police had left in the office. Heat rushed to his head. Knuckles turned white. *Snap.* He split the cane into two pieces and threw it at the antique revolver case. "I can't believe this," he said with a sigh.

The officers knocked on the door, hearing the shattering glass. They carried at least twenty evidence bags. "We got everything we need for now, son."

They only searched the top four floors, not venturing into the basement. The cops simply glossed over the many young women in Margaux's collection.

Taking a deep breath, Cecil checked the time on his Dial. He couldn't waste time thinking about his mother. "We have to find Freddy. Do you have his address?"

Ava twisted her Dial. "There's this newfangled tool called the Internet, grandpa. We simply Google."

The models began to wobble out of their rooms. Whispers trickled down the hallways like the sounds of a haunting drum. They crouched in the corners when the NYPD walked by, afraid they would be jailed or deported. The models didn't trust the police, either.

"What about the girls? I don't want them to stay here. It's not safe," Cecil said.

"Margaux has a crew of drivers she uses to send the models to Whole Foods pilgrimages and photoshoots." She searched Margaux's planner for the phone number to call the Range Rovers for pickup.

"I can send them to St. Joseph's?" Cecil asked. "The monks will help them. They need somewhere to live for now. That's a good place."

Ava shrugged. "As long as there aren't any priests."

♎

The models piled into snow-white Range Rovers with their belongings—high heels, hair ties, and a few pizzas Cecil ordered to tide them over. Thirty-two girls. No suitcases, no bags. Only an occasional ragged stuffed animal from home or a family photograph.

Four of the top models who could afford an apartment chose to rent a room together in the city. The rest of the models agreed to go to St. Joseph's Abbey.

"It looks a bit like a train station at Auschwitz, doesn't it?" Cecil asked as the girls loaded into the Range Rovers.

Ava scowled. "What's Auschwitz?"

"The Holocaust."

Ava's eyebrows sprung up. The dead glossy look entered her eyes, and she stared forward. "Oh, yeah. That." It was clear she hadn't a clue what the Holocaust was.

"What year did you leave school?" Cecil asked.

"I never went. I taught myself to read, though."

A light blush fell to her cheeks as her gaze darted away from his. She rubbed her cheek against Figaro to comfort herself.

Cecil opened the passenger door to the Rambo Lambo. "Let's go. GPS says we can get to Freddy's party in twenty minutes."

The Rambo Lambo bucked to life, rearing like a bull at a monster truck rally in Kansas. The gold shimmered like a rapper's grill, gaudy yet expensive. It roared, but inside the pristine leather and gold detailing were the seats of a limousine.

Figaro leaped on top of the gilded gearshift shaped like a racehorse. He was a fancy jockey riding with pride.

"I only ever had a goldfish," Cecil said. "She was a present for the expiration of my kidnapping insurance," he joked.

"Kidnapping insurance?"

"My dad was afraid I'd be abducted in exchange for ransom.

It isn't that crazy. Remember what happened to Frank Sinatra Jr., to J. Paul Getty III, to Patty Hearst…"

"Did you ever use it?"

"We got a few threats from Hezbollah," Cecil said, "but Margaux only reported a kidnapping once when Perdonna took me on vacation to Tahiti without her."

"Unbelievable." Ava rested her head on the backrest. "Your life is like a twisted James Bond movie."

"What was your childhood like?" Cecil asked as he stopped at a red light.

"A good day for me was digging through the McDonald's trash can and finding a half-eaten cheeseburger not within close proximity to a bloody tampon."

The prideful smile fell from his face. Car horns blasted at him for not moving on green. "I see." Cecil paused, turning on the air conditioner to cool his red face. "How did you end up modeling?"

Ava rolled her neck. She was tapping her feet up on the dashboard like a bored, antsy child. She smacked her lips together, thinking. "I was in this poor, provincial town. My dad was an inventor. But my mom died when I was six."

"I'm sorry."

"Yeah, whatever. Please don't pray for her," Ava said. "And then… My eventual model agent abducted my father and put him in a cage. I sacrificed myself in his place. The agent set my dad free and caged me up when I was thirteen. Eventually, I fell in love with the agent, though."

"That's *Beauty and the Beast*."

"Yep. It's based on me."

Cecil sighed and rested his head back against the headrest. "Hollywood must love your life."

Ava nodded. "*Ratatouille* is about Figaro."

"Oh, stop," Cecil said. "Stop lying. If you don't want to talk about your life, that's fine. But stop giving me movie plots."

Ava shrugged. "You're a monk. You believe Bible stories are real, so I thought you'd believe Hollywood ones too."

Cecil patted his fingers against the steering wheel angrily.

"Have you Googled me?" she asked.

"Why would I do that?"

"To find out why I went to prison."

"You are who you are now, regardless of what you did."

She bit her lip and gazed out the window. Jackhammers and cranes constructed the latest towers surrounding Central Park. But Ava only looked at the sky.

♎

Art galleries and brownstone mansions lined the side streets of Chelsea. The moon rose, reflecting white light off the autumn leaves. Chelsea Market, a large warehouse full of food and luxury clothing stores, lit up several blocks in a yellow hue.

Google Maps put them in front of a six-story mansion.

"Are you sure it's this block? Freddy can't afford a townhouse in Chelsea on a model agent's salary," Cecil said as a doorman swung open Ava's passenger door.

Cecil expected to see a party of drunken thirty-somethings. Or a lost generation of depressed millennials who vied to be an extra on a reality television show.

Instead, silence greeted them. Complete darkness. No chatter.

"Maybe we should rethink this," Ava said.

With the first step inside, they smelled a disgusting perfume. "Why does it smell like a dead animal? Is it a cult?" Cecil asked.

"The only cult Freddy belongs to is the 'Fans of Hello Kitty and My Little Pony.'" Ava let out a loud sniff. "I think it's cow manure."

"We're a few days before Halloween. Could it be a haunted house?"

Suddenly a series of spotlights shot down into the hallway one by one. On the floor, a brown substance coated car tires, mirrors, and BMW license plate frames. Trash was mounted on the walls. Gold-and-silver Crevier wrapping paper. Starbucks Pumpkin Spice Latte cups. And crushed Coca-Cola cans.

Photos of men dressed in Ku Klux Klan uniforms were crumpled, burnt, and covered in slop. Skeletons and zombies with barcodes on their heads sat in front of a television, dressed in Fifties-style fashion with TV dinners in their laps. Mannequins lined the walkway with bloody knives and cotton balls sticking out of them.

Neon condoms were stretched over lightbulbs in rainbow colors. And written large on the walls in a neon pen: SAY NO TO SIZE ZERO.

"I think it's modern art," Cecil said with a grimace.

A doorman called to them from the end of the hallway. "Hello. Please enter by walking on the runway through the installation. Please keep all arms, legs, and creatures on the runway at all times."

18

Cecil stared at a full-sized cardboard cutout of Kim Kardashian. A Dial was hanged by a noose beside an Osama bin Laden action figure, and a fanny pack sat in a locked display glass case with a spotlight on it.

"So Freddy is against commercial America?" Ava asked.

"Is that what this 'art' is supposed to be telling me?"

The hallway opened to a grand foyer. A rose-gold chandelier rained down into spokes of Crevier crystals. Palm trees and vertical kale gardens encircled the fountain, towering to the top of the two-story entrance. It was a high-fashion greenhouse, meant for decoration instead of growing food.

A doorman dressed in a suit and tie dragged them to the corner. "Hello. Good evening, lovely guests," said the greeter. "Would you like to draw a square for our square wall?"

He handed them two sheets of paper.

On the wall, black squares covered white papers to form a group-made art piece. Fifty drawings looked down on the guests like square googly eyes. All squares somehow ended up being the same size, orientation, and color, as if every guest thought alike.

Cecil drew quickly on his paper and handed it to the doorman. He squinted at it and then sniffed it like it was an acrid dish made by a top chef.

"This is a diamond," he said with disdain.

"Diamonds and squares are geometrically identical," Cecil said, turning the paper so the image looked like a square.

"But you drew it like a diamond."

"I decided to be different. I thought that was the point of the test. I thought maybe it was a passcode to get into the party?"

"No, dear," the doorman scoffed. "The point is to look the same as everyone else." The greeter handed him a new piece of paper. "If it's different, it ruins the piece. Try again."

Cecil gave a startled grimace, feeling like he was being fingerprinted at a police station. He half expected forensics to pop out and use his square drawing as a writing sample.

"I think I'll pass, thank you."

The man folded his arms. He lifted up the guest list. "I don't see Cecil LeClaire on my list."

"We're not invited to the party," Cecil said. "I need to talk to Freddy, please. Is he here? It's an emergency."

The man cocked his head. "One moment, please. I need to ask the hostess. Wait in the gallery. Do not move from the sofa."

They were sat in a white marble art gallery with a gold-leaf ceiling. Louis XIV furniture sat among blue Chinese vases and ornate rugs that were almost certainly made by a child labor force in Mongolia.

There were dozens of artworks by Rothko, Picasso, Baranga, and Broz. The frames were haphazardly tossed around the room. Some were propped up against walls, others hung from the ceiling by rope.

The doorman walked through a closed door at the end of the art gallery. Cecil could hear the heels clacking on the marble. The clanking glasses. The fake laughter from the guests.

"I should've combed my hair for this," Ava whispered.

"Tell them you're a piece of art. Mauve Mona, like the *Mona Lisa* but with more secrets and worse hair."

Ava's eyes turned to crescents, and her mouth curved up into a fake smile. She was a walking, breathing emoji.

Cecil turned his nose up at ceramic pigs with peacock feathers shooting out of their backs. Gnarly yellow fingers made up the handles of floral teapots and cups, like the ones from a grandmother's cabin. And Cecil's least favorite was a piece of toilet paper stuck to the wall with a pin entitled *Charmin on White*.

But he was focused on the largest painting in the room—a canvas with two dark orange squares, and two light yellow ones, purposefully painted with a sloppy stroke.

"This looks like a child's finger-painting exercise," he said to Ava.

"Excuse me," a man said as he burst into the art gallery. He wore teal-blue sunglass shades and had a white beard that looked like snow on his dark skin. "It is my painting."

"Congratulations. How long did it take you to paint it?" Cecil asked.

"*I* didn't paint it. It's a Romdinger."

"I'm sorry, I didn't know." Cecil clenched his teeth together, afraid they would be thrown out right then.

"Ethero Romdinger is one of the greatest artists of his time, young man. Which member of the club invited *you*?"

"No one," Cecil said. "I'm looking for Freddy."

The man clicked his tongue against his teeth. "Frederick can't see anyone right now. He's grounded."

"He's thirty-two..." Cecil said. "How can he be grounded?"

"It's my house, my rules," he said. "Until he moves out."

Cecil's eyebrows rose. "Oh. You're Freddy's dad? This is *your* party."

"Jim Condon," he said, shaking Cecil's hand. "I can't believe he's my son, either."

Cecil stared at the blurry lines, the three blocky colors like stripes on a canvas. To him, there was no difference between a Romdinger and a painting from Ikea.

Jim flared his nostrils. "So you like the pompousness of Renoir and Manet and Goya, I suppose?"

"I like the classics. Art that requires talent and technique," Cecil said.

"Romdinger is about intellect, theme, something deeper, which you might not respect because you are a murderer!"

Cecil sighed. He struggled to keep calm. When he looked to Ava for support, she gave him an unblinking stare. Figaro was safely hidden somewhere underneath her dress.

"Some murderers have great taste. Look at Hannibal Lecter," Cecil said.

Jim did not appreciate the joke. He lowered his blue shades and placed them inside his checkered jacket. "You don't see *any* beauty in the mood-setting colors?"

Cecil glanced at the white title placard. *UNNAMED (Dark YELLOW, ORANGE, Crayola YELLOW, Light ORANGE).*

"It's just not my taste," Cecil said.

Ava jabbed him in the side as Jim looked at his own painting. "Please lie," she whispered into Cecil's ear. "Lie, lie, lie. Now is the time for white lies."

"I've invested thirty-eight million dollars into this artist. I've paid for his schooling. His apartment and studio. His food. A billboard in Times Square. I'm sponsoring him to be a star. Was I wrong to do so? What does the painting look like to you? The sunrise over the Sahara? The inner workings of happiness?"

"An orange juice stain?" Cecil asked. "Maybe a Kanye West album cover?"

"You're a monk. No one would invest ten dollars into you."

"Well, actually... People do give the abbey donations so technically—"

Cecil felt Figaro's rat feet climbing up the leg of his NYPD sweatpants. His tiny little nails dug across Cecil's leg.

"Hello, Cecil," came a lilting voice. The door swung open, revealing a petite woman with an ebullient smile. "I'm Frederick's mom, Addy."

Addy wrapped her arm around his waist, leaning in uncomfortably close to his face. He could feel her makeup powder rubbing off onto his cheek. It felt like the powdered sugar off of a donut. "Oh my God." Her hands ran up Cecil's chunky blue NYPD sweatshirt. "Is this from the new Visage line?"

"No. It's just an NYPD sweatshirt," Cecil said.

"So cute," Addy said. "Do you think they'd give me one if I got arrested?" Her over-exaggerated laughter echoed around the room. "Sorry you can't see Freddy. We promised we would leave him alone. He says he's about to have his big break. We're not supposed to let anyone up to see him."

Figaro scurried out of Cecil's sweatpants and back up Ava's leg. Cecil's eyes trailed Figaro as he made the quick switch. Thankfully neither Jim nor Addy noticed the fluffy white rat scurrying across their home gallery.

"Freddy wants to take over for his father someday as the Director of Painting and Sculpture at the Museum of Modern Art."

"That man-child will never," Jim said.

Addy put her hand on Cecil's shoulder. "Curating models and curating art are sister businesses. Even though he's just Margaux's personal assistant, we hope he becomes an agent someday."

"Right." Cecil nodded. He picked up a piece of parmesan and a napkin to munch away his stress. "And Margaux would *really* want Freddy to speak to me now," Cecil said.

But when he crumpled the napkin in his hand, Addy shrieked.

"What do you think you're doing! Put down that napkin," Jim said.

The bearded man's neck shook, and his cheeks puffed out. He spat in his hand and tried to clean off the parmesan from the napkin.

"How dare you! That is a piece by Gregor Hunter Klingerbass!"

"The napkin?" Cecil asked.

"The artwork is called *Millennials Killed the Napkin Industry.* You are unfortunately proving his point."

"I'm very sorry," Cecil said.

Jim crumpled up the ruined napkin and slammed it onto the ground. He tapped his fingers on his bearded chin and scrunched up his nose like a pit bull ready to fight. "Okay. You think you're better than Romdinger? He's here tonight. Beat him."

"Oh. I don't think I'm better. I—"

"Paint. If you paint better than he does, I'll let you talk to Freddy."

Cecil folded his arms. "I don't understand."

"The purpose of the club is to select the next great artist," Jim said. "We invite painters to compete, and whomever wins on the night gets their debut in the Museum of Modern Art."

"I don't think I'm talented enough," Cecil said.

"Then no Freddy."

Ava plopped onto a couch. She tossed her head back against a pillow. It was as if she had used all her possible energy reserves just to stand for the conversation. "It's just a painting. Didn't you do art at the monastery?"

"I copied other peoples' art into Bible manuscripts." Cecil shrugged. "Doesn't make me an artist."

"How hard can it be?" Ava asked. "Paint an orange juice stain."

"Great," Jim said, clapping his hands together. "Addy, can you ask the board for another volunteer?"

"Another *volunteer*?" Cecil asked.

"You'll see," Jim said with a churlish grin.

Jim opened the door beyond the gallery. Club members gathered on a ruby-red spiral staircase swirled to the upstairs. They were adorned in pearls and cuff links. And most of them wore tweed Ami jackets that must've debuted before the Great Depression. The few attendees under the age of sixty wore skinny jeans and T-shirts paired with $200,000 special edition Dials.

When the door opened, Jim clapped his hands together. "We have a late entrant—Cecil LeClaire."

Three people dropped their wineglasses, and bits of glass shattered onto the floor. Some flipped open their Dials and shot a picture of Cecil wearing his NYPD sweat suit. The room fell into a fit of laughter. It felt vicious, like a pack of hyenas attacking from above.

But they weren't nearly as disturbing as the showpiece. A long table stood in the room's center, like the dining table at the Last Supper. Red thrones sat behind with a creepy royal vibe.

But it was the three women sitting on those domineering red chairs that really worried Cecil. They ominously cocked their heads, faces covered in white Venetian masks. Their hair was hidden underneath white silk shrouds, and their bodies were wrapped in white tunics. Only the shadows of their curves showed through the fabric.

They looked like ghouls presiding over a ballroom. "If this *is* a cult," Ava whispered into Cecil's ear, "Figaro is my priority. I will let them murder you in a heartbeat."

"Comforting," Cecil said.

On the table before the masked women, jars of paint were organized into rows. There were two paintbrushes, a ball of yarn, and a roll of silver masking tape.

"What do we paint?" Cecil asked Jim. "Canvas?"

Jim clicked his tongue against his cheek. A deep chuckle shook his entire belly. "One of the women. You paint her body."

19

Jim Condon gathered the artists and guests around the masked women.

Cecil's competitors looked to be his opposites in every way. They wore black army boots for the war on microaggressions. Their hair looked "undone," but they spent two hours a day gelling it to a spiky point. And they smoked cigarettes while wearing plastic "Stop Climate Change" pins.

And then there was Cecil—with his white-male-of-privilege haircut and NYPD sweatshirt. He was the enemy.

"To my right, we have George Cassimatis the Fifth. He's the son of George and Hilda Cassimatis. And he is the ArtBlock Prize winner, the Berlin Review Art of the Year winner, and his art is featured in the Chelsea Gallery."

The guests quietly applauded, fingertips tapping their wineglasses. Cecil's heartrate ratcheted up to meet the energy. He could already tell this was going to be an embarrassment beyond his wildest imagination.

He gave a quick look to Ava, hoping to find support. But she was tap dancing, counting the number of stripes in the marble beneath her feet.

"This is Eliza Ellish. She studied classics at Harvard University. Her father is the CFO of Buratti. Her art has been featured at Art Basel and—"

Before he could finish, a door slammed shut. Another masked woman entered the room. Her hair scarf shimmered with subtle gold glitter, and nude suede heels poked out from beneath her white tunic. Her mask had an enigmatic pout, a coquettish pucker. It was more friendly than the dead faces on the others.

Freddy's mom held her hand and led her to the last red throne. She took her seat beside the other three women.

Cecil trembled at the sight of them. There was something intimidating about the women. They were domineering, white statues that shouldn't be touched. Completely covered from head to toe with a shield of fabric, they *allowed* painters to touch them. They were anonymous. They knew Cecil, but he would never know them. These were not Margaux's girl models. These women had the power.

"Welcome," Jim said to the woman.

She nodded her head down in a regal dip.

"Next," Jim said, "we have Ethero Romdinger."

The crowd gave an extra loud applause, which made Ethero wink. He had a signature cocky shuffle. Every time a spectator glanced at him, he sort of wriggled at the hips like an overexcited elf. It was extremely disturbing—a puppet that only comes alive in the spotlight.

"He's the Turner Prize winner with us from London. He's also the Pierre Lazard Prize winner, the Art Grazia winner, and *the New York Times* artist of the year. His works have been featured in the Frieze Art Fair and the Whitney Museum. And last year, he was honored by Queen Elizabeth."

Cecil slowly closed his eyes until a burst of shrill laughter broke through.

It was Ava, pointing at Cecil, giggling, almost like she was drunk. She had wrapped herself in someone's Ami scarf, and she sipped at a glass of champagne.

Everyone stared at her. Mystified. She must've been thinking the same thing—Cecil didn't stand a chance.

It seemed that whenever Ava found herself in an uncomfortable position, she left her body and found a character to take over. She was a chameleon, changing color to keep herself safe.

"And finally," Jim said with a smile, "Cecil LeClaire."

"Ow, ow, ow," a younger member of the audience jeered. The whole room erupted in laughter, mocking him.

"Cecil LeClaire. *The monk*," Jim said.

People keeled over. Cecil was once again the public's punching bag. It was a familiar scene. Even though he stood in one room, he felt like he was surrounded by the entire world, cackling at him.

He thought about what Perdonna would do. How she redirected jeers before they even touched her skin.

"Well," Cecil said, silencing the crowd, "if you believe the papers, three days ago *Cecil LeClaire* debuted the skin coat. And this morning was the world premiere of *Dead Body in Oil*... I'm on a roll."

The club members gave a light chuckle, eyes softening. The evil glares turned to thoughtful glances. And the smile fell off of Jim's face.

"The rules," Jim said with a cough. "You'll be given paints and one of the four tools—yarn, masking tape, the sponge, or the paintbrush. This year, we've decided the added challenge is that you will paint in the dark. You'll each have forty-five minutes. Any questions?"

Cecil had many questions. None of which he'd dare ask out loud.

♎

The butler led him down a purple hallway filled with blank white canvases. Those unfinished papers were probably worth more than the entirety of St. Joseph's Abbey. Cecil clutched his golden cross in his hand, murmuring prayers under his breath.

"There is a time for everything, and a season for everything under the heavens: a time to weep, and a time to laugh; a time to tear down and a time to build, a time to mourn and a time to dance; a time—"

The butler tapped Cecil's shoulder. "That's a nice song you're singing," he said. "Did you write it?"

"It's a Bible verse," Cecil said.

"Cool of you to put religion into a song," the butler said. "Very retro."

Cecil raised his eyebrows as the butler left him in front of a room.

"Remember. Forty-five minutes. Good luck."

Cecil held his hand on the doorknob for several seconds. "God, help me," he whispered before walking into the room.

A small fire crackled raindrops of gold. The room was small and dark, cast only in fiery shadows. It felt like a cinnamon grotto with rocks of cedar-brown book bindings. And the woman's silhouette looked like a glowing angel's, white cloak sweeping around her. Golden light bounced off his canvas. He could only see the shape of her, the statuesque silhouette of an angel.

"Hello," he said in a nervous whisper.

She was silent. But her white mask cocked slightly at his voice.

"Do I take off your cloak or—"

The woman tapped her fingers together. After a hesitation, her arms gracefully rose from out beneath the cloak. She fiddled with the clasp behind her neck. And the cape fell to the floor with a whoosh, like a Broadway curtain debuting something beautiful.

Her white bra and underwear glowed in the dark, a contrast against the room.

He stepped around her, stumbling through the shadows. There was a loud clang as he stepped behind her. A stool crashed to the floor when his kneecap hit the metal.

"Sorry," he awkwardly whispered. "Excuse me."

He noticed the tray of paints. And beside them, a round ball. When he touched it and felt the rough string, he gritted his teeth. It was yarn. *Yarn.* He had no idea what to do with yarn.

"Shit," he whispered.

He felt a soft hand tap his chest. The woman ran her hand gently over his shoulder and onto his arm until she found his hand. Her smooth fingers grasped him softly, and she stroked her thumb over his palm. She was reassuring him.

There was something strangely intimate about the gesture.

"So," Cecil said. "I was planning to paint, but we have yarn. It seems like sacrilege to cover your body in brown yarn. So...?"

He felt her shudder with laughter. They stood so close they could feel each other's energy. Her hand bumped his neck and swept up across his pulse. He felt her index finger press into his lips, cold like a chilled popsicle.

"You can't talk?" he asked.

The woman remained silent.

Cecil panicked. He could keep her in the lingerie and decorate her bra in yarn, but that certainly wouldn't win the competition. There weren't even scissors to cut the string.

But then he felt her hands caress his arms once again. She was slow and warm. And he felt chills run over his body. She wrapped his hands to her front, where she rested his fingertips over her belly.

She tensed like a board beneath him as she gently guided his fingers in strokes across her belly button. Her hips lightly bumped against his waist.

"You want me to paint you with my hands?" Cecil asked with disbelief.

He felt her nod against his neck, her satin hair scarf brushing up against his skin. Her heart pulsed through her stomach.

A knock came at the door. "Thirty minutes," the butler shouted.

Cecil's heart beat through his ears. "I can do a cheetah print dress or something?"

The woman shook her head violently, hair scarf spraying glitter into the air.

"Yeah, too trashy. Snakeskin?"

The mask rocked back and forth in contemplation. The coquette expression seemed to mock him, the shadow of the cocked lips more visible than the eyes.

"I can do a snakeskin print fastest. I had to do it at the abbey for all of the Adam and Eve scenes."

A muffled chuckle came from beneath the mask.

"So, snakeskin dress?" he asked.

The woman shook her head. Her fingertips traced the outline of pants in the air.

"Jumpsuit?" he asked.

The mask nodded, and the woman held onto her hair scarf to keep it in place.

"You spend a lot of time designing?" Cecil asked, trying to gauge a reaction from the plaster mask. But he was met with nothing but a statue. Even though he could barely see the outline of the mask's eyes, the inanimate face spooked him.

He squinted at the paints in the dark until he found white, black, and brown for the snakeskin and placed them on the stool for easy access.

He dipped each of his first three fingers on both hands into the paints to save time.

He stood behind her to avoid looking the mask in the lips. And then he wrapped his hands around her wrists. The tips of his fingers massaged paint across her veins.

Her pulse was throbbing. It felt like a tiny ball of nerves jumping beneath her skin with excited jitters. She leaned back into him slightly to keep her balance, and her scent suffocated his senses.

Her perfume washed over him like a rainbow of happiness. Vanilla, the scent he loved most. And the musky wood burning around them gave a toasty flavor to his tongue.

Goosebumps rose over her skin as his fingers massaged scales over her forearms. She rested her head back onto his shoulder.

She felt alive and loving, like a familiar kiss against his neck. It was his first interaction with a stranger that didn't begin with her calling him a murderer.

Instead, she wanted him to embrace her. It was as if they were communicating through touch. She adjusted her arms beneath his fingers, helping him stroke the checkered snake pattern across her body. He massaged every hair upon her arms. He stroked every nerve.

It felt like being in the confessional—a moment to escape his problems.

He found himself resting his head against hers as he moved to her shoulders. The paint slid across her skin like oil across velvet. A strand of her hair brushed his nose. And sea salt collided with vanilla, the smell of ice cream on the boardwalk in summer. It took him back to swimming with Perdonna in the ocean, tossing her into the waves and smelling her vanilla hair.

He stroked the rigid strip of her collarbone. His fingertips traced the plush of her breasts swelling out from the bra cups. Dashes of black paint made diamond checkers in a plunging neckline.

The snap of a clasp made him jump. Through the shadows, he could see her arms pulling down her bra. It fluttered to the floor, a white rose petal into the fire.

He felt her pulse against his chin. Her chest heaving in front of him.

"I can paint—" He stopped himself as his voice cracked. "I can paint over the bra."

"Fifteen minutes," the butler said.

The woman grabbed his hands and placed them over her breasts.

"I'm... I'm not sure I'm comfortable with this," Cecil said.

She dragged his fingers over her breasts in the snakeskin pattern, exactly matching his strokes of before. They moved together in perfect synchronicity.

She leaned closer into him. Their hands flicked over her nipples, and she huffed deep in her chest. He cradled her breasts in his hands.

He could feel her holding her breath. Her hips subtly gyrated in front of him, as if they searched for him.

"It's okay," he whispered hot into her ear. "It's okay if it feels good."

He was saying it as much to himself as to her. She let out a small whine, and Cecil found himself massaging her breasts with paint as she pressed her hips into him.

"Five minutes," the butler yelled.

Cecil swallowed deeply.

She leaned over and dipped her own fingers in paint. She began painting her own stomach and front. Cecil started on the back of her upper thighs, painting shorts.

They massaged together, dragging their fingertips across her body in a shared rhythm. Hands slipping over each other in the most intimate way. Skin slapping against paint. The tops of his fingers slid up to the lace between her thighs.

Her whole body seemed to nod. His palm cupped her hips. He painted over her, pressing harder than he had to just for the design. He loved the feeling of her quaking against him. The shameful moans echoing from her chest.

She grabbed his hand and slid his fingers between her legs. Cecil painted snakeskin over the lace between her thighs. She grinded her hips into his hands.

He rubbed his fingers over her front, palm cradling her between her legs. Her whole body gyrated over his hand. He heard her hands collide with the wall in a primal slam. She pressed into him hard, writhing faster and faster.

"One minute," the butler said.

They both paused, an outside voice bringing them back to reality. But then Cecil put a reassuring hand on her butt. She let out a quiet moan. She bucked into his hand faster and faster. Paint smearing everywhere. It was the smell of sterile paint. The smell of vanilla. Of saltwater. Of her.

She gave a frustrated groan.

"Come on," he whispered. Her whole body shivered. She quaked against him. And a small scream echoed through her closed lips.

She collapsed with a huff against the bookshelf. He could see the shadow of her arching back, trying not to smear the paint.

"Time's up," the butler yelled.

The door opened, and she seemed to try to look at him through the mask. But he was whisked away.

Ω

Cecil had never felt so much shame in his life. When he walked back into the room filled with guests, his face was completely drained of color. The other three artists stood with the guests, and Cecil clamored back to Ava who had now removed the scarf and was back to her normal self.

She dropped pieces of cheese down her dress, presumably for Figaro.

"What's wrong?" Ava asked. "Did you murder her? You have a really guilty look on your face."

Cecil shook his head. "I don't want to talk about it."

"Did you do *that* badly?" Ava asked.

"You can be the judge."

The first woman walked out. And Cecil started coughing hysterically. His face flashed from pale white to red.

"What's wrong with you?" Ava asked.

The first woman was still wearing her cloak. The artist had painted onto the white canvas of the dress, not the skin. Cecil was mortified, and his model hadn't even walked out yet.

"I think I misunderstood the challenge," Cecil said. "When Freddy's dad said paint their bodies... I took that literally."

The first canvas was painted in a purple starry night, almost like Van Gogh. Cecil wouldn't have been able to paint it even in daylight.

Cecil held his breath as the second model came out. *Praying* it wouldn't be his. It wasn't.

The next model wore a white tunic with silver masking tape snowflakes overtop it. It wasn't anything particularly special, but it wasn't awful. Even so, the audience erupted into boos. Cecil jumped at the sound.

The third model walked out in her tunic, which was covered in blocky orange colors, exactly like Romdinger's canvas painting. The audience clapped enthusiastically, yelling "Bravo" even in the small space.

Ava covered her face with her hands. "Welp. I guess we'll have to get the files some other way."

"Can we just go now?" Cecil asked, looking toward the door.

"You look like you're going to die."

"I am. I *really* am." Cecil nodded. His arms were shaking so much he could barely even function.

"Let's go," Ava said. They walked toward the art gallery and opened the door slowly so it wouldn't make a sound. Cecil tried not to smudge wet paint off his sweater onto the walls. The moment they left the room, they heard absolute silence. No one whispered. No one sipped champagne.

"Your model must've walked out," Ava said with a laugh.

But after the long silence, there were a few whistles. And the audience erupted with raucous applause. Cecil walked back to the door and peered in from the gallery.

The snakeskin glimmered beneath the light. The paint managed to look like a real cloth romper. The woman looked elegant, not the slightest evidence she was naked at all.

"That's genius," he heard someone in the audience cheer.

Ava opened the door, and they walked back into the crowd, her eyes bulging open when she saw the outfit.

Ava gave a beaming smile, shaking Cecil's shoulder with enthusiasm, shocked he might've pulled this off. "Why do you still look horrified?"

"Does that look like Perdonna?" Cecil asked.

Ava shrugged. "She's hot like Perdonna. Like really hot."

"She smelled like Perdonna."

Jim walked back in front of the models, admittedly staring at the woman in snakeskin a little too long.

"A lot of women have vanilla perfume."

"But hers isn't normal vanilla. It's like a crêpe suzette vanilla. It's specific."

Ava put her hands on her hips. "You have one hell of an Electra complex. I mean *wow*. Perdonna wouldn't be caught dead participating in this," she whispered.

Cecil crossed his arms, closing his eyes. He'd never wanted to disappear so much in his life.

"Were you fantasizing about her?" Ava asked with a smile. "You were, weren't you?"

Cecil didn't answer.

Jim glanced over the audience. "Well. I think we all know who the winner is."

The audience let out nervous chuckles.

"Who did the snakeskin?" Jim asked.

No one claimed the piece. Cecil felt his heart beat out of his chest. Everyone looked around the room nervously, and Ava jabbed Cecil in the side.

"I did," Cecil said.

20

=====

Still covered in wet paint, Cecil waited impatiently with Ava outside of Freddy's room. They could hear Freddy fighting with his mother...Freddy stomping his foot indignantly...Freddy throwing throw pillows.

"You love models," Addy was saying. "You love that their rib cages look like overcooked baby back ribs."

"All right!" Cecil knocked on the door.

Addy let them into Freddy's lair. It was quite cozy, despite a plastic smell of latex. But the chemical stench wasn't the result of a sex dungeon. It was from the many latex beanbag chairs tossed around the room. Freddy sat on his beanbag by the fire when his mother left. But Cecil's eyes darted over the many options. Sheepskin throw pillows? Alpaca body pillows? The room was like a children's library set up for story time.

Freddy's sweaty face glimmered next to the light, curls flopping over his forehead like limp noodles.

Cecil wiped off a bit of blue paint that clung to his eyebrows. "Why didn't you answer my calls?"

Freddy poked at the fire with his tools. The embers crackled to life, and Ava bent down to the warmth. "I panicked. I took the files, and I panicked. *Panicked*."

Freddy sat in front of the fire and parted his legs, forcing Ava to catch a glimpse of the hair trailing around his belly button.

Cecil gazed into the fire, hunching against his own knees, frowning at himself. He was lost in his own thoughts.

"What's wrong with *you*? Did my parents embarrass you or something?" Freddy asked, looking at Cecil.

"Long story," Ava said. "But why did you take the files?"

Freddy made a low grumbling sound like a cat that lost a mouse. His face twisted into wiry disgust, and he looked up to Cecil pleadingly. "Erm...well." He fingered his mouth anxiously and spat when he tasted the fresh varnish on his hands. "Can I take the guilty plea, or nah?"

"No," Ava and Cecil said simultaneously.

"Phone a friend?"

Ava grabbed his head by the curls.

"Careful, bitch. My nose is made of plastic, not cartilage." Freddy folded his arms. "Why should I tell you?"

"I can fire you," Cecil said. "Margaux's in jail, so I'm in charge now."

Freddy sniffed hard. "I see. Okay. Calm it. I can explain."

He flipped his Dial and a photo projected onto the wall. Freddy tapped the image of Margaux at the Visage show, and the scene played like a movie screening.

The Visage oil vat sat untouched. Only a dim light lit up the space. But Freddy and Margaux happily scurried around the runway.

"This is so fricking kewl," Margaux shrilled, doing a bouncy catwalk across the runway. Freddy followed after her, clapping his hands. He took her cane and held it out for her to limbo underneath. Margaux threw her head back and shimmied her chubby little arms beneath the pole.

"*You put your left foot in. You put your left foot out. You—*"

"That's the Hokey Pokey."

"Yeah?" Margaux glared.

"This is the limbo."

She took the cane and smacked Freddy in the ass with it. When he whined, she dipped her finger into the oil and drew a mustache on his face.

"Why are we watching this?" Cecil asked.

"You'll see."

Margaux flopped onto the runway, looking up to the ceiling. She dipped another finger into the oil and drew black hearts along the runway.

"Should I try paging Jordan again?" Freddy asked.

"I think she's a goner," Margaux said. "Might as well burn her magazine covers. And burn the few tiny remaining scraps of my love for her."

Freddy paged Jordan's Dial.

The loud alarm went off, and a tiny bright light shone up from beneath the oil. Margaux spat at the light. "Why did you do that?" Freddy asked.

"I don't know. Thought maybe the spit would penetrate the oil and show us how deep it is."

Freddy raised his eyebrows but was clearly too afraid to mock her.

She dipped her cane into the oil and prodded the light. She stirred the cane around in the oil like a witch stirring her kettle. "There's something long and cylindrical under there."

"Like a cane?"

"Errrm. Fatter." Margaux shook her head. She tried to wedge the cane beneath the heavy thing, and then she squatted to heave the object up and out of the oil. But she wasn't strong enough. Freddy yanked the cane out of her hands and she wiggled her fingers in disbelief that he took it so easily.

"Don't," Margaux said.

"Don't what?"

"Don't scoop it up."

Freddy huffed at Margaux. He thought about it, but he lifted Jordan's oil-soaked body to the surface.

"Ah! Put her back! Put her back!" Margaux yelled.

The video paused with Margaux mid-scream.

"So," Freddy said to Cecil and Ava. "That happened."

Cecil leaned back against the wall. "You found her before the show and didn't tell the police."

"Because I assumed Margaux murdered Jordan," Freddy said. "She pretended not to know where Jordan was all day, and then didn't want me to lift her out of the oil. I didn't want Margaux to kill me. And I didn't want the police to think I had anything to do with killing Jordan."

"You were also the last person to see Jordan alive," Ava said.

"Oh God. Oh God," Freddy said. And then he took a deep breath. He made the drinks without a single tinge of anxiety, though the left side of his mouth twitched from being perpetually cocaine-ridden. He was certainly a party boy. "I let her outside for a smoke break. She bribes me with baseball cards that she gets...got...from a photographer friend."

"That's true," she said. "Freddy did let Jordan out pretty often. It wasn't just that night."

"Okay. But who was filming you?" Cecil asked.

"That's where things get interesting. For you, not for me. A man came up from behind me after the Visage show. He put his hand around my neck, and he said I had to take portfolios from LeClaire and give them to an emissary of his. Or... They would show the police this tape."

"Do you know who the man was?" Cecil asked.

"Didn't see him. I was too busy shitting my pants."

"Are you okay? I can imagine that was scary," Cecil said, putting his hand on Freddy's shoulder.

Freddy put his hands up and stepped back. "Margaux tells me never to trust religious people."

"That's pretty backward," Ava said.

"We're talking about Margaux here," Freddy said. "Her life motto is: offensive is the positive of defensive."

Ava squinted her eyes, cocking her head. "Margaux has a lot of mottos."

Freddy smacked his lips together. He plopped back onto the beanbag and slowly sank into the folds, contemplating his situation.

"Could the man who threatened you have been VD?" Cecil asked.

"CD? Those are so pre-iTunes," Freddy said with a flick of his short curls.

Ava gave a cautious glance to Figaro, who scurried over to a sheepskin beanbag.

"Hey, Figgy. Figgy, piggy, Figaro," Freddy said, scooting next to Figaro and stroking his cheek. Freddy rubbed his nose into Figaro's little snout.

"VD is the person we think abducted Annabelle Leigh," Cecil said. Freddy twiddled his fingers nervously, eyes twitching back and forth. He clearly knew who VD was. But he didn't want to say. "If you tell me," Cecil said, "you can be promoted."

"Oh," Freddy said. "*That* VD."

"Who arranged the Annabelle Leigh abduction?" Ava asked, already knowing the answer.

"It was Margaux." Freddy nodded. "I had just started working for her, but since I'm her personal assistant she still confided in me."

"Why did she do it?" Cecil asked.

Freddy scrunched his nose. "I'm the only one in the agency who knows Margaux ordered the abduction, but I don't know why. I always assumed she just didn't want Annabelle to be with Cecil. You were pretty close for fourteen-year-olds. It *was* a little weird."

Cecil cocked his head. "Why does she send girls to VD in the first place?"

"Great commission," Freddy said. "We make four times on the girls we send to VD versus what we normally make on our top models."

"What does he do with them?"

"He's not usually referred to as 'VD.' People gossip about several theories. Some say he takes the models people don't use. He's a 'garbage' man who takes the waste and destroys the toxins before the police find you. Some say he runs a mafia ring in Italy. The editor of *Yuji* magazine told me he harvested kidneys, hearts, and other things from them. I've even heard that the Illuminati uses this VD's girls when they want to fake a tragedy like a plane crash, or a moon landing. They just put the girls in the scene.

"But I will warn you." Freddy paused, and the first hint of seriousness crossed his mouth. He pushed the shaggy hair from his eyes. "Don't underestimate these people. Don't let the beautiful cheekbones, the glossy Photoshopped skin... Don't let the yachts and choppers and smiling pictures in St. Tropez fool you. People don't buy $20,000 shoes because they're pretty.

"People buy them because they're tickets. They're a step in the door," Freddy said. "Fashion is a three-*trillion*-dollar industry. That's trillion, with a *T*. Who wore what to the Oscars? What patterns are trending and who's the hottest celebrity... It's all a facade. The only thing superficial about the fashion industry is the ability to make everything *seem* superficial."

"Why would VD want these files? So he can own their passports? Their social security cards? Visas?" Cecil asked.

Freddy wriggled his tongue in between his cheeks. "He wants to steal models. Own the identities, own the girls."

"So where are the files?"

"I was supposed to deliver them tomorrow night. But, honestly I'm kind of chickening out now that it seems very possible Margaux killed Jordan. I would love not to have to be the delivery man."

Freddy dropped a giant binder of modeling portfolios in front of Cecil's lap.

"What time and where?" Cecil asked.

"Salon de Ming—the bar at the top of the Peninsula Hotel. Eight o'clock tomorrow. The delivery man has to wear a white jacket to be ID'ed."

"I'll do it," Cecil said.

Freddy's eyes lit up. "Thank God... And Cecil, for the record, I guarantee VD is someone you know. I bet he's been around you for a while. I keep thinking about it. There has to be a reason he kept Annabelle Leigh alive for ten years."

21

Cecil flopped back into the Rambo Lambo. With a deep breath, he huffed and dropped his forehead to the steering wheel. The horn blared, and dogs barked back at it. People stared. Taxis stopped mid-drive. It wasn't a typical car horn. It was the roar from the MGM lion.

Cecil stared at the wheel, imagining a tiny lion inside. He cautiously pressed the horn with his thumb again, and it was indeed the king of the jungle. A golden tank *roared*.

"That's nice," Ava said as she got inside. "Not sure it will be helpful in stopping a tractor trailer from hitting you, though."

He doused his hands in chlorine-scented sanitizer and tried to massage the paint off his skin inch by inch.

"You can't scrub off all this paint with hand sanitizer," Ava said.

"Watch me."

She opened the door to the Rambo Lambo refrigerator and found a water bottle inside. With a long chug, she made a show of sloshing the water in her mouth. Then, when Cecil looked up, she spat a stream of water in his face.

He buried a drenched face in his shirt.

"Disgusting."

"But look, you're cleaner."

When the engine revved up, and the Rambo bucked on its blinged-out tires, Cecil could still hear the cackling laughs from the party guests.

Ava paged through the names on the paperwork that Freddy had given them.

"I recognize some of the names on these portfolios, but not all," Ava said. "VD must be trying to poach these girls."

"Should we turn the passports over to the police? Tell them where to find VD's emissary tomorrow night?" Cecil asked.

"It wouldn't guarantee the girls actually ever get their IDs back." She tossed her feet onto the dashboard defiantly, revealing her tattered black playground sneakers. He only realized how fragile and weak her body was when she kicked her leg against the car. The calf muscles were so atrophied that they looked like gooey frosting coating bone.

"The girls should have their birth certificates for darn's sakes."

"Oh gosh *darn it*," Ava mocked. "And the police wouldn't move forward on finding out who VD is. They don't care. They just need an indictment in the murder of Annabelle Leigh. We have to meet this person at Salon de Ming. Yes, Clara put the skin coat on me. But she probably didn't murder Annabelle because she's a heroin addict, and her priorities are more about heroin than murder. We know Margaux set up Annabelle's abduction and gave her to VD, but we don't know why. But none of that matters to the police. I guarantee you Detective Roosevelt will continue to pin Annabelle Leigh's murder on Clara Royds to make this a clean and easy case for the papers. They need a scapegoat."

Figaro once again climbed onto the stallion gearshift, riding it into the sunset of Manhattan. He was in love with that gearshift. A rat riding a stallion. It would make a good children's story.

Ava continued. "We won't know why Margaux sent Annabelle to VD. We won't know where Annabelle was kept for ten years. And we won't know for sure who killed her unless we find out from VD ourselves."

Cecil was starting to realize why Perdonna hired Ava. Common sense was her strength. While Ava pretended not to be paying attention, she always was. Like a baby in a cradle, she knew more than she could say.

As the car rumbled along, pedestrians clambered down below like ants, reds and yellows from the traffic lights flashing across their disenchanted faces. Cecil looked up at the afterglow of skyscrapers.

There was a Taylor Swift billboard. The Coca-Cola polar bear. Crevier diamonds. Twinkle lights in October. Limos trailing like beetles, delivering celebrities to their devotees.

Ava's feet fell from the dashboard, and her legs crossed like a mouth zipping shut. She wouldn't budge. She wanted him to squirm.

"What would you say qualifies as betraying God?" Cecil asked.

"I know nothing about religion," Ava said. "Though I'd say painting a woman's naked body is borderline, but okay. A few prayers should get you by."

Cecil rolled his neck, feeling his face flush. "What if she thrusted into my hand?"

Ava's eyes squinted. She drummed her fingers against the disco shards on the car wall. "What do you mean, thrust? Women don't thrust."

"Rubbed, then. What if she rubbed into my hand?"

"Did you stop her?"

"Not particularly."

"That's a problem," Ava said, continuing to drum. She clicked her teeth together and whispered, "Tsk, tsk."

"And then she may have directed my hand to...well, you know."

"Not really, but sure. Continue."

"And then I, well, you know..." Cecil trailed off.

Ava looked up to the ceiling and then abruptly stopped drumming. She quickly turned down the radio and all they heard was the honking car horns of New York City. Then she seemed to have worked it out in her head. "You fingered a stranger with paint?"

"Sort of."

Her eyes bulged out and she took in a deep, deep breath. "Oh my God. So what now? Do you get kicked out of religion?"

Figaro scurried on top of her head. It was not the time to be cute. Cecil could feel himself shaking once again, like his whole body was on fire.

"Did she climax?" Ava asked.

Cecil glared. "You can't ask that."

"What? She's a stranger. Or Perdonna—if we're living in your fantasy."

Ava studied his face, putting Figaro on her lap. "She did. Good. I feel like God would want men to make women orgasm. It's only fair."

Cecil took a sharp right turn into an alley. Ava fake squealed as the car tires whirred. He stopped the car on the spot. Right in front of a homeless man eating bits of cardboard off a McDonald's Happy Meal box.

"What are we doing here?" Ava asked.

"I need a second," Cecil said, leaning his forehead against the steering wheel and wheezing.

"You're really upset about this, aren't you?" Ava shoved the fluffy white rat at his chest. "Here. Cuddle Figaro. I don't do emotions."

Cecil shook his head, so Ava plopped Figaro on Cecil's lap. He ran his fingers through the fluffy white fur, but then bits of a purple putty substance ended up all over his fingers. Ava winced, and then grabbed the whole hand sanitizer bottle.

"Thanks I—" But Cecil grimaced as Ava lathered Figaro in the sanitizer, not Cecil's dirty hands. "Never mind."

"Okay, wait," Ava said. "I *have* seen *The Sound of Music*. Isn't the whole Christian deal that you have to marry God *or* a human?"

"Something like that."

"Maybe you were supposed to marry a human." Ava blew air at Figaro's fur, trying to dry it off from the hand sanitizer.

"I thought I was going to marry Annabelle."

"You were fourteen. You can move on, you know?"

He watched as the homeless man threw the chicken nuggets onto the ground and stomped on them. He supposed the cardboard probably had a better flavor anyway.

"I did. I moved on to St. Joseph's."

"Is hiding moving on?"

"Look," Cecil said, leaning back. "My whole life vanished. I needed some answers about why everything I loved..." He trailed off and tried to push the car seat back so he could relax, but Margaux had replaced the lever with a twirling ballerina figurine. "My last few years in Manhattan were a weird daze. I couldn't even grieve Annabelle's death because I was constantly trying to defend myself against murdering her. I miss building model trains with her, and driving them off into rivers. I miss making the little cities and inventing the townspeople. I miss sledding with her in Central Park, laughing at the rich moms who froze to death because they wouldn't wear fattening winter coats. I miss buying those awful-tasting SpongeBob popsicles and spitting the blue gumball eyes at each other. Okay?"

"I wish I had a childhood friend like that," Ava said. "You're lucky."

Cecil scoffed and then he saw her bottom lip wriggling. She blinked like crazy to keep tears from spilling out. *Lucky* was the last word Cecil would've ever chosen to describe his childhood. One where he almost never saw his mother, and his own sister practically abandoned him. One where he became famous for being a murderer.

His headmaster asked him "kindly" to be homeschooled because he was a distraction. He needed a bodyguard to go to the library. And there was not a single parent in Manhattan who would allow their child to befriend Cecil LeClaire.

But maybe he was lucky. He was lucky to have known Annabelle in the first place.

"If you didn't deal with Annabelle, that also means you never really processed your feelings for Perdonna," Ava said. "You were too traumatized in your teens from Annabelle disappearing."

"I don't have feelings for Perdonna," Cecil shouted. When he noticed Ava with her giggling eyes, he lowered his tone. "A crush is not feelings. *Lust* is not feelings."

She raised her eyebrows. "Maybe you're just a good monk. But I've seen a lot of men interact with models. And you're the least lusty man I've ever met."

He clutched his golden cross in his palm. And he realized that Abbot Joseph had not sent him to New York to solve Annabelle Leigh's murder specifically. He was no Batman. He was no James Bond. He wasn't living a superhero comic.

It was time to grow up.

♎

Salar de Uyuni, Bolivia. Three years ago.

Amid the Andes in southwest Bolivia, Salar de Uyuni was a magnificent salt flat. Bright white saline, rock sculptures, and islands. It was one of the world's largest natural mirrors as the water over the salt reflected the gorgeous pink and purple hues that swirled in the clouds at sunset.

Sitting in the water, Cecil felt like he was floating in the clouds, suspended in a dreamlike air. He stared at an image of himself within the white billows of the sky. The waters swept over his legs like a blanket, the sand curving to the shape of his body.

He lifted his eyes only to see a flamboyance of flamingoes flapping toward him, their brighter pink mixing into the blue hues and softer yellow-pinks. The mirrored image of Perdonna's scorched eyes seemed to grow beneath the flapping pink wings, as though she were Mother Nature herself.

Vanilla and salty beach mixed well.

Perdonna slept in the wet sand. Her back arched like a cat's, and she raised her arms above her head, tossing curls over her shoulders. The white bathing suit rode up her hips, and her curves reflected across the mirror, across the blues and pinks. She was a Madonna, waist tapered inward, body like a pillar streaming toward the sky. She was a siren rising from the clouded seas.

Cecil clutched his pencil tighter. He had been sketching her in dark blue watercolor pencil. The arch of her legs. The way her white parasol hat shaded her hair.

"Sit still a few more minutes," Cecil said.

Perdonna kicked her legs into the air, stretching like a kitten rising from sleep. Her fingers traced the plunging neckline of her bathing suit while he continued. She slowly edged the straps down as he sketched. But before she pulled her top down, they both broke into a fit of laughter.

"It was all feeling very *Titanic*. I took my moment," she said.

She pulled the straps back up and twirled toward him. He couldn't take his eyes off hers. It was the first time he had seen them scarred in person. They seemed almost like pearlescent oyster shells, swirling with whites and light blues. Her iris still moved beneath the clouds. So he could see where she was looking.

"Are you really not going to tell me how you hurt your eyes?" he asked.

"I've been telling people the Sheikh of Omar burned them."

"But—"

"The real story is quite pathetic. So you'll never know." A coy grin fell to her lips.

She traced her fingers along the pencil marks, assessing the drawing. "You're a bit generous with my ass, don't you think?"

"If anything, I haven't done it justice."

He wrapped his arms around her from behind, and she drew circles on his palm with her thumbs. Her touch sent shocks through him.

"Do beautiful things like this inspire your designs? How are you still designing if you can't see?"

"Beauty does not make beauty." Perdonna shook her head. "When I want to make a masterpiece, I think of my most horrid memories—the darkest, most gruesome maladies of my life." She pointed to the swirling sky, the cumulonimbus clouds floating above. "If I were to make this sky a dress, it would be a false copy, a collection of fabrics that could never live up to God." Her salty finger rested against his lip, teasing him. "It would be a lie."

"What terrible things do you think about?"

With a coy smirk, she drew figure eights with her toe in the water. "Nothing I can speak of."

Cecil took a long gulp that didn't go unnoticed by Perdonna. Her white teeth flashed like a shark, a smile she only gave to him.

"What's wrong, bellino?"

He waited to respond.

Like a snow angel, Perdonna sprawled on the sand, letting the water rock her.

Night came quickly. Stars, like red and gold glitter, filled up their world in all four dimensions. She rubbed his shoulders to keep him warm in the night, and then she nestled her head against his chest, the pearl necklace dangling over his belly button.

"I don't like to think about Annabelle. That's my terrible memory. Does that mean I can't create anything?" Cecil asked.

Cecil never understood Annabelle's abduction as a vicious murder, never imagined the gruesome atrocities that might've been committed. To him, Annabelle Leigh simply disappeared like the way dandelions blew away in autumn.

"Art is the only way *to* process it," she said.

"And religion," Cecil corrected.

She smacked his chest, her skin making a loud slap. He heard the echo throughout his whole body. She laughed in an angry way.

"It's true," Cecil said with a smile.

Somehow, an hour had passed. Then another, until it was midnight. And Perdonna was wrapped in his arms, lying on top of him. Her chest pressed against his, every inch of her warm body flush with his. It had gone that way every night for two weeks.

His hands tangled through her hair. Her feet wrapped around his ankles. His finger tracing circles on her lower back. Her breath in his ear. Touching her felt different than it had when he said goodbye to her at eighteen.

She was forbidden on one hand—she was his godmother, he was becoming a monk. But on the other hand, of all the hundreds of millions of devotees, he was the only one who could touch her in this loving but platonic way.

"I like this," Cecil whispered. "I think it's the longest I've spent with you uninterrupted by paparazzi, foreign diplomats, or crazed fans."

Her face shone with a golden hue beneath the stars. "Don't get used to it. You'll have to share me when we get back to New York tomorrow."

Cecil's hands froze. "Back to New York?"

Perdonna sat up, rolling off of him and onto the sand. She wrapped herself in a blue Visage towel to keep warm. "We agreed. You'd try the abbey for three years. Then you'd design for Visage."

He raised his eyebrows, shaking his head. "Wait, wait, wait. Is that why we're here? I'm here because this is the last time I can leave the abbey for *vacation*. I'm taking the next steps in monkhood."

She shrugged. "Why are you wasting your life spending eight hours a day praying with old men?"

"Wasting my life? Is that what you think I'm doing?"

Perdonna threw down the towel. The heat of her anger did all the warming she needed. "If there is a God, why do people die of Ebola and AIDS? Why do hurricanes kill thousands of people? That's one *hell of a guy* to be supporting."

Cecil leaned back into the sand. "It's complicated. People... hardship pushes them forward in life. It teaches them lessons."

"What lesson is a five-year-old child learning when her father molests her every night?"

"That's the Devil."

Perdonna threw her head back with laughter. "The Devil is God's favorite angel, my dear." She wrapped her arm around his shoulder. "How deep does this go? Do you believe in creationism? Do you believe Adam and Eve over evolution? Was Noah's ark real? Is it wrong to be gay?"

"I don't believe in *all* of the Christian rules," Cecil said. "I believe in morals."

"So riddle me this," she said as she knelt before him. Her face came close to his in the dark. "If you were to kiss me, or suckle my breasts, would that be wrong?"

He was thankful she couldn't see him salivate. But he knew she could feel his quick breaths. "Me suckling *you*, or are we talking about any theoretical woman?"

"What difference does that make?" she barked, pushing him back into the sand.

She threw her hands up and stood, pacing. He couldn't remember ever seeing her frazzled. She was always the picture of power. But now, *frazzled* was the word.

"You can find another designer," Cecil said. "I haven't painted in three years anyway. Nothing spectacular. Nothing worthy of Visage. All I do at the monastery are manuscripts."

"Intrinsic talent doesn't just go away. And it's rare. I can't go find it on a street corner."

Cecil stood from the sand. "I'm happy at the abbey."

"Are you?" she asked, putting her hands to his cheeks, tracing her fingers over his jaw.

"Not as happy as I've been here. But this isn't what life at Visage would be. This isn't real."

"I suppose it isn't. Goodbye, bellino. Maybe I'll see you at my funeral," she said.

And that was their goodbye.

♎

When they pulled up in the Rambo Lambo, Cecil was surprised to find Perdonna's mansion untouched by time. The same Italian stalker from his childhood stood outside, and the same security guard, with gun in hand, nodded to him.

White orchids decorated the windowsills and he could smell the freshly baked cookies from outside.

Tonight, there were five black SUVs with United States Army badges.

Ava waved goodbye, agreeing to meet at the LeClaire Mansion before going to Salon de Ming at eight o'clock the next day to meet VD.

Then he saw Perdonna through the window, covered in a tight black suit, shoulders in crisp points. She looked like a stingray. Army generals sat before her giant white desk.

She couldn't have set up for a meeting in time if she had been the masked woman at Freddy's party. She wasn't the painting canvas.

22

As dawn cut through Margaux's barred window, she struggled to keep her hair from frizzing inside the holding cell at the New York City Police Department's Nineteenth Precinct. It sat at 153 East Sixty-Seventh Street and provided her with no view, no beignets, no beautiful girls. But worst of all, she had to sleep on *Third* Avenue, which Margaux had deemed Suicide Avenue.

She had worked hard for her rightful domain between Fifth and Madison. But the NYPD took her back to a street full of Rite-Aids and delis instead of Brunello Cucinellis. The Central Park Conservancy didn't plant flowers or put Christmas lights on the *lesser* avenues. Instead, construction refuse littered the dark and grimy world outside her prison cell.

To Margaux, the people of Third Avenue were those who *almost* worked hard enough to afford Fifth and Madison Avenues, but not quite. They earned second place in the race for riches, a depressing and devastating failure.

Residences on Third Avenue averaged about $2,000 per square foot, and it was still one of the richest places in the United States. But it was not a *Margaux* place.

The *Lesser Avenue* dwellers couldn't afford a country house or anything more expensive than a BMW. They lived one block too far away from Central Park and far too many blocks away from Madison stores. Somewhere along the way, they chose to have a childhood instead of taking the summer internship with Goldman Sachs. *Third* Avenue denizens opted to study accounting instead of Wall Street. They became psychologists because they didn't have the guts to go to medical school and become psychiatrists.

Margaux was now an alleged murderer residing on Third Avenue, the street of suicides and failure. This was the least fashionable, cruelest, and most unreasonable punishment that could have been dealt to her.

She sang "Animal Crackers in My Soup" to herself in her lonely holding cell while resting on a pillow that smelled of spoiled cheese and musty socks. Even Shirley Temple couldn't save her.

Ω

Cecil loved Third Avenue. He strolled by J.G. Mellon and smelled the classic hamburgers through the windows. Barbequed meats and baking pizza crusts wafted through the autumn leaves. Each apartment building was decorated with spider webs, inflated white ghosts, or animatronic witches that sprayed water from their boiling pots.

Yes, there was the pervasive scent of dog urine, but it was a happy diversion from the oppression of Park Avenue—the avenue that was too expensive for a grocery store. Only home to plastic surgery practices and fertility clinics.

But he cowered in front of the Nineteenth Precinct. He felt that sinking dread he got as a boy being called to the principal's office. He signed his name in at the front desk and waited patiently in a lobby coated in red, white, and blue.

Roosevelt stepped out with a mustache of sugary donut powder.

She touched her lips noticing Cecil's charmed expression, and quickly turned her face away.

They walked to another dull room with plastic black chairs and white walls where Chandler was hunched over his computer in the corner of the room. He glared up at Cecil like a black cat ready to pounce. Or more like a Chihuahua about to start a squealing, barking fit.

Roosevelt set a tray of bagels and donuts before him.

"Coffee?" Roosevelt asked. "Or... Oh. I'm sorry. I shouldn't have offered. Are you... Are you still a monk? How does that work?"

Cecil laughed. "It's still nice to offer." He stepped up to the hot water and poured himself a peppermint tea. He took half a bagel and began cutting it up into his twelve tiny pieces.

Chandler studied him, his eyes lighting up as if Cecil's behavior somehow indicated he was a sociopathic serial killer. "Why are you doing that?" he asked.

"Monks have a strict diet," Cecil said. "I'm being extra restrictive today."

"Why?" Chandler asked, standing and coming around the table. He looked like a mouse next to Roosevelt.

"Repenting."

"Repenting for what?" Chandler asked.

Cecil looked to Roosevelt but her eyes never blinked. She suddenly looked focused, homed in on the words. There was a stark contrast between the two detectives. One pretended to be his friend, and the other wanted to intimidate him.

"Did you call me in to question me?" Cecil asked.

"No, we—"

Roosevelt was cut off when Chandler smacked his hands onto the table and leaned forward like an overzealous cop from the movies. "Repenting for what? Murdering a girl?"

Cecil watched as his tea splashed up from Chandler's Godzilla-like pounding.

"I spent this morning and afternoon in prayer. Praying for Jordan, praying for Margaux's models, asking God to forgive me for developing an addiction to those Toasted Vanillas."

Chandler squinted his beady little rat eyes. He looked like an evil version of Figaro. "Do you know what Margaux's canes are made of?"

"Margaux says ivory. She used to joke that they were made of my dad's bones. She only started carrying the canes after he died in the car bombing."

Cecil dipped a piece of bagel into peppermint tea. He soaked it and then popped it in his mouth. The soggy wintergreen flavor took him back to the comfort of the abbey.

"It's interesting the skin coat was only made of Annabelle Leigh's skin. Isn't it?" Chandler asked. "Where's the rest of the body?"

He sipped the tea, but it burnt his tongue, the sting remaining as he opened his lips to let the air cool his mouth, panting like a dog.

Roosevelt lifted an ivory cane with a handle shaped like a naked woman lying on her back, breasts propped where Margaux's hand would naturally caress and grab. It was wrapped in an evidence baggie.

"Does this look familiar?" Chandler asked.

"It's the cane Margaux took to the Visage show," Cecil said. "It was covered in oil."

"Have you ever held it?" Chandler asked.

Cecil looked to Roosevelt for help, but she seemed to study his hand placements, the direction his eyes drifted, and his tapping feet.

"You're not obligated to talk to us," Roosevelt said.

"I don't think I've held the cane."

"But you split one of Margaux's canes in half when we searched with a warrant."

"Yes."

"So you *do* break canes when you're angry? In fact, we've seen you express bursts of anger *many* times," Chandler said.

Cecil looked at Chandler with an angry disbelief.

"Our forensics team was quickly able to determine that based on the shatter patterns in Jordan Jones's skull, the murder weapon was a skinny, long, cylindrical object," Roosevelt said. "At first we assumed it could've been one of the poles holding up the curtains around the fashion show venue. But then, I remembered you saying you saw oil on Margaux's cane. Forensics show that it is the murder weapon."

"How many times do you suspect she hit Jordan over the head with that cane?" he asked with a low drawl.

"Why would you ask that?"

"If Margaux only hit Jordan once, it could've been a heat-of-the-moment thing, a burst of anger. If she did it multiple times… then, Margaux's even worse than I thought."

Roosevelt licked her lips again, as if white powder still covered her face.

"About fourteen times," Chandler interrupted.

The teacup fell from his slack hand. It seared his thighs and spilled down his calves. He jumped out of his seat, trying to quell the feeling, holding the fabric away from the skin.

Roosevelt didn't blink, but she opened her mouth to say something and closed it. "I ordered tests on Margaux's cane. After we examined the outside, the oil and Jordan's DNA, I wanted to test the actual cane itself. Ivory isn't often acquired legally, and if I could get her on an extra possession charge, I would." Roosevelt paused. "I used Annabelle's DNA from Dr. Imogen and—"

Cecil put his hand up. "The LeClaire doctor is Tibolt. Perdonna paid Annabelle's medical bills. She went to Dr. Tibolt."

"Her records and muscle biopsy are with Dr. Imogen. She works with the models. Margaux claims she wanted a female doctor working with the girls."

Probably for the best. Dr. Tibolt was not the most scrupulous medical professional. He did Margaux's facelift at the LeClaire Mansion, without a sterile environment. Once, he wrote Cecil a note claiming he had autism just so he could get extra time to take his ACT and SAT tests. And there was the newly discovered ADHD debacle.

"Turns out, the ivory in Margaux's cane is a mix of jaguar bone and Annabelle Leigh bone."

"I'm sorry, what?" he asked, hoping he heard incorrectly.

"Margaux has been carrying around Annabelle Leigh's bone in her hands like a trophy."

"Who would mold a cane out of a dead body for Margaux

LeClaire? And in such short time?"

"We assume it's the same people who sewed the...Annabelle Leigh garment that appeared on the Visage runway. For all we know it could be Margaux herself."

Cecil covered his face in his hands.

He imagined his mother standing in LeClaire Model Management again with a revolver at her waist and a cane in her hand. Most of his life, he'd most feared the revolver, but he finally saw the cane as a bloody and threatening wand, stabbing people and stomping the floor.

Roosevelt's puffy eyes searched him for a reaction. "How does this make you feel?"

"Is there a *chance* someone framed her? Now it seems to me like a frame job. I mean, I've found enough evidence for myself that Margaux is not an outstanding citizen, but doesn't that make it *more* likely someone would frame her? She has plenty of enemies. I don't think Margaux is sadistic enough to carry around human bone in her cane. It seems over-the-top even for her."

"It's interesting you bring up framing," Chandler said. "Have you spoken to Clara Royds since she was released?"

Cecil rubbed his burning thighs. "Clara's out on bail?"

Roosevelt watched his eyes, seemingly satisfied with his surprise.

"We have reason to believe she only acted in putting the skin coat on Ava Germaine. Her involvement ended there."

"But she's the one who *hated* Annabelle. She was a grown adult jealous of a fourteen-year-old. And she's a heroin addict. Doesn't that fit into a murder profile?"

Roosevelt and Chandler remained silent.

"The LeClaire Mansion is officially a crime scene. If you have belongings you'd like us to bring you, make a list and we'll decide what can be cleared," Roosevelt said. "Do you have another place to stay?"

Cecil nodded with a morose, sagging face that seemed to directly contrast Chandler's doughboy smile. "These are my only belongings," Cecil said, clutching his NYPD sweats and the little dog Aberto. "Oh, and please have someone feed the fish at the mansion."

"What's in the briefcase?" Chandler asked.

Cecil felt his first tinge of nervousness. He was beginning to think that Ava was right about the police. He tried not to let his eyes drift away or shuffle in his seat. "My Bible. Prayer sheets from the abbey," Cecil lied. It was full of model passports and files for VD.

♎

"Margaux is a fuc—gosh darn monster," Cecil yelled.

Ava stood in front of the glittering gold Rambo Lambo tank wearing her usual black cylindrical dress. This time she didn't wear twinkle lights in her hair and Figaro was nowhere to be seen. She clutched a full suit for Cecil.

"There was Annabelle Leigh bone in her cane. How did that get there? Did she literally saw her up and bring her to a cane maker?" Cecil asked. "She hit Jordan over the head fourteen times. *Fourteen* times."

Ava opened the Rambo door. "I mean, she is a racist."

"She's not racist, she just says racist things for shock value because it gets her more views on YouTube. She's like Archie Bunker. Her most important confidant is a gay black man."

"You can have black friends and still be racist," Ava said.

"But being racist doesn't make you a murderer. A monster, but not necessarily a murderer."

"I think it's definitely a risk factor."

Ava combed out her hair with her fingers. It seemed she had a grudge against hair brushes.

"Clara was released on bail," Cecil said. "Do you have a phone number for her?"

Ava kicked her feet onto the dashboard of the car. There would forever be sneaker streaks across the expensive leather. "She's basically homeless. It'll be hard to track her down. But it fits with my theory. Clara was just a means of getting the body onto me. It's easy to talk a junkie into committing a crime."

Ava handed Cecil a white velvet jacket and black jeans embroidered with a white stripe down the side. Then she plopped a bulletproof vest onto his lap.

"What is this?" Cecil asked.

"Perdonna being overprotective."

"You're not wearing one."

"I see a bullet before it even walks into the room," Ava said. "I can sniff guns. I was trained like a bomb-sniffing dog to detect firearms, bombs, and cocaine. When I was a kid in Pennsylvania my dad was a drug dealer. I had to know what was coming into the heroin den so we didn't get killed."

Cecil leaned back into the car seat. He rubbed his eyes long and hard. "Is that true?"

Ava scanned his eyes. "Does it sound true?"

Cecil shrugged and Ava gave a pleased grin.

"Where is Figaro?"

"Isn't safe enough for him. Perdonna's maid is bathing him in glitter dust."

Cecil changed into the outfit, and immediately felt like a glowing white polar bear. He looked out onto the dark streets of Manhattan where dusk was setting. Orange glowing lights lit up from carved pumpkins and plastic ghouls.

"Why a white jacket?"

"You have to stand out so the VD employee knows to get the files from you," Ava said. "You'll give them the empty folder, and I'll follow them."

Within minutes of them sitting in the car, cameras surrounded them. News reporters began popping up from behind apartment buildings.

"I think we're on foot," Cecil said.

They walked along Fifth Avenue in a mass of tourists and dinner-goers. The fast shuffle was something Cecil missed. He had to shove and jostle a crowd of one hundred strangers just to walk a block, but at least he could be close to people.

Central Park bloomed with autumn reds to their right. Fall trench coats and scarves were as abundant as the leaves. One white horse carried tourists in a canopied cart complete with fuzzy winter blankets.

Cecil locked eyes on the Apple store that rose from the cement in a glass cube. He sniffed as they passed hot dog stands and warm waffle carts.

And then there was the Peninsula Hotel. They rode the elevator up to Salon de Ming.

23

Smoke snuck up Cecil's nostrils and seeped into the waterline of his eyes as he stepped into Salon de Ming. The smell of simmering pork dumplings and jasmine fried rice mixed with flowery perfumes from Ami and Pierre Lazard. The Shanghai decor, in deep reds and golds, floated over the glowing lights of New York City's skyscrapers outside.

It was a glass bar on the top of the sky, a red bubble about to burst if it hit one of the towers surrounding it. This was the edge of luxury.

Cecil felt the sweat pooling around his shirt collar, making him itch. His watch felt heavy on his wrist. Atonal music from Asian stringed instruments came from behind a black curtain. They played as if they were out of tune, a dark medieval clashing of rattling chords.

Anyone in the room could've been VD—any girl applying red lipstick, any man with semen dripping from his fly. The woman playing a tiny harp could've used a string to slice his throat. His mind reveled in chaos.

People mindlessly Chattered about a movie star's latest social media post and complained about the prices of their new Ferraris. They gossiped about the *shalls* and the *shall nots*, the *haves* and the *have yachts*.

All couples in attendance were identical. The husband begged to leave. The wife showed off her new four-thousand-dollar breasts in a four-thousand-dollar Visage blouse. And the mistress counted her cash.

Cocktails seeped into the scene as fried rice sat half-eaten, pooling oil over napkins.

The sound of laughter competed with the atonal clashing of strings. It felt violent, threatening, as the crowd's collective rumbling voice stretched and crescendoed like a rubber band. A silent competition formed. Who had the skinniest woman on his arm? Whose business made more money? Whose husband or boyfriend had cheated less? These things, of course, were not being heard over the shrill laughter.

"Let's split up," Ava yelled over the noise.

"Wait. Where should I—"

She cut him off by twirling into the crowd with a grin.

He was overwhelmed by the delicious smells. The dreaminess made him squirm. The other diners seemed bored and blasé. Perhaps to them this was normal. Or maybe they were depressed.

He sat at a round black cocktail table that faced the stage. It was only then that he realized the portraits were hung upside-down. He cocked his head to look at George Washington, who was featured on an upside-down dollar bill painted red.

Black marble bookshelves hung from the ceiling, clinging to the walls. Except instead of books, they held liquor bottles backlit in indigo.

He was about to stand up and search when a woman dressed in a long black silk dress sat across from him at the cocktail table. "Is this seat taken?" she asked.

He quickly studied her. Could she be the VD liaison? Her curly hair was pulled into a tight bun. Her dark skin glimmered with gold glitter, and her eyes seemed to wink whenever she talked. She was tall and lanky, definitely the model type.

"I loved the snakeskin," she said, shuffling her shoulders. "You should paint me sometime."

She puffed on her vape pen and seductively pouted smoke into the air, draping her neck backward over her chair.

"You were at the Condon party?" Cecil asked, sitting up.

"I'm Freddy's sister, Tasha."

Cecil held out a hand. "I'm—"

"I know who you are," she said with a laugh.

She moved her chair closer to his and popped her legs up onto the cocktail table. Her Lazard heels glimmered in neon red. They were so long and thin they looked like daggers.

"Are you close with Freddy?" Cecil asked.

"Pft," Tasha scoffed. "Even asking that question is insulting. Of course not."

If the siblings were not close, it was possible Freddy didn't know Tasha worked for VD.

"What brings you here tonight, Tasha?"

"Work," she said with a flirty drawl. Her legs peered out from the slit of her dress, which clung to her like a nightgown. Lacy white garters wrapped around her upper thigh, clasping her flesh like a hand.

"What do you do?" he asked.

"I think it's obvious, isn't it?"

A waiter dressed in a white dinner jacket, almost identical to Cecil's, approached the table. "Anything to drink, sir?"

"A water, please."

"I have Acqua Panna, Perrier, Aquadeco—"

"Just tap water."

The waiter gave a quizzical glare.

"Bring him a Diet Coke," Tasha said with a smile. "And I'll have a Corpse Reviver No.2."

"Is that a real drink?" Cecil asked as the waiter turned away.

Tasha nodded, her chandelier earrings jingling around her neck. "You're so cute."

It was twelve minutes past eight. Cecil scanned the crowd, but no one was even glancing at him. Then Ava appeared over his shoulder and whispered something in his ear. "She has to be VD.

There's no one else here. Don't fuck this up." She scurried away without so much as another look to Tasha.

"Who's that?" Tasha asked.

"My...cousin."

Tasha gave a skeptical squint and laughed it off. "Whatever."

Cecil reached for his briefcase. "Should I give them to you now? Or should it be somewhere private?"

Tasha traced her fingers over Cecil's hand. "Payment can wait."

He jerked his hand away. "What is it you do for VD?"

Tasha laughed hysterically, twirling her feet about. She grabbed both of Cecil's hands and leaned in to him. "You don't know? I'm a prostitute."

The curtain lifted to reveal two beautiful ballet dancers. The man was bare-chested and wore skin-colored leggings, and the woman was covered in a nude leotard. Jazz replaced the strings, and suddenly the couple did modern ballet en pointe.

The muscles in his arms bulged as he lifted her, and she wrapped her legs around his chest, toes flexing with all their might. It was euphoric.

"But you're rich," he said. "Why are you a prostitute?"

"I charge six thousand an hour."

His jaw dropped and he sipped at the Diet Coke as his cheeks flushed.

"What? You think I'm not worth six thousand?" she asked, folding her arms over her chest.

"I think you're worth more than money," he said. "Everyone is."

The female dancer kicked her leg into the air and raised it to her ear. Her limbs made perfect lines, like the spokes of a wheel. The muscles couldn't have been more stretched, her feet more flexed, her knee more hyperextended. But it all looked simple above one dainty pink shoe.

Her back arched and the muscles of her neck rippled. The male grabbed her between the legs and raised her above his head, twirling her in the split position.

They were human bodies at their best.

"Did you have sex with that woman you painted?" Tasha asked.

"No," Cecil said, folding his hands beneath the table to check his nerves.

"I don't believe you. That woman was beautiful. One of the sexiest bodies I've ever seen. And I've seen *a lot* of bodies."

"I'm a monk."

"And I'm a neurologist. Doesn't mean I can't also be a lady of the night."

"Really?"

She sipped at her Corpse Reviver, polished fingernails wrapped around the centimeter-thin martini glass. Her fingers were so manicured there was not a single loose piece of flesh, not a single callous. It looked as if her hands were massaged in baby's blood everyday by a team of forty servants.

"I'm a genius or whatever," she said. "A prodigy kid. Graduated high school at twelve. Did a few PhDs. So now I spend my days helplessly watching kids die of muscular dystrophy, then I come out at night to play."

There was a red ball at the bottom of the cocktail glass. It looked like a heart with its throbbing bobs whenever Tasha twirled the glass in her hands. The white drink seemed to steam up to her lips. It must have been anti-aging like the Toasted Vanillas.

"I hold dying four-year-olds in my hands every day. Little Samantha sat on my lap today. She asked me if she would marry a prince when she grew up. She wanted a castle in France with croissants and snow and singing mice. In two years she won't be able to tell me her dreams because her mouth muscles will be too weak for her to talk. And in another two years she'll be dead. There's no Corpse Reviver for her..."

Tasha tipped her drink back and dangled her neck over her chair once again. She chugged the potent drink. "I used to cry every night. Now I embrace giving up my control. I love being a whore. You can buy me like a doll. Pay enough money, and I'm delivered to your door. Dress me up, do my hair, open me, and play."

Two new ballet dancers tiptoed onto the stage. The girl wore red lingerie and the man tight red spandex. Nothing was left to the imagination. Strobe lights flashed and big band music played. Drums from behind the stage rattled at a throbbing pace.

"Everyone is a prostitute. The difference between everyone else and me is that I know it and embrace it," Tasha whispered.

"I don't live for money," he said.

"You're after eternal life. You were promised heaven, so you showed up to an abbey, were dressed up, told what to eat, what to do, and followed all the rules. You're God's whore."

She puffed on her vape pen and blew the steam toward him. The little vapor trail smelled like fruit punch mixed with fried rice.

"Shouldn't sex be more than just fun? You should love the person. Sex leads to babies. It's about love and family and marriage and—"

Tasha stood up from her chair and straddled his lap. Cecil looked around but no one even gave them a second glance. She grabbed his hands and put them on her legs. She stroked them up her silken thighs to the rough white garters. The slit in her dress rode so high that her hip bone peeked out.

"How much does this cost?" Cecil asked sarcastically.

"You're right. But men do only fuck women they love," she said. "When they're with me, they're fantasizing about fucking the second grade teacher they loved. Or they're imagining I'm the woman who got away. They're dreaming of making love to the woman they love. It just so happens, the woman they love is almost never the one they're with."

The red ballerina spun in the man's arms, her hips swinging beneath his palms. She threw her head back, neck dripping with sweat.

"I'm the embodiment of men's fantasies. I'm the embodiment of your dreams... What's wrong with a little bit of fantasy?"

She wore a diamond and ruby choker necklace with her dad's name engraved on a gold plate. She ran her fingers over the necklace that dangled before his eyes. Her perfume smelled of absinthe. And hydrogen peroxide.

"It's the best sex in the world," Tasha said. "Men fuck their wives. But they make love to me."

Her hands gripped on to Cecil's and she pulled them to her ass. He quickly retreated. So she pressed her arms onto the back of his chair, leaning her chest toward his face. The drums crescendoed. He heard the lips touching every martini glass. He could hear all the tapping feet. The laughter. The flirtatious leg rubbing. The eyelashes rustling.

"I'm a monk. I'll say it again. I'm in love with God. I believe we're animals, yes. We have the potential to sin. But we should *strive* to be civilized. Strive to be excellent. Strive to learn. Strive to build real things."

He huffed his words in short, exhausted bursts. It was as if he had to convince himself.

"I'm in love with God too. He's an evil son of a bitch with a penchant for hypocrisy." She picked off her heels and threw them to the floor. "Only rarely does he make something beautiful, and I forgive him all over again."

Tasha flashed her brilliant teeth. Even the way she moved her wrists to the music was sexual. "Do you fantasize at the monastery? About fucking?"

"I block it out," Cecil said. "I fantasize more about pizza than sex when I'm at the abbey."

"What about in your dreams? Who did you think about when you painted that woman?" Tasha asked.

The male dancer heaved the ballerina over his shoulders and she wrapped her legs around his face. It was elegant. They seemed like one machine, sweating, flexing, pumping together. And yet, it was refined.

"If you do to me right now in public what you want to do to her," Tasha said, "I'll give you what you came here for."

"I can do anything I want?"

"Anything."

A chill came over him. Suddenly all the noise faded and only Tchaikovsky fluttered through his ears. The smell of absinthe melted into roses. He felt like he was floating.

He reached up to her bun and let her hair loose. The dark curls fell down her shoulders like a wave coming into shore. The room disappeared and all he saw were the flecks of blue in her brown eyes.

He pushed a strand of hair behind her ear and stroked the backs of his fingers over her cheek. He cupped her jaw and tenderly pulled her close to him. He warmly pressed his lips to the corner of her eye and lingered there, resting his head against her temple.

When Cecil finally pulled away, he noticed the tears streaming down her cheeks. Her lip quivered. "You love her. Whoever she is. You'll go to hell for *her*," Tasha said. "The deepest, darkest depths of hell. In fact, I think you already have."

A hand tapped his shoulder and suddenly the noise returned. The raucous music. The clanking glasses. Tasha jumped away and dangled herself over her own chair.

When he looked up, he saw neon pink hair and sallow heroin cheeks plumped with Botox. "I see the dweeb was too afraid to meet me."

It was Clara Royds.

"What are you doing here?" Cecil asked.

"I'm here to pick up files. I get the l—"

As the lull of the *L* rolled off her tongue, silence followed a loud boom. Blackness.

He closed his eyes and, in a split second, felt a bullet brush past his ear, not touching him. Screams. Dishes clamored to the floor.

Clara's body lay in blood before his eyes, skull cracked open and face plastered to the floor.

Shrieks, shattering plates clanging to the floor, feet pattering.

As soon as a door closed, a stampede of at least three security guards swarmed the bleeding body, pushing people onto the floor.

Red alarms went off, illuminating the bar, and Cecil could see couples huddled together, people sheltering under the bistro tables.

Cecil grabbed Ava from beneath a bistro table and ran out into the hallway.

"You didn't see *that* bullet before it entered the room," he said, hands still shaking.

Ava nodded. "I think they were aiming for you, but missed and shot Clara instead."

"That's comforting."

Hotel security guards ran by Cecil and Ava toward the sound of the gunshot.

"Why all the games, though? If VD hired a sniper to shoot me, why do it in a public place?"

"Maybe so people would *know* you were dead. We have to follow the body," Ava said. "If there's a chance it's VD, it's worth it."

She quickly pushed him behind a trash can when she saw hotel security coming toward her.

"Miss, have you seen a man in a white jacket, tall, brown hair?"

"No I haven't, but I'll keep my eyes open."

The guard nodded his head and Ava bent down.

"Why are they looking for *me*?"

Ava shrugged. "You were standing near Clara. Everyone could've described you as a possible suspect."

Her eyes quickly scanned the hallway. She eyed the dumpster behind her and took off the lid. "Hop in."

"You're kidding."

She pointed to a security guard coming off the elevator, and he vaulted over the lip of the bin. Ava covered him in rotting sushi, and he was thankful he couldn't see the dirty napkins he knew surrounded him.

Ava rolled the dumpster away, zigzagging him away from the chaos. Silence occupied the space until he heard the pounding boots of hotel security approaching. But just when he thought the lid would be lifted, he heard Ava say, "He ran toward the kitchen. I think he's hiding there," and the boots scurried away.

The dark trash lid opened, and Ava loomed over him. "Hurry up," she said. "And take off your white jacket."

A team of four medics and security guards wheeled out the body on a makeshift gurney, covering the girl in only a white sheet. Clara had a bullet wound to the head, the red gash seeping crimson dye onto the fabric.

"Is she alive?" a guest asked.

"Yes," the medic said. "Out of the way."

They seemed to carefully but frantically push the body into the elevator.

"We'll follow them down the other elevator," Ava said.

"No way."

"What do you want to do? Run down twenty-three flights of

stairs? That looks so suspicious. They'll think we both were the shooters."

His cheeks flushed. "So we just take the elevator to the lobby and run after an ambulance?"

Ava tugged him toward the elevator line.

In the crowd of crying, terrified people, Tasha was splayed on the floor.

"Medic, medic!" a man yelled. "There's another person sick." Cecil shoved Ava's shoulder and pointed to Tasha as a stranger propped her drooping, unconscious body up against the wall. He pushed her hair away and put his finger beneath her jawbone. "Hurry!"

"What's wrong with her?" Cecil asked.

"Passed out. Overdose? She was drunk out of her mind," Ava said. "Couldn't you tell?"

Cecil watched as a medic approached and heaved her onto a gurney. He wiped sweat from his forehead. "She practically convinced me to become a prostitute."

"Drugs can convince you of just about anything."

The elevator door opened, and people piled inside, mostly the drifters who hung around the crime scene to get some sneaky photos.

Ava didn't hesitate to push the lobby button.

They stopped at *20, 18, 14,* and finally *0.* For a moment, he felt as though the entire elevator would fall into the abyss just before they reached the lobby. The strange night seemed to lend itself to that possibility.

Ping. The doors opened and Ava stepped out.

Medics shuffled the gurney down a staircase decorated with giant green ferns and palm trees as Cecil and Ava crouched in a corner by the men's restroom.

Sirens called out like warning alarms, overcoming the dulcet tones of "Dance of the Sugar Plum Fairy." A Peninsula Hotel bellhop offered to help load the body, and a medic pushed him away, accidentally swiping off his golden bellman's hat. Pedestrians stopped on the street, waiting to see if the patient were an actor who overdosed on heroin or an elderly talent agent who broke his hipbone fucking a concierge.

While all eyes were focused on the gurney entering the ambulance, Cecil and Ava scurried out onto the pavement, feeling a gust of cold air bite their faces. Wind blew Ava's hair straight up and they had to blink furiously to keep their eyes from watering.

Not a single taxi along the avenue displayed a lit sign, and the cross street was blocked by NYPD vehicles and medics.

"We need to tail the ambulance," Ava said. "I can call an Uber?"

"No, that would take five minutes. By that time, the ambulance would already be at the hospital."

Ava pointed to the CitiBike station down the block. "We'll take a bike."

The doors to the ambulance finally closed and Cecil combed his hair back with a shaky hand.

The bike reeked of acrid body odor and hand sanitizer. When the ambulance sirens blared, Cecil awkwardly squatted on the seat. As soon as he kicked up his resting stand, the bike wobbled, threatening to knock him off.

He clutched the briefcase against his chest, grabbing only one bike handle.

A huge Coca-Cola billboard lit up the side of Ava's face in red.

"Neigh, horsey, neigh," she joked.

He gazed up at the Times Square Ball as the impressions of H&M and Buratti billboards flashed by his eyes. Fox News headquarters to his right, Donald Trump lounging in Trump Tower just above his head.

Most kids learned to ride a bike by a wooded playground or a suburban neighborhood with their father pushing them down the lane. No, Cecil learned everything with glaring billboard lights shining down on him and alarm bells scaring him away.

"Seems like a long way to the hospital," Ava said.

When Cecil looked at the street sign, he noticed they had already reached Sixty-Fifth Street.

"We've passed at least two hospitals by now," he said.

"Where do you think they're taking her?"

Then it hit him. When the ambulance turned off Madison Avenue and onto the cross street, he saw the writing on the billboard.

"They're taking her to Maddox Hill," Cecil said. "It's where my family doctor works."

24

Sirens quieted as the ambulance screeched to a stop at the edge of Maddox Hill Hospital. A striking woman wearing a fitted black lab coat, rushed toward it. She had silver hair that ran perfectly straight down her back like a sheath of metal. Standing at least six feet tall, she was practically a model herself.

The ambulance doors swung open, and a medic wheeled out a blue crash cart with a black hamper attached. He pointed to a black bag that partially popped out of the hamper.

The tall woman waved the crash cart to a gated door by the hospital and handed the medic a key. He wheeled the crash cart behind Maddox Hill as the woman put a phone to her ear. With a thumbs-up, the ambulance drove away, the original gurney still in the vehicle, no police force present.

"That's Clara in the crash cart, yes?" Cecil asked.

"You follow the woman," Ava said. "I'll follow the body. I know my way around a morgue."

The hospital lobby swarmed with old folks riding hazardous motorized wheelchairs, ramming into nurses and other patients. The place smelled of cafeteria hot dogs and cough syrup–stained latex.

Cecil had lost sight of the fancy lab coat, so his first instinct was to go after the one connection he had.

"Excuse me?" he asked at the front desk. "I have an appointment with Dr. Tibolt. Do you know which floor he works on?"

"You mean Dr. Imogen?" the desk clerk asked with attitude.

"No, I mean Dr. Tibolt."

"Are you purposely trying to be disrespectful?"

Cecil squinted and gave an assuaging smile. "I think we're misunderstanding each other. I'm looking for Dr. Tibolt. He's tall and a little chubby, very pale with dimples on his—"

The clerk slapped Cecil's knuckles with a *diversity and acceptance* pamphlet. "Sir, Maddox Hill is a safe space. We do not tolerate microaggressions from the cisgendered. Please leave."

"The what? What is a cisgender?"

"That's your problem, cis-het. Read your pamphlet."

Cecil snapped open the pamphlet to find a page with the words *SIZE ZERO* crossed out above a lecture on body image and photos of models, including Jordan. The dialogue encouraged readers to Tweet: #StopTheSkinny

Then he saw it. A photo of the tall woman above a paragraph on LGBTQ at the hospital.

Upon closer look at the photo, Cecil recognized Dr. Tibolt's dimples and evergreen eyes.

"Dr. Tibolt is a drag queen now?"

The desk worker pulled her tea bag out of her chai tea ginger latte and threw it across Cecil's white jacket. "Transgender woman! Goddammit. What, cis-hets can't even read?"

"I read the hashtag *Stop The Skinny*. But I'm not sure what I'm supposed to stop myself from doing."

"Stop existing."

"You're skinny," Cecil accused.

"You don't know how I identify from my image alone."

Cecil arched an eyebrow. "What *do* you identify as?"

"I have many identities."

"Oh," he said, putting his hands up. "I'm sorry. Are you schizophrenic? I didn't mean to offend you."

"No. You know what? No." She wheeled her chair away. "I'm not trained for this. Go see Dr. Imogen. She'll fix you. Sixth floor. Fitness and Wellness."

"Thank...*you*?"

"And don't ask something stupid like, 'Why do these girls think they're fat?' or 'Why don't they like food?' And don't tell them they look ugly."

"Don't worry. My mother's a model agent. I know how to deal with anorexics."

The girl's eyes lit up. "Really? That's so cool. I bet men give them everything they want, right? I've always wanted to be a model."

Cecil scoffed. But then a softening fell over the frustrated creases in his face. "You can't identify someone's happiness from image alone," he said, repeating her own words.

He took the elevator to the sixth floor, which blinded him with bright yellow walls and pastel cloud paintings.

Only two wings, the Fitness and Wellness ward, and a Psychiatric ward, surrounded a small lounge that held a vending machine filled with carrots, apples, and steamed quinoa. Water bottles and water fountains replaced Pepsi and Snapple vending machines.

Dr. Imogen seemed to be the only MD on the entire floor. And the framed artwork decorating the halls consisted only of paisley flower patterns and sketched cartoons of rainbow-colored animals.

Toward the Fitness and Wellness ward, the colors became brighter. The nurses had puffy lips and petite noses with their hair wrapped in braided buns. It felt artificial, like a hospital made in South Beach. Or Auschwitz. Even the plants were made of plastic.

But nothing was as troubling as the black plaque sitting at the entrance of the ward that read, Donated by the Patronage of Margaux LeClaire.

♎

Seven stories below, Ava's feet pattered down the cement steps to the hospital morgue. Unlike a "movie morgue," shot in sea-green blue with shiny freezer compartments and a melancholic violin in the background, the real morgue had sterile white lights and rubber beige body bags on freezer racks that looked like something out of an Amazon shipping warehouse.

The dead baby racks were labeled in Comic Sans, which was either a sick attempt to make a slaughterhouse look like a nursery or a tasteless joke. The coroner's birthday balloons were unbelievably attached to the foot of a body bag.

Ava's death fascination came to a halt. Where were the dissected organs floating in jars of formaldehyde? The glowing lights? The eerie doctor with necrophilia? That was what she came to see. She wanted the high fashion version of a morgue, one off which she could model her and Figaro's future home.

She put on a white lab coat, covering her black dress. When she turned the corner, a smell worse than a sewer made her gag.

"What is that?" she asked a coroner who stood before her, a woman with light blond hair and a naturally Glamorama-ready face.

"Decaying shit."

Ava peered at the table to see a male body ripped into six pieces, head crushed in halves.

"Poor guy ran in front of a moving train. I'm supposed to sew his body back together for the family. No one embalmed all the separate pieces properly, so shit has been decaying in his gut for two weeks."

"You're the student from Columbia, right? Pre-med?" asked the male mortician on the other table, working on the makeup and embalming of a once beautiful woman.

The mortician looked like a cocaine-snowman because he had covered himself in baby powder, presumably to block at least some of the smell.

When Ava noticed the black body bag in the corner with a crash cart beside it, she said, "Yeah. I'm the med student. Name's Bertha."

She put on latex gloves, and the coroner pulled a tendon in the corpse's arm to make the dead, purple finger beckon toward Ava like an earthworm humping the air.

"Come, child," the doctor said.

When Ava stood closer, she noticed that the coroner had scraped away liters of yellow, liquefied subcutaneous fat so she could make the corpse "skinnier." The oily, liquefied fat lubricated every surface—their gloves, shoes, coats. It even made the pages of an anatomy textbook translucent.

The coroner prodded a nerve near the eye socket with a scalpel and the eyes looked straight at Ava, swirling around as if the body had been possessed.

Ava gave an unimpressed look back at the corpse as if to say, *I look better dying than you do.*

"You'll get used to it," the mortician said. "Promise."

Ava pointed to the black body bag. "Why is that body not on the racks?"

"It just came in," the coroner said. "Her uncle called and he's coming by tonight to identify the body."

The mortician injected a red dye into the body's lips and brushed a mascara-like fluid over the eyelashes.

One body looked like spoiled clumps of meat from a slaughterhouse trash can, and the other looked like a camera-ready celebrity.

"Who is embalming really for?" Ava asked. "God? The dead person?"

"Brilliant question." The nerdy mortician clasped his hands together. "Some say embalming is for the family. The corpse, dressed and lively as it can be, gives a memory picture so relatives can cope with their grief and get over the denial of their loss by seeing that the corpse is happy, but not living."

Ava scoffed. "I think people are just superficial...even in death. They want to be as pretty as possible."

"We get special requests sometimes, left in wills. I've had dead people ask me to remove crow's feet, give them breast implants, do the nose job they've always wanted. People aren't so worried about money when they're dead," the mortician said.

The coroner pointed a blood-covered scalpel at Ava. "That's why I think the fashion industry is using these dead-looking, skinny models. Youth, death, beauty... They're all linked."

The adolescent, dying girl aesthetic was not a new trend.

Fashion was capitalizing on ideas as old as Plato: a love for beauty and youth, and a fear of death.

"Do you want to be embalmed or cremated?" the coroner asked.

Ava was lost in thought, eyes glazed over. "Oh, you're asking me?" She twirled her hair. "I'm sick. I don't want to celebrate my body. Before my body kills me, I want to throw it in front of a train and chop it up into ten pieces like that guy."

Just as the coroner's jaw dropped, a heavy knock came at the morgue doors.

A man with a Quirk Model Management briefcase stood in the entryway, holding a camera. Ava recognized him from meetings with Perdonna. He certainly wasn't related to Clara, but he could have been her "uncle."

25

Dozens of hospital beds were crammed into Margaux's Fitness and Wellness ward, not unlike LeClaire Model Management itself.

Skeletons slept on their gurneys. IVs and feeding tubes snaked into their bodies like an irrigation system. Sunken blue eyes and jaundiced skin peeked out from under the sheets. They slept because they didn't have enough energy to open their eyes. Under their beds, they hid fashion magazines and Dials for Instagram like teenaged boys and middle-aged husbands hid pornography.

The smell of bile wafted from the garbage can.

"Cecil," a croaking voice echoed from across the room, "did you find what you were looking for?"

Cecil turned to see Jordan's friend, one of the models from LeClaire Model Management, attached to an IV pole and shivering underneath her blankets. A yellowish rash crept over her neck and down her arms.

"Are you okay?" he asked.

"I'm fine, ignore the tubes. Size *double* zero. Better than ever."

"Your skin is jaundiced."

"Battle scars," the model said. "I'm tough enough to endure it."

"Were you anorexic before you modeled?"

The model stared at him with cloudy eyes. "Margaux recruited me from the hospital when I was sixteen. It was my first stay in an eating disorder ward. Margaux and Freddy stood outside the hospital with an LMM clipboard. When she came up to me, I was still attached to feeding tubes, still wearing a hospital gown, still in my wheelchair. She offered me a job as a model, said she preferred to get anorexic girls because she didn't have to spend the money to make them thinner."

"Excuse me?"

"It happened a lot. And obviously she had a lot of girls to send back to the hospital when they stopped eating more and more. So eventually she made a contract with Dr. Imogen, and now she owns her and this floor."

A sterile beige cubby of drawers held the pearls and Visage heels that once adorned the models. Now, instead of pearls on their necks, they had bloody holes where the tubes drilled into their airways.

"A model is supposed to make you happy, to make you buy things," the model said. "The more you buy, the better chance we have to survive."

He thought back to Jordan. Perhaps she was selling herself to him—selling herself to VD.

Gloomy clouds once hid behind Jordan's eyes, the same depression that spurred the happy exterior onward.

Margaux abused young women to the point of anorexia and depression, and she hid them in her own personal hospital wing.

Cecil scoured the beds, lifting sheets and growing queasier with each body he saw.

A wiry finger tapped his back, and he spun to see two sunken eyes shoot wide open. She didn't have the muscle to lift her arm more than an inch off the bed.

"You..." he said. "You look like a corpse."

"Thank you. I look like Twiggy now."

He saw a protein bar next to the bed. "Here. Eat this. Why would you want to do this to yourself? If this is what it's like..."

The girl collapsed against the bed with a frown. "My dad used to say I was ugly too."

"You're not ugly. No. You're pretty."

She climbed out of her hospital bed, wobbly. Neck unable to support her head, she used her hand to prop up her skull. "I've been practicing my poses."

Her knees buckled and she collapsed against Cecil.

"Uh-oh," she said.

Her heart monitor beeped louder and louder with the seconds, and she fell to the floor.

"What are you doing here?" the nurse asked Cecil.

"I work for Margaux. I was just checking on a few girls."

The nurse sighed, holding the model up with strong arms and checking her blood pressure. She shot something into the IV.

"Be more careful with them," the nurse said. "Tell Margaux they all need at least another two weeks before they can do editorial. And maybe a month or two before runway. She's in jail, I heard, so it should be easier for you to stall her."

He couldn't help his jaw from dropping. "You put these girls in front of cameras?"

The nurse laughed. "You're new, huh?"

Dr. Imogen knocked on the window outside, black lab coat glimmering like a runway piece. "I see you've found your mother's stable?"

26

Clara's "uncle" chewed bubble gum that stunk up the morgue. Spearmint and formaldehyde did not mix.

"Good evening," the man said. "My name's Maxwell Bourgeois. I was told you have one of my bodies...I mean girls." He tapped his thighs and made the *ba-dum-tish* sound while laughing at his own joke.

"Are you here to identify the body? You're a family member?"

The man flipped his Hermès briefcase to hide the *Quirk Model Management* engraved on the front. "Indeed, indeed. Clara's uncle. Ugh, this is all so heartbreaking."

"You work for Quirk Model Management?" Ava asked.

The corner of the man's mouth turned up. "I'm here to identify my niece's body."

"*And* you work for Quirk," Ava said.

"Who are you?" Maxwell asked.

"She's an intern," the coroner said. "I apologize for her behavior. She's meant to *observe only*." She pointed the scalpel at Ava with a warning look, but Ava hissed like a cat under her breath.

The coroner rinsed liquefied fat and skin fragments from her hands. No matter how much she shook her hair, bone bits stuck in the curls. She suited up in new gloves and wheeled the bagged body forward.

"Now, Mr. Bourgeois, I must warn you that the sight of a body, especially the body of someone you know, can be troubling. If you need a chair, TUMS, speak up. No need to protect your masculinity."

"I'll be fine, ma'am. I've seen bodies before."

She unzipped the body bag, and Ava guiltily stared at the red blood dripping from Clara's pink hair. It looked like maple syrup glazing cotton candy.

"That's my Clara," he said.

Bourgeois ran his hand through his luscious blond ponytail. He wasn't related to Margaux or Clara or Cecil.

"What a shame. I was sure Clara would show up tomorrow morning to tell me she bedded a photographer or movie director at the hotel overnight. Instead ... I'll never speak to her again," Bourgeois said.

"We're very sorry for your loss, Mr. Bourgeois. Thank you for coming here at such a late hour."

"Of course, ladies. But if I could ask a favor, would it be possible to steal your *intern* for a quick chat?"

♎

Atonal Eastern music played in a soft, meditative tone as jasmine incense burned inside black pots. Buddha statues bathed in fountains filled with rainbow bubbly water. And ivy branches swirled around posters that read, "Beauty Doesn't Matter" and, "Say No to Size Zero." The room felt like a trance, like LSD-induced hypnosis for teenaged girls. It was Dr. Imogen's office.

Dr. Imogen shielded her suspicious closet door with her whole body, arms stretched out across the length, while sipping a two-liter bottle of Diet Coke through a purple bendy straw to look more casual. Her eyes blinked rapidly as if she were trying to remove a loose eyelash, or trying to convince Cecil she was flirtatious and loving instead of malicious and calculating.

"Beauty doesn't matter?" Cecil asked. "I don't know if that's true."

"It's a phrase my patients use in therapy daily." Imogen sipped her Diet Coke, tapping her two front teeth on the plastic bottle. "After everything you've seen on the LeClaire ward, you still think it's okay to defend your mother's business?"

He noticed a shiny purple polish on Imogen's shaking fingertips. "We both wish beauty didn't matter," Cecil said. "But it does."

Imogen anxiously looked through a peephole in her closet door. "So which one sent you? The Cockatoo or the Eagle?"

"Excuse me?"

Imogen huffed. "Have you been sent to help me, or are you here to berate?"

"Here to help."

"So the Cockatoo," Imogen said. "But why *you*?"

Cecil hoped that Imogen's own panic would blind her from his pause. He had no idea who the Cockatoo was. Yet, he needed Imogen's trust if he wanted to see the body for himself. "Margaux is in jail," he said. "And on the corporate documents, she named me the president of LeClaire Model Management in her place."

He leaned back in the chair, ironic bird chirps and incense penetrating the stress in the air.

"You're really the new president?" Imogen asked, leaning over the table. "Where does Margaux store the model passports?"

"In the basement. In a room surrounded by photographs and a world map," Cecil said without missing a beat.

"What cellphone carrier does she provide the girls with?" Imogen asked.

"None. The girls aren't allowed cell phones… What is this? I have to pay the troll toll to cross the bridge? I get by if I solve three riddles? I'm your *boss* now. Do you think this is making a good impression?"

Imogen frowned with thick red lips. Her eyes traced the dripping condensation that coated the fountain, but her hand still held the closet door.

"One more," she said with a skeptical lilt, a menacing smile. "How many people has Margaux LeClaire killed?"

Cecil paused. In the past week alone, she could've killed at least Jordan and Annabelle. For all he knew, his mother's body count could've been off the charts.

"I don't know," Cecil sighed.

"If you're the president, you'll know." Imogen's hand tightened around the door handle.

"Directly or indirectly?" Cecil asked shakily.

"Directly. Come on, Margaux would've told her president her life policy."

Policy. The word *policy* was close enough to *morals,* and that might have been the only relieving word uttered in his entire stay in New York City. Margaux may have at least had one admirable rule in her code of conduct. "Zero? Margaux's never killed anyone."

"Oh, thank God," Imogen sighed, finally loosening her grip on the closet. "I'm sorry, it's just, Margaux always told me she wanted to keep you *away* from the business. And that asshole Freddy once tricked me for access. So you can imagine my surprise when it's *you* who comes to do the cleanup."

"Yeah." Cecil nodded wearily, imagining having to drag anorexic girls out of a hospital as the police burst in.

"Even though all of the LeClaire models usually get brought to Maddox Hill, I do expect a police interrogation in a few days. We need to clean up *now.*"

2 7

Drip. Drip. Drip. Water trickled from a crack in the morgue ceiling, spattering onto the metal carts. Maxwell Bourgeois led Ava to the staircase. She could smell the Pierre Lazard cologne seeping through his pores. They stood so close that his wispy blond hairs rubbed up against her cheek.

He stared at Ava as if she were a Weimaraner trying out for Best in Show. Swiftly, he tore the doctor's coat off her shoulders to reveal the black dress underneath.

"All dolled up, are we?" he asked. "You're not an intern, are you?"

"No, I'm not."

"Then what? A cancer patient whose dying wish is to visit the morgue? An anorexic visiting a dead friend?"

"I have sex with the bodies," Ava said without an ounce of sarcasm. Her big eyes stared straight up at Bourgeois's.

"Pretty and funny. How tall are you? Five-foot-nine? Five-eight? Eh, short, but doable." He lifted her chin and placed a finger gently on her nose. "Your eyes sell you best. So caramel, but so glacial."

He wrapped his hands around her rib cage, just below her breasts. To see her waistline, he pinched her ribs and cinched the skin. One hand snaked down her lower back and wrapped around the plush of her ass, shaking the cheek to make sure there wasn't too much fat.

She hid her eyes from his gaze.

"But you *are* sick?" he asked with a strangely churlish grin, bright white, perfectly spaced teeth glimmering. "You're sallow, smoky, like Marion Cotillard. You have the heroin chic look with none of the track marks."

"I'm sick. My former model agent drugged me to keep me thin past puberty."

"Oh, wow," he said, folding his hands together. "So you'd stay that thin forever? How lucky."

"Lucky?" Ava asked. "I'll probably be dead by fifty."

"But who cares? With me, you'd peak as a supermodel, enjoy a few years as the sexiest thing alive. You'd be famous until thirty, when most models die figuratively anyway. Why not die at your natural expiration date?"

He tugged her to the metal refrigerator that reflected her appearance back to her.

"I do recognize you. You modeled for Visage. Did a few *Glamorama* covers back in the day, right?"

"And I wore the skin coat. I model for LeClaire, but I'm fielding offers," Ava said with a proud head tilt.

"Oh, what a find *you* are."

His hands stroked over her sore collarbones. A pinky finger pushed her cheekbone, feeling nothing but skin on her bone. Ribs rolled against his fingertips like the bars of a summer grill. And even Ava looked at her own sharp jawline in the reflection—boxy, seemingly floating above her neck.

"How old are you? Seventeen? Eighteen?"

Ava looked away from her body, too afraid she'd hate herself if she inspected it a second longer. "So the peak of beauty is a dying girl. That's the end of civilization, I think."

"The skinnier the better," Bourgeois said. "As long as you're breathing and you can walk. The Asian customers respect hard work. They live to work. And Asians think skinny girls work hard to be skinny, and so they look up to them."

"I'm an ex-con. That's a shit-person. Not hardworking."

"But my clients don't know that," he said. "My job is to create a fantasy that anyone can buy into."

Ava thought for a moment. If she played into his hand, if he really wanted her to model, maybe she could get information in return.

"My idol is Annabelle Leigh. Could you make me as famous as her?"

"Are you always sarcastic?" Bourgeois asked with a nervous chuckle.

"I'm serious."

His boisterous expression faded into a mischievous poker face. "Absolutely. I'm glad you know your stuff. It's important for me to recruit girls who know the industry."

"I would consider working for VD," Ava said. "Only for VD. Do you have access to him?"

He bit down so hard it seemed his teeth would crack through his chapped lips. "Quirk works with VD all the time."

Ava gave him nothing but a blank stare.

And he handed her the card.

"Here's my phone number. There's a party in two days in Chelsea. It's a group of fashion people. We hate clubs, so we pick a random location. Diners, hostels, art galleries. Always at ten o'clock. If you show up, and you're a good girl, I'll take you to the VD casting."

"I'll think about it."

"The casting is for The Mall," Bourgeois said with raised eyebrows and a wink. She assumed he didn't mean *mall* in the typical sense. He grabbed her shoulders and leaned in, smelling of bourbon, and kissed both of her cheeks.

"Call me tomorrow morning." Bourgeois gave a scathing smirk. "I'll let you know the location."

When they separated, Ava realized that Bourgeois didn't leave toward the exit. Instead, he entered the now abandoned morgue.

Chatter from the coroner and mortician had been replaced by

the thrumming gurgle of refrigerator motors and pumps.

She found Bourgeois unzipping Clara's body bag. He raised the back of the gurney and propped the body into a lifelike sitting position.

Ava noticed that whomever shot Clara made a clean kill. The bullet entered through a small hole in her forehead, but the entire back of her skull had been blown to bits.

Bourgeois fluffed the remaining hair around her head. He dipped his finger in the blood at the back of her skull, which made Ava wince.

Then the unthinkable. He traced Clara's lips with her own blood. Lipstick.

With a brush from his pocket, he added blush to her cheeks. He found a piece of missing skin in the body bag and placed it over a gaping hole in the framework of her nose. A lacy pink glove was slipped onto her right hand, hiding the purplish pallor.

Like a sleeping doll, the body posed with a lacy hand beneath her chin.

No matter how he adjusted her, bending the limbs like a broken marionette, she sagged and fell limp to the gurney.

Rigor mortis hadn't yet taken her.

With several flashes of the camera, he shot photos of the dead body.

The eyes were marbles, reflecting the sterile lights of the ceiling but lacking the spark of a soul. The skull threatened to cave in at any moment, turning her face to mush—mouth consuming her nose, eyes falling out of her head. Clara's skin had turned a beige cellophane, and her purple veins crept through like spider legs. Yet with her bloody lips and blushed cheeks, she still had her youth.

He removed the cloth from her chest, laden with goosebumps and a scattered painting of blood. Red droplets painted over the bruises on her breasts, the scars on her stomach.

Snap, another photo.

The body was the masterpiece of a serial killer, the product of luxury.

Ava felt queasy, not only from the smell of formaldehyde.

It seemed Clara Royds would not receive respect in life nor in death.

The famous cousin of Cecil LeClaire now sat in a morgue, rotting, untagged, without glamour, without a shot of vodka in her hand, without ever walking the red carpet.

♎

Dr. Imogen approached the closet door in her office with three separate keys on three separate Native American dream catcher rings. She opened each lock like a prison guard entering solitary and entered a passcode onto a touchscreen.

"What are you hiding in there? A freezer full of heads?" Cecil asked.

Imogen didn't laugh. She cracked open the door to reveal a plastic surgeon's office. The space was even larger than the anorexia ward. Dim red lights shone down on modern waterfalls that lined the wall like oversized sconces. Faux leather covered the gurneys, and many of the medical utensils were made of rose gold. A marble desk sat in greeting with shiny black mannequins on either side, saluting to visitors.

Gold placards with the names "LeClaire Model Management," "Quirk Model Management," and "IMR Models" sat beneath the photos.

"What the fuck is this?"

"A surgical suite for my, or shall we say *our*, VIP clients."

Framed photos of Jordan Jones, Anastasia Mondo, Jorelle Corbin, and Karolina Krün walking the runway in sheer black Visage gowns, hip bones jutting out from underneath the dress slits, lined the hallway.

"Will I need to bribe Maddox Hill to make sure they continue to support LeClaire Models being here?"

"Your mother is a major donor. Maddox Hill prefers not to send its employees up here to investigate. Especially now with the body from Salon de Ming downstairs, they don't want to know."

Copies of Leonardo da Vinci's *Vitruvian Man*, mathematical models of the human body, decorated the hall. Golden ratio. The height of a model's front teeth should be 1.618 times the height of each tooth.

"I lied about beauty being subjective," Imogen said. "I just say that to get the models to eat... Now, I need you to help me bring all of my surgery records downstairs."

On photos of Imogen's plastic surgery samples, Cecil noticed intricate stitching around the nose and brow line. The embroidery itself was beautiful, as though it belonged on an Ami coat.

"Detective Roosevelt mentioned that the stitching on Annabelle's body was medical stitching," Cecil said.

Imogen shrugged. *"Of medical quality.* They assumed your cousin did the skin coat as her *masterpiece."*

"We both know that isn't true. Clara barely had the mental capacity to remember her own name."

"You think *I* sewed Annabelle's skin together?" Imogen asked. "That *I* paraded the body for Visage? For Margaux? I wouldn't do such a thing. I hate your mother. She just pays my bills."

"Fine. Then who killed Annabelle? Was it VD?"

"No."

"You say that pretty confidently. How are you sure?"

"I'm sure," Imogen sneered.

"Did Clara?"

"No."

Cecil paused. "Did *you?*"

"No!"

Cecil's eyes locked onto Dr. Imogen. In the past, she was the person who had touched his body, who had kept him healthy his entire childhood. The person who had given him physicals and throat examinations.

"You were the one who confirmed that the body on the runway was Annabelle Leigh's. Did you do this through DNA analysis? Blood samples?"

"Yes."

"But..." Cecil sighed, feeling his head spin. "But why would you have blood samples *stored*? And she was never sick."

"But she was injured. You remember," Imogen said. "It was that Fourth of July in the Hamptons. Clara pushed Annabelle off the stage after she sang the national anthem."

"She fell off the stage," Cecil said.

"If that's how you'd like to remember it, then so be it," Imogen said. "After Clara pushed Annabelle, she went to the kitchen and tried to kill herself by cutting."

Cecil's face screwed up, and his jaw clenched. "Either way, Annabelle broke her wrist," he said. "You didn't draw blood."

"Yes, I checked calcium levels."

"I came to the hospital with you. There was no blood drawn."

Then he noticed something that didn't belong. On a medical tray, there was a set of gelatinous blobs meant to be nipples. But Cecil had learned that high fashion models were flat-chested. A bottle of body glitter sat next to them. Fashion models were pale. Their breasts couldn't grow beyond an A-cup.

"Cecil? Is there a problem?"

His face went blank. He walked toward a cart of silicone implants. Behind it, a black sheet covered a countertop.

Cecil whipped the black cover off. Polaroid snapshots of the girls—their bare, childish faces—sat next to magazine tear sheets from *Glamorama* and *Fashion Weekly*, which sat next to Polaroids of their spread legs, thin underwear barely covering them.

"It's not child pornography. It's medicine," Imogen joked.

There was one lone photo, without a headshot or tear sheet. A mole sat on the inner left thigh. He knew that mole.

"Vaginal reconstruction?" Cecil asked knowingly. "Why does it matter what models look like naked?"

The pieces had come together. Annabelle working in Shanghai. The lingerie photos VD shot. The hymen replacements. The breast implants. It all made sense.

He covered his face, leaning against the countertop. "I guessed some models were involved in prostitution, but I assumed it was by choice. Though, the girls' ages, they're too young. They come here thinking they'll be rich and famous but—" He paced the room. "It's sex trafficking."

"You didn't know?" Imogen kicked over a rack of bloody Louboutins. "You said you were president! Margaux's going to kill me."

"I am president, legally, just not officially. I'm here to find out what happened to Annabelle."

"You always have been an uncontrollable little bastard child," Imogen said.

"Prostituting these girls is despicable. They're innocent. They're so young."

"It is. I agree. But it's not my choice. Hedge fund managers aren't paying to fuck regular schoolgirls on the Lolita private jet. They're paying for a brand name, *high fashion models*. A girl opens the Visage runway show, that's twenty thousand to fuck her. The Bugatti and Lamborghini of pussies. A man doesn't want to fuck a whore. He either wants to fuck his mother or his daughter. Modeling caters to those who want the daughters."

"This is the 'side' business VD works on?" Cecil asked.

"Girls who don't bring high enough returns for the modeling agencies are sent to work in the sex industry. Top models are sent to fuck occasionally for the premium clients—Wall Streeters, movie producers, politicians."

"So let me get this straight," Cecil whispered, feeling his throat tighten up. "My mother sent my first love into prostitution?"

"*Sex slavery*...is more accurate. Fucking an abducted girl is a fantasy, like fucking JonBenét."

Cecil kicked the cabinet hard and tossed all the photos to the ground.

His eyes didn't leave the scalpel resting on the cart until he lifted it toward Imogen. Without thinking, he rushed toward her like a bull and pressed the knife to her neck, trapping her.

Jasmine incense and hairspray were mixed with the scent of fear.

"You're a monk," Imogen said. "What are you going to do?"

Cecil shaved hairs off her neck with the scalpel. A little pressure, a little tap of the blade tip. The scalpel nicked Imogen's skin.

"You don't have the strength to kill me," Imogen chided.

His eyes seemed to shake, hands gripping Imogen so hard he

might as well have broken the bones.

Slash. Blood dripped in slow drops. It splashed to her skirt. Imogen twirled the curly tips of her hair, and her lower lip trembled.

"I don't do this for Margaux...the genital plastic surgery," Imogen whispered. "She only fixes noses and faces on her models."

"Who killed Annabelle?" Cecil asked.

"I can't tell you that."

"But you *know*," he said. "You faked the DNA results, didn't you? You didn't have Annabelle's blood on file to identify the Visage skin coat."

"I had other means of identification," Imogen said, her eyes glittering like a coquettish teenage girl.

Cecil gripped her wrist and held the scalpel above her hair. "What identification?"

"I won't say."

Cecil grabbed his own Dial. He tried to message the police, but Imogen stepped on Cecil's foot.

"You don't want to do that."

"Why not?"

"I've been helping your friend escape," Imogen whispered. "I've been doing a good thing. If you call the police, she won't be able to escape."

She pointed to a red closet. Cecil tentatively opened the door and found a cheap blue cooler along with designs for the potential skin coat covered in oily fats.

"Open it," Imogen said.

A corpse sat cut to bits on ice. Feathers and sequins, rope and stitches covered the guts that fell out of the body. Purple Sharpie indicated lines where skin should be removed.

They were the remains of the corpse after the Visage skin coat had been made. But the body was male. The body was not Annabelle Leigh's.

"You faked Annabelle's death." Cecil gasped for breath as he leaned against the doorframe. "She's still alive."

28

Cecil took Imogen's Diet Coke out of her hand, and he chugged the rest of it. His hand shook as he held the bottle to his neck, trying to cool down as his heart throbbed in his chest.

He heard the muffled cries from a girl in the anorexia ward—resigned, prolonged whimpers. He closed his eyes and imagined Annabelle lying on the gurney. She was a doll—fucked, broken, and refurbished in a consumer's cycle. He feared that when he saw her in person, he would turn her head for a kiss and two beady, lifeless doll eyes would replace her caramel hues, and a line of crude stitching would replace her lips.

"Are you okay, Cecil?" Imogen asked.

"Why fake her death? What happened?"

"Look, I've changed. I'm not the man who I was. Ever since I became Imogen, I got nicer."

"You call *this* nicer?"

"I do the plastic surgery reluctantly to pay the bills… I do the anorexia ward to help the girls. They would die if they couldn't come here. I helped Annabelle too." Imogen nervously rubbed at her eyelashes, pulling apart the hairs that stuck together from her mascara. "She had just returned from several grueling years in Shanghai when I met her. You have to prove yourself there first, get training in modeling and in sex, before you work in New York.

"VD's assistant, an agent from Quirk Model Management, called to say he had an injured girl. High profile. They said no nurses could see us bring her in or out of Maddox Hill.

"In came Annabelle Leigh. She had a compound fracture to the collarbone, two broken ribs, and chlamydia. And even then, she had that confident look.

"She wasn't afraid to tell me that your mother orchestrated the abduction. She told me she was a slave. And I couldn't save her. No one could. Not even the police. I thought at first that she was simply paranoid, maybe insane. But I kept in contact with her.

"Because of Annabelle's fame, she couldn't model for major fashion brands. But in the sex market, a famous child abductee can bring in big bucks. She's smart. She bargained with clients. You could whip her until she bled if you gave her a cell phone. And she blackmailed employees for higher positions in the agency, hoping that with more power, she could escape. But more and more it seemed impossible.

"If she escaped, she'd have evidence to put Margaux and VD in prison. And the entire fashion industry would fall under legal scrutiny. She could only escape if I helped fake her death. As you know, we succeeded, except for the framing element. We intended to implicate Margaux and Clara. And Annabelle was supposed to take care of VD, but she failed. Now she's trapped, and I've lost contact with her."

"Trapped? Where? She never told you who VD was?"

"VD works from behind a curtain, like the Wizard of Oz of model trafficking. Annabelle didn't know who he or she was."

Cecil threw a scalpel across the room, and it snagged on the curtain and slid down the fabric, creating a gash. "How do I save Annabelle?"

"I don't know if you can save her, but all of the girls are showcased in an event called 'The Mall.' This is Annabelle's last year."

"Where is it? And what is it, exactly? I'm guessing it's not *actually a* mall?"

Imogen rolled her eyes. "It's usually on October 30th. That's all I know." She walked to her refrigerator, hips swaying underneath the dress. She pulled out another Diet Coke and handed it to Cecil.

"I just don't know what to do next," he said.

"Find VD and kill him."

29

Everyone lost himself in Manhattan. Whether he was lost in a celebrity apartment tour or in the winding rambles of Central Park. Whether he lost himself among the cookie-cutter Ferragamo scarves on Fifth Avenue or the commercial molds of skyscrapers.

New York City was bigger than itself. It was a brand, not accounting for the fact that fresh air in Manhattan smelled like body odor and stale garbage. Not accounting for the shop on Thirty-Fourth and Second Avenue that made ice cream designed to look like poop. Not accounting for the homeless man at the Sixty-Eighth Street station who wore Mickey Mouse ears and sang "Black Skinhead" a cappella.

Cecil never saw stars in the black Manhattan sky, only a bright moon called *the light at the top of the Empire State Building.* And a sun called *the New Year's Eve Ball.*

Matter did not exist in that galaxy called New York City. Anyone could hide within the towering, concrete plumes—even Annabelle Leigh.

It was half past ten o'clock.

Wind bit at his face and autumn leaves stuck to his coat. Billion-dollar glass skyscrapers towered high above, penthouses lit in golden hues. Manhattanites rode the ticking clock of short-winded elations, of false desires and deluded aspirations. Women paraded sculpted hair and Tiffany diamonds, while sugar daddies carried their shopping bags. Images of solemn fashion models towered twenty stories high with lavish hair and perfect skin.

Madison Avenue had one insurmountable power—through a single store window, it could display everything that America held dear: money, sex, and Christmas.

The street level of Manhattan reveled in consumerism, in superficiality. But as you climbed the skyscrapers, the more money you found, the more intelligence you gained, the more corrupt you became.

The trees lining the Park Avenue partition lit up in twinkling lights. Yellow taxis buzzed at one another like bees. The Milky Way, an avenue of blurring lights.

Then the cars dispersed as if into a black hole. NYPD vehicles casually slid into place along the cross streets.

A tourist who wore a camouflage vest and a burly beard walked near Cecil with his daughter. "Is that a Christmas pageant? Already? At this time of year?"

The man pointed to a series of flashing lights near Sixtieth and Park Avenue. Eight motorcycle outriders flanked a white Mercedes-Maybach S600 Stretch. A stout NYPD Dodge Charger flashed blue disco lights. Black Escalades and Suburbans flashed suppressive red lights and drove in a slow, parade-like military fashion.

"That white car. Santa Claus is in there?"

"No. A Middle Eastern sheikh," Cecil replied.

The man's face screwed downward. Six machine guns pointed out of the open Escalade windows. More NYPD Chargers joined the motorcade that spread four city blocks. The flashing lights did seem like a Christmas parade, when in fact, it was a show of military strength.

The man's face turned red, and he held his daughter's hand tightly, hiding her behind him. "Just like home, eh?" he joked.

Cecil froze. "Yeah." He robotically chuckled. Motorcades and diplomats were once a normal part of life for Cecil, like seeing the mailman or garbage truck. "Actually, I grew up here."

"I'm sorry to hear that." He flashed a sympathetic pout. "But looks like you turned out okay anyway." The man awkwardly tipped his hat and shuffled away. "Merry Halloween."

When Cecil watched the convoy, he imagined Annabelle lounging casually on top of the Mercedes-Maybach, a mojito in her hand, blues and reds lighting her bruised face. Even with armored cars and machine guns, safety wasn't guaranteed.

How lonely Cecil felt. He existed on an island, Manhattan. An island that three billion dreamed of living on, but only one-point-six million did. A place where lost souls could hide from one another and themselves among the world of show business.

He checked his watch. He had messaged the update to Perdonna. Annabelle was alive and held captive by sex traffickers.

♎

Ava messaged him to meet at the Carlyle Hotel.

Bemelmans Bar at the Carlyle Hotel upheld the classic New York City that Frank Sinatra lamented. A time when cocktail parties were a way of life, and white-glove service seemed a beautiful necessity. When women wore pearls to lunch, and men smoked cigars in a languid haze. When barstools were made of leather, and the Gershwin played "My Funny Valentine"—softly, so you could hear your lady speak. Lights shone a dark golden hue. There was no place like Bemelmans. It made Manhattan magical again.

The bar was named for Ludwig Bemelmans, the author of the children's books about the French orphan, Madeline. Murals of Bemelmans's ice skating elephants, Christmas villages, and picnicking bunny rabbits were sketched in gold over the walls. Carousels, striped parasols, and magical forests adorned lampshades. Illustrations collided with chocolate-brown leather banquettes and a twenty-four-karat gold-leaf-covered Art Deco ceiling. The characters provided a warm touch to an otherwise burdensome amount of extravagance. It was decorousness and whimsy, childhood cracking through adulthood. A family-friendly watering hole.

Sentimentality dripped from the dulcet notes of the piano as Cecil crunched into salty cashews and downed an entire glass of Perrier with mint. He felt guilty about the mint.

There was a cold rush down his throat. How he dreamed of a cigar at that moment.

He closed his eyes, feeling the cool marble of the bar against his palms. The music felt like cashmere to his ears. Rich, oaken perfumes and apple tart.

Then his mind wandered, and he felt a frail hand on his neck. A warm breath tickled his ear. "There lived twelve little girls in two straight lines... The smallest one was Madeline."

He turned to see Ava with smeared red lipstick and wild, frizzing hair. She blended in with the illustrations, stick arms and anime eyes.

Ava sat at the bar, below the illustration of Madeline and her school friends in blue coats. "The police are trying to find us. To question us about Clara's shooting."

"NYPD wouldn't dare disturb Bemelmans, not even to catch Harvey Weinstein." He shook his head. "It's sacred."

"Okay, so I was looking at my footage. I think that sniper at Salon de Ming was shooting for you and missed. It doesn't make sense that VD's men would want to take out their own liaison."

"That would make sense."

"But, I have good news to counterbalance."

"At least one of us does."

"I know how to get to VD. A model agent named Maxwell Bourgeois came into the morgue to identify the body and—"

Cecil cut her off. "Does this Bourgeois happen to work for Quirk Model Management?"

"Yeah. How'd you know?"

His eyelids drooped. "Keep going."

"Bourgeois wants me to model. He says I can get to VD if I make it through casting for this thing called The Mall." Her eyes lit up. "We'll prove you're innocent, find Annabelle's killer." Breath caught in her throat when she saw his hands quaking. "What's wrong?"

His gaze traced over her delicate neck, the soft bridge of her nose, and the tender bones of her breastplate, framed by the black dress.

"Stop it. I'm the only one who can be silent for multiple seconds at a time," she said. He folded her hands into his palm like a cradle. Pulse bursting through her fingertips, she slithered her hand away from his. "What?"

"We don't have to find Annabelle's killer anymore."

"You know who it is?" Ava asked, tossing multiple peanuts into her cheeks like a chipmunk and crunching down on them. "What? They're free. I have to eat the whole bowl."

"Annabelle's alive. She's trapped, being held prisoner. She's going to be in 'The Mall' in three days. Whatever the hell that means."

Ava twisted her red watch and typed into her palm to Perdonna. She didn't show any sympathy. She didn't even bother to show any emotion on her face whatsoever.

"That was the good news," Cecil said.

"And the bad?"

"VD works in sex trafficking."

Ava's face paled to such a white that she seemed transparent, dissolving back into the mural behind her.

"I should've known," Cecil said. "It explains why some models are so valuable, why they have to be illegally shipped in from Brazil, why they have to look like twelve-year-olds—Saudi billionaires and financiers will pay top dollar for young virgins.

"And because she graced *Fashion Monthly* in a twenty-thousand-dollar gown, they can say to themselves, 'I'm not fucking a whore, I'm fucking a luxurious, high fashion model.'"

Ava grabbed a handful of peanuts and tossed them into her mouth. She tilted her head toward the barman. "Can I have a Corpse Reviver?" she asked.

"ID?"

Ava shook her head. "No one cards me when I have my rat." She put her feet up onto the bar counter in retaliation.

"Do you think Annabelle's okay?"

"No. Not even remotely."

The jazz singer began Frank Sinatra's "Strangers in the

Night," accompanying the chipmunks making snow angels on Cecil's coaster.

"Now would be the time to lie," he said. His fingers traced the dewdrops that clung to his refreshed Perrier glass. He popped them, little balls of water exploding in his hands.

"Annabelle's best hope in there is dying. She probably tried to kill herself a few times. Not a very successful chick, apparently."

He gave a hooded glare. "You don't know what it's like there."

"Wanna hear a story?"

"Is it *The Lion King*? *Sleeping Beauty*?"

"Hey, don't knock my stories." She grabbed the lime from Cecil's Perrier and squirted it in his face. "You have Bible stories, I have Disney stories. Both teach morality. Both teach how to survive. Get off your high horse."

"What's the story?" he asked, still wiping lime juice from his eyes.

"There was this little girl called Bertha. It was October the second. It was her sixth birthday. Six is a big deal. Obviously. It's like that birthday you remember, you know? So she wakes up, and she hops off her mattress. The house smells like sugar cookies.

"But then she realizes her mom isn't actually baking sugar cookies. It's the plug-in scent diffuser called 'A Child's Wish' by Yankee Candle. So there's mild disappointment for a minute.

"It's okay, though. Because she's got a *birthday girl* party hat all ready to go from her kindergarten teacher. And she's super excited about this hat because her teacher remembered she liked puffins. And there are golden puffins on this hat. GOLDEN puffins.

"So, Bertha asks her mommy, 'Is there presents?' Mommy says no. Bertha cries. She has those big round chubbsy cheeks. So, hysterical tears are bouncing off cheeks that look like baby butt cheeks. It's important to know that to get an accurate idea of how sad this was."

"Tears bouncing off butt cheeks. Got it," Cecil said.

"BABY butt cheeks," Ava corrected. She sat up on her stool and wrapped her legs around for stability. "Bertha's mom has like overly greasy mop hair that sticks to her face. And she wears a giant sweatshirt for most of the day. She's the villain here.

"'Shut the hell up,' Mom says. But when it doesn't work, she adds, 'Your dad's coming to meet you. He'll have a present for you.'

"'Ahhhhhhh,' Bertha screams. I mean she SCREAMS like a cow. This child *cries* she's so happy. Children don't cry from happiness very often. This one did.

"She asks in this cute little pleading voice: 'I'm gonna get to meet my daddy?' She's still screaming.

"'Yeah. But you ought to be nice to him, hear? He might not love ya if you're a brat to him like you are to me,' she says. 'You gotta do your hair all nice. And put on that new Old Navy dress I bought you. With the polka dots.'

"So Bertha's heart is pumping. She might as well be loaded on Pop Rocks at this point. She puts on this pink dress with polka dots. There were new barrettes and ponytail holders in the bag. Which she was really excited about. She tried for forever to make her hair into braids. So she went with pigtails.

"'Mommy, is there gonna be a cake? Or cookies? Or ice cream?'

"'Can't afford that shit,' said mom. She was watching *Golden Girls* for the seven hundredth time on their brand-new television. Bertha and mom lived in a trailer.

"So Bertha pouts, but she climbs onto the kitchen counter. The whole kitchen is like a stale yellow wood. She gets up there, and she empties the cabinets. There are M&Ms, potato chips, cigarettes, gummy bears, leftover mashed potatoes, and a bottle of ketchup. She takes a Fisher-Price plastic blue hammer and smashes those M&Ms into bits. She kneads apart the gummy bears with her sticky little fingers. The gummies mixed with potato chips and potatoes and crushed M&Ms.

"On the top, she wrote *Welcum Hoom Daddy*. The only thing she spelled right was Daddy. And the only reason she spelled it right was because all she wrote about in kindergarten was about missing her daddy.

"Bertha stuck a cigarette in it as a candle. Boom. She put the cake beneath her bed. She wanted to surprise him.

"'You gotta let him hug you,' Mommy said. 'You can't do this no I'm-too-cool act you do with me. You gotta curtsey to him. Be sweet. Don't be a bitch. Ya hear? Be Sleeping Beauty, not a dumb bitch.'

"So then he rides. It's a dirt path along the woods. He rides up on a motorcycle. Bertha thinks that's pretty cool. Her little hands were suctioned to the windows. She almost broke her nose trying to push out.

"He lifted off his motorcycle helmet. He was young, like her mom. With a goatee and a cool buzz cut. Bertha ran to get her cake.

"She lit the cigarette candle with her mom's lighter. She carried the ketchup-laden *Welcum Hoom Daddy* cake toward them, running with excitement. Smoke filled the air and mixed with 'A Child's Wish.'

"And then Mom grabbed the cake out of her hands and threw it onto the floor. The concoction spilled all over the carpet, and the cigarette smoke snuffed out beneath gummy bears and moldy mashed potatoes.

"'What the hell is that?' Mom said. 'You're embarrassing. How stupid are you?'

"Bertha tried not to cry. She bit her bottom lip. That's what she always did. She bit her bottom lip until her outer pain was bigger than her inner pain.

"'Hey there, little one,' Daddy said. And then in that minute, it didn't even matter. Bertha was the happiest Bertha alive. Her daddy picked her up in his arms and spun her around in circles.

"'You excited for our fun time?' he asked her.

"Those baby butt cheek cheeks puffed out like frickin' tomatoes. Her pink dress flailed all around her.

"'Do you have a present for me, Daddy?' Bertha asked.

"Daddy looked to Mom. 'You told her I was her dad?' he asked.

"Bertha thought that was weird. But she didn't really care. She was too happy to have her daddy there with her. 'Present?' Bertha liked presents.

"'I got something, but you gotta do something for me first. We're gonna go outside and have some fun. Give your mommy time for herself.'

"Daddy gave Mommy a one-hundred-dollar bill. And they were out of the trailer. He took Bertha down into the woods. He asked her to show him how she skipped. They danced together.

They played Ring Around the Rosie on the way to the woods. And then he put down a blanket.

"'Do you like kissing?' Dad asked. 'Do you have crushes on any boys in school?'

"'My teacher Miss Cynthia kisses my head,' Bertha said. 'Every day before I go home.'

"'Do you like it?'

"'A whole lot. Miss Cynthia's my favorite person in the whole wide world. Well, except for you, maybe.'

"Then he rubbed his hands together. Fast and with a ton of power. An excited adrenaline rush. It scared Bertha a little. 'Well, I'm gonna kiss you on your head too,' Daddy said. 'And between your legs.'

"For the next hour, Bertha bit her lip. She bit her lip so hard there was more cut than lip. He gave her a present, though. A Tootsie Roll. But you know what the saddest part was?"

Ava looked to Cecil, whose veins were popping out of his forehead. He didn't move an inch of his body. A hundred people were gracing an elegant jazz bar, clanking glasses, singing songs, and he didn't hear a beat of it.

"The saddest part was she couldn't even eat the Tootsie Roll. Because her jaw was broken."

Cecil put his hands over Ava's, but she pulled away with a quizzical look. "That story is about you, isn't it?"

"No. It's from a novel."

"What novel?"

"I don't remember the name of it. It's a Chinese novel, I think. Or maybe a Russian one. Those Russians are dark bastards. The book follows her whole life. She wants to be rich and famous. Because then she won't have to smell the earthworms and the fish gut soil."

Cecil leaned back. He had never trained as a priest, but he occasionally shadowed classes in the seminary school. He had heard many people tell horrific stories. But it bothered him how many tiny details she remembered.

"I told you because... You gotta know what Annabelle's going through. This isn't CSI sex trafficking. Or a television special. You have to know the emotions. It's not the raping that's the torture. It's the slavery. As a kid, Bertha didn't have any rights. She couldn't protect herself. She didn't do anything wrong. Her mother was her slave owner."

"How does that story make *you* feel?" he asked.

"I think about it a lot. I always have the same question," Ava said. She sucked on the lime from Cecil's Perrier. *"Why was Bertha worth a hundred bucks and a Tootsie Roll to that Stranger Man, but she wasn't worth it to her mom?"*

Ava's fingers toyed with her hair, and she stared off at a painted elephant, wearing pointe shoes and twirling on a tricycle. Her jaw seemed to unhinge itself as she inhaled deeply.

"Quirk Models is awful," Ava said, changing the subject. "Their 'Margaux' is called Andre Blancas. Except he's much worse."

"Worse? How? Have you met him?"

A little girl sat only two feet away, sitting on a woman's lap, crunching peanuts in her mouth and sipping a pink Shirley Temple. Ava stared at her with that wicked vacant expression on her face.

"He was my agent...from when I was a kid. From before I went to jail."

"Could he be VD?"

Ava took a Corpse Reviver from the person beside her and guzzled it. "You better pray he isn't VD."

"Why?"

"He's a monster." Ava scrunched up her nose and squinted her eyes like an anime character. "And I love him."

Cecil caught the illustration of an adorable hippopotamus floating away with a bunch of balloons.

Ava took the last swipe of salted peanuts from a golden bowl. "I'll pretend I want to model for Quirk. That will be our way into The Mall."

"If we send you to VD, we'd be sending you into hell. You could be killed."

"I've been through worse," Ava said.

3 0

"Did you ask Perdonna if I could stay here?" Cecil asked as he stood outside her mansion. Bouquets of white macarons sat in the windows, the smell of buttered brioche seeping through the door. Perdonna demanded that the house smell of lemon, sugar, crêpes, and vanilla. Scents served as her inspiration, but she hated the artificiality of candles. Immacolata warmed lemon juice and sugar in crystal bowls with vanilla extract in every room.

This was home.

"Believe me, *you* have an open invitation. At any hour," Ava said.

The door swung open, and Immacolata, Perdonna's most trusted servant, stood in the entryway. "Señor LeClaire!" she exclaimed, so shocked she covered her mouth. "The señora will be so pleased to see you. I will put crêpes on right away."

"I appreciate that, but it's late—"

"Extra butter and chocolate sauce, just the way you like it. Or do you want snickerdoodles? Maybe red velvet ice cream? The chocolate soufflé will take longer, but I promise it will be ready for breakfast tomorrow." She rushed a stream of indiscernible words, Spanish sprinkling into her English.

"The crêpes will be perfect," he said.

Immacolata kissed his hand and held it tightly. "So truly nice to see you." She rushed off to the kitchen, feet moving so fast it seemed they'd run away from her chubby body.

"Your visit is like the second coming," Ava said.

"You'll eat the crêpes, please," Cecil whispered to Ava. "Or give them to Figaro."

Perdonna's mansion was a natural marvel. Water ran down the foyer walls in a constant stream, a lullaby of rain. The chandeliers were made of pink Himalayan crystals. And the softest white alpaca rugs covered the floors.

The rooms felt imbalanced, as if no *thing* had a boundary and the mansion was simply one with the natural world. Peacock feathers framed door entryways. White aspen tree bark was substituted in lieu of wallpaper or paint. And a gold-painted velociraptor fossil graced her atrium.

The rejected bits of nature—fallen leaves, shattered deer antlers, loose feathers—were formed into a spectacular mansion. Perdonna took God's work and made it better. She took all the best and threw out the rest.

Beetles became emerald beads for sconces. Aspen made the world's most beautiful wallpaper. And white swan feathers and gold leaf became a coffered ceiling.

The staircase was made of backlit quartz that looked like cracked ice. And beneath the rock, mirrored watch cogs were lit in gold.

Cecil walked up to the second floor hallway. The walls were covered in bright watercolor dress designs by Perdonna. Indigo feathers were draped over a Cinderella ball gown. Bright green beetles covered a cocktail dress. There was even an outfit made of crushed conch shells.

He found Perdonna in her bedroom, covered in mesh netting overtop her white lingerie. She clutched indigo feathers in one hand, and sketched a feather-covered dress with the other hand.

Her rose-gold hair was pinned up into a loose bun, instead of her usual waves. She was an innocent Juliet, bare-faced and exposed. The feathers were stroked between her fingers the same way Ava twirled her hair. She brushed the feather over her neck, a languid caress over her throat. She bit the purple tips into her mouth, eyes twirling to the ceiling. She was studying the texture, brainstorming the dress's construction.

Feathers cascaded down her hips as she bent down and lifted up her dress skirt. She traced a feather up her inner calf, over the inside of her thigh, and weaved it over her belly button.

"Ahem," Cecil said.

"*Excuse me,*" Perdonna said, shielding her mesh-covered body with her arms.

"Excuse you," Cecil said. "Margaux runs a sex-trafficking ring?"

"Oh, please. Margaux couldn't even work a NuvaRing."

"What is—"

She put her hand over his mouth, brushing her fingers over his lips. Her palms cupped his face, and she closed her eyes. She felt his temples. His jaw. His cheekbones. She was decoding all of the details of his face she couldn't see. Her nail polish smelled of bergamot. He inhaled as the band of her tanzanite ring slid over his nose.

His eyes traveled to the framed blue butterflies mounted above her head. He didn't want to look her in the eyes when they were only an inch from his.

"Your cheeks have slimmed a bit," Perdonna whispered.

"Is that a good thing?"

"Not for a celibate monk." She bit the feather between her two front teeth then weaved it into the mesh over her shoulder.

"Did you know about the sex trafficking?" Cecil asked. "Did you know about my mother?"

Perdonna placed an indigo feather in the mesh along her hip. She spread her fingers across the feather, spreading the fibers like she was petting herself.

"Of course," Perdonna said. "I don't condone it necessarily."

"What do you mean, *necessarily*? Anything short of condemnation here seems—"

"Trafficking is more complicated than you might think," she said. "Visage has a factory in Uganda, for example. It's a significant trafficking hub. Traffickers sell people to Saudi Arabia, Egypt, all over. It's a significant form of income for Uganda. If dozens can eat and go without starving because one girl became a slave, I would take that deal."

Cecil tore off his white jacket and slammed it to the ground. "Are you trying to justify selling girls for rape?"

Perdonna squinted, scraping a feather across her lips, biting into the fibers. The purple strands gave way to her bite, leaving an imprint of her lips in the feather. "Well, yes."

"Uganda needs a better export then. Some education. No amount of money justifies sex trafficking."

"I don't care to be the arbiter of righteousness. I'm not a monk."

Cecil grabbed a Crevier vase from her nightstand. The rage built up inside him as he ground his teeth together. He had to release the energy. He threw the vase toward the far wall.

An explosion seemed to happen in slow motion. Shards fell to the floor in rainbows. Metallic blue wings fluttered down like they were flying off the walls, blue reflecting across her mirrors like neon lights. When the little butterflies hit the floor, they became even more lifeless than they were as bodies mounted on the wall.

Blue wings were splintered by shards of glass, turned into worthless pieces of glitter on the ground.

"Thank you," Perdonna scowled, throwing her arms up.

He carefully picked up a butterfly. It was large, almost the size of his hand and felt as light as an autumn leaf. It was a brilliant blue that seemed almost impossibly natural.

He spread the butterfly over her veins and gently wrapped it around her wrist, studying the shape in the mirror. But the wings split off into a thousand tiny flecks that sparkled into a glittery blue. The butterfly body turned to dust, furry ink staining his hand black.

A body turned to ash in his palm.

"Unethical... Says the man who just desecrated a body," Perdonna said.

His fingers wrapped around Perdonna's wrist, and he felt her veins beneath the wiry fabric. It felt like an allegory for their relationship. There was always a bit of tough, abrasive mesh between him and her.

"You should make the dress out of the butterflies."

"I'm doing feathers," she said, pointing to the part of her stomach already covered.

"It's terrible. You look like an Easter basket," Cecil jabbed.

"Well, then at least I'm more religious than you've been lately," Perdonna said. "Though it wouldn't take much." Her eyes dazzled with an acidic glint. It was as if pools of yellow sulfur dripped into the clouded eyeballs.

With a scowl, she deplumed herself, unpinning the feathers from her stomach, hips, and feathers. She knew he was right. Cecil took over, his hand holding her waist to keep her steady. He felt the curve of her hips in his hand. He plucked the feathers from her stomach, carefully removing pins from around her belly button. She shook beneath him, not from arousal but from anger.

"If a homeless family cannot feed their four children, if the babies are chewing their thumbs because they're so hungry, I cannot blame a father for selling the oldest daughter. One dead child for three live ones, instead of four dead, is a good deal," Perdonna said.

Cecil pinned the butterflies tightly to her shoulder. He would've rather focused on designing than the argument. The black rims of the wings looked like stripes over the metallic blue. It was only when he looked close enough that he could see the butterfly shape. They looked like luxurious fish scales from afar.

"And then you have the girls who want to be models. They could've worked as a waitress. Could've become nurses. Become accountants or mothers. Instead, they wanted false fame. *They* didn't read the fine print."

"But we have to protect them. They're young girls. They're not even legal. It's one mistake. One mistake shouldn't end their life."

"We all have free will. Safety isn't a right. It isn't a guarantee," Perdonna said. "And that's what makes life exciting… Being a victim for a moment is a tragedy. Remaining a victim is a choice."

Perdonna swatted away his hand. She manipulated the shape of the butterfly over her arm. Their hands fought each other to adjust the piece until it sat perfectly flat. "Keep it in line with the index finger," she barked.

"They're slaves! They don't want to be victims." He had to be careful not to poke her with the needle in his hand. Carefully he had to puncture the butterfly without tearing open her bare flesh. "So you won't save Annabelle? You'll let her die? Where was her choice when Margaux sent her away? Where the fuck were you?"

"Don't you dare accuse me of hurting Annabelle. I would've destroyed my own company if it meant stopping her abduction."

"Was it Margaux?"

Perdonna crossed her arms. "Not intentionally. Maybe accidentally."

"Accidentally?"

Cecil brought the scissors to her chest. The energy of the argument only propelled the creative synergy. They moved quickly, grabbing at each other's hands. She kicked him in the shins when an antenna pointed in the wrong direction. Angry hands making staccato movements over her body.

He drew over her breasts where he thought the neckline should be, plunging to the bottom of the rib cage. She ripped the marker from his hand and drew a more conservative scoop neck.

He stole it back, grabbing her wrist.

He drew a neckline in between his and hers. "Compromise," he said, cutting the fabric between her breasts. Her chest heaved at his touch.

"The modeling industry is cunning. Stupid people are animals. Animals are exceptionally cunning. If VD wanted Annabelle to turn profits, well... Margaux likes money," Perdonna said.

His fingertips danced along the outline of her bra, placing butterflies along the cut neckline. Perdonna cut the tips of the butterfly wings along her collarbone to expose more of the neckline. "Yes? No?"

"I'm always in favor of more chest," Cecil said with a wink.

She elbowed him in the gut.

"What is The Mall?"

Perdonna moved her bra to cover more of her breast. Goose-bumps appeared over her upper-half. "I don't know. I know the word, of course. I make money in more beautiful ways, so I wouldn't know."

"I'm going to go in," he said. "Ava will go as a model. We know there is one more spot. I'll get her in, and we'll save Annabelle."

"Oh, you're so naïve," she said, taking the needles from his hand and jabbing them forward.

"Careful," he said, pointing his scissors back at her.

"Are you insane? A billionaire pedophile just committed 'suicide' in prison over being jailed for fucking teenagers on his private island. He was murdered. Murdered to keep quiet about all of the other billionaires and millionaires sleeping with adolescents. Annabelle wasn't found because no one wanted her found. You cannot just walk in and pull Annabelle out. These people are not only above the law, they are above your God. And no amount of prayers will help you."

Her lips came close to his as she breathed heavily. He took the needles from her hand.

"I can't call the police because they think I'm a suspect," he said. "No one will believe me when I say Annabelle's alive. There's no evidence. I'm her only shot to live and escape. I have to go in and try to save her. Even if I die. It's what God wants."

"Then, I guess... Welcome to LeClaire Model Management, bellino." A sadness drifted into her voice.

Perdonna's fingers traced over the butterflies covering her top and arms. Even half-made, the dress was striking. The glittering blue looked like the most expensive fabric that had ever been crafted.

"You'll work for your mother, but you won't work for Visage."

"Working for you is more complicated," he said, blowing the black butterfly fur from his hand.

"More complicated than invading a sex-trafficking ring to save Annabelle Leigh?"

He collected the rest of the whole butterflies from the floor, careful not to step on glass. Then he turned to meet her eyes. "Yes."

She presented her back to him. "I'll finish the rest myself," she whispered with a dash of disdain.

He unbuttoned each conch shell along her back, delicately holding her stomach so she wouldn't fall. She smelled like sea salt. Like toasted marshmallows roasting on a campfire by the oceanside.

Cecil's hands wrapped around the bottom of the dress carefully. It was like handling a bubble, a fragile rainbow.

"Close your eyes," Perdonna said. "You can't see me naked."

"Afraid I'll find a wrinkle?"

"I'm afraid you'll decide to traffic *me*. I would return a pretty penny."

He closed his eyes and lifted the dress over her head. His hands slid over her smooth legs. Over the curves of her hips.

He heard footsteps and the sound of a drawer opening.

"Open," she said, taking the dress from his hands. She hung it on the door, the mesh still an elegant outline of her silhouette.

"The nightgown is...short," he said, staring at her thighs. She had put on a teddy made of golden spider silk.

"I thought I should give you something." She sprawled out on top of the bed. The base was made of mussel shells, and the sheets glimmered with spider silk. She untucked the bedsheets and shuffled inside. Her bun was messy against her pillow, and only smeared remnants of mascara dotted her bare face.

In that moment—eyes garnished with wisdom lines, manicured toes peeking out from beneath the sheets—she was an innocent version of herself.

"This seems inappropriate for a monk. You shouldn't be in my room," Perdonna said.

"Well, I painted a naked lady this week so... I'm due for confession anyway."

Her fingers tangled through her silken hair and released it from the bun. The rose-gold hair fell in waves.

His eyes traced the remnants of gold glitter that was brushed over her red scars.

"Ava mentioned that."

He scanned the fluffy bed. This was not his monastery cell, not a bare-bones mattress. The sheets smelled of lavender and vanilla. They smelled like her.

"I painted snakeskin. But the woman helped."

"I'm sure she *did*." Perdonna grinned.

With lotion from the nightstand, she lathered her feet, fingers tracing over her toes. The lotion being warmed in her wringing hands made a delectable slushing sound like two bodies making love.

"Did you enjoy it?" she asked.

"A little." He looked to the floor.

Her nightgown rose over her underwear as she rubbed lotion onto her thighs.

"Sex isn't always awful, you know? Sometimes it keeps the human race going," she said.

"I've had sex." He shook his head. "With Annabelle."

"At fourteen?" she asked, stopping her lotioned hands around her knees. The motherly tone slipped into her accent.

She hugged her hands around her shoulders, massaging around her collarbone. Her neck arched backward as her fingertips raked along her scalp.

"So you knowingly eschewed sex for stale bread and incense. Shocking."

Her toes curled up against his calves.

"So you *do* have sex?" he asked.

"You thought I didn't?"

"You never dated anyone. Not that I met," he said. "Or are you like a black widow spider? Do they all end up dead?"

She pulled the gown over her head and lathered lotion onto her stomach.

"You don't have to be married to have sex, darling. I only sleep with men who can't talk about it afterward. And only four times each."

"Why four?"

"After four, they become too attached."

Cecil took the lotion from her hands and motioned for her to spin onto her stomach. Her eyelids dropped. The bit of shattered iris remaining in her eye traced triangles around his face. It was as if she was trying to see every grimace. His right eye twitch. His left eyebrow raise. Even if she couldn't.

She turned onto her stomach, resting her hands beside her head on the pillow. He warmed the lotion in his hands. His fingertips gently massaged her neck and shoulders. Her bra straps rolled beneath his thumbs.

His fingers scraped along her neck, sending shocks down her spine. The heat from his core wrapped around her lower back.

"You never wanted to get married?" he asked.

"I don't like many people."

His fingers tangled into her hair and his knuckles brushed along the nape of her neck. She rolled onto her side and took the lotion from him.

"I imagined you…when I was painting that woman." Guilt glazed over his eyes. "I'm sorry I—"

"Did you want her?" she asked, not betraying any emotion.

Her chest heaved, and he suddenly noticed the red flush along her neck. Her legs quivered. He couldn't believe her question. "It's why I can't work for Visage." He brashly slid his hand down to her lower back and whispered in her ear, "I wouldn't be able to stop at four." His voice cracked at a low grumble. The tone surprised even him.

He rubbed his hands down her shoulders in quick succession. It was frustration. It was deciding whether to push her back onto the bed and make love to her. He walked away with his heart beating through his ears.

"Are you allowed to masturbate?" she asked.

"Of course not," he said, turning back to her.

She took steps toward him and reached out her hand. She found the waistband of his pants, and a sharp fingernail ran beneath his belly button. "Then I'll try to scream your name loud enough for you to hear me when I touch myself tonight."

A seductive voice rumbled from deep within her chest. She held on to the door, but when she tried to push it closed, he held it open for a moment. A sad little smile crossed her lips.

"Goodnight, Cecil," she whispered.

"Goodnight, darling." He kissed her cheek and brushed a finger over her jaw. And as he walked away, he was surprised by his thoughts. His only regret was not holding her longer.

31

Light burst through Cecil's window and gleamed over the duvet. It was seven o'clock, and Immacolata had already prepared chocolate soufflé and banana pancakes. He wanted to rest in Perdonna's mansion forever, head under the covers.

A collared navy shirt sat folded above cream pants on the bed stand.

He sent a message from his Dial.

Cecil LeClaire: Have some evidence you might want to look at.

Det. Fran Roosevelt: Meet me at the precinct. Outside. Don't come in the building.

♎

Cecil stared at a giant sculpture of a purple Halloween spider eating a cupcake in front of an apartment building. He clutched his briefcase just like all of the other Manhattan commuters. But there was one major difference. Commuters held spreadsheets and calendars, Cecil held portfolios of teenaged girls and fake visas.

He felt an arm wrap around his. And suddenly, he was being tugged through a black gate along the precinct's alley.

Roosevelt led him down a set of dusty stairs full of tiny spiders and cobwebs.

The room below felt like a military storage unit. SWAT cars and emergency service vehicles sat in lines like army men. Weapons sat in secure storage. An eerie yellow light shone down on a wrecked, dilapidated police car with shattered glass and rusty metal in the corner.

"You gotta be quick. I don't have much time," Roosevelt said. "Whatcha got?"

She hopped onto the hood of an ambulance, and unscrewed a jar of honey. Her bare fingers dunked into the golden goodness. She reminded him of a grizzly bear. At first, she seemed cute and lovable, and then he remembered she had giant claws and a pistol.

He showed her the briefcase. Roosevelt concealed her honey-coated fingers in plastic gloves and opened the case. She fingered through the passports, the birth certificates, the all-too-disturbing slave contracts.

"They use these fake visas to take girls over country borders without being tracked," Roosevelt said.

"VD wanted these files from Margaux," Cecil said.

She slurped the honey over her tongue, puffing out her cheeks. And then she clicked the briefcase closed and handed it back to him.

"I can't take these," Roosevelt said with a somber drawl. "They'll get me into trouble with the higher-ups."

"Can't you use this as evidence? Or find missing girls through the names on the birth certificates?" he asked.

"Your mom was let out on bail this morning. She got cleared to stay at St. Joseph's Abbey," Roosevelt said, scrubbing a hand through her short hair. She spiked it up into adorable horns, using the honey as gel. "She has an ankle bracelet but... Doesn't seem right, does it?"

"Are you kidding me?"

His eyes scanned the dusty, unused vehicles throughout the room. Hundreds of thousands of dollars of taxpayer money sat in the trenches.

"There are a lot of people here with conflicting interests, kiddo. I can collect evidence. I can make a case and indict people. But the moment the arrest is made, it goes to the district attorney's hands. I ain't got no more power."

"But how can they let her out on bail?"

Roosevelt shook her head. "Margaux will get the blame for Jordan's murder. But she's not a flight risk. Prosecutors will claim Jordan made the *fake* skin coat. *She* sent the invitation to you. And to retaliate, Margaux killed Jordan. Then, for Clara's death, they'll blame someone like you. For trying to protect your mother. And everyone will believe it because they already think you're a murderer."

Roosevelt hopped down off the ambulance. Her sticky fingers grabbed on to Cecil's hands. "You gotta be careful, kiddo. I like you."

"But what about Annabelle?"

"Annabelle will be forever *missing*. The district attorney doesn't want to talk about sex trafficking. He can't reveal that half of the political donors are screwing teenaged girls. You won't see the words *sex trafficking* anywhere but on a fictional television special."

"She's alive," he said.

Her eyeballs sunk into their sockets. She paused, staring him in the eyes. "You sure? Where is she?"

"Don't know yet. But Imogen gave you fake DNA results so Annabelle could fake her death to get away."

Roosevelt grabbed a notepad and began jotting down notes. "I need evidence. No one can argue against evidence. If you can bring her to me, we can take down the whole circle who put her there. I can get her in protective custody. She can name names. I can arrest on *evidence*."

"I'll have her in front of you in two days."

She reached out for a handshake. But then she pulled him into a big hug. She patted him on the back so aggressively he actually started coughing. She sniffed up her tears and put on a tough face again.

His Dial buzzed against his wrist.

Tazia Perdonna: Meet me at LMM. Margaux's out.

Beignet sugar covered Margaux's floor like a dusting of snow. Curtains, ripped and tattered, dangled from poles. Boot stains sullied the carpet. Trinkets and collectible pressed pennies from Disney World were scattered around the room. The NYPD had ravaged Margaux's office.

Margaux crammed her giant Visage suitcases with canes, Marshmallow Fluff, cashmere blankets, a *Mary Tyler Moore Show* boxset, and three pouches of Philly Cheese Steak Hot Pockets. She had to pack swiftly. She could only take the essentials.

Paparazzi and news teams were minutes away from swarming LeClaire Model Management to catch Margaux's fall from grace. Margaux covered her face by pulling the turtleneck of an oversized Tom Gray sweater over her head, hair sticking out from the faceless black neck like nappy blond pubic hair.

She tossed on her Pierre Lazard backpack, black combat boots by Buratti, and a leather jacket from Eco. Clad in her military uniform, she was ready for war.

Margaux strolled through her chaotic office, never touching her stuff, only placing a rainbow of Post-it notes on trinkets. Occasionally she scribbled a note in gold ink. The room was covered in Post-it confetti, messier than before.

"What is she doing?" Cecil asked as he and Perdonna peered in through a slit in the door. "I've never seen her do this."

"Mostly organizing...a little cleaning," Perdonna said.

"I don't see a vacuum. Why isn't she putting her dolls back on the shelves?" Cecil asked.

"She is. Each Post-it note is a color code for the suelas."

"*Suelas?*"

"Margaux is all about dehumanization. Her housekeepers

aren't people. They're Suela Uno, Suela Dos, and Suela Tres."

Margaux crawled under her desk trench-style to put an orange sticker beside a lollipop that fell out of her candy tray.

"That means *pick up*," Perdonna said.

She wrote in gold ink on the lollipop *NO EATO PORFAVORITO*.

"Her maids aren't even Hispanic," Cecil said. "Samantha's from Nebraska."

Perdonna's tongue clicked against her teeth, and a puff of a chuckle escaped. "Maybe the corn confused her."

Margaux kissed the lollipop and shuffled in reverse trench-style from beneath the desk.

"But she spent all that energy climbing under there," Cecil said. "Why doesn't she just pick up the lollipop?"

Perdonna shook her head. "Margaux doesn't clean. Suela Dos cleans. Green is for Windex. Yellow is for Clorox wipes. Pink is for vacuuming. Purple is for reorganizing."

Margaux's body tensed like a stretched rubber band when Perdonna knocked on the door. She spun around and ran to Perdonna, throwing her arms around her.

"That prison was so horrid, you would've thought Idi Amin was running it. The bathroom stalls didn't have doors, and they wouldn't give me shampoo. Entrapment, I tell you. It was absolute entrapment. My prison guard made Pol-Pot look like Santa Claus."

"Can't be worse than how you treat your models," Cecil said.

"Yes, but I'm Margaux *LeClaire*, not some Amazonian prostitute. Let me paint the picture for you." She dramatically flailed onto an ottoman. "You know how depressing it is to see a kid in a wheelchair carrying a plastic bag with a dead carnival goldfish inside? Well, picture me in an orange prison jumpsuit. I was the dead goldfish."

Margaux took a handful of stale cheese balls from a silver Tiffany's tray and shoved them in her mouth. A ring of orange powder stuck to her lips.

Her eyes had pink tints to them. Her bun seemed extra scraggly, with hairs flowing outward and sticking to her face, lacking the normal volume from her dry shampoo.

Freddy yelled into the room, "Five minutes, Margaux. *Glamorama* is only three blocks away. We have to get going."

"The police have been harassing me all through the night. *Margaux, did you kill... Margaux, are you depressed... Margaux, what's your biggest fear*," she said, putting her face in her hands. "I was being attacked by an ugly, lesbian shrink with no manners. It's entrapment, I tell you. They say, *We know you killed her.* They ask, *Have you hit your children in the past?* They say, *We know what happened, just tell us and we'll help you.* It's entrapment. Absolute entrapment. Everything should be wiped from my case."

Margaux held a broken pink fingernail out to him like a dog with a broken paw.

"You deserve it! You *killed* Jordan," Cecil said, taking the fake broken fingernail from her and tearing it in half. "I saw the tape of you lifting her body out of the oil."

Margaux put her hand over Cecil's mouth. She leaned into his face with artificial cheesy puff breath. "No, I didn't. I don't kill people. *Ever.*"

"Just because you say—"

"She doesn't kill. To a dangerous degree, she *refuses* to kill people. I've seen many times she should have."

Perdonna's eyes danced up to Cecil's as an iciness came between them.

"Then who did?" Cecil asked.

"VD, probably," Margaux said.

He picked up Margaux's favorite malachite music box. When he opened it, a carousel of naked ballet dancers twirled to *The Nutcracker Suite.* He lifted it up and threatened to break it.

"But who is VD?" Cecil asked.

Margaux's right eyelid twitched at the name, as though that one eye had been personally attacked. She lunged at his arm, struggling to tear him from the music box.

"I don't know. I just give her girls, and she gives me a commission."

"*Her?* VD is a woman?"

Margaux shrugged. "In my mind, she is. All bad people are women. I hate women."

"Why did you send her Annabelle? Why would you have your son's best friend abducted?"

Margaux's lip trembled, and she wiped the sweat from her forehead. "I didn't do it."

"But you knew where she was, then. You were getting money out of this." He ripped one of the ballet dancers from the music box and threw it on the ground.

"I didn't cash those checks…most of the time," Margaux shouted. "I sent her to a modeling gig. Then she disappeared. I wish I could've brought Annabelle back. But there wasn't a way." She looked up to the corners of the ceiling. "And I can't tell you more because the police might be bugging me."

He put the music box down.

"Three minutes," Freddy shouted.

"Do I *have* to go to the monastery? I can head Visage Charity." Margaux grumbled through chewing. "To fix the LMM image."

"The last time I let you run a charity event, you gave mink coats to starving, homeless children from the Bronx instead of the college scholarship money I had given to you," Perdonna said.

"Hey, I heard Oranjelo sold his polar bear fur for twelve thousand dollars on the black market. That's twelve thousand orders of French fries from the dollar menu."

"No."

"What do you mean, *no*? *No* what?"

"Just…no," Perdonna said, folding her arms. She cleared an ottoman of beignet dust and sat on it. Her skintight shagreen dress barely allowed her to cross her legs.

"I'll call Abbot Joseph and apologize," Cecil said.

"I already have. I told him that we are sending him a cheese puff, and the models are coming back to the mansion," Perdonna said. She put a puff in her mouth from Margaux's tray, and immediately spat it back out. "It tastes like mold."

"*Cheddar* mold," Margaux corrected. "Artificial bleach cheddar mold. It's the flavor of nostalgia. Crunchy nostalgia."

She licked the orange crust from her lips. Her tongue was so white from all of the beignet sugar that her mouth looked like an orange creamsicle.

"Why aren't we sending Cecil back to the monastery too?" Margaux asked. "Talk about bad PR. The psychopathic monk who murdered his fourteen-year-old girlfriend. Can't get worse PR than that."

"I wish we *could* send him back. But he's on a suicide mission to save Annabelle."

"Who's gonna run LeClaire while I'm gone?" Margaux asked.

"Cecil," said Perdonna.

Margaux gave a bulging-eyed glare. She whipped out her revolver and shuffled it between her hands. Perdonna grabbed the shaft, her scarred eyes meeting with Margaux's.

"Temporarily," Perdonna said.

Cecil looked out into the hallway where suited agents strolled with intensity, screaming into their headsets for possibly no reason at all. A breath caught in his throat.

"Annabelle's going to be at The Mall. Cecil is going to be Ava Germaine's agent, and they want to try to free Annabelle."

Margaux dropped her gun. Her head cocked in a serious, slow way. "You're going to The *Mall*?"

"Do you know what it is?" Cecil asked.

Margaux looked out the window. One reporter had begun setting up his lighting equipment with a cameraman. She rubbed her hands together with a nervous clap. "It's like the convention of the fashion industry," Margaux said. "I've been trying to get an invitation for decades."

She grabbed her favorite music box and threw it against her desk, shattering it. Cecil jumped, but Perdonna remained frozen on the chair, typing messages into her palm.

"Ava Germaine, the lifeless vampire, got an invitation, and I can't? I'm one of the top model agencies in the world. How the hell does that happen?" Margaux asked.

"They want her to model in it," he said. "We followed Clara's body to Maddox Hill, and we found one of VD's people."

"VD puts The Mall together?" Margaux asked.

"You seem woefully undereducated about this," Cecil said.

"I'm woefully undereducated about a lot of things." Margaux nodded solemnly. She cradled her malachite music box in her arms, suddenly regretting smashing it. She seemed to worry he would take it from her again. "Ignorance has gotten me far. Can't be blamed for anything if I don't know anything."

"Are you really giving girls to VD without a clue what he's doing with them?" he asked.

Margaux clicked her teeth together and shrugged. "The Mall is a once-a-year thing. It's held the day before Halloween. I think it's like what New York Fashion Week is *supposed* to be. All of the reality show stars and D-listers started coming to Fashion Week so we needed something better. I think The Mall is an insane, underground fashion show for the elites. Like Woodstock but in a bunker."

"If that's it, then why haven't you been invited?" Cecil asked.

"Maybe model agents aren't allowed. If VD is a model agent, she wouldn't want the competition."

"So then who do you think runs The Mall? Who is VD?"

Margaux's eyes squinted with delight. "A short woman. With ugly blond split ends. She's got blue beady devil eyes. And she looks a bit like a troll doll. Every word she says is a lie."

"So you're VD?" he asked.

"No." Margaux glared. "Hillary Clinton."

"Oh, for God's sake." Perdonna covered her face with her hands.

"People think Bill's the rapist. And sure…he is. But Hillary's a model agent. I'm sure of it. How else does a foundation make that much money? The Clinton Global Initiative is about recruiting models from Haiti. Lock her up, baby. *Lock. Her. Up.*"

"And on that note," Freddy said, stepping into the room and grabbing Margaux's suitcases. His ears had turned bright red with anger. They were little red Christmas lights to match his skintight plaid pants.

"I agree with Perdonna," Margaux said. "You shouldn't sneak in. You're an outsider. It doesn't matter that you're Cecil LeClaire. Or that you're a monk. They'll probably sacrifice you to Chelsea Clinton."

"They said it's Annabelle's last year. I only have this one chance."

"Then they'll kill her *and* you. It's not worth it!" she shouted, her hands slamming down to her sides. That dreamy, crazed look left her eyes. Freddy tried to tug her away, but she wrapped her arms around Cecil's chest. Her hair smelled like sulfur. He couldn't remember the last time she had embraced him. He wasn't sure whether they had ever touched at all.

"Keep God close. You're going to need her," she said, fingers tapping the cross around his neck.

She walked to Perdonna and threw her arms around her shoulders. Her forehead rested against Perdonna's, and her lips pressed to her temple. Perdonna stroked a curly strand of hair behind Margaux's ear.

"I love you," Margaux said in a sweet whisper. "Keep him safe."

The fourth-floor cubicles sat empty like windowed cages. The regular golden mood lighting was turned off. And the translucent floors no longer glimmered. It seemed like a mall without mannequins.

"Do you remember when Annabelle decided to turn your basement into a butterfly garden?" Cecil asked as he tapped on an empty cubicle.

"Which part?" Perdonna asked. "The dead caterpillars and chrysalis shells you hadn't bothered to clean up? The moss you stapled to my ceiling? The actual pond water you dumped onto the floor? The black bear that snuck in through the doors you left open?"

"I was thinking of the bear," he said, leaning against the wall. "I remember it sneaking in. The fear. The sounds of breaking glass. You thought it was a stalker coming to murder you. I remember us all going down there. I grabbed the rifle from under your bed. But when we got down to the cellar, and the eyes looked back at me, I couldn't shoot it. The bear could've mauled you or Annabelle. And I couldn't kill him... I keep thinking about that. If I couldn't kill a bear, what's going to happen at The Mall?"

"I'll come save the day and shoot him." Perdonna pressed the elevator button. "If you're going to do this, I might as well help you."

The elevator doors swung open to reveal Gisele already in her black underwear. Except now, she wore a big golden cross around her neck. And her skin was no longer deathly white. She had a subtle rosy glow.

"You don't have to stand here in your underwear anymore," Cecil said. "I'm in charge now."

Gisele put her hands on her hips. "Why? Are you firing me?"

"No, no, you're still a model. You just don't have to do this all day."

"But I love it. It is my...occupation. I am doorman. I am proud elevator model. Please don't fire me." She pouted and crossed her arms over her chest. Tears started to form in her eyes. "Margaux gave me extra Toasted Vanillas for this job. I love it."

"I'm sorry. Really sorry. I didn't realize." Cecil waved his hands. "I thought Margaux forced you. Now I understand."

A scoff escaped Perdonna's lips. "The attic please, Gisele."

Perdonna closed her eyes and leaned her head back against the shattered purple mussel shells. Her fingertips stroked the watch hand on the elevator wall every time it twirled above her head. She leaned into Cecil's ear. "You'll find people don't like it when you take away their way of life."

The doors opened to a small nook that looked like a dressing room for Cirque du Soleil. Vintage mirrors tarnished with golden rust covered every square inch of the ceiling. Trolleys of discarded Visage runway creations lined the walls—a top hat with a Styrofoam billiard ball on top, a makeup case shaped like a pistol, shoes made from discarded cigarettes, a headpiece made from deer antlers, a burka made of spaghetti noodles, and a dress made of broken piano keys.

It felt like a horror set, with runway stage lights casting red and black hues over the mannequins and trolleys.

White Venetian masks hung above the clothing trolleys, half-human bastardizations. They looked like plaster molds of corpse faces, as though Perdonna had murdered girls and stolen their faces. The eyes were black holes that expressed no fear, no disdain, no personality, or soul.

That room was the opposite of white. It appeared beautiful and horrible at once, like a Stradivarius played out of tune.

When they pushed through the costume-filled trolleys, they came to a wall covered in white canvas with a projector above it.

"The Mall won't be as dangerous as you imagine," Perdonna said. "It's the people who are the problem. In that cabinet over there," she pointed to the right wall, "you'll find a DVD with 'Quirk Models: Andre Blancas' written on it."

Cecil found hundreds of DVDs. Two decades of runway shows, security camera footage, and documentaries about Perdonna, the LeClaire family, and New York Fashion Week. There were even some ancient VHS tapes sprinkled in the collection. In a drawer labeled "Lolitas" was the Quirk Models DVD.

"This is the man you need to study. I once asked Andre Blancas, then president of Quirk, to videotape his model recruitment process so I could get a sneak peek at the new faces available for my show.

"I'm showing you this tape because when you meet with Bourgeois, in order to be recruited by VD, you will have to act like a model agent. You will have to talk about Ava as if she is a collectible, a classic car you adore but want desperately to sell. The dynamic between the two of you must be master and slave, or else you will seem suspicious the moment you step into the room. You have to pretend you are the new president of LeClaire Model Management."

Perdonna started the video.

The image opened on a run-down gymnasium in Siberia. Cracks scuttled through the orange floor, brown flags hung over dust-covered stadium seats.

Model agents, dressed in fur coats of mink and chinchilla, stood in front of young girls wearing string bikinis covered in rainbows, unicorns, and stripes. Fuck-me pumps were given to them, and paper numbers were placed on their stomachs. They were cattle on display.

The girls were between the ages of eleven and fourteen—earwax staining their ears, nose hairs untrimmed, white, oozing acne around dry skin on their noses. At least half were yet to develop breasts.

Not a parent in sight.

Scabs and scars covered their knees from playing playground games. They were innocents with doll-like eyes, cheeks gray from malnutrition. Hair fell ragged with split ends.

Diamonds in the rough.

Andre Blancas, a strapping man with a thick scruff of beard and bushy black eyebrows, tanned and handsome, not at all the pervert profile, turned to the camera. "These girls are so fresh. They glisten. Wet and shiny and new," he said with a deep drawl.

He rolled a measuring tape to the top of the tallest girl's head. "Six feet tall and only fourteen years old. They've grown taller since I've been here. It's the hormones in the chicken—I swear the food industry is doing fashion serious favors."

While Blancas talked, his agents measured girls, slipping their fingers underneath thin bikini fabric. They prodded stomachs, measured the circumferences of arms and thighs, and told the fatter, darker colored girls to go home.

"They say *we need more color in fashion.* They *whine, whine, whine* about inclusion. But all the studies show that no one buys magazines with blacks on the cover. Especially not in France." Blancas chuckled. "It's not me. I'd love an African ass. It's money that makes me go for whites."

He stopped in front of a tanned blonde and pointed her to the door. *Tan* did not belong in high fashion. *Tan* was for the working class, the poor field workers who couldn't afford to avoid the sun.

"I found most of these girls by targeting mothers in whorehouses. Mommies with budding daughters would much rather their babies get famous and take pictures than fuck dirty men on bedbug-ridden cots." Blancas snickered. "Stupid bitches; they don't do their research.

"Homeless shelters are good too. We found four girls that way. Better they get a warm bed in a models' apartment than die of frostbite on the street."

Most of the girls left in the room looked to be about twelve.

Their tiny pelvises made them look like teenaged boys. Many girls had voluptuous lips and thick, curly hair.

"I have to get girls young. Train them, make them obey me, learn my ways. I tell them, show up to your casting on time, don't eat the bread at craft services, respect your photographer. Use both hands when playing with cock. Don't cry when he sticks it inside you, don't forget to say his penis is the biggest you've ever seen.

"Besides, the younger I get the whores, the more magazine covers they can do, the more luxurious the pussy. Five hundred horsepower versus four hundred."

Blancas stopped in front of one of the tallest girls who seemed to be at least five-eleven. She wore a bikini with pink hearts and smiley faces on the breasts. Her hair fell in tight blond curls. Ears stuck out from her head, large and floppy like an elephant's. And a two millimeter gap sat between her two front teeth. She looked like a bumblebee, lips so red and full they seemed to be stung. She was unique.

"Do you speak English?" Blancas asked her.

"Ye...yes," she replied nervously.

"What's your name?" he asked with a Novocain smile. His eyes brightened as though he'd just run into his high school sweetheart.

"My na-a-name?" she stuttered. "Evgenia."

"Evgenia, beautiful. Oh, you're so adorable. *So* adorable." Blancas put his hand on his assistant's shoulder. "How old is this one?"

"Thirteen."

"Oh, perfect." Blancas clapped. "She's just perfect, isn't she?"

Evgenia giggled, and her cheeks turned as rosy as they could with the anemic blood she had.

"You like fashion? Pretty clothes?" he asked.

Evgenia looked worried. She shrugged, not understanding. The assistant translated to Russian and then the girl smiled brightly, bouncing her chin like a bobblehead. "I like it. I like it."

Blancas used the measuring tape around her chest. "Do you have hobbies?"

The assistant translated.

"Ballet."

The girl lifted her arms above her head and put her leg in the air, only a few inches off the ground. She hopped up and down on her toes. Not Bolshoi material, but cute nonetheless.

"Ah. I love you, I love you, I love you!" Blancas exclaimed. "Do you know how perfect you are?"

The assistant snapped photos with her Polaroid camera: one of the head, one of the torso, and two side profiles.

Blancas grabbed Evgenia by the arms and led her to walk. She wobbled on the heels like a newly birthed colt. Her eyes went blank as she was guided down a runway like an elderly woman in physical therapy. He held her ass the entire walk, pushing her hips forward to get the ideal curvature. His other arm grabbed around her bust, pulling her shoulders back.

He scribbled on a notepad: *Evgenia – Pitch to Visage, Ami, and maybe Pierre Lazard.*

"Finding a model like that is like discovering a da Vinci sketch in your grandmother's attic. It's like knowing you've finally painted your masterpiece, like finding a rare stamp for your collection," Blancas said to the camera. "Perdonna, in two, three years, you have her open for Visage, and the whole audience will wish they were fifteen again. They will see *death* in her emaciated rib cage but feel as though they've seen God. They'll wish to buy your twenty-thousand-dollar gown so that they can live forever."

The screen faded to black. Cecil felt bile rise in his throat. He wanted to throw up, to wash away the feelings and eject them.

But then a new title card came up—RECRUITMENT: TEXAS, USA.

Blancas sat outside a toy store in a small suburban shopping mall. Dozens of teenagers walked by giggling in packs like hyenas.

"It's difficult to recruit American girls, but they're without a doubt the most valuable. They speak English, know American customs, and they can relate to the young, future luxury shopper. The downside—they are brats.

"I look for girls who are alone—ideally, crying. The ones with a nose ring or green hair are best because it means the parents are either absent or delusional—either will do for my purposes."

The camera turned to a girl crying as she wrote in a small notebook. Her hair was pink, and she wore a slutty red dress that rode up almost to her hip bone. A hint of black lingerie peeked out. But underneath all that, she had a beautiful nose and sharp cheekbones. She stood at five-ten and had a wonderfully quirky mole on her right cheek.

"Are you okay, young lady?" Blancas asked. "Anyone bothering you?"

The girl looked up, blue eyeliner trailing down her face. "I'm fine, thank you."

"Is it your parents? Keeping you from seeing the boyfriend, found out you're doing drugs?"

The girl laughed through her tears. "How did you know?"

Blancas gave her a fatherly pat on the shoulder. "You're not the only one with shitty parents. I know what it's like."

The girl rolled up the sleeves of her dress to reveal needle marks, which explained the sunken look around her eyes, the slender frame. "My dad shoots up too. That's who I got it from. Don't judge me. I'm only sixteen. I can make mistakes."

Blancas stroked her palm subtly with his thumb. "You're really pretty, you know that?"

She gripped his hand, and her eyes seemed to smile as the tears stopped completely. "Please, all the boys in school call me Big Bird."

"Because they want you, and they know they can't have you," he said. "Believe me, I'm a model agent. I know a beautiful girl when I see one."

"A model agent? For real?" A cartoon smile revealed yellow, crooked molars that would soon be ripped out and replaced with dental implants.

Blancas held out his business card. "Quirk Models, New York City."

"New York City. Like *the* New York City? Wait. Quirk Models is the agency where Carly Wooster models, isn't it? She's like a billionaire, right?"

"Carly's father abused her too. But she got over it. Now she spends her nights in the Plaza Hotel," Blancas said.

"I'd love to model. It would be the coolest thing ever. I could leave my parents' house, never see them again!"

He laughed. "I have a casting tomorrow at this mall. I'd love for you to come so I can take pictures, tell you more about modeling. You're beautiful, and I think I can make you a star like Carly Wooster."

"Absolutely. Omigod, this is so cool. I can't wait to tell everyone."

"Eh, eh, eh," Blancas said. "You can't tell your parents. What if they say you can't model? You'll be stuck here in dreary old Dallas for the rest of your life. We can't have that. Stars aren't meant to be buried under the desert."

"Fuck them. I'll run away to Manhattan and make millions. I'll get so rich that I'll never have to see them again."

Perdonna shut off the screen.

"This is insane." Cecil kicked his stool.

"The average age of a girl who enters the sex trade in the United States is twelve to fourteen, coincidentally the same age at which fashion recruits high fashion models. Twenty thousand girls are trafficked into the United States each year. I would say eight thousand of those enter the modeling industry in some capacity," Perdonna said.

"How many model agencies are involved?"

Perdonna sighed. "I would guess about half are involved with legitimate rings internationally. Others work primarily to put girls on the fashion runway, but they will organize backdoor deals for a top model to fuck an oil tycoon or a technology magnate from Silicon Valley for a high price.

"Modeling is about the agent, not about the girl. It's about the power you wield. Everyone lies. They lie about the number of hours they work. They lie about how unhappy they are. They lie about how rich they are. Now they can even fake their photographs. And the result is that everyone is self-conscious. We live in a world of low self-esteem. And so people *believe* confidence when they see it. They *believe* control. Because anyone must be stronger than themselves."

Perdonna sat on Cecil's lap, straddling him. She ran her fingers over his scalp until they interlocked behind his head. Her golden choker scraped along his cheek as she leaned into his ear. "It's all an act. Everyone who seems like they have control is faking it. Power is performance."

He pushed a strand of hair behind her ear. His palm cupped her jaw, fingertips playing with the baby hairs on her neck. His lips danced around her temple, tempted to kiss her head. "Is flirting with me a performance? Are you trying to control me?"

"Always," she whispered into his ear. "Go be Blancas."

3 2

Ava Germaine: *I have bad news. We need to talk.*

When Cecil entered Perdonna's lobby, the mansion was silent. Immacolata was nowhere to be found. Figaro's usual gnawing sounds were gone.

"Ava?" Cecil called out.

"Down here!" A muffled yell came from behind the golden dinosaur.

A tile was lifted. Beneath, a charcoal-covered staircase was lit with emerald LED lights. He climbed down into the dark tunnel, emerald lights turning him green. He came to two black pressurized doors that towered several feet above him. There were no windows. No lights coming through.

"What is this?" Cecil asked through the doors.

"Spiders," Ava replied.

He heaved open the doors and cautiously entered into... spiders.

Charcoal-colored rock covered the walls, and a dozen fake black twig trees rose a dozen feet into the air. On those twigs, golden spider webs were hung. The geometric tapestries were glowing like individual suns. Dewdrops clung to the thread, and light dazzled through the holes in the otherwise perfect circles. They were like pyrite against the charcoal background.

But the webs were not without their spiders. Fifty golden orb-weavers sat in the centers of fields of gold. Vicious Jurassic crabs. But instead of claws, they had razor-like legs with red highlights. Some of them were bigger than his hand.

They were high fashion spiders, striped with red heels.

"Is *this* the elusive security team Perdonna refers to?"

"Chill. They only bite if you offend them." She waved Cecil toward her for a whisper. "Don't insult their webs. They're all girls. They're competitive."

A puff of mist shot out of golden beetle-encrusted shoots. He looked up to find blue and gold light bulbs meant to mimic the sun.

"So, Perdonna has fully gone backyard zoo?"

"It's temporary," Ava said with a pout. "The army wants to use the spider silk to make bulletproof vests. Visage set this up as a showcase for a meeting they had."

A golden dress sat in a display case at the end of the room. It was long-sleeved with a high slit up the right leg. He brushed his finger along the fabric and immediately drew his hand back. It was softer than cashmere.

"Tug on it. It's five times stronger than steel. Perdonna invented a machine that can vacuum the silk from the spiders without hurting them."

Dried fly bodies clung to the webs, serving as warnings to all other passersby. It was quite the contrast. Beautiful golden rainbows and dried corpses.

"How big is Visage's army contract?" Cecil asked.

Ava shrugged. "Pretty big, I guess."

Suddenly a smaller spider crawled onto the web of a larger one. The big spotted gold spider sprinted across her web in defense. She jumped on the tiny spider and injected her venom. Thick white silk was rolled around the dying body, like a corpse being mummified.

"Oh, screw you, Katie. Screw you!" Ava yelled. She pointed at the spider to shame it. "You bitch." The spider tore off the other one's head and began draining the juices from it. The body shriveled up like a dried raisin inside a mummy.

Ava retaliated by grabbing a long black pole and hacking at the spider's web. It fell from the web and dangled on one lone strand of gold right before Cecil's eyes. The legs wriggled before him. He put his hand out, and the spider climbed onto him. She felt like a tiny hand, the tips of her legs scratching like fingernails. His attention left the creepy legs and eight eyes and focused on the fuzzy patch of fur behind her head.

"I thought you said we shouldn't offend them," he said.

"Well, Katie offended Stacey. She offended Stacey's head right off so...screw her."

He pulled the spider closer to his face, seeing the tiny strand of golden silk coming from the abdomen. It was thinner than a human hair. He took the pole from Ava and put the spider onto it. The spider was airlifted back up to the remnants of her dismantled web, twirling into the sky like an acrobat. She chomped on her new snack: Stacey.

Ava's laptop was open to a Christie's auction. And a giant pile of cash surrounded it.

"Are you trying to buy an antique vase or something?" Cecil asked.

She flipped open a Christie's catalogue to a giant crystal castle. It didn't look like Versailles or Vaux-le-Vicomte. It was almost an exact replica of Cinderella's castle. It stood nine feet tall. And the estimated cost was $200,000.

"I thought it would be nice for Figaro to live in his natural environment," Ava said.

"It's a castle."

"Like I said...his natural environment."

Ava scooped the cash into her arms and presented it to him. "Do I have enough? Perdonna gives me cash for Figaro. That's our deal. Housing for me, cash for Figaro."

He quickly scanned the pile of money. "I don't think you have enough."

Ava pouted and slumped into the corner.

Figaro must have known that Immacolata was about to

enter with trays full of blueberry tart, chocolate soufflé, Toasted Vanillas, and Tooth Goo. The white rat raced to Ava and scurried up her shoulder.

Ava crunched into a blueberry tart, lips staining purple. He could smell the buttery crust. But Figaro seemed to prefer the Tooth Goo, as he got his own portion served to him in a miniature crystal bowl.

The white rat became a purple rat, covering himself in purple putty.

"I see the supposed teeth whitening effects haven't helped Figaro," he said, pointing to the yellow bucked teeth.

Cecil pulled bits of crust from the blueberry tart and ate the crumbs. He didn't eat the blueberry inside. That was too luxurious.

"Thank you, Immacolata," he said as she blew him a kiss. She exited the room as quickly as possible to avoid the spiders.

"So, what's the bad news you messaged me about?" Cecil asked.

"You're gonna have to find another model to go to The Mall. I quit."

Cecil's eyes bulged so large they almost popped out of his head. He wiped the Tooth Goo right out of his mouth. "Why?"

"I saw you and Perdonna at Margaux's house. Perdonna doesn't want us to go to The Mall. I work for Perdonna. I don't work for you."

"But...after all of your experience. You know what it's like to be a victim of...of what Annabelle's going through. Don't you want to help her?"

"Not for free," Ava said with a shrug.

"How did you see into Margaux's office?"

"I see things," she said, eyes staring off into the distance. "*The Sixth Sense* is my memoirs. I'm not going to risk my life to save a girl I don't even know."

Cecil noticed the current Figaro cage in the corner of the spider room. It had fluffy white cushions and soft hammocks. There were wooden puzzles and treat dispensers, a metal running wheel and rope bridges.

"Would you do it for the crystal castle?" Cecil asked.

"Keep talking," Ava said with a raised eyebrow.

"I can bid with my Dial. The Visage Amex is uploaded to it, and I can use Perdonna's Christie's account to bid on it for you."

Ava spun the bidding screen to him. She was already logged into Perdonna's account. On one side of the screen, there was a picture of the castle and a box for the bid amount. On the right side was a livestream of the auction house at Christie's.

"The bid's at $350,000," Ava said.

A man in his late sixties with cupcake cheeks and a chubby belly sat with his young granddaughter as he raised his paddle. He wore an adorable plaid suit and bowtie.

$375,000.

"We could feed an entire homeless shelter for a year with that money," Cecil said. "Are you sure we can't find something similar that's not made by Crevier?"

"Figaro deserves Crevier."

"He's a rat."

"You're a rat."

Cecil typed $400,000 into the bid bar.

The man leaned into his daughter's ear. She looked a lot like Ava. Petite with creepy, serious eyes. But she favored pink fairy dresses over Ava's twinkle lights. The man bid $425,000.

"I'll suck a cock," Ava said. "If I need to suck a cock to get into The Mall, I'll do it."

Cecil closed his eyes and guiltily typed $450,000 into the bid box.

The little girl clenched her fists and slammed them against her legs. Her cheeks started to puff out, and she was two bids away from a tantrum. The grandfather bid $475,000.

Ava mimicked the girl's actions and slammed her fists to her legs. But this time, she grabbed Figaro and held him against her cheeks. "He deserves the castle. He's had a tough life."

"What's his lifespan, even?"

"Longer than yours," she said ominously and without any humor. Her eyes squinted into frowning crescents. "I'll walk down a runway naked. And I'll even add in my signature catwalk."

Cecil put his face in his hands. "God is crying right now."

Her pupils rolled toward her nose as she thought up a new bargain. "I'll take it in the ass."

"Ava!"

"I'll take it in the ass *five times* to save Annabelle."

His eyes turned to a dull, gray-blue. He stared blankly at the wall and felt almost like he was going into shock. It must have been the same feeling that gave Ava her aloof stare.

He angrily typed $500,000 into the bid box.

The old man put his hands up in defeat, and Ava leaped into the air to do a jumping jack. "It's yours, Figgy. It's yours."

Cecil rubbed his face. He felt like his skin might disintegrate. "We could've paid for three heart transplants with that money."

"We're saving Annabelle, at least." A big smile beamed across Ava's face, completely changing the shape. She looked like a different person. She became six years old in the most delightful way. "And I am at your service," she said with an overly dramatic bow.

The giant spider was doing gymnastics several feet above their heads, attempting to re-spin her gold web. Silk shot out of her like a bullet, and she flung herself through the air like a trapeze artist.

Ava pulled a card from beneath her laptop.

"I texted Bourgeois, the VD agent I met in the morgue, for the address to the party tomorrow. It starts at ten o'clock. I made up a modeling agency for you to represent me from."

Ava handed him a stack of Voyer Model Management business cards.

"Nice pun."

The title on the back read, "Carmen DeVoyer, President." Like a bad omen, the letters dazzled in bloodred.

"It's a masked party. So no one will know you're Cecil LeClaire. You'll be representing Ava Germaine as the best option for the spot in The Mall."

33

Perdonna's black Bentley Bentayga sped down the FDR Drive, carrying Cecil and Ava. It was a race down the edges of Manhattan. On one side, skyscrapers towered into the clouds above. And on the other, a waterway twinkled with ferries and reflective golden lights.

It felt like flying.

Dingy yellow taxis sprinted by them like angry hornets. Every loud honk was a stung person screaming.

The Pepsi-Cola sign took over the view, a stop sign among the rainbow skyscraper lights scattering across the water. It was almost magical. If you could ignore the rusty cranes, and the scaffolding, and the smog, Long Island City looked like paradise from across the river.

Henry had decided to drive Ava and Cecil to the party. The Rambo Lambo wouldn't exactly be discreet.

Henry's head hovered several inches above the headrest, and he smelled of gunpowder. But when he started humming along to "Somewhere Over the Rainbow," Cecil remembered he was the bodyguard to a fashion designer, not a Navy SEAL.

"What do you think VD stands for?" Cecil asked as he gazed out the window.

"Venereal disease has been my best guess so far," Ava joked. "I don't know. But I do have an idea about who it is."

"Who?"

Ava took Henry's dirt-stained Penn State football cap and put it on her head. "Perdonna." She let out a high-pitched giggle. It was a little nervous yelp.

"Perdonna?"

Ava shrugged and began rapidly twirling her hair until bits of dried ends split off. The little golden edges were ground into a cloud of dust.

"It's not Perdonna," Cecil whispered, glancing into the front seat, wondering if Henry overheard. "She's not sex trafficking girls."

"But she's got the money and the means," Ava said in a sing-song voice. "She's got the money, honey. Money and the—"

He tore off the baseball cap, and Ava's face went blank. She stared off into the distance.

"Ava?"

She crossed her arms over her body.

"Why did you turn into Margaux just then?" he asked.

Ava grabbed one of the flat screen tablets from the seatback in front of her and began playing Pac-Man. "I don't want Perdonna to be VD. But she would've had access to Annabelle *and* Margaux. She definitely has a dark side."

"If that's true, why wouldn't Annabelle have targeted Perdonna? Annabelle can't escape without VD being killed."

"She tried to," Ava said, realizing. "She put her 'dead body,' the most damning evidence, in the *Visage* show. It was the NYPD who put the culpability on Clara." Cecil folded his hands. "Annabelle tried to frame Perdonna. She tried to put VD in prison so she could escape."

"Perdonna wanted *you* to find Annabelle's killer," he said. "She promised you a promotion, right? Why would she want you to do work that condemns her?"

Ava's Pac-Man got eaten by a ghost, and she threw the expensive tablet to her feet. She leaned back and opened up a panel to the trunk. There was a Mulliner hamper full of caviar jars, champagne, escargot…and Snickers bars. But Ava didn't only take a Snickers. She was classy. She smothered the bar in fish eggs like she was frosting a cake and ate half of the concoction in one bite.

Bile came up in Cecil's throat. Caviar and chocolate smells did not mix.

He leaned back and looked into the refrigerated bar. This was not the Rambo Lambo. The white leather interior stretched along the seats and floors, and beautiful chrome panels lined the windows. A Dial with a Bentley button was built into the dashboard.

Ava clicked the Bentley icon and turned on her seat's massage settings. She leaned back and her body bobbed with the force of the vibrations.

"Perdonna's testing you. She wants you to be her prodigy," Ava said.

"I know you think Perdonna is God. But she's only a fashion designer."

"And she's from one of the most powerful mafia families in Italy. She's seen some dark shit."

"Which makes her all the less likely to *repeat* the dark… nonsense."

Suddenly Figaro popped out from the passenger seat and stole bits of caviar off the Snickers.

"You brought Figaro?" he asked. "You can't bring Figaro to this."

"He's my emotional support animal," Ava said. "This is an emotionally painful situation and I need love." Figaro stole another bite of caviar and Ava hissed at him. "Love is complicated."

Cecil remained silent. He grabbed a Snickers bar from the hamper and took a bite. Then he leaned over to Ava's Dial projection and tried to turn on his massager.

"Heat or cold?" she asked when he fumbled.

"Heat, please," he said with a guilty mumble.

She turned on the settings, and he felt like he was in a spa. The seats rubbed the tension out of his shoulders.

"You know," Ava said. "One time, my mom locked me in the basement. It was a farm, so there was a lot of hay. She told me that if I couldn't turn it into gold, she'd cut off my head. So this little green goblin came and did it for me. But I promised him my health in exchange."

"I do actually believe *that* story is about you," Cecil said. "But you're not the girl. You're Rumpelstiltskin."

"Touché," Ava said. "Touché. At least I give a better deal. I do favors for crystal castles instead of firstborn children."

Ava did look sick. Her arms were tiny white aspen branches. And her eyes were so purple and rippled that they looked like tiny caverns.

"Perdonna has a lot of men over," Ava said suddenly, squinting her eyes. The words came out with more force and volume than usual. The childish veneer slipped away. "They're always older than her. And she fucks them in her home office. She's never let a man in her bedroom. She keeps her dress on. At most, she takes her pants off. Yet she let you touch her half-naked."

"How do you know?"

Ava looked straight at Figaro and remained silent.

"Hello?" His shirtsleeve dipped into Ava's caviar, and he sucked the fabric clean. He quickly spat out the salty fish eggs, surprised they were a delicacy.

"I see things," she said. "What's the deal with you two?"

"We're friends. On top of her being my godmother, she's my friend."

"Look, all I know is that Perdonna wanted you in New York. You're in New York. Doesn't matter to me either way," Ava said. "Even if it turns out Perdonna's selling little girls, I'm on whichever team she wants me on."

DANGER.
HEAVY EQUIPMENT MOVING.
NO SMOKING BEYOND THIS POINT.
CONSTRUCTION AREA.
AUTHORIZED PERSONNEL ONLY.

Google Maps had led them to a construction site in TriBeCa. Two large red cranes dangled above like oversized robot giraffes. An unfinished building, covered in reflective glass, towered thirty stories high. Exposed beams protruded out like broken, silver bones. The glimmering blue panels that would someday make up the facade sat dusty and covered in white plastic on the street. Sweat and man hours were building that luxury hotel building, and it showed in the handprints that covered the mud around the base.

The handprints would disappear the moment "Corporation X" put its name on their hard work.

Yellow tape and green plywood fencing surrounded the entrance.

DANGER. PEDESTRIAN WALKWAY TO THE RIGHT.

A forklift and a bulldozer blocked the main entrance.

"This can't be the right address. I should've guessed Bourgeois set you up," Cecil said.

"It's four-eight-nine. That's the number Bourgeois said."

"It's a construction site. Fashion gurus don't have parties in places where sawdust and wet paint can stain their Manolos."

A BMW sedan pulled up to the mouth of the yellow tape. Out came a suave Indian man dressed in a full white suit and a furry, dead raccoon hat. The woman beside him wore a dress made to look like raw meat and yellow American cheese slices. The Glitterati indeed.

"On the other hand..." Cecil said. "Fashionistas would shave off their lips with a nail file if it was on trend."

Ava wobbled on her heels as she dragged him to follow the meat dress.

Henry nodded to the two. "Good luck. Prayin' for you."

They shut the doors, and Cecil gave a happy, naïve grin. "I didn't think Manhattan had believers."

"Henry has to be a believer. He's killed like a hundred people. If there's no forgiveness, he's going straight to hell."

"You believe in the Devil?" Cecil asked. "But not in God?"

"Yeah," Ava said. "I'm not a satanist. I don't pray to him or anything, but he's for sure real. How else do you explain fire?"

Ava handed Cecil his mask. It was a seafoam splatter-painted

Venetian mask, the same shape as Margaux's models' masks. Ava wore a black half mask covered in red lace.

She had traded her regular black dress for black jeans and a black tank top without a bra. Her hair was pulled back into a tight ponytail. The model uniform. Except she kept her golden twinkle lights in her hair.

"You have to keep Figaro," Ava said, holding him out to Cecil. "I don't have anywhere to put him."

"He hates me," Cecil said, waving his hands. "You should've left him at home."

"Bonding time," she said, stuffing the rat into Cecil's black denim jacket. "He's had caviar, so he'll be less bitchy."

When she tried to walk toward the party, Cecil put a hand on her shoulder. His head was bowed in prayer. He grabbed her hands, and she rolled her eyes.

"St. Michael the archangel, defend us in battle."

"Wait," Ava said. "I thought you were married to God."

Cecil squinted, trying to figure out what she meant. "Yes?"

"Then who is this Michael fellow? Are you cheating on God with Michael?"

"St. Michael is the leader of all the angels and the Army of God. He's the one who will lead you to heaven when you die."

Ava crossed her arms over her body. "And you believe this shit?"

Cecil huffed and held her hands again. "St. Michael the archangel, sorry for Ava. Please defend us in battle anyway."

"Wait, wait, wait," Ava said. "How does he feel about rats?"

"What do you mean?"

"Is he gonna take Figaro to heaven? If I don't pray to him, will Figaro go to hell?" Her eyebrows scrambled across her face like caterpillars until they kissed above her nose.

"Yes," Cecil lied.

Ava quickly flipped open her Dial, and the Pearl projected Google onto her hand. She searched for the prayer and found the words. Knowing she couldn't read well, Cecil spoke slowly so she could follow.

"Be our defense against the wickedness and snares of the

devil. May God rebuke him, we humbly pray, and do thou, O prince of the heavenly hosts, by the power of God," they said.

"Thrust into hell, Satan!" Ava read by herself with enthusiasm, stomping her foot.

"And all the evil spirits," they said, "who prowl about the world seeking the ruin of souls."

Ava threw her hands into the air. "Great, now we won't die. Why doesn't everyone pray?"

A man wearing a raccoon mask and a woman with a confetti mask lifted yellow tape to enter the lobby. The couple stopped in front of a bouncer who handed out yellow hard hats to the guests. Cecil could've sworn he heard the couple introduce themselves as Sigmund Freud and Eva Braun.

When the bouncer checked off *Freud* and *Braun* on the guest list, Cecil and Ava locked arms and prepared for a performance.

Electronica blasted through the hotel's skeleton, shaking the few chandeliers that already hung in the lobby. Sawdust covered a checkered red floor, and brand-new velvet curtains, still covered in packaging wrap, cordoned off the space. A ten-foot-wide painting of a classic Visage timepiece sat half-covered in bubble wrap, ready to be hung over the welcome desk.

It was hard to say whether the hotel was new and soon to be dazzling with luxury or abandoned to rot—tough to say whether it was close to the open or the close.

"Names, please," said the bouncer, who looked like a construction worker in his plaid shirt and orange work boots.

"Ava Germaine."

"And the Graffitied Phantom of the Opera over here?" he asked, pointing to Cecil's mask.

"Carmen Voyer. My plus-one. Mr. Bourgeois told me to bring my agent."

The bouncer tapped a tumorous brown mole on his nose. "Could I please see your face, sir? They told me not to let any ugly plus-ones in here."

"Who are you to say who's pretty or not?" Cecil asked.

"I am Jonah Delemote, chief creative director and photographer for *Couture Italia*. Yes, I'm dressed like a construction worker. But do I *look* like someone who voted for Donald Trump to *you*?" The bouncer pressed his face so close to Cecil's mask that their noses touched.

His Adam's apple bounced in his throat.

"Now, Mr. Voyer, let's be honest with the man." Ava pointed to Cecil's nose and laughed. "He got a nose job yesterday. He can't show his face."

"Oh, I get that." The bouncer pursed his lips. "Explains the agitation too. But, I have an idea... What celebrity does he most look like?"

"A young Clint Eastwood. Everyone says so."

Ava's gaze splashed across to him, steel cloaked beneath puddly dark eyes, playing coquette better than a Bunny played the Playboy.

"Oh. Why didn't you say so? Come in, come in," he said. But before they could pass, the bouncer tapped the plastic mask. "You have an actual plastic nose too. Ha, get it?"

Everyone in fashion had the same nose, that plastic nose. The perfect nose.

The bouncer pointed to a hole in the far wall of the lobby that led to a cemented cavern.

"You first," Ava said.

He couldn't hear Ava calling to him as he stepped into a narrow, boisterously loud hallway.

Graffitied flowers and posters of voluptuous faces and large breasts clung to the exposed concrete. Paint chips dusted each guest's hair. Sheetrock panels leaned against the wall next to pallets of decorative stone tiles, and metal beams dangled from wooden blanks.

Like a funhouse, the foundation seemed to quake and morph with each throb of the bass.

When he finally reached the end of the tunnel, he found the dingy construction site transformed into a chic urban club. Oriental rugs covered the concrete floor. Vintage mirrors and old Hollywood movie posters covered the walls. And playing in the corner were three DJs, *the Three Wise Men*.

It was designed for blabbing socialites. A mobile, marble bar top stood in the center with reclaimed-wood barstools.

All Hallow's Eve was the trend. Twinkling orange Halloween lights decorated the cracks in the cement. Crystal skulls served as sconces. And the scarecrows looked like actual corpses of beautiful people. Instead of hay, they were made of a goo that resembled purplish flesh. Their Visage dresses were splattered in blood. Their eyes were lifeless marbles. And they even smelled slightly like rot covered by air freshener.

It was the definition of high class originality—impoverished, dying chic.

The place suffocated Ava—the heavy smog formed by smoke machines and perfume, the flashing rainbow lights shining down on contorted faces, twitching from cocaine. Pearls and diamonds dripped with languid luxury. Sweating patrons mingled violently, drenching the floor.

There was a distinct aroma about Manhattan clubs—Cheese Balls. Pink Daisy. Dirty Socks. Jasmine. Salty Semen.

Each guest was too disillusioned to care; they had photoshoots to book.

Pants ballooned out in harem styles, and boots came up past the knee. Women wrestled with rogue bra straps showing through their dresses, and men complained of sweating underneath vicuña wool.

Cameras flashed, not from paparazzi, but from Instagram documentation. A photo with Margaux LeClaire earned +900 Instagram followers, +1,000 likes, +90 comments. A photo of Harvey Weinstein, -200 Instagram followers. A photo with any girl who claimed to be a "model" because she did a mattress commercial one time: +400 Instagram followers, all of whom also followed accounts about binging, purging, food porn, and anorexia.

Cecil caught Ava trying to sneak her already blistered foot out of her high heels: "Do you see Bourgeois anywhere?"

A hand tapped Ava. They turned to see a peace-sign mask. A man with long blond hair and an expensive T-shirt stood with a Theory Models briefcase. "Ava Germaine?"

She nodded. "The skin coat bitch, yes."

"Funny. I'm Laurent. I've never met a funny model before... Is this your agent?" he asked, looking at Cecil.

"Carmen," Cecil said. "Voyer Model Management," he said with less confidence than he would've liked. Saying the word *Voyer* out loud was less kitschy and more unbelievable.

Laurent's head cocked like a confused chicken's. "Voyer? Why haven't I heard of you before?"

"Well...I'm small. I mean. The agency is small. I'm just starting out."

"You're young. Is that why you're just starting out in the modeling world? What industry did you come from?"

"Wall Street."

"I was an analyst for Tsai Capital for years. Where were you?"

Cecil couldn't name a hedge fund.

Laurent took a few steps away from them. Cecil could practically hear Ava breathing harder. And Figaro scraped his paws along Cecil's chest.

"Archangel," Cecil said.

Ava rolled her eyes and stroked back an imaginary strand of hair with her shaking hand. Laurent's eyes scanned Cecil's body. His hair. His jacket. His shoes. But the eyes stopped on the watch. He was sure they would be kicked out that second.

The rosary beads. The detail on the Dial. It was like a giant billboard screaming: *I'm Cecil LeClaire.*

But all the skepticism vanished. "Nice Dial. Custom?"

"Yes," Cecil said with a deep inhale.

"Awesome, dude. You must've been a great trader. Ava's a great get. And...since LeClaire's a shit storm, I'm sure she was cheap."

The guy slapped Cecil on the back. He smelled of bourbon.

"*Couture Italia* brought the furnishings; the hotel gave us permission to be here," he screamed over the blasting music. "We do this 'pop-up' biannually around Fashion Week. This location's particularly Brooklyn-hipster-chic, don't you think? Like Andy Warhol meets white homeless man's asshole—bright and tight with a little shit mixed in."

They were pushed toward a group of yuppie thirty-year-olds meant only for a Christmas catalogue. The group shouted. They loved to hear themselves talk, and it was otherwise impossible to hear their voices over the music.

"It's becoming such a drag to travel. Where am I supposed to stash my cocaine if I have to take off my shoes in airport security? Decent restaurants at JFK have been replaced with McDonald's and deli sandwiches. Planes are too democratized now, I say. Private jets should have their own terminal," the tallest man said.

"Trump's evil. Climate change is a problem! Too much carbon emissions. Like, the entirety of fucking California is fucking burning, and he's denying global warming."

"I heard Trump wants to end food stamps. Like, what kind of monster is he?"

"I love that jacket. So hobo chic."

They were social swans swooning. It wasn't even clear if they were talking to anyone but themselves. It was never clear which mouth was producing sound.

"I know what you mean. I vacationed for four weeks in South Africa last winter, then flew to Dubai to buy these shoes I couldn't find in Manhattan, and ended in Paris for six weeks. It was just too much travel. I was exhausted by the end. Traveling is miserable. I can't wait for virtual reality. Then I don't have to share an airplane with a grimy fat man in steerage who didn't work as hard as I did to earn first class."

"I'm all about helping poor people. Diversity. Equality. We have so many feminist strides to make."

"She looks like a fat cow."

"College should be free. Everyone should go to college."

"What do you do for a living? Oh… You're an assistant? That must be humbling."

"Everything is too democratized, not just airplanes. The electoral college is bullshit. It gives poor flyover states full of obese farmers the same political power as the highly populated rich cities that actually contribute to the economy. Rich people have better education, and therefore, we have better morals. Should have triple the votes, I say."

A woman in the group took a round of forty selfies, a camera flash for each wrinkle and imperfection she sought to hide.

"I read an article in the New York Times, or I don't know if it was the New York Times; I just say that every time I mention an

article because it's a reputable newspaper. For all I know it could've been on BuzzFeed or fake news. But anyway, I read an article that said democracy is dead. America has fallen. So basically, we're gonna turn into a third world country, and France will once again be the trendiest fashion queen of the world, bitches."

Cecil knew this game vaguely, whoever could concoct the worst problem or whine the most won the morality contest. It was an instant cure for nouveau-riche-itis. He hated that behavior, that vapid nothingness that actually had a whole lot of damaged subtext hidden underneath.

Suddenly the entire group turned to Cecil. It was as if he was watching a movie and suddenly it was paused. And all the actors turned to him for input. Except, he wasn't exactly sure what he was supposed to say.

"Um...man. I didn't really follow politics at the monastery," Cecil said.

Laurent suddenly resumed his skeptical glance. His nose seemed to redden and swell. His chin jutted out like a judgmental turkey.

"Um. Fuck Trump?" Cecil stated like a question.

"Yeah, fuck Trump," a drunk man said.

"I hope someone assassinates him," someone said.

Cecil tried to stop his eyes from bulging out at the viciousness.

"Is there a bathroom somewhere?" Cecil asked Laurent. He pointed to a corner where the dead scarecrows sat on black spray-painted hay cubes.

As Cecil made his way through the crowd, a woman tapped him on his shoulder. "Cecil LeClaire?"

How had he been recognized with a mask? He turned to see a group of very stylish fortysomethings huddled in a half-circle. "Um. No, sorry," Cecil said, trying to mask his voice with a higher pitch.

"It's you," a cat-masked woman with emerald green eyes said. "Omigod, it's Cecil LeClaire."

Cecil shut his eyes at the name. The jig was already up.

3 4

Ava and Cecil found themselves in the middle of Dante's *Inferno*, a circle of middle-aged women who had "retired" from the industry. One mask was an ironic dinner plate smashed to bits. Another dressed as Coco Chanel.

But the creepiest was the Eiffel Tower mask. It twinkled gorgeously with blue lights until it exploded. Fire shot out of the top of the mask, and bits of plastic showered onto the people around her.

Ava jolted backward and hid her face. "It's an ironic terrorist attack," the mousy-voiced woman explained. The top of the Eiffel Tower snapped back into place and the fog dissipated. "It goes off every ten minutes. Sometimes tiny bloody people shoot out of it."

She bent to the floor and picked up a little action figure of a girl with braided hair and a small dog. The dog's head was blown off, and the girl's arm was burnt and bloody.

"Why would you choose to dress up as a terrorist attack?" Cecil asked. Ava elbowed him in the side, but she accidentally elbowed Figaro who squealed and squirmed up to his shoulder. Several of the women noticed a creature under his jacket, but no one spoke up. Figaro was born for this environment.

"Terrorism is so on trend," the woman said. "An attack happens almost every week. Art isn't about beauty. It's about meaning. About being in touch."

Cecil squinted through his mask. He was grateful for the splatter paint hiding his reddening, angry face.

The woman with a cat mask and emerald green eyes tapped Cecil's shoulder. "Are you here for the casting?" she asked.

"Yes," Cecil said. "But I would appreciate you not telling the casting agents who I am."

"Why not?"

"I'm afraid there might be a stigma associated with the LeClaire name."

"Oh." The Eiffel Tower nodded. "You mean because of the monk thing?" Her voice fell to a soft whisper despite the deafening music.

"No..." Cecil stopped himself from saying something offensive. "From Annabelle Leigh's disappearance."

"If there's a stigma... It's *definitely* the monk thing."

Cecil blinked rapidly to calm his nerves. "Here's the truth. I'm trying to help someone. Someone who will be at The Mall. I'm afraid if the casting agents know who I am, I won't be able to go and save her."

A long silence fell among the ladies. The Dinner Plate pulled out a bag of bright yellow candy corns and began throwing them out into the crowd of people like confetti.

"Just...please. Please don't tell anyone you recognized me."

The women awkwardly cowered their heads, eyes searching their friends' expressions. Who would snitch on Cecil LeClaire first? The room began to fill with dense purple smoke. And green slime dripped from the sconces along the wall. Cecil looked to Ava, who shrugged.

"Who do you think the casting agents are? Who chooses whether or not I go to The Mall?" Ava whispered into his ear.

"Maybe Bourgeois? That group he was with?" Cecil asked.

The Eiffel Tower scrolled through her phone. "Ladies, Bergdorf clearance is on sale."

"If there's a sale on a sale, you know it's a good deal," said the Dinner Plate.

One woman with blond curly hair extensions and a big red bow in her hair, looking like a human rag doll, took a minuscule bite of a brownie at the bar. She said, "I hate this health craze. Lettuce, gluten-free, exercise. Who cares? I prefer the old fashion way. Vodka soda, cigarettes, and cocaine."

She is afraid of that brownie, Cecil thought.

"I don't exercise at all. No, thank you. Only way I'm bending over is to pick my Pierre Lazard heels off the floor," said the Dinner Plate.

She has a personal trainer three times a week, and she walks up and down her staircase obsessively when her daughter isn't watching. She walks the long way to her nail appointment. She counts the steps.

Cecil became transfixed by the ladies. His eyes couldn't leave their masks. He imagined even if they removed the papier-mâché or the plastic from their faces, they still wouldn't look human.

"All these little girls are anorexic now. It's so sad. I read in *Cosmo* that there are more eight-year-olds than ever who count calories. How terrible."

Her eating disorder developed when she was nine.

"I mean, what's a little candy, huh? I try to have a square of chocolate every day."

One square of chocolate. 99% dark. Zero fat. No other solid foods for the rest of the day.

"I hear food doesn't even make you fat, and exercise doesn't make you skinny. It's all genetic."

She doesn't believe that. She gets lunchtime liposuction once a month as a replacement for her now inactive menstrual cycle.

Cecil squinted at the brownie. Blondie hadn't touched it since the conversation about weight and eating started. "Don't you like the brownie?" Cecil asked, trying to solicit a reaction.

"I'm full. Do you want it?"

Cecil handed it to Ava. She shoved the entire brownie into her mouth and swallowed it whole like a snake.

"How are you so skinny?" the Dinner Plate asked in shock.

"I'm sick. Probably muscular dystrophy or something."

Most of the women gave sympathetic frowns, but one piped up and said, "Lucky. See, I told you skinniness is genetic."

Sadistic delusion.

One of the fatter women leaned against Cecil's chest. She wore a heart-shaped mask with Visage Libra logos all over it. "My husband used to be as sexy as you. Now he has a beer belly, and he's losing his hair. What a mistake I made."

She doesn't care about the beer belly. She's sad because he doesn't love her anymore, choosing to sleep with his best friend's daughter instead.

"Are things better with Sebastian, Sandra?"

Sandra chugged the last drop of vodka. "If you're referring to the disgusting rumor, it isn't true. We're perfectly happy. We're dressing up as the yin-yang symbol for Halloween this year."

Sandra caught her husband having an affair with two gay shoe designers in St. Tropez.

The women's heads turned to a tall Russian girl with a black bob cut. She wore a striped black-and-white dress so short that her ass cheeks peeked out from underneath. Her laughter was so loud it pierced through the noisy room. She rubbed her breasts against a photographer's chest and stuck her tongue out for the camera he pushed in her face. A mustache of cocaine stuck under her nose. Got milk?

"I don't miss that age," the Eiffel Tower muttered. "Little girls who don't know what they want from a man. She's lost."

She wants nothing more than to be seventeen again.

"I used to look like that."

Just a little fatter and a lot shorter.

"She opened for Ralph Lauren's most recent collection. I think she's a bit strange-looking, though. That nose is too flat, and her eyes are too far apart. She looks like a cockroach. Why designers are hiring such ugly models lately is beyond me."

She thinks the girl is beautiful. She's jealous. She wants nothing more than for her eyes to be that beautiful.

"We shouldn't be commenting on appearances. This is all Instagram's fault, I tell you. We're used to looking at people's edited fashion photos. Now we have a skewed beauty perception. I hate Instagram."

She checks Instagram seven times a day but doesn't post so people think she's not self-absorbed. Women have been insulting each other's looks since the Ice Age.

"I only really look at Instagram to keep up with my daughter and people who live abroad."

And to read about detox teas, check anorexia pages, read about the supermodels, track intarsia sweater trends, and check for new exercise fads. She looks at her friends' photos and thinks: why don't I have a body like that? My life is so boring.

Cecil finally put his hands up. "Stop it, all of you!" he shouted. "Stop it. Can I be honest with you all for a second?"

They paused sharply like preprogrammed robots, ears quivering at attention, their interests piqued.

"You all have eating disorders, so you don't have to hide it with each other anymore. You all have problems at home with your husbands and children. You all have an Instagram and Internet and gossip addiction like everyone in the United States of America. Your lives aren't perfect, and neither are your friends' lives. You're all hurting inside, and instead of talking around those issues, you should connect with each other and ask for help. You *are* better than this. You *deserve* better than this."

Half the women went slack-jawed, as much as was possible given the surgery and Botox. They cautiously glanced at friends' faces to see if it were true. Did they all feel that way?

Blondie muttered, "Wow."

Bourgeois suddenly came up behind Cecil and Ava, draping his arms around their shoulders. "I see you've met the casting agents."

Cecil covered his mouth with his hands. He was subconsciously trying to pull back his proselytizing. Ava's face somehow turned an even paler shade of white. She gave him a hopeless pout.

"Take off your mask, Ava," Bourgeois said.

Ava removed the mask and hopelessly tossed it onto the floor.

"Well..." Bourgeois said with a stupid grin. He shook Cecil's shoulder. "Introduce her."

"Ava Germaine," he said with downcast eyes. "She most recently was featured in...in the Visage Fashion Week..."

"Wearing a skin coat. Doesn't she need a break from modeling? She was kidnapped and dressed in a dead body a week ago," the Eiffel Tower said.

"She's fine," Cecil said. "She's been through worse."

He tugged on Ava's waist and pulled her toward him. "She's twenty-four, yes, but she's incredibly thin. The clothes will fall on her well. She's got the ghostly look you want. She looks like a prepubescent boy. And she's got the name recognition."

"Does she behave?" asked the Dinner Plate.

"Behave?"

Suddenly Figaro rushed out from beneath Cecil's jacket and climbed up Ava's leg. The Cat Mask jumped into the air. She yelped so loud half of the club turned to look at her.

"Was that an armadillo?" she asked.

"No. It's an elephant," Ava said with an angry glower.

Cecil put his head in his hands. But then the women started laughing among themselves.

"Why do you still want to model, Ava? Isn't it time to retire?"

Ava pouted. "I need the money."

"She likes playing characters," Cecil corrected. "She likes playing characters and dressing up beautifully because she can't bear being herself."

Ava squinted her half-moon eyes, but Cecil continued. "Like me. I'm a monk because I can't handle the thought that Annabelle Leigh died, and there wasn't a purpose to it. I needed to run away because I couldn't bear to face my family."

The Eiffel Tower caressed Cecil's hands and stared with wide eyes. "You're like the Messiah," she whispered. "Can all monks read minds?"

One woman took a long chug. "I have a confession to make… Richard left me a year ago, but we've been pretending to be together. I hear him fuck a different prostitute in our bedroom every night while I sleep in the guest room."

Gasps. Blondie wrapped her arms around the woman while she cried into her neck.

The Eiffel Tower piped up, tears threatening to spill over. "My daughter has had three abortions in the past year, and I secretly hope she gets sent to juvenile prison so they can fix her. I don't even know if she can have children anymore. I'll never be a grandma."

"Awww," they cooed. Tears streamed down, mascara mixing in like runoff from a coal mine.

"Sometimes I sit at home all by myself for days on end. My housekeeper can't even clean the bedroom. I just zonk out and read Facebook posts and fill out personality surveys to see whether I'm an oak or a maple tree. I think I'm depressed."

"I tried to overdose on Advil, but I stopped after three pills because I was afraid they'd make me fat."

"I ate three bags of salt and vinegar potato chips yesterday because I hadn't had a potato chip in a decade… When I had one, I couldn't stop. I'm fucking my twenty-five-year-old trainer, but I know he fantasizes about my daughter when he's inside me. I caught him sniffing her underwear."

"Sometimes I cover myself in peanut butter so my dog will lick me. That's the only sex I've had in three years."

Sympathetic frowns. Shaking heads. Desperation. The women hugged, tears filling their eyes aided by several slurps of vodka and gin. When the tears and the shivers ended, Bourgeois finally raised his hand.

"What in the actual hell is going on?" he asked.

The group turned their attention back to Maxwell Bourgeois. "We want Ava in the show," the Cat Mask said. "We can't pass up the opportunity to bring Cecil LeClaire into the fold."

Bourgeois took a sip from his martini glass. He conspicuously leered into the slits of Cecil's mask. "You really are the president of LeClaire now?"

"May I speak to you for a moment?" the Cat Mask asked.

Cecil nodded as she grabbed him by the wrist and pulled him to the side of a cheap blow-up skeleton. It wore a red leather Buratti suit and handmade Italian sunglasses.

"You see these scarecrows?" the woman asked. "They're corpses for a reason. It's not a joke. It's not irony. They posed your cousin for editorials after she was shot by the sniper at Salon de Ming. And they'll do it again."

"Who are you?" Cecil asked. "How do you know this?"

"I'm Andre Blancas' wife."

She wore a simple black turtleneck and black leggings. Her curled hair was pulled to the side in a delicate ponytail. Cecil knew very little about Andre Blancas. But he expected his wife to be fifteen years old and a model. Not this gorgeous woman.

"We're worried Ava will be taken advantage of at photoshoots," Cecil said. "We've heard prostitution and modeling go hand in hand. So is there a risk?"

"There's a formal sub-business for it. Run by a VD. I don't know what the title stands for. Vice Director? The current one is pretty militant, more dangerous than previous ones."

"He? Are you sure it's a he?"

She shook her head. "I've only heard things. This VD is out of control. He's reckless, dangerous, mowing down bodies like blades of grass... Someone tried to shoot him down at Salon de Ming, but it failed."

"VD was the target at Salon de Ming? I thought it was him shooting at me."

The Cat Mask cocked her head. Her ears seemed to flick in his direction even though they were plaster. "It's only what I've heard."

"Does he have connections to my family?" he asked. "Either Margaux or Perdonna?"

The woman nodded her head cautiously.

"I don't know what The Mall is. But. You should know... They're going to kill Annabelle tomorrow. It's her last year in The Mall."

The Cat Mask flipped open her Dial and projected a photo of Clara with her pink glove, dead in the morgue. Cecil felt acid rise in his throat.

"I overheard Andre's assistant talking about Annabelle dying. I... Please don't tell anyone I told you. I just... Andre would want Ava to be safe."

Bourgeois once again snuck up behind Cecil. He was like a ghostly pilgrim with that long blond hair. He handed Cecil a card with an address scrawled across it. "Make sure Ava is here. Four o'clock."

Cecil nodded. Ava came up beside him, studying his face. She cuddled Figaro to her neck.

"We should talk about LeClaire playing a more significant role in The Mall next year," he said. "Margaux always refused to do it."

"Margaux *refused*? She told me she was never invited."

Bourgeois' eyes bulged as he shook his head like an angry dog. "We begged her to bring all of her models on. But she only lets some of them go to VD."

Cecil gave Bourgeois a fake nod.

"I love your mom. She's so funny. She's all mouth, you know? She likes the shock value. Any way she can feel less inferior to Perdonna, Margaux LeClaire will take it. Grab that headline, girl."

Ava overheard the conversation. She snuck into the spot where Bourgeois had stood. And Cecil pulled her close to his ear. "They're going to kill Annabelle tomorrow if we don't save her."

Ava covered her body with her arms. "What the hell are we walking into?"

35

Steam seeped from beneath a manhole cover, wet and slimy. The smoke puffed up toward the apartment buildings and townhomes, fogging the hundreds of cubed windows in the sky.

Cecil and Ava were dropped off several blocks from Perdonna's home.

Somehow the nights in New York City only amplified the chaos and the glamour. There were no golden stars here. It was a black, smog-lit sky. There were no singing crickets or groaning frogs. Instead, the cars honked louder. And everywhere there was marble. There was concrete. Limestone. Only a small cube of grass was allotted for anything natural, a display case for the world.

"Cecil LeClaire," a voice yelled out. "How does a monk become president of a modeling agency in a week?"

The reporter for *Glamorama*, Jeremy White, appeared from behind a lonesome tree. There were no cameramen. No microphones. No razzle-dazzle.

"I'm not," Cecil said.

Jeremy flipped his Dial and projected a long social media feed onto the sidewalk. He scrolled through the feed and clicked on a video that appeared to be from the club.

The video showed the back of Cecil's head, a black ribbon tied from his mask. Ava stood by his side and the women surrounded him. But despite the blaring music, Cecil's voice could be heard crystal clear.

"She's fine," Cecil was saying. "She's been through worse." He tugged on Ava's waist and pulled her toward him. It looked like a dominant move. An aggressive, dictating gesture. "She's twenty-four, yes, but she's incredibly thin. The clothes will fall on her well. She's got the ghostly look you want. She looks like a prepubescent boy. And she's got the name recognition."

Jeremy scrolled through the chat forum where all of the comments looked something like: *Creep. Child murderer. That pedophile should be in jail for murdering Annabelle Leigh. I'd still fuck him.*

Cecil kicked the tree trunk to his right and immediately hopped back onto his foot. He started running his hands over his jacket. He reached into his pockets. There wasn't a microphone.

"Who could've recorded that?" Cecil asked. "Someone must've had a microphone on me. There's no other way I could've been heard over that music."

He looked to Jeremy who wore a skeptical, shit-eating grin.

Cecil threw his hands up. "No comment."

"*No comment?*" Jeremy asked. "Were you Annabelle Leigh's model agent too? How long have you been an agent? Did Margaux teach you the trade? Is it a family business?"

Cecil grabbed Jeremy by the collar. And his hand writhed with anger. "Shut up. Listen. You want a story? I'm not a story. I'm a punching bag. Tomorrow, there *will* be a story."

Jeremy pushed a button on his Dial band and tapped his wrist to Cecil's. "You have my number," he said, tugging his shirt collar out of Cecil's hand. He walked away with a jaunty gait.

"Ahem," Ava said as she stood at the edge of the avenue. She pointed to Perdonna's house. A dozen news crews huddled behind a line of NYPD officers. "You should go in alone. I'll go in the side entrance."

Cecil felt the cracked skin split open on his knuckles. Ava gave him an awkward but almost comforting pat on the shoulder as she strolled away.

The moment Cecil stepped onto Perdonna's sidewalk, the black cameras wrapped around him like a blanket. The camera necks seemed to bow from the warm, sweaty hands. They were like inanimate heads craning toward him. Their lenses were the marble eyes of taxidermy, glassy and almost real. Coughing fits, were the lens shutters closing by his ear.

The camera was kinder to him than the people holding it.

The police officers tried to keep the cameramen from whacking Cecil in the head or running him over in a stampede. They parted the crews for him. And Cecil walked through the parted pile of humans, like Moses in the Red Sea.

"Are you going to murder Ava Germaine too?" one reporter shouted. "Is that why *she* wore the skin coat?"

"Are you no longer celibate?"

"A Chatter poll shows seventy-eight percent of people think you should be in jail."

Cecil stood before Perdonna's door and spun around. He rubbed his own hands together so hard that the chapped skin on his palms turned to red rashes.

"Tomorrow, I'll bring you the person who abducted Annabelle. I'm going to bring him to you. Right here! And you better abuse and torture him the same way you've ruined my life for ten years."

Cecil slammed the door closed.

Visage suitcases covered in Libras lined the foyer of Perdonna's mansion like toy soldiers. The pink rock salt lights were dimmed, casting shadows like footprints on pristine white fur carpets. Even the fireplaces had been smothered, and Cecil could see his quick breaths puffing vapor into the chilled air.

No light scattered along the gold leaf or the white swan feathers. And the fibers on the ceiling looked almost like cobwebs.

"Hello?" Cecil's voice echoed through the mansion. "Anyone here?"

"Bellino."

He looked over his shoulder to see Perdonna materializing from the shadows darker than coal with a black draped blouse and knee-high boots atop her leather pants.

"You look…"

"Like a Thai nightclub worker?" Leather-clad hands twisted her locks into a bun. "I have to fly to Shanghai. Emergency."

"You're going *now*? Is Shanghai more of an emergency than *this*?"

"I shouldn't be staying in New York while...this is going on." She pointed to the doorway and the mob of reporters who threatened to break down her windows. "It doesn't look *spectacular* to the investors."

She plucked a cookie from a crystal vase in the hallway and suckled her fingers to clear the rogue sugar. She strolled past the golden velociraptor, brushing her cheek lovingly along the bone.

"They're going to kill Annabelle tomorrow night," Cecil said. "That's why she's been trying to escape."

"We'll find her. My team is watching over you and actively searching for Annabelle. There's nothing I can do here that I cannot do from Shanghai."

The dining room table was set for one, adorned with pussy willow branches and white rose petals. The table was a glass aquarium filled with rainbow corals and piranhas. Their teeth jutted out like angry toothpicks. The air smelled of beach: fish and caviar, sand and seaweed.

Mirrored panels covered the ceiling, reflecting Perdonna's black attire like a rain cloud.

"My jet leaves in an hour." She unfurled her red napkin and it waved toward him like a matador's red cape. It was a warning. "Sit," she said.

"I can't eat at a time like this."

"Sit," she repeated. "I have some advice for you. I want to give you a parting message in case you die," she said with a half-smirk.

His hands brushed over the roses on the table—how similar the petals felt to the flesh on a woman's wrist. Perdonna's eyes lingered like a cloudy sunset above the pussy willow buds.

"Someone put a microphone on me at the club," Cecil said. "I just don't understand. What could I have done to deserve this? Do I have an evil face? Home is hell for me."

"There's no place like home," she said wistfully. "Unless you live in North Korea. Or Syria. Or *most* of Africa."

Cecil chuckled despite himself. "My life could be worse, huh?"

"Much worse, bellino. Much worse."

A rattling sound echoed from inside one of the covered silver platters on the table.

"What's that?" Cecil asked.

"Dinner."

"Immacolata made it?"

Perdonna shook her head. "God made it."

The rattling continued, not different from the sound of rats scurrying through walls or subway tunnels.

He tried to lift the lid, but Perdonna placed her hand on his. "We have some time. No rush." Her thumb stroked the tops of his knuckles. His hand never moved from the silver lid for fear that if he even flinched, she'd stop stroking him and he'd lose that familiar serenade of her pulse.

"Someone wants to kill you," Perdonna said. "Most likely because *they* want to enjoy killing Annabelle Leigh. If you save her, what's the fun in that?

"You stare at my eyes too much," Perdonna said, moving the pussy willows from her face. "I can see a bit, you know?"

Cecil felt his pulse speed up. "*All* men stare at you."

"Not at my eyes," she said, a light rose-gold glitter coloring her cheeks. She looked up to the reflective ceiling. "Even mirrors refuse to look me in the eye."

A sloshing sound ricocheted from the other silver platter. Salt seeped into their nostrils. Swish. Swash. He felt like drowning.

When she removed her thumb from his, he saw goosebumps dotting the skin of her neck, like sand granules around her pearls.

"I hate that eating has become so complicated." She fingered her fork. "We used to eat for fuel. We ate because we were animals that needed to fight for life. Today, the rich eat for pleasure. We drink wine because it's sensual, eat sugar because it makes us feel sweet... Sometimes I just want to *have* to eat."

Vanilla-infused drops of sweat trembled on her chest with each of her breaths.

"Sometimes I forget that I'm alive," Cecil whispered.

Clatter. Trickle. Slosh.

The silver platters.

Perdonna's hair tumbled out of her bun like a crashing wave. A gust of perfume escaped her as she stroked his ear with her forefinger. "Ask me what you want to ask me," she whispered.

"What?"

The red scars around her eyes seem to glow like coils on a hot stove.

She finally lifted the lid. Spotted red shrimp danced upon a garnish of ivy leaves and conch shells. Angry red whiskers writhed against insect-like legs. They might as well have been tarantulas.

"I think someone forgot to cook them," he said.

She used silver tongs to place the live shrimps on their plates. The critters tried to scurry away, but were stopped by an ornate lip on the plates.

Perdonna grabbed her shrimp by the tail, and with no hesitation, she tore the shrimp's head from its body. Juice rained onto the plate. The tail contracted and writhed, decapitated. But the head remained alive, still moving its tiny mouth. Flicking its antennas like a dying butterfly would.

She put the eyes in her mouth and sucked, lips glistening with juice. Her tongue flicked around the head. And her gaze never left Cecil's.

The tail went into her mouth whole.

"You're going into The Mall with a false sense of security," Perdonna said. "You think God will keep you safe. But he won't. Not necessarily."

"Why not?"

"Life is very simple. God is very simple. God wants the best. He wants the strongest, the most beautiful, the smartest. Whoever or whatever eats the small, ugly things wins. The jury is still out on you," she said.

Snap. He split the shrimp in two and felt half its life break in his hands. The tail felt gooey in his mouth, and the twitching legs tapped his teeth like fingertips. When he sucked at the head, he felt the pulsing muscles on his tongue. The heartbeat. He could see the shrimp's fearful eyes below his nose. But he slurped the salty juice.

His jeans tightened around his crotch.

"How involved are you in all this?" Cecil asked. "How much power do you have? How—"

"I have power today because the wind blew in my direction," she said. "Tomorrow, I may very well be the shrimp."

She opened the last platter, and a slimy leg crawled up the silver. Tentacles and suckers sloshed and slurped.

"You're joking," he said.

With white chopsticks, Perdonna fished her octopus out of the water. She gripped the tentacles hard and twirled them around the sticks like she would spaghetti around a fork.

"The trick is to bite the head hard and fast, killing the central nervous system. If the suckers latch on to your tongue and cheeks, it becomes difficult to swallow."

She slid the octopus into her mouth headfirst and munched for what felt like minutes. The octopus refused to go down without a fight.

When she finished, her chest was flushed, and her lips were swollen red from gnashing the octopus to death.

"Your turn," she said with a smirk.

"No way."

Perdonna fished the second slimy mollusk out of the water and put it on his plate. Purplish with a bulbous head, the squirming sack of mucus hardly looked appetizing.

"Try it."

Cecil tried to hold the creature in his hand, but it slipped away and rushed down the table.

"Fish are friends, not food," he chided. "Because food doesn't run away."

The octopus wrapped around two of Perdonna's fingers, and she carried it to him. "Open up," she said.

Cecil laughed, eyes trailing down to her engorged lips. The tentacles slipped to his face from her fingers, and he opened his mouth. Slime dripped into his mouth, and he sucked the octopus off Perdonna's fingers. Her warm pulse melted into the octopus's cold meat.

"Don't worry about biting my finger," she whispered.

The muscled tentacles pushed against his cheeks, and he felt his throat contracting, trying to swallow the thing whole. He waged war in his mouth, with vanilla fingertips caressing him along. The metallic flavor of blood flooded his taste buds when he nipped Perdonna.

And it was delicious.

When she removed her fingers, Cecil felt the urge to reach out for her body, to whisper in her ear. But instead he asked, "Are you VD?"

"I have five minutes left with you. Is that really the question you want to ask me?"

No. But he couldn't bring himself to ask what he truly wanted to know.

"Do *you* think I'm VD?" she asked genuinely.

The scars that marred her eyes seemed to disappear, leaving baby-soft skin. He traced his fingers over the fabric of her blouse, and he leaned in to hug her, feeling the cushion of her body.

"Do you trust me?" she whispered.

He swallowed hard, seeing the dark passion in her eyes. "Yes."

His lips danced close to her mouth, but when he leaned in, she presented her cheek.

"Then I'm not going to tell you whether I'm VD," she said. And as soon as her body broke from his, he felt empty again.

When they walked to the hallway, they found Immacolata red-faced, listening.

"Señora, your car is here. And you're late," she whispered and scurried away.

Her manicured nail tapped her Dial. "Well." Perdonna's lips brushed his cheek as the suitcases were carried to her car. "Goodbye, bellino. *In bocca al lupo.*"

"Into the wolf's mouth."

She paused for a moment and cocked her head. She looked like a cat careening toward a hummingbird. "Do you know what it means? I've been saying it to you for your whole life. But you don't know, do you?"

"I assumed it was a cute threat."

"It means good luck."

36

A screeching roar bellowed outside Cecil's bedroom window. He pushed back the scale-covered curtains to see a rusty crane heaving a crystal castle above car traffic and pedestrians.

Cecil looked up to see Ava pushing open her French doors so the crystal castle could be dragged inside. Apparently, the palace was too wide for the elevator.

Tiny white curtains covered in Crevier diamonds sparkled over the backdrop of manhole steam, black garbage bags, and racing yellow taxi cabs.

Cars honked as a taxi driver stopped to watch the crane try to heave the castle through the French doors four stories into the air.

Cecil drowsily trudged up the quartz staircase to find Ava's bedroom.

White alpaca seemed to be Ava's only color scheme. Alpaca floors, alpaca lampshades, alpaca comforter. Even the sconces were covered in creamy puffs. It was a white wonderland, except for the tiny splashes of black on the aspen bark that lined her walls.

Henry sat on the floor wearing work boots, a hardhat, and camouflage sweatpants. But it wasn't dirt or gunpowder covering him, it was glitter. He applied sparkle and stickers to a treehouse for Figaro's castle.

"You didn't leave with Perdonna?" Cecil asked.

"I had more important work to do," he said with a serious nod. "Building rat hammocks and feather beds."

Bridges, climbing ropes, and rat toys sat scattered around him, along with power tools and screws.

Ava undid the straps that clung to the crystal castle, freeing it from the crane. Autumn leaves whipped into the white cloud. Cecil realized Figaro had been camouflaged against the furry white comforter the whole time.

"But why didn't you leave with Perdonna?" Cecil asked. "She's in Shanghai. She needs protection. You have to be with her at all times."

"She took one of our other guys. Giorgio."

"If she's in Shanghai, doesn't she need more than one bodyguard? She's not exactly popular there."

"She thought you needed me more."

"She's not in Shanghai, is she? She lied about where she's going."

Ava was completely oblivious to the tension. She switched on her Dial, setting the hologram to film Figaro's first steps in his crystal castle. She filmed as he ran through the many miniature ballrooms. It was meant to be a dollhouse, which seemed to be ideal for a rat. He whipped up the crystal staircase and jumped onto the second floor where a miniature chandelier hung. He leaped onto the swinging crystal circle and rode it like a tire swing.

She fixed her hair over her Visage pajamas that were covered in Libras. Then she turned the camera onto herself. "This is Figaro, the gentlemanly rat. Signing off."

It was a Chatter video.

Cecil looked Ava over. Her eyes were puffy, and her hair was a mess. She rubbed her neck and wrenched her back in pain. And the twitching muscle in her cheek looked like a beetle trying to escape through her mouth.

"I got up early this morning to help Henry build toys for Figaro," Ava said.

"We're about to go into a mysterious fashion party run by a sex trafficker, and you're building rat toys."

Ava squinted her eyes into tiny rat circles.

"We could die. Annabelle could die."

Ava shrugged with a blasé toss of her hair. "I don't die."

"Everyone dies."

"Not me. Not yet." She craned her neck in front of his face, showing off a black choker necklace. "Anything look suspicious about this?"

Cecil fingered the strap; a black jewel sat in the middle, just below her chin. Two decorative screws garnished the sides. No wires. No visible lenses. "I assume there's a camera in here, but I don't see one."

"It's the screw," Henry said.

He squinted. The screw head couldn't have been bigger than a millimeter. "Well done."

"Look at her ears," Henry said, standing up and dropping decorative pink puffs from his pockets.

"I don't see anything but earrings."

"Take them off her."

He pinched the earring to undo the clasp and held it in his hand, turning it over in his palm, putting it up to his eye. They looked like plain pearls. Not a cord, wire, or microphone.

"I've been waitin' to use this for years," Henry said. "It's a molecule microphone. I embedded dibenzoterrylene and anthracene into the earring. The electron clouds create waves. A computer will track those shifts and monitor the frequency of sound. Through a headset and your Dial, you'll be able to clearly hear everything that's said around her."

"That's incredible." Cecil clipped the earring back on her, and Henry gave him a laptop and an earpiece. "But what if they make her take the earrings off?"

"We can pin a small backup to her inner ear, if you feel better with that?"

Cecil nodded.

"You'll be able to track her on the laptop too. So you can follow them to help you break into The Mall."

Ava combed her hair with aggressive strokes. It was so long that she had to scrape at the ends until entire knots seemed to break apart into dust. "My safe word will be *Hitler.* If I say 'Hitler,' come get me," she said.

"A more ironic sentence has never been spoken," Cecil said. "Hitler?"

"I can work 'Adolf Hitler' into a conversation better than any other word. *Marshmallow, president, fairy, Hamilton, bacon*...no. People love talking about Hitler, just look at the History Channel lineup."

"Our grand plan for taking down a sex trafficking ring is to talk about Hitler?"

"Yep."

♎

They took the subway to the meeting place.

The downtown 6 train station smelled of urine, and the walls looked so dirty that they might as well have been in a sewer. Garbage packed the railways, threatening to start a fire and set all of public transportation ablaze. Yet New Yorkers loved their subway. If they didn't use it, they would be stuck in a taxi in midtown traffic, watching tourists gawk at Times Square.

People packed into the train car so tightly that they could feel each other's sweat leak through their shirt fabrics. Stomachs pressed to asses, and grimy hands touched on the metal handrails. While Cecil chose to stand, Ava pushed people out of the way for a seat.

She peeked over the shoulder of the girl next to her who edited a photo of herself in a bikini, erasing the cellulite bumps that covered her thighs. Her pimples melted away with the touch of a button. She magically shrunk her waistline. Even the head and jaw needed thinning. Breasts enlarged and shadowed, abs drawn on like squiggly lines.

"You don't have to do that, you know," Ava said. "You can post baby animal pictures instead."

The girl posted the photo to Instagram. #Beach #SexyBeach #GirlOnBeach #ModelOnBeach #AnorexiaJK #VogueREADY. She scrolled through other profiles and wrote comments like, "Gained weight? Check out my diet tips," and, "Feeling heavy, get #VogueREADY. Follow me."

"Never mind. Screw you," Ava said.

"Excuse me?"

The doors opened at the Fifty-Ninth Street stop, and Cecil waved Ava out of the train car. She put up her middle finger and stomped out, pushing past a homeless man on her way.

They stood among tourists holding shopping bags from Givenchy, Crevier, and Visage. The cobbled streets and the colorful lofts made the area feel like a luxury village surrounded by concrete skyscrapers. Light shone down on the cobblestones, air smelling like roasted almonds and popping kettle corn. It was a peaceful scene despite the mood.

"This is where I leave you," Cecil said.

Ava handed him a long piece of paper on rose gold and seafoam Visage letterhead. "This is my will. Henry wrote it up for me last night."

Her will was written in scratchy, terrible handwriting. But Henry had spent a lot of time on it, judging by the precise spaces between the words and lines. The will read as follows:

*Please use my piggybank money to pay for Figaro for the rest of his life. If there is money left over, please pass that money on to any of his future babies.

*Figaro must eat Mazuri rat pellets. Don't buy him the cheap pet store shit.

*Love Figaro. Or please find someone else who loves him.

"So you have been worried," Cecil said with a sad huff.

She nodded. "I'm worried. Just not about my life. About Figaro's. Nobody took care of me. But I take care of Figaro. Nobody loves me, but I love Figaro. I might not be worth much, but Figaro is. Because he's loved."

Ava pulled Figaro out of her big black bag. She brought him

to her face and rubbed her nose into his bedhead fur. "Don't eat rhubarb," she said to him. "Promise. Don't eat rhubarb ever."

Tears started to well up in her eyes, and she handed him to Cecil.

"We shouldn't do this. I can go to the address alone," Cecil said. "I can be incognito and try to follow the models into The Mall without you."

"That won't work. Look, it's still a fashion show. Run by a known sex trafficker, yeah. But still a fashion show. There is probably as much chance that I die in a car crash."

"It's run by a sex trafficker who killed Jordan Jones and tried to shoot me at Salon de Ming."

Ava shrugged. "I was just trying to make you feel better."

Neither of them knew what to say next. Cecil opened his arms for a hug, but Ava wrenched up her nose, repulsed.

Taking in a deep breath, she gave a thumbs-up. "*Sieg heil.*"

Cecil smiled despite himself. "*Sieg heil.*"

♎

High fashion models were easy to spot, all wearing the same uniform. Large bags strapped onto their backs held heels, multiple bras, and nude Spanx with gross beige tights. Their heads poked above the city crowds, usually with dyed hair in silvers or reds.

When Ava stopped in front of the address written on Bourgeois's card, she didn't like what she saw—cracked windows covered in dirt and wrappers from Wendy's. Loud techno music blasted from inside the building. Rags dangled from broken windows, and two bloody needles sat on the sidewalk. No business license hung near the stoop.

It was exactly like every other modeling job she had attended.

A large man wearing a red-stained wifebeater and a glowing dildo hanging from a pocket chain stood outside.

"Excuse me, is this number forty-two?" Ava asked.

"Yep, you got it. You here for Demarchelier? Or are you a new girl?" the man asked, a teddy-bear smile on his face.

"New girl."

He swung his dildo on the chain like it was a car key. "Then welcome, welcome, little lady. I'm Jesus. Used to drive tomato trucks, now I manage this place. So let me know if ya have any problems with anyone, like if a girl stabs you with a heel or puts the black plague virus on your hair thing. That shit happens." He gave her a bug-eyed look as if to say, *Trust me these bitches are crazy.* "Boys inside will help with whatever you need—water, chocolates, hairspray. Hell, we even got pimple concealer for you pale kids."

"Thank you."

"Hey," he said, eyes leering close at her face as if he were inspecting an antique at the Met, "you've got special eyes. And those stickin'-out ears will make *you* stick out too. You're a cool-lookin' chick. How old are ya?"

"Eighteen," Ava lied.

"Hmm, little old. Tell them you're sixteen. You can pass. Then you've got a real good chance."

"Any other tips?" Ava asked.

Jesus pursed his lips, bobbling his head like a turkey, his thinking face. "I like you. So I'mma tell you something." He leaned in to whisper, smelling of cigarettes and cheese puffs. "If the model men give you water, don't drink it. I've seen shit happen."

Inside, gruff men sat around on barstools. Their shirts had holes and beer stains, and their beards grew so long that little food particles tangled in the hairs. Trash covered the floor. Slot machines covered the walls. It looked like a Nevada biker bar, especially because of the neon Playboy Bunny signs on the walls.

The floor was black and white, but the white tiles had yellowed after years of being covered in beer.

"Hey, hey, hey," a chubby man said, clapping his hands. "What you here for, little mama?"

"I'm going to the model casting," Ava said.

"Third floor. Studio B. Good luck, sweet honey."

She walked up a tight staircase with creaky wooden stairs.

Crinkled posters covered the walls, and strobe lights blasted in her face.

Ava had never been inside a crack house, but she imagined they smelled and looked something like this. Naked photos of voluptuous women with large, highly altered breasts peeled off the grimy walls.

Loud pop music blared from a photoshoot. A high-pitched male voice radiated from the studio. When Ava peeked her head in, she was shocked to find a fashion shoot straight out of a Hollywood movie.

Four giant fans blew pink and purple silks into the air. It was a full photo studio set, including softboxes, reflective umbrellas, and three separate cameras. At least twenty men—stylists, hair, makeup, lighting—made up the crew, just to shoot one model. Makeup mirrors came equipped with hundreds of brushes, each one shaped for a unique effect.

Designers pinned fresh roses and daffodils to the model's white gown. She crouched in the commotion, wearing makeup so thick that she looked like a scarecrow in person. But on camera, she looked like a princess.

The photographer hopped up and down every two seconds. He changed the lighting obsessively with each click of the camera shutter.

"Yes, darling. Fabulous, fabulous!" he called. "Flip the hair forward. Harder! Yes! You're beautiful. Think supermodel. Be Heidi Klum, be Heidi! Give me Heidi."

Ava was transfixed. She remembered those days, and part of her longed for them. The good parts, at least. The photoshoots shot in luxury Park Avenue buildings or chic Brooklyn lofts. Most of the abuse leveled by Blancas should've been erased from her memory.

She walked up the next flight of stairs to a studio on the third floor.

Girls aged thirteen to nineteen sat on cheap metal folding chairs with school backpacks and water bottles. Some had raggedy clothing with holes at the knees, others had Gucci dresses and backpacks from Buratti. They stared into their cheap flip phones, trying to catch their reflections in the darkness. Side-eyed glares were given to the prettiest girls.

No parents attended. Not even a nanny.

Some girls picked their nails, others twirled their hair. Each girl stared at the next, comparing the shape of their eyes, the size of their waists.

Size mattered when the industrial revolution created clothing for the mass market, and fabrics were no longer cut and sewn at home, no longer tailored to a specific body. When there were only sizes small, medium, and large, small became the best size.

Why would you want to be medium when you could be small?

Size became a competition.

And then makeup became a paint job. And we valued angular cheekbones and youth because bridges made of triangles seemed to work best. And new, shiny, updated gadgets had the most value. Girls were mechanized, as angular as the machines that made them, sitting in a room, waiting for a valuation. They waited to find out how much their bodies were worth.

The girls showed up to work to be the best. They were competitive. They were destructive.

"Okay, girls, bikinis and heels. Be ready in two," a man said through closed double doors.

Only the booming music from downstairs gave a rhythm to the floorboards.

She watched as the girls stripped their clothing down to bikinis. They wore a variety of suits, paisley patterns and geometric shapes, and even cheap "Corona" bikinis purchased on the Jersey Shore.

Ava chose to go in a bra and underwear. She thought it would get her extra points.

"Excuse me?" a little blonde girl asked. "Does anyone have an extra bikini?"

No one acknowledged her. And when the nerves got the best of her, the little girl started to cry. Her silver barrette slid down from her hair because she didn't pin it in properly.

"If any of them did have an extra, they wouldn't give it to you," Ava said.

The girl shuffled in her seat. She wore a fancy golden dress, not the jeans and tank top uniform.

"Go in your bra and underwear. People do it all the time," Ava said.

Still, the girl cried.

"You're gonna have to suck it up," Ava said. "This is the easy part." The girl began wailing and hid her face in her fluffy golden skirt. "What's your deal?"

"Huh?" she asked.

"Your story. Name. Agent. Where you from?"

The girl pouted. "Lilly Blake. I don't have an agent yet. One just came up to me at my school today. I went with her to here."

An Ami clothing label was attached to the inside of her dress skirt. "Do you have a nice home?"

"Yeah," Lilly said.

Girls aggressively tugged tangles from their long hair. They smacked their cheeks to put some last-minute rosy hues onto the bare skin. Some even lathered themselves in petroleum jelly. The extra glimmer made them stick out.

Models' bodies incurred severe damage from stylists pulling at their hair and applying and scrubbing away their makeup sometimes six times a day for different photoshoots or runway jobs. Teenaged girls required serious upkeep.

"Then go to that home. This isn't what you think it is."

Ava slipped off her jeans and tank top to reveal a black bra and underwear.

"But my mom and dad are at work," she said.

Just when Ava was about to push her back down the steps, Bourgeois walked into the holding area.

"Alright, girls. Let's get started."

37

Cecil was stationed at the closest coffee shop. The Tea-Pea.

It looked like a hairball vomited up by the Cheshire cat from *Alice in Wonderland*. Twinkle lights hung from the ceiling, and bright pink covered the walls. Cecil sat in a white plastic chair covered in fake flowers with a table shaped as a smiling clown face. Mickey Mouse danced on the television screen on a loop. The place felt like LSD for teenyboppers.

The tea served had enough sugar in it to give Type 2 diabetes to two sumo wrestlers, and the scones were covered in shells of caramel and chocolate.

Cecil wore a black hoodie, trying to conceal his identity.

There were girls, all under age ten, and all wearing princess dresses for tea with their American Girl dolls. Every parent complained about Cecil's creepiness to the management. But no one kicked him out or called the police because Cecil's excitement for the poster of *The Mary Tyler Moore Show* charmed the old lady owner. Maybe he would have been better off in a Starbucks.

He could overhear through his earpiece everything that Ava experienced—the footsteps, doors closing, even the sounds of backpack zippers.

The girls auditioning looked no different from the girls dressed in their tea gowns, and Ava didn't look much older than the Tea-Pea birthday girl. But they found themselves in different worlds, with different struggles.

One girl worried about whether she'd get the American Girl dollhouse for Christmas, the other girl worried about seeing December alive.

Cecil began to pray as Ava waited in the holding room.

♎︎

The casting room looked like a ballet studio, equipped with mirrored walls and a barre. Pearl-hued linoleum tiles and pink trim. It evoked Barbie packaging, a pink cardboard box held together with translucent plastic.

Girls lined the mirrored wall like skinny soldier slaves. Each had a white piece of paper tied to her bikini top, which read #575, #22, and #44.

The room smelled of strawberry lip gloss and flowery body spray. To Ava, the teenaged models looked like poppies in a field. Their stems were white, their petals colored in pink, yellow, or brown.

Ava knew the narrative in Bourgeois's head. Gorgeous pelvic bones. Perfectly curved femur bones. Which sack of flesh was best in show? Does it smell like a rose or honeysuckle? Does it have voluptuous lips, or thin, villainous ones? Does it smile when you look at it, or shiver with fear?

White Venetian masks—full-faced, resembling the ones Margaux made her mannequin models wear—sat at the feet of the girls. *Bauta* masks with strong square jaws, covering the entire face. *Moretta* masks, complete with black veil, the "mute maidservant." And the *Volto*, the mask so carefully sculpted to mimic flesh, cheekbones, and nose that she could've mistaken it for being a humanoid face.

In the mirrored panels across from Ava, she could see legs, thighs, and breasts reflected kaleidoscopically. Jagged images of arms clashing with collarbones, a pair of breasts reflected above heel-clad feet. Judging a model was like chopping up a body in a morgue.

Most of the agents would've preferred to take a piece from each body and assemble the perfect girl.

Occasionally, Ava would see the reflected image of a teary eye. No number of youthful chins or hourglass torsos could compare to the flash of a blurry brown iris. In brief moments, a spark of expression would pass behind those vacant stares. A model's soul was a dying lightbulb flickering beneath glass.

When Ava looked down the line, she realized they all looked the same but with variations. A tall girl with wide eyes and tiny shoulders. A tall white girl with wide eyes and tiny hips. A tall girl with wide eyes and a body thinner than a strand of hair.

When each girl was equally lovely, she could only be defined by her flaws.

Bourgeois inspected the girls like fine china, while his assistant, a short Indian man wearing lifts, jotted notes. Bourgeois could've been one of the girls lined up, with long blond hair and prominent cheekbones...the body of an adolescent boy. His black jeans were so tight that his legs looked like a black mermaid tail.

"Welcome, ladies! Congratulations, Mall first-timers. This event will be life-changing for you. It's an interactive show, so it won't be anything like what you've experienced modeling before."

Bourgeois leaned into his assistant's ear and whispered as he pointed at model #55. He pointed at her greasy, unwashed hair and gesticulated. Suddenly a woman wearing a black suit appeared and took #55 out of the room.

"Things will become clearer throughout the night," Bourgeois said with a smile, ignoring the interruption. "But there is one rule more important than them all. You'll hear it fifty more times. *Don't let the client take photos of you.* Photos will be shot by our in-house fashion photographer, and the client can pay extra to take those home. You have to stay with the client for the full time period. Treat the client with kindness and respect, be charming, and look your best."

The woman who took #55 out of the room re-entered and continued whispering to Bourgeois.

Suddenly Ava felt like they were lined up as cattle at a farm show, waiting to be graded like prime steaks chopped at the slaughterhouse.

"You're nervous," the girl next to Ava whispered in her ear. "Don't be. My former agent said VD doesn't want to kill us. We're too valuable. Most of the clients are millionaires with reputations. And it's a seven-hundred-thousand-dollar fine if you go missing or die during The Mall."

"How many have died?" the little blonde Lilly asked, overhearing.

Just before the girl could answer, Bourgeois shaped his hand into a pistol and pretended to shoot her in the head. He stroked the blond hair in his ponytail. "Right. I'm going to select girls for Masterpiece."

"If you weigh more than one hundred and fifteen pounds, stand to the right, please," Bourgeois said.

Six girls moved to the right of the room.

He walked up to a voluptuous girl who stayed in her spot. She couldn't have been larger than a size two.

"You're a lying whore," he whispered in her ear. He licked his lips in front of her face as if he were going to tear open her mouth and stick his tongue down her throat.

"But I'll let you stay. Only because you have nice eyebrows."

Bourgeois snapped his fingers at the assistant, and music played. Electronica thrummed with a pulse so rapid it reminded Ava of being on speed. The lights dimmed to a less sterile hue.

"Put on the masks," he said.

The girls bent down, almost in synchronization, afraid to do anything wrong. They put the masks on, hiding their faces, and an eerie, sickening feeling fell over Ava. Innocence vanished from their bodies. Any ounce of a soul that once squeezed through their fearful eyes was nullified by masks.

Blankness.

Armored soldiers, muted maids in black veils of mourning, jokers with daggered noses.

Ava could no longer compare her anxiety to the experience of the other girls. She was alone despite being in a crowded room. Alone, with Cecil a block away.

"Each time my assistant claps, change your pose," Bourgeois said.

He clapped, and instantly each girl bent her body into an awkward shape. Some put their arms above their heads, some were sexy, some hunched their shoulders over, posing their elbows into triangles. They stood like pieces in one mosaic.

When a person's face was taken away, it became easy to focus only on their product. On their body.

The circumference of a body's thigh was in focus. One body was brown-eyed with a mole above its belly button. Another had a weird left middle toe. This one has a nicer uvula than the white girl. This one has a pretty patella. This one looks like a meerkat.

Bourgeois clapped to get everyone's attention. "If I tap you, please move to the left."

He started at the far end of the room, and the music changed to a soft orchestral piece. Chopin.

But just as the romantic, calming music began, so did the horror. While he tapped most of the girls on the shoulder, he hurt the ones he didn't touch, shoving them to the right.

He approached a tall Asian girl. "Beautiful. Where is home for you?"

Through her muffling mask, she said, "My family."

"I mean geographically."

Her mask cocked to the right, showing she didn't understand. "Geogr...geo...what?"

Like a vise, his hands clutched her head. He said, "Bend over, face the wall."

With a rough tug, he spun her around and made her bend at the waist, putting her ass directly on his hips. He wrapped a measuring tape around the fat part of her butt. But his fingers lingered just below her center.

"Thirty-five inches," he said. "What does your family feed you? Fried rice and dog fat?"

His hand crashed against her ass, and she squealed, causing a visible reaction in all the other girls.

He grasped her ponytail like a horse's lead. She stayed on the ground, coughing, pretending to be sick so she wouldn't have to move. "Stand up!"

When she stood, a voracious smile crossed his face. "To the right, please."

He walked back to the center of the room and looked on at them.

"Less than one percent of the girls in this business make a living. One percent of the one percent get houses on Park Avenue and an extra vacation house in St. Tropez. Before that, you have to suffer. You have to prove you're obedient, that you're willing to work hard to be the prettiest girl in the world. You can either eat half-eaten hamburgers out of the McDonald's trash can, or you can eat a penis here and there."

Ava scoffed out loud, which she later regretted.

"Have a problem?" he asked as he approached her. "Cecil LeClaire should lash you for being a bitch. Bet religious men aren't too good at keeping models in line."

"He makes me pray. That's a bigger punishment."

He looked her up and down as if she were a sculpture. His eyes stopped at her belly button, staring at the one orifice he couldn't stick anything into, the forbidden sexual organ. Ava felt heat stick inside her mask like the uncomfortable moisture under a rain poncho.

She could barely see him through the mask. She saw him as a separate player, a third *thing* outside of herself. But when his hand touched her stomach, she became painfully aware of her body and the cage it represented.

His fingertips toyed with her bra clasp. The smirk on his face meant to ask her if she would allow him to demean her.

When his fingers undid the clasp, she cracked her hand across his cheek, making him roll his jaw.

Though Cecil couldn't say a word, Ava knew he was watching.

Bourgeois tore off her mask in anger and tossed it all the way across the room. It smacked into one of the mirrored panels and fell in a corner, reflecting on all mirrored surfaces equally.

"Girls on the right, you're the Poppy group. You'll go with Rajesh. Girls on the left, you'll be with Sarah. Your group is called Carnivale. And the middle, Masterpiece group, you're with me."

38

Shirley Temple was back and black.

Heidi played on the screen in the Tea-Pea, where the new generation of younger girls barely knew the child starlet who once wore ribbons and frilly little pinafores.

Her beaming smile, her maturity, her swaying hips, her ability to enchant even middle-aged men... Cecil scanned the babes holding their dolls at the Tea-Pea. What was a ten-year-old like in 1930? Certainly different than an iPhone-wielding youngster of today.

In *Heidi*, Shirley played a bouncy child, drifting through the Swiss Alps, hand in hand with a creepy old man.

In *Wee Willie Winkie*, Shirley played a bouncy child, drifting through India with a creepy male prisoner.

In *Little Miss Marker*, she played a bouncy child, drifting through horse racing tracks with a creepy male librarian.

A recurring theme.

Were animal crackers in her soup?

Cecil watched his own Shirley on the computer screen. Four girls were chosen from the casting, but Ava was taken away separately.

Ava whispered into her earpiece as she followed Bourgeois

up a staircase. "I got the pretty group. I got the pretty group," she taunted with pride. "I'm like ten years older than this little blonde, Lilly, and I'm still hot."

Bourgeois brought Ava and the other Masterpiece girls to a grimy corner that looked like an amusement park bathroom. A wrinkled black backdrop was stained with beer, and no sunlight shone on beige tiles.

But the Polaroid pictures that hung on the wall had "Couture" written on them in plain red ink. They looked like a stalker's collection of teenaged porn.

Young girls straddling poles, stools, and men. They wore wet white tank tops with nipples peeking out. They posed bare-chested, wearing only black lacy panties and heels.

And two of the four Kardashians?

Cecil looked closer. Famous leading ladies appeared in the trashy collection. Did VD make private sex tapes for celebrities? But Ava didn't point to Kim Kardashian. She pointed to a blonde, about twenty-two, whose pose somehow managed to be regal, despite being completely naked among trashy girls. The photo was a faded Polaroid bursting with pastel colors, thoroughly of the eighties. Was he supposed to recognize her?

Ava's finger slipped down to the only accessory—a watch on the girl's wrist. *The* watch.

Tazia Perdonna.

The Frenchman flew in with a flick of the black curtain like Count Dracula and handed Ava a water bottle.

"Come on, Ava. It's hot in here. You've gotta be thirsty."

Bourgeois smirked, twirling the tips of his blond hair in sync with Ava biting the tips of her own. "You've done incredibly well, Miss Germaine. Surprisingly well, in fact." He shoved the water bottle at her, forcing the rim to her lips.

He lifted the curtain for Ava to go back first.

"Standing still and posing is pretty easy," Ava said. "My only talent is looking like a ghost on crack."

"And trying to save Annabelle."

Bourgeois took the microphone out of her ear and stripped the earrings and choker from her.

"VD doesn't want you too involved, Ava."

"How does VD know me?"

"She knows Cecil." He hesitated and then looked around the room, leaning in to whisper into the earring. "Cecil, I hope you haven't burned your tongue on that Swedish Fish Chai Latte. Because you'll want to be in top form. You won't be finding Annabelle tonight. And don't even think about calling the NYPD."

♎

Cecil dropped his headset and sprinted out of the Tea-Pea. His heart beat through his ears. The New York traffic seemed to suddenly slow down. He rushed across the street, frantically waving his arms, praying the cars would stop.

The car horns blared so loudly they sounded like screams. One taxi came to a screeching halt and still managed to bump his calf.

"What the hell, man?" the driver yelled, opening his car door and jumping out.

But Cecil had already made it to Jesus, who stood swinging the red dildo on a chain.

He tried to rush upstairs, but Jesus grabbed him by the shoulders.

"No one allowed up there," Jesus said.

"A woman's being abducted," Cecil said. "The sticking-out-ears girl. She was talking with you about an hour ago." His words barely escaped between the nervous huffing.

Jesus rubbed his hands together. "Yo, Don," he said, waving his hands at the other men who sat in the bar. "They snatched that girl. That girl they carried out. They be stealin' her. Bastards."

"It was only a minute ago. He hasn't taken her yet," Cecil said. "He just threatened me that they would take her but—"

"Nah." Jesus shook his head. "The other girls at the casting went out like thirty minutes ago. They kept the little ghost one here for a while. Then just a minute ago, snatched her out at the speed of light."

Cecil put his face in his hands and leaned back against the grimy wall.

"Sorry, man. We thought it was strange. Just didn't want to get involved. Wish we had," Jesus said.

"Do you mind if I just check for myself?" Cecil asked.

"Yeah. Course, man."

Cecil sprinted up the stairs. The grimy checkered floors. Empty photoshoots that left behind glitter and duct tape. And an abandoned ballet studio. But all he could hear were his own footsteps.

Ava was gone.

39

Water flowed down the glass walls in shades of aquamarine. Men tried on winter coats made of white moss. And a girl stared up at the ceiling aquarium, where three giant stingrays swam above like bats in the night.

Cecil rushed into the Visage flagship as a sweaty mess. His hair looked like a wet, brown rag. Half of the customers inside stopped and shot pictures of him.

"I need Perdonna," he yelled across the room to the sales assistant. "Get her on the phone, please."

The small girl cowered behind the desk encrusted with tiny blue mussel shells. "Can I get security to the front now?" Her eyes nervously traced over Cecil's flushed face and crazed huffing.

"I'm Cecil LeClaire," he said.

"I told you," he heard a little girl whisper loudly to her mother.

"It's an emergency. A life and death kind of emergency," he said. "I've tried calling her. She's not answering. Don't you have an emergency pager for her?"

"One minute, sir. I'll get someone to help you," the sales assistant said, escaping behind a door.

Cecil leaned against the desk, feeling his hands sink into the cold stone.

A giant portrait of Perdonna hung above the desk. Her naked body sprawled out on the ocean shore, covered in seashells. Her hair tangled with the white foam of a wave crest. It felt strange to watch customers take selfies with a seductive portrait of her.

He wanted to cover her with a giant black curtain so no one else could see her.

Cecil walked around the desk to knock on the door. "Emergency," he said. "*Urgent* emergency."

For a brief moment, he thought he would collapse on the floor. He felt light-headed. He wished he was in a trance. And in Visage, it felt like he was.

A woman broke into tears upon seeing Perdonna's own blue diamond Dial displayed in a marble case. Guests stood in front of mirrors, clicking through options as a robotic "Perdonna-voice" recommended clothing based on their body types.

"Excuse me," a man said, tapping Cecil on the shoulder. He held out a shopping bag topped with white feathers instead of tissue paper. "Could you sign this? My daughter's a huge fan."

Cecil felt his guts sink into his feet. Suddenly he went from being light-headed to flabbergasted. "I'm a suspected murderer. I'm not sure you should support your daughter's fandom."

"Hey. At least you're not in a boy band."

He gritted his teeth and signed the bag.

"We don't think you killed Annabelle Leigh, though. You don't seem the murdering type. A little rapey, sure. I could see you molesting some teenagers. But not murder."

Cecil squinted his eyes and felt a big groan escape his lips. "Thanks."

The sales assistant came down the stairs with a strapping Indian atelier. He wore an all-white lab coat covered in fish scales. "Perdonna's in Shanghai."

"I'm aware. Can you page her, please?"

"We're not allowed to page her today. She said we can't page her under any circumstance."

"Someone's been abducted. I think Perdonna might have

information that can help me get her back," Cecil said in a rush.

The atelier gave a worried look to the sales assistant.

"*I* didn't abduct her."

His claims did not unfurrow the atelier's brow.

"I need to speak with her right now."

When the atelier didn't budge, Cecil walked behind the desk. He began toying with the miniature mirror at the entrance.

"Sir, you can't go up there," the atelier said.

The mirror was similar to the one in the LeClaire mansion, but it didn't paint faces. Instead, it seemed to scan Dials.

He flipped open the Dial, and the mirror sketched his rosary bead design in gold. The door unlatched.

He sprinted up the staircase, feeling his feet slide against the stone.

"You shouldn't run," the atelier said. "The flowers make it slippery."

Above, hundreds of vines of purple wisteria encased the ceiling and the walls. The staircase shimmered with indigo malachite. The deep purple ridges gleamed like the world's most expensive purple Pop Rocks. He had to shove through the creamy vanilla-scented flowers to reach the first-floor hallway.

The wisteria enclosed the entire space of the staircase in a tunnel full of purple feathers.

They reached a keypad at the entrance of the first floor.

"What's the code, please?" Cecil asked.

He noticed the atelier's face redden. His feet seemed to tap along to his quickening breaths.

"What's your name?"

"Om."

"Om. Nice to meet you, Om." He held out his hand. "Perdonna programmed me into the system. She doesn't care if I come up to the studio."

Om clacked his teeth together. "You'll take the blame if she's angry?"

Cecil nodded.

"It's 0-8-0-2."

The door swung open and led to a long hallway surrounded

on all sides by an aquarium. Bright red-and-blue corals shot up around them. Stingrays and tiger sharks cruised by. It made him feel grand. He felt like a king walking through water.

Two giant mirror touchscreens sat along the walls.

"You can page her from here," Om said.

Cecil touched the screen, and suddenly a robotic image of Perdonna appeared on the screen. "Hello. Please let me know how I can help."

His skin crawled at the sound of her elegant accent. The voice was a creepy mimicry of hers. But the emphasis of the syllables and the seductive timbre in her voice was lost. It felt cold. Like an abstraction of the woman he loved.

"Page," Om said.

"Tazia Perdonna has turned off the paging capability today," the mirror said.

Om gave a pout to Cecil. "She'll kill me if I override this."

"How long have you worked here?" Cecil asked.

"About four years."

"How often does she turn off her pager?"

Om's eyes floated up to the ceiling. His lips moved as he counted through his own mental calendar. "About once a year."

"Is it always October 30th?"

Om's bushy eyebrows jumped. "Yes. Yes, I think so. Why is that?"

"Just a guess." Cecil pressed his hand against the aquarium glass. His fingers curled up into a fist. "Can you override it, please? I'll take the blame."

"Page. Override," Om said with a whimper.

Golden sparkles floated over the screen as the pager rang. Cecil worried about what he might see. Would she be standing above a model, pushing them out into The Mall?

She appeared on the screen dressed in a long-sleeved black velvet dress. There were so many diamonds in her hairband that she could've fed the entirety of Africa. Her makeup was done in a smoky black, and her lips were a nude pink.

She was dressing for an event, perched on the edge of a hotel bed.

"Hello, Om," Perdonna said, putting diamond earrings on.

"What's wrong? If the building is not on fire, *you* are fired."

"Ava's been abducted," Cecil said, stepping from behind Om.

"Forgive me, bellino. But wasn't that part of your grand plan?" She wrung her hands. And the nail of her index finger began scraping at the white polish on her French tips.

"To have them take her *and* for me to follow. They caught on to us. Bourgeois took her. I have no idea where she is."

Perdonna's face clenched up. Her arms moved frantically like she wanted to grab the air and strangle it. She bent down, took off her heel, and threw it. A smashing explosion sounded like the heel crashed into a mirror.

"I'll call Henry. He will go to Quirk and look for her." She stood from the red canopied bed. A white smock covered in rainbow handprints sat at her feet. "Well, Cecil. Are you happy? Now you have to find Annabelle *and* Ava tonight."

"Tazia," a voice said from the hotel bathroom. "Are they ready?"

Suddenly the screen went black. But the sounds from the room remained.

"My guys are finishing the last one now," she said.

"Alright, love. You look absolutely ravishing, you know. What would it take to fuck you against Grand Central tonight?"

"Get me more media coverage than Ami."

"Certainly motivation."

A door clicked shut, and Perdonna reappeared on the screen.

"Was that Tom Gray? Selling sex is for the models, you know?"

"My price is much higher," Perdonna said with a scowl. "I wouldn't be criticizing my morality. Not when you've just sent a girl to be raped."

"He said *Grand Central*. You are definitely not in Shanghai."

Perdonna clicked her teeth together. "Go save Annabelle."

"I don't know where to go!" Cecil shouted, throwing his hands into the air in exasperation.

The screen went black, and Perdonna disappeared.

Cecil banged his hand against the glass. One of the stingrays dived toward the pounding and rolled over the outline of his hand.

Om looked down at his shoes. "You two have an...interesting dynamic."

"Yeah," Cecil said, patting Om's shoulder. "Let me know if she yells at you over the pager."

The atelier nodded as Cecil treaded back down the stairs.

He quickly dialed the monastery, hoping he could reach the end of prayer hour. The projection of Abbot Joseph appeared above the purple malachite staircase.

"Brother George!" the abbot said with enthusiasm. Cecil felt relief just at the sound of his better name.

The abbot spun the camera around to show the refectory, full of monks and Margaux. The young red-headed Billy played with a feathered cat toy as Margaux cuddled Muffintop.

"I need a prayer, please," he said. "And advice. I've made a terrible mistake. I'm trying to save two people, and I don't know how to—"

"Hello?" Abbot Joseph said. "Hello? Brother George? We can't hear you."

Cecil reached the bottom of the staircase and pushed into the store level. "Sorry. I was saying I'm trying to—"

The abbot shook his head. "You'll have to call us back tomorrow. Bad connection. Sorry. We miss you. May the Lord be with you."

The projection shut off, and Cecil collapsed against a rack of leather jackets in the showroom. Then, to add insult to injury, Cecil noticed two paparazzi outside.

Cecil ran and slammed the door shut behind him. He kicked the curb and stood right in front of their cameras. "Look. I'm not a role model. I'm not a murderer. I'm definitely not an artistic genius. It's time to stalk someone who is."

He had snapped. He strode away in a manic frenzy, until he heard a deep voice. "You could use a little Jesus."

"I'm a mo—" Cecil stopped before calling himself a monk. He wasn't worthy of the dignity lately.

Coins jingling against a glass jar broke through the hiss of wind. Cecil turned to see the face of a battered man wearing a ratty shirt that revealed skin, cold and blue from the autumn chill.

His cardboard sign read, "US Army Veteran. Please Buy My Art."

From a distance, he saw garbage, French fry containers from McDonald's, and Coca-Cola bottle caps on a folding table. Crinkled H&M shopping bags and Hershey's chocolate wrappers.

Cecil walked toward him. Cecil pulled out all of the cash from his pocket and put it on the man's table. Four hundred dollars.

"Thank you, sir. Which do you like?" the man asked.

Pieces of dead butterfly decorated the table, mosaics of body parts. Fast food wrappers and other garbage made the disassembled butterflies into gorgeously strange mosaics.

Thin bodies had fishing line attached, as though they were arrows with spears coming out of the heads. Some were made of three different butterflies stuck together—one Painted Lady wing, a caterpillar body, and a bottle cap for the left wing.

"People crush the world. I pick up pieces," he said.

Cecil looked closely at a blue butterfly with yarn unraveling from its body, repairing the broken black torso and swirling down like an anchor. The black thread spun down until it connected back to a fractured golden cocoon.

"It's like he's still attached to the fear," the man said. "He turned into a butterfly, but he can't fly away."

The man wrapped the blue butterfly carefully in a McDonald's Big Mac wrapper.

"I can take it unwrapped. I really have to go, I'm sorry," Cecil said.

"Hurrying is overrated."

"Someone's in danger. My friend's just been abducted."

"*Abducted* is not so bad. I'm starving," the man said. He tied the butterfly into the Big Mac wrapper with a dirty shoelace.

"She could be raped."

"Maybe by me. I like them young."

"Excuse me?"

He tapped the edges of his table. "I can *help*, Cecil."

When looking more closely, Cecil saw a Pierre Lazard handkerchief, stained and torn but unmistakable inside his sweater.

Though the man looked dirty and smelled of soil and rain, he wore Visage shoes with ruined Libra symbols and holes in the soles.

"You know who I am. So the Jesus remark really was a jibe?"

"Bothered you, huh?" A smirk spread across the man's face. It was an expression he recognized. A big toothy grin that should've looked happy but instead resembled a Halloween mask.

"What's the foundation of Christianity?" he asked.

"Good triumphing over evil."

"Okay then..." the man said, rubbing his fingers through his greasy hair. "The first-floor lobby of Christianity?"

Cecil folded his arms. The dreaded thought crossed his mind that this really was an insane homeless man. Was Cecil insane for listening? But then, he remembered what the abbot had told him. "Truth," Cecil said. When Cecil looked up, he noticed Karolina Krün posing on a Visage billboard, lit up and hanging over the Henry Hudson Parkway. To Cecil, she desperately pointed at the VD House, asking someone, *anyone*, to *please* pay attention.

At the edge of the desk, there was a crumpled, dirty flyer. It was a fourteen-year-old Ava Germaine posing in a ripped T-shirt on the cover of *Glamorama*. She posed in lush black lingerie with a strand of diamonds seductively cushioned between her lips. Her sharp cheekbones stood out in red, and her finger gestured toward the sky. Her expression would seem coquettish, lustful to any man on the street. But to Cecil, she looked dead.

"Right. Truth," the man said. "And in my view, during your week in New York, you've just been chasing down a rabbit hole." The man unwrapped the butterfly. "This is you." He clutched the cocoon in one hand and dropped the insect. The butterfly unraveled down, fluttering its wings as it fell. But it stayed attached to the cocoon. It couldn't fly away.

"The truth is hard to face. But it's right in front of you."

"Forgive me. But I'm stressed. Abstractions aren't—"

The man pointed at a yellow taxi. "You are facing it. It's literally right in front of you."

On the car, there was a poster for Tom Gray: *Masterpiece*. Two models with painted faces covered in a Jaguar pattern stared back at him.

"Masterpiece. That's the name of the group Bourgeois put Ava into."

The man scooched his eyebrows like they were two bushy caterpillars. Cecil folded his arms. "Who are you?"

"A risk taker," he said. He roughed up his grimy hair and picked dried blood off his cheek. "Look where that's gotten me."

Cecil nodded to the man. "Thank you."

"I didn't do it for you," he said. "Don't tell anyone this happened."

Cecil nodded and headed for Madison Ave. The Tom Gray store sat just an avenue and a few blocks away from Visage.

He pushed through rowdy tourists and jaded businessmen shoving their way through rush-hour foot traffic. As he walked toward Madison Avenue's high fashion stores, the noise quieted down. The chaos. The smell of garbage. The sound of the roaring subway grinding beneath him. It all faded away into a milky white limestone.

The buildings got shorter and more elegant. And suddenly he noticed that most of the Christmas lights had gone up that morning. It was a day before Halloween, and already twinkle lights were strewn over the avenue. Lighted red bows decorated Buratti and "We Wish You a Merry Christmas" played loudly on the sidewalks. Even the trash cans had sparkling gift boxes hovering above them...just in case you forgot about how many handbags you had to buy before Christmas Day.

Cecil noticed a horde of Asian tourists standing outside the Tom Gray store. They excitedly took pictures and shouted to one another. When Cecil finally pushed through the crowd, he realized why this event was called "The Mall."

A model posed in the store window, motionless like a mannequin. She was for sale.

40

"You have to pretend you like it when his thing's inside you, even if it hurts."

"Yes. But client want model. He want meek. Make feel like rape. She cry."

"Then pretend like you don't know nothing at first, then moan and groan and please him so VD gives you a bed tonight."

Ava sat in a small white room along with other models from the Masterpiece group. Two armed security guards stood by the exit door. Ava stared at them with a vicious glare, hoping that if she kept her gaze without blinking, she would disturb them just a little.

Some girls blabbered nonsense to calm their nerves, while others sat shivering on cold metal stools.

The room smelled of Froot Loops, flavored electronic cigarettes, and nail polish remover. The girls sat waiting in bras and underwear for hair and makeup to make them beautiful. Green-sludge face masks of cucumber and mint, bathrobes, and cotton balls.

No different than a backstage runway show, the girls prepped and primped, gluing on eyelashes and covering their abs and thighs with golden contour powder. Stylists lathered sculpted thighs and waists in satin lotion while photographers shot "back-stage" photos for the clients.

Like thoroughbreds in the paddock, they were being saddled before the race. The clients waited in The Mall, ready to place their bets.

Most of the models sat silently, unable to speak English. But then there were the others: "It's not so bad, you know," said one as she sprayed a chemical in her underwear to protect her from STDs. "Two girls have landed spots on *The Bachelor* from fucking one of the producers in this house. One became Pierre Lazard's closing girl at Fashion Week. So, you know, it's like, you have to pay your dues to be famous. Kim Kardashian's famous because of a sex tape. I'll be famous after working at a whorehouse. The key is that you have to promise not to squeal about what goes on with us young girls. Once we get to the top, we can't talk about how we got there. It's like the Illuminati or something."

One girl cried in front of the makeup mirror for at least fifteen minutes, and the stylists had to reapply her eyeliner before it slid down her face. She looked like a clown.

A girl with big curly hair leaned over to Ava. "Are you nervous? I'm so nervous. I was taken from Theory Models. We get to go back to our other agency after this, right?"

"I'm not nervous."

"Why are you staring at the security?"

"I have mind control powers," Ava said without any irony. Her eyes never drifted from the guards. Little water droplets formed like dew on her lower eyelid, but she didn't blink.

"Seriously?" the girl asked, pouting her lips so she could brush pink blush under her cheekbones. "That's so cool. You should start a YouTube channel about it."

Ava rolled her eyes and walked away from the girl without any acknowledgment of her presence. She missed Cecil not believing a word she said.

A stylist, a man wearing bright green hair and white gloves, approached her with two outfits. She recognized him from helping organize Margaux's closet at the LeClaire Mansion. He lived as a regular fashion stylist by day.

"Are we thinking more innocent babe with a sexy side or like Madonna fishnets with Tom Gray boots?"

"This is leading to prostitution, right? Shouldn't I just be naked?"

"You're a high fashion model. This ain't the Red Light District. We put our girls in Givenchy and Visage with *real* leather whips."

The stylist shuffled through clothing racks of black lace corsets and garter belts. Leather whips by Buratti and cashmere teddies from Loro Piana.

"I suggest Agent Provocateur. It's a good brand for you. Oh, I got it...some lacy white panties. We put your hair in sexed curls, half bun, and we do a smoky eye with a nude lipstick."

As the stylist prepared Ava's look, Rita, the assistant, came by with a notepad.

"I have to go over quick rules, okay? You have to stay with the client for the full time period. Treat the client with kindness and respect, be charming, and look your best. No photographs. Do whatever the client says. But please don't allow them to murder you."

Ava raised her hand as she was removing her current bra and underwear and number tag from the Bourgeois casting. "How do you disallow someone from murdering you?"

Rita's eyes skimmed down the notepad. She made an exaggerated frowning face and shrugged. "Doesn't say on the sheet... We don't allow murder in this section of The Mall. Remember, no murder. If your client is interested in...*that*...tell him or her to contact his liaison."

Ava raised her hand again, her other arm covering her bare chest. "Wait a second. Is there a section in The Mall where murder *is* allowed?"

A quiet silence fell over the room. Rita looked nervously to Ava's stylist.

"How many sections of The Mall are there?" Ava asked. Her hand shook as she tried to spread lipstick on her lips, making her look like a vampire with bloodstains on her chin.

Rita ignored Ava and continued reading from the notepad. "You must stand still in your position for thirty minutes at a time.

Do not make faces. Do not speak to the clients. Do not fidget or twirl your hair. If you cry, cough, spit, laugh, or vomit in your position, you will be punished. The bidding process will continue for the clients for three hours. But you will only be stationed for thirty minutes."

Ava raised her hand again, but this time Rita ignored her. Ava turned to the stylist instead. "We're mannequin modeling? What does she mean about 'bidding'?"

The stylist nodded. "You'll see."

Ava stared at herself in the white panties and pink bra. Somehow it seemed to give her skin color. The slight yellow shades peered out from beneath her gray-white skin. She hated seeing herself in underwear. She never had any good associations with being sexy.

The fabric indented by her belly button. It showed off the bones on her rib cage, the tiny spur along her right elbow. But what made her feel most like a Christmas present was the ridiculous red heels with red ribbon tied up her legs.

Rita waved her hand, and suddenly a door opened.

A dozen girls entered in white bathrobes. They moved like sleepwalking robots. Their eyes were cast down, and their faces covered in bruises.

Ava almost didn't recognize the last girl to enter. Her signature curls were pulled back into a tight bun. Golden eyes sat in the crevices above sunken cheeks. She looked nothing like her fourteen-year-old self.

But Ava was sure. It was Annabelle Leigh.

Outside, an army of fairy-lit nutcrackers began marching on the Tom Gray roof.

The window displays were eccentric and outlandish.

Models posed in a twinkling sleigh with animatronic white

reindeer. Two girls shared a hot cocoa while looking into each other's eyes. They held on to a fuzzy white Tom Gray blanket as flurries fell onto their faces from a snow machine. The snow landed and melted all while the girls were frozen themselves.

The second Christmas window featured a beautiful white-and-gold Christmas tree. And around it, models froze mid-unwrapping presents. A redheaded girl wore a giant smile that never budged except for the quivering edges of her mouth. The strain had taken a toll. Another blonde girl had her hands thrown up into the air, raising a garland to the ceiling.

At first, it appeared they wore ugly Christmas sweaters and pajama pants. But when Cecil managed to shove past the tourists, he realized the clothes were painted onto the girls' naked bodies.

Tom Gray had managed to mimic the weave of a sweater through body paint. One Christmas sweater featured a grumpy cat face and squirrels, and another Santa Claus sticking his tongue out.

But it was the middle window that had the biggest crowd. A giant golden crucifix was splattered in red paint to look like blood. Two models dangled limply from their wrists nailed to the crucifix.

Their bodies were painted to look like anatomy. One featured the skeleton in detail with the organs showing behind. And the other appeared to have broken bones. Her entire rib cage was smashed, and her heart had somehow been ripped out. A giant gaping red mess was left in the center of her chest.

The third girl sat at the base of the cross, on a bed of real snow. Cecil could tell it was real by the reddish-purple hue that crawled up the girl's legs from the cold. Purple lacy underwear was painted over her body. Convincing bruises covered her jaw, and pieces of her wig appeared to be ripped out.

A sign in the window read: "Don't forget the Christ in Christmas."

They were people who only had their bodies. They might as well have been corpses posed in the windows. It would've been more efficient than forcing human beings to turn off their brains and their souls.

"It's genius," a tourist said to her friend. "Really makes you think. The world's so awful lately. We forget what Christmas is supposed to be all about."

Cecil rolled his eyes. "Tom Gray is an atheist. He just wanted an excuse to make a murder window."

The final window featured a golden ballroom, lit up with snowflake chandeliers. Girls held a waltz position like robots, their arms wrapped around dashing male models.

The tuxedos were painted on, but clearly meant to shadow and show off the abdominal muscles and biceps on the young men. And the women wore painted-on corset bustiers, with real tulle skirts pinned to their bottoms.

Cecil had often seen models posing in luxury windows for promotional events. Stores did it to drive traffic to the clothing. He wondered if it was always for sex.

He approached the arched doors of the Tom Gray store. But when he opened them, he found a small blond man with a clipboard and headphones. "Sorry, sir," he said. "Private event."

Behind him, a tall man wearing a Visage tie and Buratti shoes approached. Without much of a glance, he was waved into the store by the blond man.

"How can I get an invitation?" Cecil asked.

"You would have to find someone to sponsor you."

"Thank you," Cecil said as he rushed back through the crowd of tourists.

He ran his hand through his still-sweaty hair. He rubbed his hands together. Could he rush the blond man, sprint into the store, and rush out with Ava and Annabelle? No.

Then he noticed white strobe lights coming from Buratti across the street. That in and of itself wouldn't have piqued Cecil's interest. Blinding strobe lights were quite normal for Buratti. However, the shirtless male models in golden boxer shorts were new.

"Take me home for Christmas" was written in black paint across their chests. One of the boys held a stuffed animal of a Pomeranian puppy. Another held a twenty-four-karat-gold toilet plunger that had BURATTI bedazzled in crystals.

An elderly Chinese tourist screamed at the sight of the young men and pressed her lips to the glass windows. She threw herself into a photo and took selfies with the boys.

A block away, Cecil could see another crowd forming around the Ami store.

There was an energized buzz to the high fashion blocks of Madison Ave. that night. It was rare that an entire sidewalk could be filled with stopped people in Manhattan. It was usually a mad rush of bodies moving quickly like schools of fish.

Instead, vendors sold kettle corn from tented carts. Rolls Royces and taxi cabs alike slowed down when they passed the stores. Women giggled with glee at the sight of Christmas cheer.

The Mall was trick-or-treating for adults. Each high fashion store had a different body for you. You could jeer at it, take photos of it, and even, like many of the young boys, knock on the expensive windows.

"Hey, what's your number, princess?" a teenaged boy yelled at one of the male models in the Buratti windows.

His friend took his skateboard and pretended to throw it at the glass. One of the models twitched in fear. The pack of boys laughed hysterically. "Pussy!" they yelled.

Cecil grabbed the skateboard out of the kid's hand. With a stomp, he split the board in half on the curb edge. And then he threw it in the trash can.

"What the fuck?" the green-haired twat asked.

"He's doing his job," Cecil said, pointing to the model. "He probably has to do that. You're an entitled brat. Go home and get your costume ready for Halloween tomorrow."

There was a peculiar mix of people on the street. Tourists and locals who had heard about the windows, passersby, and extraordinarily elegant rich people. There were always wealthy people on the Upper East Side. But today, they all seemed to be dressed for a ball.

A middle-aged couple was welcomed into Buratti by the girl guarding the door. The blonde woman wore a mink coat with a Visage dress made of white feathers. And the man wore a tuxedo.

Cecil felt something bump his back. He turned to find a twelve-year-old girl wearing a child's puffy white winter coat and jeans. Her mom was the type of person who you can prejudge immediately on appearance. She wore a J.Crew tweed jacket with pearls and had a blond bobbed haircut.

"Hi. Um, Cecil LeClaire?" the girl asked. "Nice to meet you."

Cecil felt himself soften. The rush of adrenaline settled when he heard the girl's soft voice. "Hello," he said.

"Um… Sorry, I'm really nervous." She looked up at her mother, and then hid her face in her mom's arm.

"She's wondering if she has what it takes to model," the mother said.

Cecil's anxiety returned with a furor. She was a beautiful little girl, but clearly, she was never good enough for her mother. She was already almost five-foot-eight. Her lips were big and pouty, and her cheekbones barely stood out against the baby fat still on her cheeks.

"I… I'm sorry. I'm busy tonight. But call the agency if you want," Cecil said, already starting to walk back toward Tom Gray's store.

"You think she's not pretty?" The mother folded her arms and puffed out her lips like an angry duck.

"I… What? No, she's beautiful. Of course. You don't need a model agent to tell you that."

"I want her to model. It would be a great way for her to work during college. She wants to go to Columbia."

"That's great," Cecil said to the girl. "Columbia's a wonderful school."

The adorable little girl blushed and looked away. But as Cecil continued walking to Tom Gray, the mother kept following.

"Is she not your type?" the woman asked. "You don't like blonde women? You think we're stupid?"

"This seems to be more about you than your daughter," Cecil said.

The woman clicked her tongue against her teeth. Cecil walked faster, and she picked up her pace as well. He finally stopped and turned.

"Is it her breasts?" the mother asked.

"Excuse me?" Cecil screeched.

"She'll fill out, you know. She hasn't gone through puberty yet." The woman stroked a hand over her own chest and heaved up her boobs.

"We don't exactly go for curves in fashion," Cecil said.

An old man wearing a golden top hat stepped up to the Tom Gray doors. And this time, Cecil noticed the blond kid checking the man's Dial projection.

"All she wants for Christmas is to try modeling," the mother said. She suddenly tried to unzip her daughter's jacket.

"Hey," the girl said, gripping on to her mom's hand.

"Show him your body."

"No," the girl said, shaking her head.

"Look," the woman said. She leaned into Cecil's ear, breath uncomfortably irritating his skin. "She's a tomboy. She doesn't have any boyfriends. All she does is hang out with her soccer friends. She won't wear dresses. She won't try makeup. I'm afraid she'll never get married. Modeling might—"

"She's like twelve. You're an adult. Stop trying to live through her."

Suddenly a man exited the Tom Gray store with a beautiful six-foot-tall teenaged girl attached to his arm. Cecil waved his hand up to him. "Excuse me, sir. Could you tell me what time it is?"

Cecil tried to catch a glimpse of the Dial time. The man shrugged his shoulders. "Sorry. My watch hasn't been working." He flashed a hologram of the clock onto Cecil's palm. "It's been stuck at 11:04 all week. See?"

"11:04," Cecil repeated with a knowing tone.

The man gave a pursed-lips smile in return and winked.

"Sorry," Cecil said to the young girl. "I have to go."

He rushed back up to Tom Gray. He set his Dial to 11:04 and approached the door.

"Welcome, sir," the doorman said.

41

Tears smeared pale foundation down Lilly Blake's cheeks. The white paint mixing with tears looked like melting snow. Lilly's hand wobbled as she tried to apply mascara. A streak of black cut down her eyelid like a scar.

The first-time model was a sad clown.

Ava stayed in her makeup chair while the stylist finished her hair. She stared as Annabelle Leigh moved behind Lilly, watching the girl nervously design her face.

"Do you want some help?" Annabelle asked. Her voice rang deep from within her chest, oaken and earthy. She sounded like a warm bass drum, a motherly vibrato thrumming beneath her words.

"I'm okay," Lilly squealed through her tears. She hid her face in her arm, blond curls catching the white paint on her face.

"A hug then, maybe?" Annabelle asked.

Lilly wrapped her own arms around her body, hesitating. Her lower lip blubbered, and then she held out her arms. Annabelle scooped her up onto her lap and wrapped her in an embrace. All Ava could see was Lilly's blond curls nuzzled into Annabelle's arm.

No one paid them any attention but Ava. The stylists went about their business. They didn't even blink at the sound of a wailing girl.

"I'm scared," Lilly said, wiping her eyes with her hand. Makeup smeared into her eyeball and looked like a white cloud on her blue eyes.

"First time is always scary, hon," Annabelle whispered. "It's okay to be nervous."

Annabelle handed her a tissue. Instead of using it to wipe her tears, Lilly clutched the Kleenex to her neck like a safety blanket.

"Is this going to be fun? The agent lady who picked me up from school told me modeling would be fun," Lilly said.

Annabelle's eyes seemed to fall to her nose. She rubbed her fingers over Lilly's shoulders and kissed her forehead, not knowing what to say.

"How 'bout we rub this gunk off your face, huh?"

She used a makeup wipe to gently stroke Lilly's face free of the mask. She gently stroked her forehead, her temples, wiping off the tears with the grime.

"There you are," Annabelle said with a small smile, holding Lilly's head in her hands.

Ava felt a pang in her stomach. All she ever wanted was a mother to cuddle her like that. The only time Ava's mom did her hair was when she wanted to sell her.

"Imagine we're getting ready for prom," Annabelle said. "What color do you want on your eyes?"

"Pink," Lilly said with a little smile. She gazed over the eyeshadow colors like a child picking a lollipop flavor. "Maybe some gold sparkles."

"Oooh. Good choice," Annabelle said. "Gold sparkles are my favorite too."

Lilly smiled as Annabelle covered her eyelid in glittering color, turning her eye into a sparkling Christmas ornament. But Lilly peeked up at Annabelle with her free eye. "You're so, so pretty," Lilly said. "I wish I was as pretty as you."

"You're beautiful too," Annabelle said. "You're still a baby. You'll be much prettier than me. People will say you're so, so gorgeous tonight."

"What's going to happen tonight?" Lilly asked. "Girls were talking about S-E-X? What does S-E-X have to do with modeling?"

Annabelle's finger gently patted Lilly's lips with a light pink gloss. "This is a...different kind of show."

"Do we have to kiss boys? I don't wanna kiss boys. They're gross."

Annabelle frowned and closed her eyes. She rolled her finger-tips within Lilly's curls and combed her hair out with her fingers. Lilly leaned back into Annabelle's embrace. "Sometimes...you have to do... You have to do things to stay alive."

"I have to kiss boys to stay alive?" Lilly asked with wide eyes.

Annabelle's hooded eyes blinked in rapid succession like a malfunctioning robot. She braided Lilly's hair, gently massaging her scalp as she twirled the locks. "Maybe. A boy is going to choose you. Like a boy at recess. And then you have to keep him happy. You have to be polite. Smile a lot. Be cute."

Lilly still clutched the tissue in her hand until it became a tight snowball. "When do I get to go home?"

"Sometimes if you're extra, extra nice to the boy who picks you...They let you go home. But you have to be very good. Do everything the client tells you."

Lilly nodded, tapping her hands together worriedly, the same way she probably did before a math test. "Do you get to go home?"

Annabelle shook her head. She sucked her cheeks into her mouth like she was trying to swallow herself whole. "No. No, I never got to go home."

"Were you bad to your client?"

"Yeah." Annabelle pushed down the edges of her bathrobe off her shoulders. Red patches of skin sat like mountainous veins to form scars where she'd been lashed. Cigarette burns trailed from her shoulders down her back. Her body looked like a used-up punching bag.

But Ava saw them as battle scars. She watched in admiration. Each of those gashes, each burn represented a moment when Annabelle survived. It was how Ava imagined her own body in her head. Each abuse left an imaginary mark.

Annabelle parted a segment of her hair at the top of her head.

She showed Lilly a giant scar. Her skull was dented in at the top like a cracked egg. "This was my first time in Shanghai."

Lilly gasped and covered her mouth with her hand. A drop of lip gloss smeared across her chin, leaving it shiny like a doll's porcelain skin.

"But this won't happen if you do what they tell you. Here, this is a trick I use: what's your favorite memory? You can play it in your head while you're doing something you don't want to do."

Lilly thought as Annabelle brushed sparkling highlighter over Lilly's cheeks.

"I don't know," Lilly said. "What's yours?"

"I think of my friend," Annabelle said. "We used to run around in the Hamptons. We'd spend all day outside. I imagine all the details. The color of the yellow daffodils. The way the gardenias smelled of vanilla. I remember flipping over rocks and searching for salamanders. My friend and I would build little habitats for lizards. Then we'd take them to the beach and make fake leashes. We'd race them across the sand and make bets about which salamander would win.

"I remember dancing with him along the ocean. Hearing the crash of the waves. I remember how his hands felt. I can see him painting step by step. He could create entire worlds with his fingertips. And those worlds were so much more beautiful than ours."

Lilly smiled again. "Oh. I know what I can do. I can think about my mom. She has cancer right now. But I see her at the hospital every day. She's so funny. Whenever she's too tummy sick to eat, she makes puppets out of the food and does shows for me. She makes dinosaurs out of saltine crackers. She even did a little ocean show with noodle soup."

"There you go," Annabelle cheered, lightly tapping Lilly's shoulders. "You're going to be great." She picked up a blue lacy princess dress from a clothing rack. "This is perfect for you." She helped Lilly take off her bathrobe, and she tied up the buttons in the back.

Lilly looked like a beautiful doll. A porcelain princess ready for a prince.

"Good luck, little one," Annabelle said. "I'm sure you'll see your mommy tomorrow."

Lilly nodded with an emphatic smile. She hugged her tightly, and Annabelle gave her a kiss on the head.

Annabelle strode across the room like a jaguar in the jungle. She was the pride leader, the oldest veteran.

"Annabelle? That was really nice of you," Ava called out, but she didn't hear her. Ava followed behind in the crowded room. But as she pushed by a purple-haired stylist, Annabelle tapped Rita.

"Send the little blonde girl to Mr. Sterling," Annabelle said.

Rita's face paled. "He almost killed the last one."

"I got a million bucks out of him," Annabelle said. "If he *doesn't* kill her, I'll give him a quarter million back."

"She's not even a teenager," Rita said.

"He likes them young."

Rita hugged the clipboard to her chest. "I... I don't know if I can do that."

"You wanna take her place?"

Rita cowered into the corner as Annabelle swerved out into the hallway.

Ava rushed out into the hallway, guards chasing after her. Suddenly her illness didn't matter. She had all the adrenaline in the world. "*You* are VD? *You?*" Ava asked.

Stomping heels passing by them in the hallway sounded like dinner knives clacking against champagne flutes. It added to the thrumming in Ava's ears.

Annabelle stepped toward her with a happy smirk on her face. "I decided I didn't like being raped. So I took VD's spot. And now I fuck everyone else over."

42

―――――

Cecil nervously walked toward the cable-knit sweaters. He pretended to feel up the navy blue cashmere while he scanned the Tom Gray store.

It was elegant but minimalist. Bloodred curtains lined the walls, draping over a frigid black marble floor. The clothing was hung in black onyx closets instead of clothing racks. In the middle of the store was a swirling white grand staircase. It felt cold, like a modern Dracula lair.

The Tom Gray store was meant to be a castle. And you could live in it...if only you owned a $4,000 pair of leather loafers.

It seemed like a typical shopping day. Women in pearls and diamonds, men with Crevier cuff links and Bottega Veneta briefcases. The buyers scoured shelves of handcrafted handbags. Or they sat on fluffy white ottomans, drinking champagne and licking lobster butter off their lips.

It took Cecil a few seconds of staring to realize the mannequins posing on mirrored platforms were human beings.

The model above him sat still on a red lounge chair. She looked cozy and warm, body curled up with a book and hot chocolate.

She wore velvet leggings and a fluffy purple suit jacket. A saccharine smile clung to her lips. But the longer she had to hold the expression, the faker it looked, the creepier it was.

The models' skin was coated in oil and glitter to make it shimmer like a doll's. The limbs seemed to lose their life, existing on hinges. Arms bent to their hips to show off their asses. Legs were parted into balletic forms.

Cecil approached a white canopied bed. A group of models was frozen mid-pillow fight. Lacy white-and-pink lingerie covered their bodies. Pillows burst with feathers. One girl held another in a chokehold, fake laughter plastered on her face. Another girl's head rested on the lap of another.

He felt an urge to poke them. To say hello. To tap their shoulders and embrace them in a hug, hoping they would reanimate. He sniffed the air to be sure they smelled like humans.

Two blonde twins froze in a playful kiss, while another model pointed and laughed.

It looked like a private moment. One he shouldn't have been allowed to see.

Long black eyelashes were glued to the eyelids. And when Cecil looked closer, he noticed some of them had taped their eyeballs open so they didn't blink. Their eyes became marbles, almost completely dry on the colored surface.

The two kissing girls had saliva running down their chins from being stuck in a pucker, leaving little lines of spittle through their makeup.

A group of young male models sat in a mock office. They wore velvet suits. Their faces were so closely shaved that their pores had disappeared. They looked like young boys playing at being men. Cigars to their lips, legs and arms spread wide.

They were Ken dolls for a CEO Barbie collection.

Cecil pretended to look at a velvet tie. Rita clapped from behind him, and he jumped.

"Welcome, Mr. LeClaire," Rita said. "I'm Rita. Is there anything I can help you find?"

"Just looking," Cecil said with a nervous nod.

A suited waiter carried a golden plate of raw oysters to him.

"Hors d'oeuvres, sir?"

"No, thank you."

Rita rubbed her hands together and flipped her black pony-tail over her shoulder. "Champagne? Toasted Vanilla?" she asked.

"Maybe in a moment."

Rita's eyes shone a bright green, so light they almost looked yellow like cat's eyes. They stared him down, leering over his shoulder. "Would you prefer something white?"

"I'm not a huge fan of white. I gravitate more toward darks. Blacks. Navy. Aquamarine. Evergreen. Seafoam—"

"I meant skin color," Rita said with a nervous laugh.

"Oh." Cecil gently rubbed the sweat off his eyebrow. "No preference."

"No preference? Everyone has a preference."

"I'm not racist."

"Have you ever slept with *any* black people?" Rita asked.

"Well, no… I haven't but… It's not that I *wouldn't*."

Rita raised a questioning eyebrow. "I'll find you something white."

She waved him up the white staircase. As he swirled up the cold steps, feet stomping against marble, he couldn't help but look down. There was a gaping chasm of existence between the moving, drinking, laughing folks and the frozen ones.

Rita stopped in front of a glass display case that covered the entire upstairs wall. "This is the 'buy now' section."

Men and women posed behind locked glass, like diamond rings in a jewelry store. They wore everything from velvet tank tops to ball gowns to lingerie. It looked like a showroom at Madame Tussaud's.

"'Buy now'?" Cecil asked.

"These models have set prices. The others on the floor are sold through silent auction. The silent auction models rotate every thirty minutes. So if you don't find what you are looking for right now, new ones will come out soon."

"I see."

"Can I show you anything?"

"I think I'll wait for more to come to auction."

Then Cecil noticed the center window. Models were made to be celebrity look-alikes. There was a Leonardo DiCaprio. A Marilyn Monroe. And a Kim Kardashian.

All of the celebrities wore lingerie.

But one in particular caught his eye. Tazia Perdonna. A rose-gold wig was attached to her head, and the stylist even managed to mimic the golden flecks in the hair. Makeup sculpting recreated the pink scars across her face. But the eyeballs were all wrong.

Perdonna's eyes maintained their cornea and iris, like a pearl in an oyster shell. The model's were murky marbles. Contact lenses could never do them justice.

"Would you like to see her?" Rita asked.

Cecil shook his head.

"Too weird to sleep with your godmother?"

"Something like that."

"Good. She'd set you back two million dollars and about seventy-five grand in extra fees. She's our most expensive one. She always sells."

Of all the girls, it disturbed him most to see the fake Perdonna. It disturbed him that someone would pay a small fortune to fuck a copy of her. The girl was at least twenty years too young to have the grandiose presence of Perdonna. The most brilliant business-woman in the world, and even she couldn't get respect.

"You have the lingerie wrong," Cecil said in a monotone drawl. "It's plain. She likes lace."

"We'll make note of that for next year." Rita's mouth twitched like a nervous rabbit's. "Can I just show you one? There's one I think you'd adore."

Rita lifted a set of golden keys from her jeans pocket and approached a glass window. She put a key in the gate, and pushed open the display. The four models inside didn't flinch. Rita pointed to a young girl with curly brown hair. She wore a sheer pink nightgown with a white garter.

"Wanna see her?" Rita asked.

"Um...I don't think so." He paused for a second. "Well, what happens when I buy her?"

"Before you buy her, you can take her back to the changing

room and try her on. Then, when you buy, you get to dress her up. A stylist will do her hair and makeup however you like. Then you get to take her home. You return her at midnight tomorrow.

"Or you can also take her to the VD House and spend the night there. There are all kinds of activities on Madison tonight."

Cecil tried not to swallow his own throat. This was like Build-a-Bear workshop for wealthy perverts. He had to buy the girl just to set her free.

"Can I buy more than one?" he asked. "Bid on a few? Buy a few?"

"You can buy more than one," Rita said. "But you're limited to three."

Cecil nodded slowly. "Let me see her."

"Great!" Rita said with a cheer. She squatted down to the model's feet. It was only then that Cecil realized all of the models were chained to their pedestals.

Rita manhandled the girl's feet and lifted up her legs like a horse trainer shifting hooves. She smacked the girl's behind and pushed her out of the window, then grabbed her hand and pulled her forward.

The model posed with her hands on her hips. Her eyes stared away from Cecil's.

"She's given twelve glasses of water a day. Her skin is exceptionally hydrated. Top of the line smoothness. Feel," she said, lifting the model's nightgown. She tapped the model's stomach. "Baby soft."

Cecil shook his head. "I can see."

"But you have to feel. It's like satin."

Cecil reached out for the model's hand. But when his fingertips brushed against her, it felt uncanny. Based on her stillness, his brain expected to feel cold plastic or steel, a mechanical hand. Instead, it was a warm pulsing wrist. A textured hand complete with moles and scars.

He flipped his Dial and subtly filmed the rest of the exchange. He wanted the evidence for later.

"Her hair is one hundred percent human hair."

He let out a small chuckle. "What other kind of hair would it be?"

"Hair extensions can be synthetic."

"Ah."

Rita grabbed the model by the shoulders and spun her around. "She has a lovely peach-shaped butt. And I just love the shape of her thighs. She's what we call a 'violin silhouette.'"

He felt somewhere between devastated and confused. It was complete disbelief. He walked in front of the model's face, and she finally blinked at him.

"She's what we call 'premium' because she's a virgin."

"How can you know for sure?" Cecil asked sarcastically.

"She comes with a certificate guaranteeing that her hymen is still intact. If you find it is not, there is a full money-back guarantee."

"You're joking."

Rita shook her head. "She comes with a whole care package." Rita pushed open a set of curtains in the back. "Try her on?"

"When will the next girls come out onto the silent bidding floor?" Cecil asked.

"A bell will chime whenever there is a rotation."

Cecil noticed three extra windows at the back of the store. They were lit red, and the models inside wore those eerie white Venetian masks.

"Why are they masked?"

Rita shook her head. "You can't have those. Club members only."

Cecil raised an eyebrow but didn't bother asking more. When he walked toward the dressing rooms, he expected the model to follow, but she didn't.

"They don't go anywhere without instruction," Rita said.

Cecil took a deep breath. "What's your name?"

The model didn't answer.

"You name her when you check out. It's part of the dressing-up process."

"What's your real name?"

"She's not allowed to say."

Cecil already had a headache. He waved toward the dressing rooms, and the girl followed him.

A man stood by marble chambers with black curtains. "Need a dressing room?"

"Yeah," Cecil said.

"How many items are you trying on?"

"One human," he said, spit flying out of his mouth with anger.

"Right this way, sir."

Through the curtains he passed, Cecil could hear bits of the strangest conversations:

"I really liked philosophy in school. Yin and yang and all that."

"For necrophilia, I recommend blowup dolls. Cold, plastic, and lifeless."

"Your mom was a kindergarten teacher, right? Can she tutor my son in algebra?"

"Incest isn't my thing... But I like father-daughter porn."

"It's all fantasy. It doesn't hurt that bad."

"I want to go home."

The curtain drew back, and the model entered. It was a small cubicle. Mirrors and bright white lights felt sterile against the reds. It felt like a standard dressing room. Until music began to play, a deep bass shaking the mirror frames. The girl clumsily started a striptease.

She gyrated with her neck, flipping her freshly tossed hair over her shoulders.

She leaned into his ear and awkwardly kissed his earlobe, pushing her chest toward his face. The soft skin of her neck brushed against his cheek.

"Do you have somewhere to run away tonight?" he asked.

The girl jumped back at the sound of his voice. "Am I doing a bad job?"

"I'm going to pay them so you can run away. Do you have somewhere to go?"

The girl covered her body with her arms. "We're not allowed to run away."

"I get that. But I'm giving you an opportunity."

The girl curled up on the ground. Cecil patted the velvet bench, but she refused to sit beside him.

"There's a huge fine if you bring me back late."

"The fine is fine," he said. She didn't appreciate the joke.

"There are consequences if you don't bring me back at all."

"What do you mean *consequences*? They kill me? They kill you?"

"Consequences," she repeated. Her eyes brimmed with tears, and she stared at her reflection. It was as if even she couldn't find life behind her vacant eyes. She stared into the mirror to search for herself.

"Someone told you to say that."

"But it's probably true," she said.

"Would you rather stay here? Or risk dying to potentially have a life?" he asked.

"I cost forty thousand dollars."

"You're worth more."

The model hung her head, hiding her tears in her arm. "Thank you."

Cecil led her outside. "How do I pay?" he asked the attendant.

They were directed to a large marble checkout counter shaped like a spear. The clerk was dressed in a bright red suit. "Perfect choice. Now the dressing stations are in the—"

"Can we just buy jeans and a T-shirt? Winter coat, hat, gloves?" Cecil asked.

"You have to do the dressing station."

Cecil glared. "I'm paying a lot of money. Get me the stuff."

Two clerks ran out onto the store floor to pick out items. "That'll be $56,756.54 for the model and her accessories. She comes with this winter coat so you didn't have to pay for that."

The clerk dressed the model in the coat, and Cecil was handed a signature velvet Tom Gray backpack with the accessories he requested. He gave it to the girl.

A row of black leather purses lined the mirrored wall behind them. One was spread out onto the marble counter.

"Here is her go-bag." He lifted a set of five packets that looked like sugar packets. "Here is her food. This will last her until midnight tomorrow. She can have water or alcohol. Please do not give them LSD." He spread out a set of cotton balls. "These are for makeup removal or eating, whichever she prefers."

A morning-after pill. Condoms. Handcuffs. Lotions and oils. These were the things the clerk did not mention. But they sat in his pile nonetheless.

"We've also included a set of diamond earrings. They are signature. Tom made them only for this event. A lot of our clients put them on the model for tonight. Then tomorrow they give them to their wives. It's a win-win."

"Charming," Cecil said.

He noticed a few black briefcases, which were presumably the male go-bags. He wondered what was inside of those.

The clerk pointed to a miniature leather-bound address book. "Emergency numbers are in here. If by any chance an accident happens...call one of these numbers."

"What kind of accident?"

"If you...if you were to accidentally kill her, say. Or she had a heart attack. Or overdosed on heroin. Whatever you want to call *it*...call us. No need to get the police involved."

"Right."

Cecil paid with his Dial, and they were out the door. It was dark outside, and the Christmas lights were on full display. Animatronic reindeers launched overtop the Pratesi store. And on the next street, carved pumpkins were still lit up with ghouls.

"What's your name, finally?" Cecil asked.

"Samantha. Samantha Parkington."

"Cecil LeClaire," he said, holding out his hand. She shook it with a happy smile.

"No one's ever taken me serious enough for a handshake."

Cecil patted her shoulder and hailed a taxi. She climbed inside with an ebullient smile. Cecil scribbled into the address book he had been given and ripped out a page. "Take her to St. Joseph's Abbey, please. This address." He gave the taxi driver the rest of the cash he had.

As the car drove away, Cecil flipped his Dial. He opened Chatter and found article after article of Cecil's temper tantrum at the Visage mansion.

He fumbled his way through the buttons and opened up the post option. He uploaded his recording of Rita "selling" him

Samantha. It showed Rita describing Samantha's body shape and her real human hair. He captioned the post: "The Horrors of High Fashion."

Within seconds, comments rolled in:

> **CheetahGirl342:** *That is NOT an okay way to comment on a woman's body.*
>
> **USCgrad$231:** *This is disgusting. No model should be that skinny. This is a terrible message to be sending girls.*
>
> **AshleyMore2:** *#Feminism #Standwithwomen #saynoto-Photoshop #saynotoSizeZero*
>
> **YankeesFan32:** *Yo where are models standing in lingerie? Which store and how do I get there?*
>
> **FuckLeClaireModels:** *How dare you. Hire some models who are actually a healthy body weight please. This is an unreasonable standard.*

Minutes later, articles flew up onto the Chatter feed. *"Cecil LeClaire Posts Video of Anorexic Model to Redirect Annabelle Leigh Murder Suspicion." "Cecil LeClaire is the Ultimate Misogynist." "Cecil LeClaire starts a Chatter Profile—Proves He's the Antichrist."*

He quickly added another post. He said, "To clarify, that video is of a woman selling a girl for sex against her will. This is sex trafficking. It's happening on Madison Avenue."

More comments:

> **Beachbitch32:** *Conspiracy theorist much?*
>
> **DeDe2:** *Die. Go home, stab a knife in your head, douse yourself in gasoline, and set yourself on fire.*
>
> **PierreLazardStalkerFan:** *Dude. You just jumped the shark.*
>
> **RickJones2:** *This is like PizzaGate. It's not a thing.*
>
> **Rockstargirlforever3:** *You probably also believe Clinton raped women on Epstein island... What's wrong with you? I hope someone kills you.*
>
> **ForeverCrazy23:** *You're just saying this to cover for the fact you posted a video of an anorexic model.*

Cecil bent down into a crouch. And he screamed, very loudly in a guttural, crazed way. Tourists stopped looking into the store windows and turned to Cecil.

"Yo," someone said from several feet away. "How would you

like it if you were upheld to an unreasonable body standard? Don't pity yourself."

He flipped his Dial and added yet another post. "None of you people actually care about human beings. You post and say what will give you metaphorical and real 'likes.'"

He didn't bother to read the comments.

The bell rang within Tom Gray. And when Cecil turned and peered through the store door, he saw Ava Germaine being walked to her podium.

4 3

—————

"Silent night, holy night. All is calm, all is bright. Round yon Virgin, Mother, and child. Holy infant so tender and mild. Sleep in heavenly peace. Sleep in heavenly peace."

Christmas music played in the Tom Gray store. But the presents were yet to be boxed.

Ava's body was draped over a white grand piano. Her legs were spread open, showcasing the white lace between her thighs. They had cuffed her ankles to the piano legs with golden bracelets.

Diamond bracelets tied her arms together behind her head. And a nude-pink bra blended into her body, rising with her raised arms. Half of the roundness peeked out.

Her back arched over the piano, the silhouette of a woman mid-sex. She wore heels that wrapped around her in red ribbon. The silk braided around her calf, up her knee, and tied to a bow on her thighs.

Her cheeks were covered in a heavy pink blush, and her lips were a purplish red.

Curls dripped out of a loose bun that looked tousled by fucking.

She was the most sexualized of all of the displays. A hog-tied princess ready to go.

To Cecil, they had dressed her like a pig roasting above a fire. There was not an ounce of her spirit in that body. She kept her eyes closed so she didn't have to be there.

Her skin was as white as the piano. She could blend in like a ghost into the wall, and no one would ever know she was there.

Cecil walked around the piano to her wrists. There was the leather price tag.

Starting $62,000. Bid in $4,000 increments.

He asked a gray-haired salesman for a pen. And he scribbled: *Cecil LeClaire $66,000.*

Ava's eyes suddenly drifted toward the tag. When she glanced up, she couldn't look him in the eyes.

A young blond man approached the piano, wearing ridiculously tight black jeans. He looked like the mid-level Wall Street type—privileged and without any talent.

"Can I touch?" he asked the salesman.

His fingertips found her inner thigh. He gently stroked like he was petting a cat. Each rhythm brought his fingers closer to her underwear.

"Mm. So soft. She feels like a pillow. There's no muscle on that thigh. Just fluffy skin. Imagine putting your face between them," he said, turning to Cecil, expecting a response.

Cecil tried to stay calm, looking away as though he wasn't paying attention.

The man wrote: *James Caldwell $70,000.*

Cecil took his pen and immediately wrote: *Cecil LeClaire $74,000* beneath it.

"Whoa. You really like her, huh? Think she's worth it? How do you think she is in bed?"

"Terrible," Cecil said.

James laughed but Cecil didn't. When James realized he wasn't joking he said, "Well then why did you bid?"

"There's probably a reason they have her tied down. It isn't because she *wants* to be here."

"At $78,000? She probably makes at least half that, right? $35,000 for one night isn't bad."

"I don't think they get paid at all," Cecil said.

James shook his head, puffing on his electronic cigarette. The steam blew right into Cecil's eyes. It smelled like cinnamon and chocolate. "No way, man. Hey, sales guy. They get paid, right?"

The gray-haired salesman nodded assuredly. "Of course, sir."

"See," he said. "Of course they get paid." The young man traced the fabric of the ribbons across Ava's calf. His fingers rubbed down to the shoe, and he bent close to her toes to see the nail polish.

"Would you like to see the shoe off?" the salesman asked.

James nodded.

The salesman dutifully untied the bow above Ava's knee. He unraveled the ribbon like he would wrap up a sweater for a shopper. The ribbon fell into streams of red, and he took the shoe off her foot like she was Cinderella.

James rubbed the arch of her foot. His fingers felt between her toes. A palm wrapped around her heel.

"Very nice," James said. He scribbled: *James Caldwell $82,000.*

Without a second spared, Cecil wrote: *Cecil LeClaire $86,000.*

James shook his head with a chuckle. "What's the deal? She your high school sweetheart or something?"

James's fingers traced over the lacy waistband of her underwear. He stroked in and around her bellybutton, slipping his hands beneath the sides of her panties. He massaged her hip bones, manhandling them like those spiky pelvic ridges were his fetish.

"Is this allowed?" Cecil asked.

The gray-haired salesman coughed. He tried to adjust his aroused face. "Um, sir. Please be gentle."

"Could I see the bra off?" James asked.

"Of course, sir."

"Of course?" Cecil asked.

The salesman grabbed Ava's head and shoulders and bent her forward. He propped her up. But as soon as he released her, she fell back to the table. The salesman grumbled and pushed her up again. But she collapsed faster, like a brick onto a piano. The bang made the piano let out a nails-to-chalkboard wail.

He grabbed her hair bun and yanked on it, whispering something into her ear. When he pushed her up again, she stayed upright, a resigned expression on her face. The salesman unlatched her bra and removed it from her chest.

Ava managed to hide her emotion. She stared at Cecil's shoes.

James tried to hide the goofy smile that came onto his face. He sat on the piano, head lurching toward her chest. His hand cupped her boob, and he rubbed his fingertips over her nipple.

"How old is she?"

"Twenty-four," the salesman replied.

"She has the tits of a teenager," he said. His breathing quickened as he placed his left hand on her upper back. He massaged her harder, bouncing her in his hand. His cheek came close to hers. "Does that feel good, sweetheart?"

Ava was silent. Cecil wanted to punch him in the face, even if it meant leaving without Annabelle.

"Will you get wet for me?" James asked.

And with that, Ava spat in his eye.

"Ugh," James shouted, wiping his face. "What the fuck? That's disgusting. She can't do that! I pay a lot of money for this," he said, pointing at her. "I cannot be treated that way."

"She'll be punished later," the salesman said as Ava flopped back onto the piano.

James turned to Cecil. "You can have her."

"Thank you," he said.

Cecil leaned over Ava's face. "I'm gonna go see if Annabelle is in this round."

Ava's eyes widened, and her mouth balled up. She subtly grabbed his hand and tried to scribble something in his palm with her fingertip.

"What?" Cecil asked. "I don't understand what you're trying to say." He tried to remain calm. "Me? Are you writing the word *me*?"

She continued touching until Cecil noticed a figure standing in a leather jumpsuit. He would recognize those curls anywhere. "There's Annabelle," Cecil said.

Ava grunted, but Cecil was already several yards across the floor.

Annabelle wore a skintight leather jumpsuit. She sat on a

black leather stool with her legs parted. When Cecil moved into her line of sight, her golden eyes drifted toward him. She struggled to hide a smile.

It all felt worth it to him when he saw her smile. All of the nervousness went away. All of the pain. Even if he died that night, it would be worth it. Just seeing her smile one more time.

A deep V-cut highlighted the shape of her breasts. Her hips curved out like an hourglass. Strong and virile. She was an absolute outlier from the young girls.

A steel plaque in front of her read: *THE Annabelle Leigh.*

Cecil found the price tag dangling from her wrist.

Starting $280,000. Bid in $20,000 increments.

Ronald Huffington: $300,000

George Burns: $320,000

Rachel Jeffries: $340,000

George Burns: $360,000

Rachel Jeffries: $380,000

Cecil turned to his right to find a petite woman wearing a tartan Ami coat. She peered over his shoulder. Presumably, it was Rachel Jeffries. She was middle-aged but kept twenty with several injections of Botox.

"I guess you didn't kill her, huh?" Rachel asked.

"Guess not," he said, scribbling his $400,000 bid onto the price tag.

"She's so hot," Rachel said. "No wonder you were in love with her."

"She was fourteen when I last saw her. It was more her personality at that age."

"She was a pretty hot fourteen-year-old, though," Rachel said. "I usually go for teenagers. But I mean...it's Annabelle Leigh. I've got a whole Discovery ID, murder porn complex."

"Right," Cecil said.

"So, are you still a monk?" Rachel asked. "How are you going to have sex with her if you're a monk?"

"It *is* Annabelle Leigh. God makes exceptions."

Rachel nodded. "Right on. For sure God would have sex with her if he had a chance." Rachel looked up at Annabelle. "I feel like you should have her. Two young lovers back together and all."

"Thank you," Cecil said. "I'm sure you'll find another... I'm sure you'll find someone else."

Rachel clapped her hands with a happy snap. "I have my eye on a nutcracker. Have fun."

As she stumbled away, Rita approached Cecil from behind.

"Sorry to bother you, Mr. LeClaire. Um. I spoke to my manager. We don't usually allow this. But since you're purchasing three girls, do you want to take Annabelle to the dressing rooms? Try her on before the bid is over?"

"Yes," Cecil said quickly and with way too much enthusiasm. "Um. Yeah."

Rita unlocked Annabelle's ankles from the stool. She grabbed Annabelle by the wrist and pulled her off the platform. She was shorter than he remembered, more fragile. But she still held her head with that arrogant confidence.

Seeing her walk in front of him filled him with a strange glee. Even though she was being led by a slave master, she was walking. And for so long, he thought he would never see her move again.

Rita pushed open the curtains of a dressing room. "The bid is over in about five minutes. I will notify you if someone outbids you on Ava Germaine."

"Thank you," he said as Rita pushed the curtains closed.

Annabelle beamed with joy and pushed him onto the fluffy purple chair. She straddled him into a smothering hug. He grabbed her head, nuzzling his face into her neck. He was so overjoyed he couldn't even find the words.

Annabelle took his chin and pulled him into her lips. They were the only lips he had ever kissed. It was the most familiar warmth in his mouth.

But now she tasted of coriander instead of strawberry Starbursts.

"*I missed you* feels like an understatement," he said.

He rubbed his forehead to hers, her panting breath warming his nose, the scent of chocolate on her breath. For several seconds, his fingers circled her wrist, counting each pulsing beat to see if he'd remembered the rhythm of her heart.

"We're going to get you out tonight. I promise," he said. "And when we get out, we'll go to New Hampshire. Build that inn you always wanted. We'll make you a koi pond, a chocolate fountain, even that mini-rollercoaster."

"Mini-rollercoaster made out of *gold*," Annabelle corrected. "I always said I wanted a *real* golden rollercoaster in my backyard."

"Well, you deserve it. Especially after all you've been through." Cecil hugged her tighter to his chest. He shivered with the excitement of a young boy who had finally found his long lost puppy. "Are you okay? Are you healthy? Are you—"

"I'm fine," Annabelle said. "It wasn't all bad. Not toward the end anyway."

Cecil grabbed her hands. "I have a detective. Her name's Detective Roosevelt. As soon as we get you safe, she's going to talk with you. We can shut this whole thing down. So no one has to go through what you went through."

"Let's just stop talking." She pressed her lips into his, her breasts pushing into his neck as she scooted up his lap. And she ground her hips into his waist and rubbed his hands up and down the leather on her body.

She dragged his hands to her chest. And suddenly, he felt her exposed breasts in his hands. She had unzipped the front of her jumpsuit.

"Are you trying to have sex?" Cecil asked with disbelief.

"It's part of the show, isn't it?" she asked with a coquettish grin.

"I'm trying to save you from sex traffickers. They're planning to kill you tonight, and you want to have sex?"

"If we die tonight," Annabelle said, "then at least we should feel good."

Cecil pushed her off his lap. "I'm sorry, what? Not right now. Ava's out there. I... I'm surprised VD hasn't already sent someone out onto the store floor to attack me."

Annabelle zipped up the front of her jumpsuit halfway, still leaving some of her cleavage exposed. "VD doesn't kill for no reason. She'd probably rather you work for her than kill you."

"It's Perdonna?" Cecil asked.

Annabelle practically spat with laughter. She licked her finger-tip and wiped her smudged lipstick off of Cecil's lips. "Perdonna? No. VD is much more powerful."

"Bourgeois and his men said I know VD. So who is it?"

Annabelle shrugged as she adjusted the jumpsuit around her thighs. "I never got to see her in person. It's always her goons that abuse me."

"We have to move quickly to get you out," Cecil said. "We'll get Ava and—"

The bell chimed, and Rita knocked on the outside of the dressing room. "Bidding's over. How would you like to pay, Mr. LeClaire? Same card?"

"Yes, please," Cecil said. He pushed open the curtain and fol-lowed Rita to the checkout desk.

"That will be $400,000 for Annabelle Leigh and $86,000 for the model in pink."

The Dial beeped when the clerk scanned it.

"Oops. I'm sorry, sir. Sometimes it's a problem with our com-puter. Let's try again."

The clerk scanned the Dial, and it beeped again with a red flash.

"I'm sorry, sir. But your card has been denied."

"This has to be a...a mistake." Cecil flipped his Dial and pulled up the alert message on his palm.

Visage Card: You have a credit limit of $1,000,000.00. You have a remaining $452,000.00.

Cecil swallowed deeply and put his head in his hands. The stupid crystal castle. He rubbed his head, trying to imagine how he could quickly find cash. He groaned with frustration.

"Oh, look on the bright side. You can still get *one* of them," the clerk said, sneaking a peek at the message.

Annabelle leaned over his shoulder. "Take me. I know how we can save Ava later."

"You sure?" Cecil asked. "You're absolutely sure you'll be able to find her?"

Annabelle nodded.

"What happens to the other girl, then?" Cecil said. "Does she stay out for another round of bidding?"

"She'll go to the second-highest bidder."

Cecil's heart sank as he watched James Caldwell smoothing his blond hair with a tiny golden comb.

"Can you find her before he hurts her?" Cecil whispered.

"I'll keep her safe."

Cecil pointed behind him to Annabelle. "I'll buy this one."

"Perfect choice."

44

Annabelle hid her face in a chinchilla coat. She had the look of a feral animal, eyes darting toward each and every shopper on the crowded avenue. The scent of pumpkin spice mixed with cinnamon and pine.

She pulled the fur up to her eyes. "The VD House is on Sixty-Third. We have to hurry."

Annabelle scurried to the base of a tree and found a pebble. She tossed it onto the sidewalk and began kicking it in front of her as she strolled. The stone threatened to hit every person that walked by.

"We can't play that game anymore," Cecil said with a chuckle. "We're adults."

"Adults shmadults." She kicked the stone beside her, and Cecil stopped it beneath his foot. It threatened to hit the little boy near him who wore a vampire Halloween costume. "Around the trash-can," Annabelle said. "If you lose the pebble, you have to do my makeup for a week."

A familiar grin spread across her face, and her eyebrows danced up and down. He couldn't ignore the challenge. He kicked the pebble in front of him as they walked. He tried to swerve around a stroller and a mom. But he kicked the pebble at the back of the woman's heel.

"I'm so sorry," he said, trying to hide his face so she wouldn't recognize him.

The woman didn't even notice. It was New York. Strange objects hit pedestrians all the time. A pebble was preferable to poop.

He swerved the pebble around the trash can with a laugh and kicked it over to Annabelle. "Around a dog. If you lose the pebble, you have to visit a church with me next week."

Annabelle giggled. She kicked the pebble faster. Then she spotted a shih tzu. She waited until the owner wasn't looking, and then she kicked the stone in front of the dog. But the pink bow-wearing fluff ball pounced on the pebble. She sniffed it for a few seconds. And then she swallowed the stone whole.

Cecil bent over with laughter, clapping his hands together.

"That dog just ate my pebble," Annabelle said with disbelief. "That doesn't count. It doesn't count!"

"It counts!" Cecil said, face turning tomato-red.

"Excuse me." The owner of the shih tzu tapped Annabelle on the shoulder. "Did you just kick a rock at my dog?"

Annabelle buried her face in the chinchilla coat. She paused for a moment and then sprinted forward through the mass of people on the street. "Hey. Hey!" Cecil shouted. "I don't know where I'm going."

She waved him forward. Annabelle had an amazing gift when it came to shoving people over. She was the type of person who tackled in touch football. Cecil chased after her, ears turning red with embarrassment. All the while, he prayed no one recognized them.

He bumped into shoulders. Jumped over rogue dog leashes that dragged on the street. And apologized every time he crashed into someone's shopping bag.

Annabelle ripped apart the bridge created by a cute young couple's clasped hands and dashed between them.

It was exhilarating. Although it was dark, it felt like the sun was shining on him. The warmth beat against his skin and into his lungs. He used to say that when Annabelle disappeared, the sun went down. The paparazzi came out in the dark. There was a never-ending cold. And it all felt like a nightmare.

Annabelle stopped in front of Sixty-Third Street with her hands on her hips. "Beat you," she chided. Cecil scooped her up in his arms and spun her around. Her hair whipped behind her, and her feet flew up into the air.

He put her down, and they laughed in each other's arms. "Did I mention I missed you?" Cecil asked.

"Not enough." She pointed to Sixty-Third Street toward Fifth Avenue. "The VD House is beside Margaux's house. That's where they'll bring Ava. It's above Café Ami."

"The VD House was my *neighbor*?" Cecil asked.

Annabelle shrugged. "Guess you didn't look for me hard enough, huh?"

The words dripped off her tongue like acid. A glare peered out from the side of her eye.

The LeClaire Mansion looked as it always had. The mirrored windows reflected tree branches like eerie ghost fingers. The snaggle-toothed lions were smashed to bits from angry tourists.

"I...I should've known Margaux would push you into modeling," Cecil said. "It's all my fault. I'll spend the rest of my life apologizing to you. I—"

"Yeah. It's okay. You'll make it up to me," she said with a playful giggle.

Café Ami displayed olive trees draped in twinkle lights. Croissants traveled on golden trays, and espressos threatened to overflow from crystal glasses. Rose-flavored macarons decorated the window display. It looked like a normal night. Except the patrons were dressed in tuxedos and gowns instead of winter coats.

Annabelle opened the door. "After you."

Prosciutto and Gruyère drowned buttery croissants. Slurps of spaghetti carbonara were louder than the piano. And old men rubbed their fingers over their mistress's thighs beneath rose-covered tables. Nothing seemed out of the ordinary.

"A lot of the businesses near Fifth and Madison do The Mall," Annabelle whispered as she tugged him toward the back of the café. "The Beacon Royal Hotel has a ball. And in the back, there is a strip club for you to use your 'recent purchase.' The movie theater has a porn showing. And they bring in big-name directors so you can film a porno with the model you just bought."

They swerved through tables of macarons and daisies. Annabelle plucked a daffodil from a vase and stuck it in her hair. "The most fucked-up event is in Griffin's, the children's store. In the back, there's a ball pit and a jungle gym where you can fuck your model. Because, if you're going to be a pedophile, do it right," Annabelle said.

"How do you know that guy will bring Ava here, then?" Cecil asked.

"Because this has the best event of them all."

Annabelle moved to a Visage mirror. It reflected a Rothko painting in gold until Annabelle waved her hand in front of it. A keypad rose onto the screen. She dug through her go-bag and pulled out the folder that came with her.

"What are you doing?" Cecil asked.

"Typing in your order number," Annabelle said. "Each purchase comes with a code. That gets you in everywhere at The Mall."

She typed in 1-8-9-2-0, and a handle magically burst through the white brick. And Cecil noticed that there had been the outline of a door there all along. She opened it and led him forward.

The hallway was dark, except for two blinding square lights. They were faced toward a male model and his seventy-year-old grandma client. A fashion photographer squatted at their waists, pointing his camera at them like a hipster sniper.

The boy had a dusting of scruff around his jaw. His eyes were so vacant they looked translucent. He couldn't have been older than eighteen.

His six-pack abs had been dusted in glitter. On one shoulder was draped a black bear hide, grizzly teeth and muzzle still attached. He posed with his thumbs in the belt straps.

"Derek," the photographer said. "Lick your lips, please."

Derek tried to appease, but his lip licking looked more like a young boy sticking his tongue out. The client had her spider-veined hands over the boy's crotch. And her lips left lipstick all over his neck.

His clothing gave off sexuality, but he never once smiled, never winked, never looked the client in the eye. He was Michelangelo's *Derek*, a modern image, that of the prostrated male fashion model.

Just a few years ago, Derek played in the stream behind his house, chasing rabid raccoons for fun. Good kid, the kind who asked his dad permission to keep his high school sweetheart out past midnight.

But the family needed money. He couldn't be a schoolteacher.

Derek was terrified of modeling, but he had to be a strong man. *"Boys your age go to war, and you're bitching about takin' pictures?"* his father would ask.

When Derek said modeling would score him some hot chicks, his father would reply, *"Son, I work sixty hours a week drilling concrete. Your job's not that hard. You don't need a psychiatrist."*

Derek thought he had control. Instead, a millionaire Manhattan socialite was about to purchase his body and stick a dildo up his ass.

He couldn't tell his father about the abuse, couldn't ask for money because Dad thought Derek was making thousands a month.

Cecil could've been Derek. There wasn't much distance between becoming a monk or becoming a model.

"It's hard to watch," Cecil said.

Annabelle scoffed. "Men love sex."

"Rape and enslavement are just as bad for men as for women," Cecil said. Annabelle rolled her eyes, pushing open the door at the end of the hallway instead of listening to him.

Turquoise lights shone down onto water. Steam filled the room in a foggy haze. And the floor and walls were covered in deep blue rocks. It felt like an underwater cove.

A saltwater pool covered most of the floor with tiny rippling waves. Circular Jacuzzis covered in crushed shells surrounded it. There were nooks carved into the rock walls for sitting and fucking. You could rock climb to thirty feet in the air and cozy into your own special cove.

It smelled of the outdoors, a cool breeze biting his lips.

Waterfalls poured from a glass dome. The ceiling seemed never-ending, as though the building reached up to the sky. The sound of a conch shell played over loudspeakers. But the conch lullaby was drowned out by the moans.

Over one hundred people filled the space. Models wore their bras and underwear, while most of the clients wore swim trunks.

Topless girls swam through the water. Clients suckled their breasts. Girls were bent over against the rock walls and fucked beneath waterfalls.

Models fondled each other's breasts and kissed each other's lips. Naked models filled the Jacuzzis, their long legs wrapped around clients' heads.

People fucking in the caves above looked like an art piece. Nameless bodies pumping into each other aggressively. Mews and sighs echoed over the roaring conch shell and the sound of falling rain.

"Pretty cool, huh?" Annabelle asked.

"Not...no. Pretty *disturbing*."

A peculiar group sat in a shallow black pool to the side. Shiny black masks made them look like guards. Two men wore black Speedos, and a woman covered herself in blue mesh. The coverup wrapped around her entire body, even her hair. The only bit of her that could be seen was the black nose of the mask.

The woman cuddled onto one of the men's laps. Her back arched over his knees, head falling back into an inch of water. The blue mesh revealed her full black mask. She parted her legs from beneath the mesh. She kicked out into the water like she was making a snow angel.

The man's hand stroked her inner thigh as black water splashed over her feet. His other hand burrowed into the blue mesh at her chest. He uncovered her breasts and began rubbing with his palm. Her head dipped back, and she let out a light moan.

His head dipped to her breast and kissed the nipple. He moved his palm to her belly and stroked her.

"Who're they?" Cecil asked.

"Elites," she said as if that one word explained everything.

"Do they pay extra? Is that woman a model?"

"No. They just *are*. And no, the woman isn't a model."

Suddenly a girl screamed. A fat bald man had his hands wrapped around her neck. He pushed her up against the side of the pool. "I don't want to," she cried. Her face wrenched up like she was dying. "Please. Please! I'm scared."

She covered her bottom with her hands. And the man dunked her underwater. He held her there for seconds. No one even bothered looking at them.

"Hey," Cecil shouted, but Annabelle covered his mouth, her nails digging into the sides of his cheeks.

"Don't," she said. "You'll get dragged out, and then we can't save Ava."

"He'll kill her," Cecil said.

He lifted the girl back up, gasping for air. She was tiny and thin. Her black hair was kept in a little bun with white bows. She might've been fourteen at most.

"She should take it," Annabelle said. "It's her job."

"Her *job*?" he asked. "Her *job*!"

"I mean... It's easier to please the client than to die."

Her response didn't sit well with Cecil. He crossed his arms.

"I almost died here too," Annabelle said. "I was in that cove up there." She pointed to a burrow toward the ceiling. "It was my first year back in America. I fought a client. Because he dangled me over the edge of the alcove, so my head and body were hanging toward the rocks. He held me by my feet and fucked me. He rammed my body and pushed it closer to the rocks. I screamed when I started getting faint. So he pulled me back up and punched me in the face. He stuck a rock in my mouth to shut me up. When he put me back over the edge, I swallowed the rock. Because I wanted to die."

Cecil closed his eyes. He wrapped his arm around her, but she shrugged him off. "I'm... I can't even imagine."

"It's okay," Annabelle said. "I'm alive."

The little girl was pushed underwater again as the client laughed.

"Soon, I'll have to say something," Cecil said.

"The experience will make her stronger. I was too weak then. She's too weak now."

"Too weak?" Cecil squealed, eyes bulging out.

Suddenly a lanky young man approached Annabelle and tapped his chin. His eyes directly met Annabelle's.

"What was that?" Cecil asked.

"Nothing. I have no idea. He must've been a client from another time."

Cecil leaned up against the rock wall. "He gets one more minute."

Annabelle's feet seemed to shuffle. "Excuse me. I have to use the bathroom," she said.

"Is it safe?"

"I really have to go. Unless I pee in the water," she joked, "I don't have any other option."

She scurried away. And then the girl let out another shriek. Her legs kicked out, and the man lifted her out of the water. He held her in the air while she shouted. And then he slammed her against the rock. A tiny patch of blood pooled out, and her eyes closed shut.

Cecil rushed toward her. But the masked woman beat him to it. Blue mesh flew before his eyes as she scooped the girl into her arms. She carried the girl toward a set of metallic doors built into the rock. Cecil followed.

The woman gestured toward a door, and Cecil opened. She carried the girl to a fluffy white bed and laid her down. "There should be a needle and thread in the mirror," she whispered in a thick Spanish accent. "And grab alcohol off the bar. We have to be quiet."

Cecil grabbed the needle, thread, and scissors from inside a mirror cabinet, and he pulled a bottle of vodka off an onyx bar.

The woman bent over the girl, feeling her pulse. Her hands shook as she held on to the girl's hand. "Can you hear me, darling?" she whispered. Her voice didn't betray any of the shaking in her body.

"Wake up. Open your eyes. It's safe." The woman applied pressure to the wound with her palm. She doused the open wound in alcohol. Cecil threaded the needle.

The woman climbed onto the bed and put the girl's head in her lap. She took the threaded needle from his hand. She felt the wound, and then she pressed it into the skin. The two pieces of flesh came together, bloody and bruised.

She concentrated, but her hand shook as she tried to weave the thread correctly. Cecil wrapped his hand around hers and kept her from shivering. The black mask looked up at him. And he heard a deep breath suck into her chest. They finished closing the wound together.

Cecil felt the girl's pulse. "Still good."

"All we can do is wait. Wait for her to wake up," the woman said, nodding as if she was trying to reassure herself. She shuffled out from beneath the girl. Like tucking in her own child, she lifted a fluffy white duvet over the girl's legs and stroked her hair.

Cecil caressed the woman's bloody hands. He splashed her with vodka and rubbed the blood off her palms. His thumbs massaged hers, picking the gooey red from beneath her cuticles.

Little sobs rang out from beneath the mask. He leaned back onto a fluffy white carpet and pulled her to his lap. He held on to the blue mesh and stroked the rough material on her back.

He pushed the mesh from her mask. And leaned down to kiss the metal lips. Even as he gently pecked the cool, lifeless form of her, he loved her.

"This doesn't seem appropriate for a monk," she said.

"Crying doesn't seem appropriate for *you*, Perdonna." He felt her heart rate speed up. "I've never seen you cry before."

He stroked the back of her head and gently untied the black lace from between her hair that held up the mask. He slid it up to reveal her.

"What gave me away?" Perdonna whispered.

"The accent wasn't very good," Cecil said with a small smile.

She hit him across the chest. "The accent is spectacular."

"I just knew," he said. "And you had trouble seeing the wound without touching it."

Perdonna's eyes squinted. She leaned her head against the translucent wall, pressing her ear to the glass. She motioned for Cecil to do the same.

The outline of a woman circled around a smaller girl. He could see the shadows in the room. The bed. A bar. A mirror. The voices came in muffled bursts.

"Are you a virgin?" the larger woman asked.

The girl's silence made the woman clap.

"Great. Then you probably got more money." She grabbed a sheet of paper and a clipboard from her desk. "Take off your clothing down to your bra and underwear."

"Is this a hospital checkup?" the girl asked. "I'm not fucking that guy. It's not happening."

"Then I'm punishing you," the woman said. "Full body check. So I can determine whether your body is even worth selling."

The woman tore off the girl's tank top.

"Is this VD?" Cecil whispered to Perdonna. She nodded.

The girl's silhouette was emaciated like a queen sent off to starve in a prison cave. And then she removed her skirt, standing in front of VD bare. Her tiny ankles barely held the bone and flesh that towered above them.

VD's fingers grasped the girl's jaw like a vise, and she pried her mouth open with her fingers. "Your chompers look like rotting candy corns," she said.

"My father fed me corn syrup and secondhand smoke," the girl said.

"Good. When I soak your mouth in bleach, you won't scream as loud as the others."

VD hovered closely behind the girl. Her neck curved around her shoulder like a vampire ready to take a bite.

VD pressed her hands to the girl's belly. "No bloating. Good. My clients complain about models having 'cotton ball stuffed stomachs.' And since you're anorexic, you're not growing pubic hair like a yeti." Her fingers ran up the entire length of the girl's body and ended up in her hair. Long spiny fingers lifted strands into the air, massaging the head. "Keep your hair long," VD said. "I like it longer. More *you*. Untamable.

"Beautiful waist," VD whispered, her fingers dancing along the girl's sensitive pelvic bones. She traced the line of the girl's underwear, slowly, flipping up the edges of the fabric. Suddenly her hands cupped the girl's ass cheeks and massaged them. One hand rose and came down to spank her.

"If you're going to kill me, get it over with," the girl said in a cracking voice. "If you're going to rape me, kill me first."

Suddenly VD slammed the girl against the mirror, and there was a loud shatter. Cries rang out.

"Shut up and get out there," VD yelled. The girl scurried out, and VD clapped her hands before following her.

Cecil took a deep breath. "Wow."

"She's worse than the last one," Perdonna said. "Everyone thinks she's out of control."

"The last one?"

"They're rotated out every so often. This VD came into existence because she killed everyone else."

Cecil raised his eyebrows. "This would've been useful information before now."

Perdonna shrugged. "I told you not to come. But now that you're here, you have to go quickly." She stood up and waved him out.

"Is VD dangerous?"

"To you, probably," Perdonna said with a small smile.

"Annabelle's safe. I found her."

"I saw," Perdonna said curtly. "But where's Ava?"

"I haven't found her yet. But Annabelle says she's going to come here."

Perdonna gave him an angry glare.

"Don't criticize me when you lie about going to a sex-trafficking party," Cecil said.

"If I wasn't here, this girl would be dead."

"You weren't saving anyone with that man's hands on your breasts."

Perdonna rolled her eyes. "I think Tom would disagree with you."

"That was Tom Gray?" Cecil asked.

"Tom and the owner of Ami."

Cecil's eyes bulged out. "This is disgusting. How could you do this?"

Perdonna crossed her arms. "This was going *so* well," she said, pointing to the floor. "Cuddling and saving lives. And then you became a monk again."

Cecil stormed out of the cubicle, slamming the door. He found Annabelle standing right outside, waiting. She had changed out of her leather suit and into a white nightgown. Makeup that once covered her shoulders had been rubbed off. Red venous scars ran over her body. Red ridges ran over her shoulders like coils. The bones in her neck seemed to jut out with spurs.

"How much longer until Ava is brought here?" Cecil asked.

"They walked by about two minutes ago," Annabelle said.

"Why didn't you get me?" he asked. "Are you serious? Let's go."

Annabelle shrugged her shoulders. "Never smart to interrupt you and Perdonna." She led him out of the cove. "He took Ava upstairs. Shouldn't be hard to find her."

45

Ava Germaine was bent over doggy-style before her clients.

Sun-kissed hair fell in ringlets down her shoulders. Her wrists and ankles were tied in furry black handcuffs. She was a slim, swaying reed, wavering above a mucky swamp.

A pale pink, the color of an eyelid, decorated the room. It had a king-sized bed and a chest full of sex toys. It could've been a six-year-old's bedroom if only the chest were full of baby dolls instead of sex toys. If only there had been a mobile dangling stars above the bed instead of a sex harness ornamented with chains.

The clients, a husband and wife dressed in Hervé Leger and Buratti, admired Ava's submissive body as if she were a piece by Rothko. Ava was young enough to be their daughter. Perhaps that was the point.

Was that the reality of the mother and father? In the end, all parents fucked their children one way or another.

She longed for the couple to crush her body, to feel the heavy weight of the man on top of her and the woman beneath her. To be cocooned, to be crushed between them so that she would shred to bits and see nothing but darkness. To be spooned by two intelligent beings, smashed between their mandibles so that she was no longer Ava Germaine but a part of the two.

She wanted them to absorb her, put her back in the womb so she could be reborn a bouncing, baby girl—beautiful, well-mannered, and valedictorian of Harvard Law.

Suddenly the wife knelt down before Ava's eyes, a string of black pearls dangling around the neck. Her fashionable, cropped white hair brushed against Ava's cheek. A delicate, floral-scented palm cupped her face. Without a word, the woman's lips danced across Ava's.

But that was not Ava's reality. It was only a dream.

The real scene was quite different. Mr. Caldwell had gotten them a room in the VD House.

It was like a hotel. Silver-lined duvet covers, salted peanuts, a Sony television, and a bar. The only difference was that this room did indeed have a box of sex toys.

James Caldwell lay flat on his stomach while Ava rode him. But she didn't ride him quite in the way that Mr. Caldwell had expected when he asked her to chain him to the bed.

His wrists were zip-tied to the bedposts, and his pants were pulled down. Ava clutched a whip in her hand, sitting on his back like a rider on a saddle.

"Neigh, pony. Neigh." She clapped with genuine enjoyment, bouncing on his back. "Giddyup." She slapped him on the back lightly, and he whimpered. "I barely hit you. It was a tickle."

"Stop it! This is so embarrassing," James said, face turning bright red.

"You think being handcuffed half-naked to a piano was *less* embarrassing?"

"You're a whore, though," James said.

Ava took the whip and held it tightly in her hand. She whacked him hard this time. And the slap shook through the room. "Chaining yourself to a bed is never a good idea. Not getting the BDSM you expected, huh?"

She leaned over toward the bed stand and pulled out rainbow paint. She scrubbed it through his hair. "My little pony..."

James rubbed his face into his pillow. "Please. Please stop. I won't touch you."

"You'll let me leave here?" Ava asked, leaning over his head to look into his eyes. She had to be sure he wasn't lying.

"I'll let you leave. I will. Just *stop*." Ava stood up and walked to the zip ties. But then a guard appeared in the doorway.

He was so large that his white suit barely buttoned around his round belly. He wore two red bandanas around his neck, and his teeth had rotted out in the front, leaving two pink gummy stumps. "Do your job," he said.

"I don't work for you," Ava said, squinting her anime eyes.

"You do now," he said. "Or I'll kill you."

Ava shrugged. "Kill me. I would've taken euthanasia years ago if I had the chance." She walked toward him and spread out her arms. "How would you prefer to do it? Shot to the head? Decapitate me? Maybe rape me then strangle me? What's the preference?"

The guard gave a confused look, then stared off at James Caldwell's crying face. Ava thought she had won. But the guard took Cecil's backpack off his arms. It was the bag Cecil had forgotten at the Tea-Pea in a rush to find Ava.

The guard's hand roughly dug through the pouch. He pulled out a squirming Figaro by his tail. "I got word you like rats."

Ω

A bright red light lit the second-floor hallway in an eerie red glow. It was the Amsterdam Red Light District re-created in a building.

Bodies for sale.

Behind glass doors that looked like store windows, girls in lingerie posed underneath spotlights. Each cubicle was outfitted with a king bed, a sauna, hand sanitizer, and cologne that was meant to mask the scent of sex when the men arrived home to their children and wives.

Girls lined the hallway like portraits in a museum showcase.

Skin. Legs. White-gloved hands. Bedazzled garter belts. Long, wiry necks framed by collarbones. Eyes covered in black ink. Blond bobs. Long brown curls. Plumped, plastic lips.

The underground Madison Avenue—where you tried a girl on in the fitting room for $25,000, but you didn't get to take her home afterward. Where tight-fitting took on a whole new meaning.

An artsy director wearing torn jeans and a Gucci T-shirt peeked into the rooms waving suggestively at the women. He paced by the windows, choosing carefully, enjoying the shopping as much as he would revel in gambling or fucking.

When he finally chose a body and entered a room, the model flicked a switch, and the electrochromic glass frosted over, creating a shield to hide the perversions that would ensue.

"This is where clients buy girls during the normal season," Annabelle said. "This runs every day. Even Christmas Day. It's actually the biggest time of year."

She said it with some pride, leering through the windows.

Girls shuffled up against the glass. One bent over and rubbed her butt against the window and spanked herself. The cheeks jiggled for seconds after.

"They get bonuses the more men choose them. Like better food, or a nicer bed," Annabelle explained. "They sleep in the same room they work."

"*They?*" Cecil asked. "Where do you sleep?"

"Same. I have a cell too."

Cecil slowed his walking. He stayed several feet behind Annabelle. "Where do you eat? Do you spend all day in that tiny room?"

Annabelle nodded. "It's terrible. You get raped five times a day. And then you have to stay there and eat terrible food. Sometimes if we're lucky, the client buys one of the nicer rooms upstairs. So we get to sleep there that night."

"So which room do you think Ava is in?"

"The ones upstairs."

"Then why are we down here?"

"I wanted to show you this first."

Cecil leaned up against the wall. "We need to get Ava and get the hell out of here."

Annabelle pouted. She leaned up against the glass. A girl in a jewel-encrusted corset leaned into the window and pressed her puckered lips to the glass. Annabelle kissed her through the glass. "VD owns all of these models. They only leave for runway shows."

"I don't care," Cecil said. "Can we go get Ava?"

Another guest wore his work suit and carried a diaper bag in his hands. He hunched with his head down when watching the girls, terrified that someone would see him there and tell his wife.

"Aren't you just *a little* turned on?" Annabelle asked.

Muted sounds of sex emanated through the hallway. Legs spread across window ledges, sex covered by large rhinestones or thongs. Nipples poked through fabric, meant to entice like the tips of Hershey's Kisses. Bodies were covered in bruises where their last client hit them.

Girls touched themselves, rubbing between their legs, licking their lips, arms beckoning men toward them. Round, voluptuous asses shimmied on pedestals.

The VD House was a zoo full of gazelles in simulated heat.

Underneath the dancing and the smiles, an emptiness stared back. The models laughed but never smiled. They moved like ghosts, appearing when summoned, disappearing when they could.

Music, sex, song, dance—Cecil felt as if he were in a dream, an unceasing radiation of gloom and depression.

"No." Cecil's hands went cold. He watched Annabelle staring at the girls in their cages. "Do *you* like it?"

"A little," Annabelle said, giggling with a faked high pitch to make the words sound more innocent.

"Is that...Is that Stockholm Syndrome?" Cecil asked nervously. His voice wavered. He suspected the truth. But he couldn't accept it.

They had finally reached the end of the hallway, where she opened the doorway to a large black swirling staircase. Cecil studied her confident stride as they climbed higher, metal clanging with each step.

"Do you know who the new VD is?"

"No."

Cecil furrowed his brow. "But you work here. How can you not know who your captor is?"

"Oh. So *demanding.* That's new." She stuck her nails out like cat claws. "You're a grown man now."

"Are there vents I can climb through?" Cecil looked around.

"Ava can take care of herself."

He grabbed her shoulder. "You don't seem too worried about your own life, either."

"Are you accusing me of something?"

"Maybe."

"I'm not VD." Annabelle looked to the ground, red creeping up her cheeks. "It's just that I've been so beaten down, burned, raped... Dying isn't so scary. It would take away my pain." Tears filled her eyes. "I don't even feel real emotions anymore," she said, glazed eyes dancing with images of shriveled prunes instead of sugarplums. There was a real vapidity about her. A superficiality.

"You are," Cecil said, freezing on the staircase. "You are VD."

46

"What's happening?" Cecil asked, covering his face.

"Come in," Annabelle said. "See my office."

Gold-and-black brick covered the walls. A toy train zoomed around the largest wall on an intricate railroad system. Elevations and loop de loops sent the honking cars tumbling in a frenzy. The trains sped around villages covered in fake snow and twinkling lights, coal miners working the caverns and general stores of days long gone.

But this wasn't a train from a Christmas catalogue. It was a horror train.

Plastic trees had been singed. Some train cars were derailed, crashed into blood-splattered churches. Miniature people were eaten by grizzly bears, their bloody heads lying in candy stores. It was the definition of a "crazy train."

The office's far wall was covered in glass. The room hovered above the VD Red Light District. It gave a view of the models fucking their clients in the cells below. Somehow her window allowed her to see through the frosted glass downstairs.

Along her walls, the bookcases were filled with fake passports, birth certificates, and the identities of a hundred girls.

He watched as Annabelle rearranged the train tracks and sent a ladybug-shaped train up the hills, atop a rainbow that shot through plastic trees.

She pushed buttons on a cotton candy maker, and the machine roared to life.

"Where's Ava?" Cecil asked.

"Trust me, she's safe for now," Annabelle said. She toyed with a railroad track and derailed a train into the faux firehouse. The cars hit the structure and flipped over, but the wheels kept spinning. "Most patrons try to avoid killing the models. The fine is too high. But I'll take you to her if you agree to work with me."

"Is that why you did this? Cecil asked. "To make me *work* for you?"

Annabelle walked to the glass and looked down at the models. She twirled her hair and nibbled at the broken split ends.

"No. I wanted revenge. Revenge for Margaux sending me for an 'interview' with VD. Revenge for Perdonna not sending people to find me. And for *you*. For you letting me rot in here for ten years."

She lounged on a yellow plastic swing attached to the ceiling, the kind one could find in any child's playground. How eerie it was that the childish décor clashed with the depravity outside.

"Several people didn't want me to be the new VD. So I faked my death. If I'm dead, someone else must be VD. And in the process, I could fuck over the LeClaires.

"I sent you the invitation to the Visage show to bring you back to Manhattan. And, conveniently, in doing so, I could put Perdonna and Margaux in jail for my death. It was poetic, really.

"However, that junkie, Clara, mishandled the corpse we gave her. She ended up replacing Perdonna as the prime suspect for the skin coat. That wouldn't work, of course."

She paced like a lioness on Pride Rock, flipping her Shirley Temple curls like a mane as she talked.

"So I found Jordan Jones, your perfect seductress. I gave her the note from the old VD specifying Margaux's commission so you would explain everything to the police. I had to kill someone to frame Margaux, and Jordan was the obvious choice. It kept her quiet about my identity.

"You weren't supposed to know I was alive. I still don't know who shot Clara in Salon de Ming. I think they were trying to stop her from getting your files. Thankfully, Dr. Imogen is a weasel and was able to lead you here."

She pulled pink cotton candy out of the machine and twirled it around her fingers like a spider web. Saliva dripped down, disintegrating the mass into sugar sludge.

"You did well," Annabelle said. "I set up a game, and you redeemed yourself. You proved you *do* care about me. And you do have some balls."

"What the fuck is wrong with you?"

Annabelle pouted, cotton candy finger between her lips. "Excuse me?"

"You want to be VD? You want to sell and abuse girls like you were sold?"

"That's less important." She pointed her sticky fingers at him. "You're the one who stopped looking for me. How could you?" Annabelle asked. She rushed toward him and brushed her lips against his neck. "You're the one who let me rot here like an imaginary friend."

"I—"

"But it's not so bad," Annabelle cut him off. "I always did like playing with Barbie dolls. Now I get X-rated ones dressed in Chanel."

"You could've reached out to me."

"My superiors threatened to murder me if I saw you."

"You sold girls! You're a pimp!"

"Models. Managed fashion models, Cecil." She grabbed his hands and pulled him toward the bed so that their heads rested on the headboard just below the train tracks. "Oh, don't act so shocked. Everything you *have* came from selling girls."

The train whooshed by, locomotive chuffing smoke, horn sounding above their heads. The lights seemed to take on a light-blue-and-pink hue, as though the air were made of cotton candy.

None of it felt real.

"It's almost as good as the train set you had in your room," Annabelle said. "But not quite."

Cecil's father had left him a train set of handmade cars from Italy in his will. The track looped around mountains sculpted with white rock and pink quartz. Villages modeled after London, Avignon, and Sienna sat along the tracks. Big Ben and the London Eye lit up when Cecil went to bed. It was a work of art, one of the only presents his father had given him.

"You loved that train set," Cecil said to Annabelle. Part of him felt nostalgic, another part wanted to dig out her eyes with a train track.

"I did," she said. "Remember that game we used to play? When we put paper dolls of each other in different cars and tried to guess in which city our trains would cross paths. And we'd wave at each other."

He took a deep breath, eyes glancing at hers with a wistful longing. Annabelle Leigh was still in that body somewhere.

"I'm devastated it's gone," Cecil said. "I never understood how it caught fire."

Annabelle's face turned red, and she held her breath until she spilled out a string of giggles. "I *may* have set it on fire in the third grade." She covered her face like a shy toddler. "I was jealous you could have nice things, and I couldn't. And there was something you loved that wasn't me."

"*You* set it on fire!" Cecil's eyes grew wide. He stared at the flipped-over train spinning for life like a beetle trying desperately to flip back onto its feet.

Then the whole reality hit Cecil. "At my birthday party, with the ponies and cowboy costumes, *you* were the person who put the plastic snake in front of my horse."

Annabelle smiled. "It was quite funny."

"The horse tossed me off into a concrete wall. I got a severe concussion and couldn't go to school for three weeks."

"You were fine."

Cecil shook his head. "Did Clara cut her wrists in the Hamptons, or did you attack her so that you could sing the anthem alone?"

"Clara is crazy. I didn't want her around you," Annabelle said.

"I still don't, even though I needed her for this."

"How blind was I?" Cecil asked himself. He held a train car in his hand and rolled the wheels across his palm, massaging away the memories. "Choo, choo," he whispered in a dejected sigh. He looked up at Annabelle, the idealized imaginary friend. "Have you always been evil?"

"I'm a realist," Annabelle said, her posture brimming with self-adulation. "The government sees the people as upper and lower class, one percent or ninety-nine. I see them as masters and slaves. What's the difference?" She sat on a fluffy white beanbag chair. "I'm not evil. I'm a realist."

She pointed to the train across from them where tiny half-inch figurines sat in cars.

"See how tiny they are? Like little pine needles inside a machine. What would you say if I gave you just five thousand dollars for each one you crushed? And if you didn't take the offer, someone else would get the five thousand dollars and crush you instead. That's how life works."

"You used to believe in God."

"And Santa Claus," Annabelle said. "I've grown up. And I can tell you this. People are better off dead. Dead and in the ground, where they don't have to worry about being beautiful except for at the funeral."

She put a fluff of cotton candy in his mouth. "You've had a tough going. But we can take you for help. Clear your mind and start new," Cecil said.

"You know what Stalin said about how the death of one man is a tragedy, but the death of a million is a statistic? Well, millions of girls are sex-trafficked each year, only a few thousand of those girls are fashion models. I can't stop the cycle. But I can become more powerful within it until I no longer have to worry about being one of the millions again.

"I loved staring into Jordan's eyes while they closed. I loved watching her heavy body sink into the oil. And I loved sending Margaux to jail and finally taking VD's spot as Madame of this house.

"I'm a victim. These people raped me. They beat me. They locked me away. The world hates me? Then fine. I hate it."

A group of four guards dressed in white entered the room. They surrounded the perimeter. Their hands clung on to guns by their waists.

"Roosevelt said she would help you. If we brought you to her, we could bring down the entire sex-trafficking ring."

"I don't want to bring it down," Annabelle said. "I want to have my chance at power. I endured the suffering. I should get the prize. It's not fair if I suffered for *years* and never get the money. The perks. It's great to be the one *doing* the fucking."

"There are consequences to responsibility," Cecil said. "Responsibility is hard."

"It's easy. As soon as we finish here, I'm going to Milan. I made a deal with an orphanage. I'm picking up a bunch of fresh girls. We'll make millions."

"Because money will fix the physiological torment?"

"Maybe," Annabelle said. "But it will definitely make me happy. So, what will it be for you? Are you going to die responsibly or work for me?"

Cecil shook his head. "You'll have to kill me."

He dropped to his knees and stared straight at Annabelle. His heart raced. But it was more that he felt saddened for her. His heart was broken. That was more horrifying than death.

"We were good together," Annabelle said, bending toward him. She kissed his cheek and then stood up.

"Kill him," she said, nodding to the largest of the men.

They remained motionless. Cecil watched as the guards kept their heads down.

"I said to kill him," she said, tossing her hands into the air. Her voice had a tinge of toddler-whine.

"We got orders from higher up," a large man said. The guards began filing out of the room.

"Higher up? There isn't a *higher up*."

The guards kept leaving. One left a large knife on a table behind Cecil's head.

47

─────────

"Anyone would've done what I've done," Annabelle said, pressing her face to the glass window. She looked down at the girls in tiny boxes. Their skin pressed to the glass like congealed pork fat on a pan. "You haven't gone through what I've gone through. Men have beaten me. They've punched me. They've killed me inside. I'm a victim of the patriarchy."

"You can be a victim and also an abusive bitch," Cecil said. He took the knife off the table, and Annabelle's eyes drifted down to it. "Awful things have happened to Ava Germaine. You don't see her killing people."

"Funny you should say that," Annabelle said. She twisted her Dial, and suddenly a video of Ava appeared.

The guard in front of her held Figaro by his tail. A girl curled up at his feet. She wore a tattered sequin dress by Chanel and bloody fishnet stockings. Blood and splinters of skull sprinkled her tight blond curls. A crystal barrette in her hair was cracked, leaving shards through the hair. Red gashes covered the ankles and neck where rope tied the body.

The little blonde girl looked up at Ava with pleading eyes.

"What did you do to her?" Ava asked, her little lower lip quivering. "Is that Lilly?"

"You don't care if you die, fine. You get to choose," the guard said. "Lilly or your rat? Which one dies?"

Ava crossed her arms over her chest. "I'll die."

"That's not an option," the guard said. "You don't care about your own life. This punishment will get our message across."

Lilly clenched the wound on her head and sobbed. "Please. Please don't let me die. I don't wanna die. Please."

"Figaro's my whole life. He's all I care about," Ava whispered. She stared off despondently. Her eyes drifted toward the ceiling.

"So I kill the girl?" the guard asked. "How do you prefer we do it? Hammer or gun?"

"I'll fuck that James Caldwell guy. I'll follow the rules. Just don't do this."

"Too late for options," the guard said.

Figaro squealed, wriggling upside down. His little feet peddled the air like he was on a hamster wheel. "At least hold him upright, goddammit!"

Ava bent down to where Lilly lay. She clasped her hand into hers and tried to scrape some of the blood off her palm. "Here's the deal. If you live, you gotta promise me something."

"Yeah. Yes. I will."

"Hear it first," Ava said. "Things are gonna be really hard here for you. And ugly. It's gonna hurt a lot. And you're going to want to quit sometimes. But you have to bite your lip and get through it. Bite your lip and cherish the good things. Because there *are* good things. And you'll get them if you fight long enough. My only good thing was Figaro."

Ava put her palms out for the guard to put Figaro in her hands. "Let me say goodbye."

"No."

"Let me say goodbye!" Ava screamed bloody murder. Her face was bright red, her teeth bared.

The guard put Figaro in her hands, and she held him up to her face. She nuzzled the white bedhead fur to her cheek. Tears flew out of her eyes, and she drenched his little head.

"Be good, okay? When this archangel comes to take you to heaven, don't bite him, please. Maybe you'll get an even bigger crystal castle in heaven. I mean those clouds are cool."

Ava's eyes turned red. Her hand petted his back rapidly and nervously. She seemed to feel every fiber of him so she could remember. "And it's gotta be better than this, right? Cause this is some bullshit."

Figaro stared up at her. And it seemed that even in the slightest way, he cocked his head. "I love you, Figgy Piggy. I'm so sorry." Ava kissed his head. "But she's just a little girl."

She sobbed as she leaned to hand Figaro toward the guard.

But as she opened up her hands, a shiny black cylinder floated alongside the guard's head. It wound up, and the cane swiped the guard's head. He fell to the floor, eyes closed shut.

"You're right. There are good things," Margaux said, standing behind the guard, clutching her cane. "I wasn't about to let this asshole kill Mickey Mouse." She bent over and put her finger on the guard's neck to check his pulse. "Still kicking." She put two fingers up to heaven. "Screw him, though."

"Yeah," Ava said. She started laughing through the tears, completely in shock. "Screw him."

Annabelle turned off the projection. Cecil leaned back against the wall, a cocky, proud grin on his face. "That didn't go exactly as planned, did it?"

"Margaux ruins everything."

Cecil shook his head. "You wanted Ava to kill the girl to save her pet. So then you could prove that people hurt others to stop their own suffering. But Ava didn't do that. Ava did the hard thing."

Cecil's Dial buzzed with a message:

Det. Fran Roosevelt: I'm outside. By the LeClaire Mansion. Can help if Annabelle wants it/will surrender herself.

Annabelle Leigh existed as a funhouse clown, morphing into laughable, colorful shapes. She sat beneath her train table, coaxing Cecil into her spider's web.

Dozens of antique gas lanterns lined the shelves that hung just above her head. It looked satanic, not like the lanterns of a Christmas train village.

"A detective is offering to help," Cecil said. "If we turn you in, you'd probably get a plea deal to expose the rest of this."

"And then what?" Annabelle said. "I can't do anything else. I knit? I have some babies? I'm a CEO now."

"You could get psychiatric help. You could go to a *real* shopping mall again. Go to the beach. See a movie."

"I'm fine," Annabelle said. "I like it here now. Really. There's nothing more fun than buying other people. I have so many resources at my fingertips. I can toy with boys. I've always liked manipulating people. Now I get to do it with an entire team."

"You remember when we used to swim in the creek in Southampton and play mermaid and hunter?" Cecil asked. "I'd try to shoot at you with a Styrofoam gun when you swam through the branches and rocks. And we sucked on watermelon. You sucked it to be flirty, and I stole chunks from your mouth with my lips. That one time when you convinced me the raccoon we saw was rabid and would eat us alive if I didn't climb a tree with you." Cecil sighed. "Those were real, right? Those were good times."

"They were," she said. She turned fourteen again before his eyes. He spun the curly ends of her hair with his fingertips while she bit her fingernails.

"So why don't you want that?" Cecil asked.

"Because we're not fourteen anymore."

Cecil grabbed her hands and looked into her eyes. "I overheard you in the locker room," he said. "Abusing that girl. If I were to do that, you think I would have fun?"

Annabelle nodded, a light filling her eyes. "The *most* fun. More fun than you have painting with Perdonna."

"I don't paint anything original anymore. I was too depressed without you."

"You can fix that."

"By enslaving people?"

Annabelle raised her eyebrows, agreeing. Cecil took a deep breath, and after a slight hesitation, leaned in to kiss her. His palm wrapped around her cheek. His fingertips stroked her lips, resting his nose to hers.

He sat there for a moment, taking her in. Until he pulled the knife tip from his pocket and pressed it to her neck.

"Oh, now *this* is a turn." She smiled a catlike grin. "You won't kill me, Cecil. I'm the only thing that's kept you going. You tried to forget me. You were desperate to remember me. I'm here." She tapped his head. "I'm always here. I influence everything you do."

"You'll keep doing this if I don't end it." Tears filled his eyes. His hands grew sweaty and warm against her skin.

"You're a monk," Annabelle said. "I'm pretty sure killing is a sin."

"Goodbye, Annabelle."

He slid the blade and tore through her neck. Blood fell from the wound like a waterfall, gushing from her neck, spraying him in the face. But he didn't look away. He didn't wipe his lips.

Betrayal read on her face like a mask. He'd set up their favorite childhood game, but then he broke the rules.

In her final gasps, she looked especially like a fashion model, broken and dead.

He felt a wave of relief when her body fell limp into his arms. He kissed the top of her head and gently placed her on the floor.

Her hands fell into a folded clasp over her torso. A prayer. She looked like an innocent girl of fourteen.

"So long, my darling."

Cecil took a few deep breaths above her, staring at her lifeless body. He had been mourning her for a decade.

"Deliver her from every evil," Cecil prayed. "And bid her eternal rest. The old order has passed away. Welcome her into paradise, where there will be no sorrow, no weeping or pain, but fullness of peace and joy with your Son and the Holy Spirit forever and ever. Amen."

He hesitated as he rose to his knees. Worry marred his face. For the first time, he felt he might not have believed those words.

He exited the office to find the guards dressed in white. They lined the outside wall.

"Do we need cleanup?" one asked.

Cecil paused. He looked to the floor and then back up at the man's eyes. "Yes... Who do you work for?"

"You. Just for tonight," the guard said.

"Then can you please take all the files off the wall? Take all the girls you can find in this building and bring them to the LeClaire Mansion."

"Yes, sir."

♎

A private ambulance parked outside, but no lights flashed from it. And a fleet of Mercedes sat behind. Lilly was lifted up into the vehicle, along with the girl he had saved with Perdonna.

Roosevelt waved Cecil toward him the moment he exited the VD House.

"Where's Annabelle?" Roosevelt asked. She crouched behind the ambulance to hide them from traffic.

"She's um...she's passed," Cecil said, trying not to break down.

"Self-defense?"

Cecil thought for a moment. He looked down at his clothing to find little splashes of blood. He grasped the red blotches, the vein, gooey liquid staining his fingertips. "No. No, I wasn't in any danger. I murdered her."

Roosevelt looked up at his face. "Why?"

"She leads the sex trafficking... She faked her death, killed, and planted evidence to take vengeance on me, my mother, and Perdonna."

Roosevelt crossed her arms and stared down at her feet, making the bunches of skin around her neck sink together like an earthworm squeezing itself. "Self-defense."

"I didn't have to kill her."

"You did," Roosevelt said. "It was the brave thing to do."

"It didn't feel brave."

She patted him on the shoulder.

"Can you find out who owns the VD building?" Cecil asked. "The security team seemed to be controlled by someone. I want to know who it was."

"I can find out."

Cecil heard a yammering voice from inside the ambulance. He stepped in to find Ava and Margaux.

"I swear," Margaux said. "I didn't purposely get Annabelle sex trafficked. I thought I was sending her to a normal model interview with Quirk."

"It's fine."

"I didn't know they were sex trafficking. Prostitution, maybe. I thought The Mall might have some prostitution involved, which is why I never went. I have principles. Some."

"I understand."

"I wouldn't have taken a commission if I *knew* knew the girls were being raped."

"I killed her," Cecil said.

"Hm?" Margaux asked.

"I killed her. I killed Annabelle."

Margaux raised her eyebrows so high the brow tint flaked off the hairs. "You did what?"

"Annabelle is dead."

Margaux rubbed her hands together. "I don't know how I feel about that."

"I don't feel good about it," Cecil said. "That's for sure."

He heard a loud pop and saw a medical glove deflate. Ava had blown up toys for Figaro to play with. "Good riddance." Ava nodded. "Screw her."

48

Sleeping bags piled around the LeClaire Mansion fountain. Hot cocoa overflowed with marshmallows. And ice cream was ladled into golden dishes and drenched in hot fudge.

The models Cecil had liberated from VD and Quirk were huddled up with pillows and blankets. Morning light streamed through the mirrored windows.

Roosevelt and Cecil agreed not to involve the authorities, and to provide the girls with their own help. They had a safe haven here at the mansion.

Board games like Clue and Monopoly were strewn across the floor. Music pumped through the atrium.

Muffintop and Mochi, the monastery cats, bobbled their fat little bellies down the swirling staircase.

"I'm adopting the queer ginger," Margaux said, pointing to Billy. He stood by the hot cocoa, eating the marshmallows one by one. "His parents dropped him off at the monastery and didn't come back for him. So...I figured he'd be a good Freddy. Better than having to live with a bunch of old monks."

"I'm pretty sure *queer* is a derogatory term," Cecil said.

"Not anymore. Now *homosexual* is the evil word, and *queer* is the positive one."

"Six years in a monastery, and suddenly I'm from the Stone Age."

Margaux shrugged. "No. You were always just a little slow."

Billy waved at Cecil from across the lobby.

Cecil stood up on the staircase to talk to the girls. He felt uncomfortable towering over everyone. An agent gave him a microphone to speak into, and Cecil felt the cold brush up to his lips. He fidgeted with the switch.

"Ahem," he said clumsily into the mic. "Testing. Testing. One, two."

"Oh, for God's sakes." Margaux rolled her eyes. Ava stood next to them, clasping Figaro in her hands. Her hair had finally been combed, and the twinkle lights were turned on once again.

"Hope everyone is doing well," Cecil said. "I have great news to share with you. We will start helping you return home today!"

An awkward pause followed Cecil's excitement. Hushed whispers fell among the girls.

"I mean," he said. "You're free. We'll pay for flights home to your parents. Or we'll help you get an apartment."

Happy smiles were nowhere to be found. Cecil was not expecting the anxious frowns that unanimously covered the faces of once-happy girls.

A girl lifted her hand. "You're not going to hire *any* of us?"

Cecil gave a confused look to Ava. "Um. It wasn't really something we considered."

Another girl stood up from her pillow. "Can't we audition at least? Doesn't LeClaire have any openings?"

"We thought you would want to go home. Be free. Go to high school. Prom. Maybe even go to college or a trade school."

"No go home," one interrupted. "My parents, no money. I homeless. I have no skill. No education."

Another model stood. "Please no. I rather live homeless in Manhattan. My parents beat me if I go back. Shameful that I came to America, all that opportunity, and I failed? I rather be a whore."

"You can be a waitress or a nanny?" Cecil asked. "You could learn a skill, or you could go to school. We would help you."

"I'm fourteen, can't get job. I left school at fifth year. Not smart enough for scholarship."

One girl broke down in tears. She stood and stomped her feet. "What did I do wrong? Please don't send me back to my dad," she pleaded. "I'd rather die in a modeling agency than be killed by him."

Cecil turned to Margaux and Ava. Margaux threw her hands in the air and looked at the ceiling. "I told you this business is complicated."

Ava shrugged while Figaro ran up to her head and clung to the strands of twinkle lights. "We could get them educations and still pay them for modeling. There's enough space to fit them all in here."

Cecil looked at Margaux. "Would you do that?"

"Me?" Margaux asked. "I don't run this modeling agency anymore."

"Excuse me?"

"You are president now. The head honcho."

Cecil raised his eyebrow. "I'm going back to the monastery."

Margaux shrugged. "I kinda liked it there. I'm going back too. Abbot Joseph said I could help him recruit monks."

He crossed his arms. "Stop joking."

"I'm not," Margaux said, twirling her cane like a baton. "You think you can run my modeling agency better than me, then fine. Do it. I'll take the extra profits without the responsibility. You run it, I'll own it. I'll advise you and mentor."

"I don't want to run a modeling agency."

"You freed these people, Moses. They're your problem now."

His eyes glazed over with fear. He turned to Ava, who spun around and refused to look at him. "Not my problem," she whispered.

"God called me to be a monk."

"Did he, though? Because he just had you kill someone." Margaux blew big pink bubbles with her gum. A little smirk crossed her face when Cecil turned back toward the models.

"Forget what I just said. You're all hired." The girls cheered with joy. Some even screamed. They hugged each other and danced around the fountain. Three girls even jumped into it, swimming around the tiny pool.

Cecil turned back to Margaux with crazy nervous eyes. "They'll have to have a salary," Cecil said. "LeClaire can only take twenty percent of their earnings."

"Fine."

"Each of them has to have their own room. With *clean* sheets."

"Fine. But you'll go broke."

"They have to be able to call their parents and friends. And go outside on their own."

"Fine."

"No prostitution," he said.

Margaux shrugged. "I'm not the president. You do what you want. I shall keep my office and bedroom. No one can touch my music boxes, beignets, canes, or guns. And that's all."

Cecil strolled down the second-floor hallways. "Those red display cases on the fourth floor have to go too. How did you come up with having the girls model in windows if you've never been to The Mall?"

"They were Perdonna's idea. She designed the modeling agency. I decorated it."

Ava lagged behind, spreading her hands over her cylinder dress. She looked as she always had. Except somehow, her eyes were brighter now. There was a newfound confidence.

"I'm sorry," Cecil said. "I shouldn't have put you in The Mall. Saving Annabelle wasn't worth risking your life."

Ava shrugged. "The crystal castle was worth it."

"I'm sorry you had to say goodbye to Figaro."

"Makes me appreciate him even more."

He crossed his arms. "Are you still working for Perdonna?"

"I don't know. What do you have to offer me?"

"Nothing." Cecil shrugged. "Money, maybe. Depending on how much the business has."

"Perdonna has the whole world to offer me. I'm fairly certain she could make me dictator of an entire country."

"Then I guess the answer's clear."

Ava waited. She held Figaro at her neck and looked into his

tiny little eyes. "You really think you can save people?"

Cecil nodded. "We can together."

Ava shuffled her feet. "Saving people and enough Snickers to get me through the week. That's my offer."

Cecil hugged her, and she shuffled in his arms. Figaro made a strange cackling hiss sound. "Let's not get too crazy," Ava said.

Detective Roosevelt knocked on the wall behind them. She waved up her hand. A solemn expression crossed her face. "I have some interesting news."

"Yes?"

"The VD House is owned by a company."

"Quirk Models?"

Roosevelt shook her head. "It's a holding company called Aberto, LLC."

Ava's head slowly turned to Cecil, who clutched the little red dog in his pocket.

"But the strangest part," Roosevelt said, "is that you, Cecil LeClaire, are listed as the owner and manager."

Cecil sighed and hung his head. He let out an exasperated grunt.

"I assume *you* don't own the building," she said.

He shook his head. "I know who does."

He stormed into Margaux's office. Her face was covered in so much beignet sugar it snuck up her nose. Her nostrils turned red like she was snorting cocaine.

"Perdonna," he said. *"Perdonna!"*

Margaux grimaced and spat sugar over her desk. "Yeah."

"She owns the VD House. Did you know?"

Margaux leaned back in her white chair and looked up at the ceiling. She let down her blond curls from her bun and turned the crank on a music box. Little snowflakes fell from its ceiling and cycled down, while carousel reindeer trotted over wrapped presents.

"Perdonna is complicated."

"Complicated?" Cecil asked. "Those were *her* guards in that place. That's why they didn't kill me. She *owns* sex trafficking?"

Margaux rubbed her hands together. "This is worse than

explaining Santa Claus isn't real...Sit." She patted a fluffy white beanbag and cleared porcelain dolls off of it. He reluctantly sat, putting his head in his hands. "Perdonna has her hands in some... vile things."

"Worse than sex trafficking?"

"Oof. That was nothing. You can't even imagine the fucked-up shit these people do. It's like bin Laden but fancy."

Cecil's face turned bright red. "How can all the women I love be sadistically evil?"

"You're in love with God. Perdonna's my God. Sometimes God gives you bread, sometimes he gives you Ebola. Sometimes Perdonna gives you unimaginable beauty, sometimes she gives you leather boots made out of humans."

He flopped back against the beanbag. "Do I have to kill her too?"

"You love her," Margaux said. A seriousness crossed her face.

"No. I—"

"Oh. You've wanted that cunt since you could speak." She bopped her cane against the music box, and it stopped playing. "I'm trying to have a heart-to-heart here."

"It's a crush. She's twice my age."

Margaux squinted her eyes and put her finger to her head. She was doing the math. "Not quite twice your age," she said. "Perdonna was practically a baby when she came to New Orleans. She's like my daughter."

"I'm your son."

Margaux shrugged. "Eh. Son by birth. But you're too much like your dad. I was happy to let Perdonna raise you." Margaux laughed as Cecil grew ever more frustrated. "Look, I'm terrible at basically everything. I can't cook. I speak terribly. And apparently, I have poor taste. But you know what I *am* good at? I'm good at picking horses and hippos."

She pulled out her book of models and plopped it on the table. "I know who the stars are. And I mold them. That's all. I found Perdonna, and I molded her. You're a star too. You're sensitive, creative, *and* strong. When you want to be. You're empathetic. You and Perdonna are opposite creative geniuses. Trust me. She needs you as much as you need her.

"You could do amazing things together. Or you could kill each other. I don't know."

Ω

Rose-gold hair burst against the sunset. The turquoise blues from morpho butterflies spun into the sky to a beachy haze.

A photoshoot on Perdonna's balcony. She stood in the completed butterfly dress that she and Cecil had created together. It arched along her shoulders, each wing folding in toward her chest. She looked like a holographic goddess.

Photographers hunched around her like pack animals.

"I was right about the wings," Cecil said from behind the photographers.

Perdonna smiled and waved the photographers away. "Would you excuse us for a moment, please?"

She pulled a cloth screen out from the wall as people went back into the mansion. The screen wrapped around the balcony edge and turned into a digital touchscreen. Suddenly a beautiful Tuscan countryside became their view. Olive trees tangled with sunset. Bright colors and sounds of the countryside replaced a gray, loud world.

"Better than brick skyscrapers, huh?" she asked. "I can put people in whatever location they choose."

"What do you care if you can't see it anyway?"

"It's about the *feeling*."

She carefully lifted up the bottom of the skirt over her waist and climbed onto a fluffy white hanging couch. She patted for him to sit next to her. "How are you feeling?" she asked.

He sat on the fluff, and the whole structure rocked, knocking her into his chest. It felt like they were floating on the water. Her hair fell over his neck, and her legs tangled in his lap. He couldn't help but hold her tighter.

"I didn't have a right to take her life," Cecil said.

"She would've been killed last night whether you had done it or not. She had to die."

"How do we know she wouldn't have changed? Couldn't we have taken her to Roosevelt? Gotten her psychiatric help?"

"She was long gone," Perdonna said. "You took her out of her misery."

"What about your misery?" Cecil asked. "Should I kill you? You own the place."

Perdonna spun off his lap. She squatted up to her knees, careful not to damage the butterflies. The wingtips shimmered down her body when she moved, like a knife blade brandished against fire.

"I do," Perdonna said. "I also had Henry kill Clara at Salon de Ming. And I tried to have Bourgeois stop you at the entrance to The Mall. Those are the bad things."

"I'd say."

"But I also saved a girl who would've died. I stitched up her wound and took her to the hospital. *I* could've been killed for that. So who am I?"

"Why did you save that girl?"

"Because I wanted to," she said.

"But you facilitate the rape of other girls."

"I didn't like actually *seeing* it. I didn't like watching her suffer. It wasn't fair."

"It wasn't fair?"

"No. It was disgusting. You saw."

"Is rape *ever* fair?"

"It's equitable, maybe." She leaned over him, holding on to the ropes that held up the chair on either side of his body. "Everyone has someone pulling their puppet strings. You have a choice whether to cut them or not. Annabelle chose to make more puppets."

"But shouldn't we help people cut their strings? Instead of making *more* strings? You own a sex-trafficking ring," Cecil said. "What else do you do?"

Perdonna's hands slid down the rope. "You can't even imagine."

"You basically run a crime syndicate."

Perdonna shrugged. "Along with a few other people."

"Why?"

"It's complicated. You'd have learned why if you hadn't become a monk."

"I'm not going back to the monastery yet... But there is *nothing...absolutely no* reasonable, good explanation for running a sex-trafficking ring. What else do you possibly own that is *worse* than a sex-trafficking ring?"

"Well, my dear. Let's take stock of what *you've* done this week. You spent half a million dollars on a crystal castle. You've fucked a naked stranger and started a body-painting trend in the sex-trafficking community. *You* got the LeClaires involved in The Mall. You sent Ava to die to save *one* girl who turned out to be Satan. And you slit Annabelle's throat."

Cecil pushed Perdonna off of him and onto the other side of the couch. She flopped back and bits of butterfly wing flew off around her. The glittery blue shrapnel flew up into the air like sparkles around her. He gripped the chair rope by her head, leaning over her.

"I also saved a bunch of people from slavery."

"Good deeds have consequences." Perdonna shrugged. "If you want to make moral judgments. If you want to play God, as you'd say it. Then you have to take responsibility for acts of God."

"Killing a murdering, sex-trafficking boss in Annabelle Leigh is not the same as funding a sex-trafficking ring."

Perdonna gave a chuckle and cocked her head against the rope. "Then fight me. Hard." He felt his breaths heavy in his chest as her smirk grew. "I do hope you paint me again, though."

"It *was* you?"

"Of course it was," she said, squirming out from beneath him. She pulled the dress over her hips and slid off the couch. "You knew it."

"Well, I've already used one of my four goes. Then you put me out to pasture with all of the other men."

"I would give you ten," Perdonna said with a wink. "Too bad you're a half-monk."

Cecil climbed off the bed. "What if I have to kill you?"

Perdonna placed her hands into a prayer. Her dress spun around her.

"*In bocca al lupo.*"

Made in the USA
Middletown, DE
10 October 2020